OFF-LIMITS CRUSH

KELLY SISKIND

First edition: published under the title Stud January 2018

Second edition: CD Books November 2019

The author is not responsible for websites (or their content) that are not owned by the author.

ISBN 978-1-988937-03-8 (ebook edition)

ISBN 978-1-988937-02-1 (print on demand edition)

❧ Created with Vellum

PRAISE FOR KELLY SISKIND'S ONE WILD WISH SERIES:

"Addictive and refreshing." ~ Rebecca Yarros, #1 *New York Times* bestselling author on He's Going Down

"I devoured this book." ~ *USA Today* bestselling author Brighton Walsh on He's Going Down

"It was impossible not to lose my heart (and occasionally my breath) from this sexy, smart, wholly consuming story." ~ Bookgasms Book Blog on He's Going Down

"Siskind knows how to write characters that have off-the-charts chemistry." ~ RT Book Reviews on Off-Limits Crush

"Funny, charming, and hot as hell." ~ author Beth Anne Miller on Off-Limits Crush

"Sexy, funny, and at times heart-wrenching. I loved every moment!" ~ author Rachel Lacey

"An emotional rollercoaster, with sexy highs and what-will-happen-next lows. The perfect mix of romance, friendship, self-discovery and mystery." ~ *USA Today* bestselling author Stefanie London on 36 Hour Date

ALSO BY KELLY SISKIND

One Wild Wish Series:

He's Going Down

Off-Limits Crush

36 Hour Date

Over the Top Series:

The Snowflake Effect

One Degree of Perfect

Slammed into Focus

Showmen Series:

New Orleans Rush

Don't Go Stealing My Heart

The Beat Match

The Knockout Rule

The Bower Boys series:

Fall in love with the Bower brothers! A decade after being forced into Witness Protection, they're finally allowed to return home and fight for the women they lost.

Visit Kelly's website and join her newsletter for great giveaways and never miss an update!

www.kellysiskind.com

CHAPTER 1

AINSLEY

A four-letter word meaning a horny covering.

I went to type *Bull* into my crossword app, but that didn't make sense, horns notwithstanding. Neither did *Knob* or *Flap* or *Fang*.
Beak
Peak
Deck
Wing
No. No. No. No.
Frustrated, I tapped my toe while decadent wafts of melted chocolate curled around me. Another minute and I'd be a floating Minnie Mouse, my nose led by the decadent scents. If heaven had a chocolate shop, it would be Aazam's Sweet Treats. Towering truffles, smooth peanut butter cups, and mouth-watering bark lined the shelves, nut clusters drenched in choco-late teasing me. Aazam was a genius with the cocoa bean, *and* all his products were vegan.

A man after my own heart.

The virtuoso held up a finger to tell me my order would be out shortly. I allowed myself a deep sigh. He really was gorgeous. As delicious looking as every morsel in the place. Dark hair and skin, a beard that was sure to tickle, not scratch. Eyes so soulful they practically sang the blues. His lips should be downright illegal, plump and smooth as they were. They had me thinking up other four-letter words for horny things.

Kiss

Suck

Hump

Lick

I nearly wrote *Muff* into my phone, but erased each letter. My G-rated crossword app might explode. I'd become addicted to the word game recently, a way to pass the time while waiting for the doors to open at a Tiffany's sale or a secret pop-up store. As I was about to admit defeat on the horny covering—*Bark? Bibb? Clip?*—Aazam assaulted me with his killer smile.

Wow. Heart, meet belly.

He lifted a brown box tied with bright green ribbons. "Ready for you."

Not only was he ready for me (God, how I wished), but he slid over a piece of my favorite seventy-percent chocolate with candied violet. High from his smile and the rich smells, I took a bite before thanking him. Double wow.

When I stopped moaning and opened my eyes, I said, "Are you sure you're gay?"

If I didn't know better, I'd say my chocolatier was blushing under his dark scruff. "Last I checked."

"Like, really sure?"

"Yep."

"Not even bi? I promise I'm great in bed."

That had him chuckling. I added a bottle of his chocolate-spiked perfume to my order. A couple dabs on my neck always put the sexy in my step.

He ran my credit card, then locked his John Lee Hooker eyes

on me. "If I were straight, I'd be all over your offer. Especially with that outfit of yours. Make sure you flaunt it today. Any heterosexual male in a thirty-mile radius will trip over himself to get your number."

My gingham wrap dress *did* give me cleavage for days, but the only two men who'd dialed up my lust-o-meter recently had proven poor choices. Emmett, the Adonis at the gym—*gay*. My heavenly chocolatier, Aazam—sadly, *gay*. Gwen and Rachel had pegged Emmett's sexuality right away, my best friends razzing me endlessly. My denial lingered until I'd witnessed him locking lips with a man. Aazam had blatantly turned down my dinner-date offer. He'd sent me home with chocolate, a hug, and a mildly bruised ego.

My gaydar was clearly broken, the instrument fogged up by raging hormones.

I needed to find release.

Finishing off my piece of *almost*-better-than-sex chocolate, I turned with a wave, but swiveled back. "What's a four-letter word for a horny covering?"

Aazam scratched his bearded cheek, then clapped. "Nail!"

"Nail? Like"—I fluttered my manicured hand—"*nail*, nail?"

"I think so."

I'd never been a language geek, unless *Prada* and *Gucci* were involved. But my new hobby had fired up my synapses, transforming me into a well-dressed linguist, who often cheated to finish puzzles. Aazam, however, was a total word savant. I'd once asked him for a five-letter word for a coastal feature, and he'd said, "Bight," in two seconds flat.

Apparently a horny covering didn't involve licking muffs (dammit). Horny coverings were *nails*.

"You're a genius," I called as I hurried out the door.

I hit the road, two unpleasant errands left to round out my day. I tapped my horny coverings against my steering wheel, the edges of my nails clipped and buffed to perfection. Ms. Mae's hand massage this morning had rendered my skin soft as silk, my mind nearly comatose. And her polish job? My tiger-striped French tips, with their flamingo-pink highlights, deserved to be hung in the Museum of Modern Art.

Picasso had nothing on my nails.

He also had nothing on the azure blue Versace draped over my back seat. I'd strip my nails bare for a night in that dress. It was perfection personified, and the slit up the front would highlight Mrs. Arlington's legs—her greatest asset. She would be thrilled, which meant her husband would be thrilled, which meant I'd deserve the hefty bonus coming my way.

I should be sale-at-Sephora giddy.

Except for the box of chocolates hijacking my passenger seat. Another gift purchased on my client's behalf, Mr. Infidelity himself, Thomas Arlington the *third*.

His most recent mistress had a soft spot for sweets. In particular, Aazam's eighty-percent dark chocolate bars sprinkled with cayenne pepper and pistachios. I noticed the packaging in her trash the first day we met, along with a broken pocket mirror. A replacement mirror, with similar gold detailing, had arrived on her doorstep that week, the chocolates following regularly, all punctuated with love notes from her doting philanderer.

Clamping my jaw, I drove faster and turned up the music. Nothing like a little Pat Benatar to lift my mood. Love was a battlefield, all right. A battle I had no interest in joining. Not when it was littered with duped women and lying husbands. Count me in for the pillaging afterward, though. If it came with a straight Aazam, or hunky men in kilts whose Scottish accents could slip into my Victoria Secret Cheekinis, then giddy-up.

Unfortunately, these days, all my *oh-my-God-yes-yes-yeses* applied to stellar purchases, not savage plundering.

I parked near the Arlingtons' house. Thomas's Porsche wasn't on the street. He could be working or golfing, or invading enemy fields...

I pulled the Versace from the car, cradling the plastic-wrapped fabric like a Fabergé egg.

A doorbell ring later, Sloane swung the door wide. "Just the lady I wanted to see."

She ushered me past a pair of dirty work boots, the clanging from above hinting at construction work. Remodeling their bathroom, if I remembered correctly. She disappeared into their modern townhome, and I laid her dress over their leather couch. I checked and rechecked my watch, urging the second hand to tick faster.

Spending time with Sloane was always uncomfortable. She'd chat about her morning playing tennis, and I'd smile and answer while thinking, *your husband is a lying sack of shit*. A sack of shit who helped pay my bills, which allowed me to wire cash to my parents.

My golden handcuffs were cemented in place.

Sloane returned with an envelope and presented it to me. "Thank you."

I took it by the edge and looked up at her. Even in my pink Manolo Blahniks, I was a head shorter than the statuesque brunette. "Thank you for what?"

"For that dress, for one. Your eye for clothing is remarkable." She ran her fingers over the clear plastic. "And for always going out of your way for me. I know you work for Thomas, but your help with the shoe emergency was above and beyond. Plus, you've become a friend. So, thank you."

Running over a pair of heels because hers had snapped in the middle of a fundraiser wasn't part of my job description, but the friend part of her comment had me wanting to slither out of the room. Friends told friends when bad things were happening. Friends saved friends from future heartache. Having been on the receiving end of a cheating manwhore once, I didn't wish it on anyone.

Without opening the envelope, I pushed it back at her. "Thank you, but I can't. I'm happy to help."

Please, get me out of here.

A loud bang blasted from above us, and we both winced.

"Bathroom reno is turning into a bit of a nightmare. And"—she raised a sculpted eyebrow at the envelope I was attempting to refuse—"I'm not taking that back. It's a gift." She picked up her dress and hugged it to her skinny frame, a body she kept painfully thin (green-vegetable diet), likely for her scumbag husband. "It's spectacular, Ainsley. Thomas will love it."

That part I didn't doubt. Give me ten minutes in someone's home, and I could list their favorite beverage and coffee addiction, where they purchased their linens, judge their waist, hip, and bust measurements (Sloane was a size celery), and the jewelry they coveted all with a nod and a walkthrough. Which is why Thomas had passed my cards to his friends, and why I mainly shopped for overpaid lawyers who "worked late" and had unscheduled "business meetings."

I was to personal shopping what Walter White was to methamphetamine. I was *great* at my job. I loved scouring stores for that *oh-my-God-yes-yes-yes* item. I also contributed to the downfall of society and needed cash. (Instead of *Breaking Bad*, my HBO series would be called *Killing Love*.)

Insert heavy sigh here.

"The dress will look stunning on you," I said. "Have a fun night, and you shouldn't have gotten me anything, but thank you." I saluted her with the envelope, like an awkward army recruit, and hurried toward the door, speed walking so quickly I nearly slipped on a nail. *Not* a horny covering. I picked up the offending piece of metal and hightailed it to my car as fast as my heels would allow.

Now I had to gift chocolate to the mistress.

Once that joyful deed was done, I sat in my Mini Cooper and opened Sloane's envelope. Two tickets to the San Francisco Ballet's *Cinderella*. Not only was she sweet enough to buy me a gift, she also ran a small bookkeeping business. She could walk a red carpet with enough confidence to draw paparazzi...and her husband was cheating on her.

I slumped into my seat, unsure how much longer I could

keep this up. I loved aspects of my job—piecing together clues to discern the perfect gift or outfit, helping someone look his or her finest—the rest of it was a giant pile of suck that paid well.

I picked up the metal nail from my passenger seat and flipped it through my fingers. If I had to write a crossword clue for this sucker, it would be:

Four-letter word for a pointed spike I'd like to jam into my eye.

I couldn't quit my job just yet, but I could do something to lessen this sticky feeling. Like I'd been sprayed by a rogue perfume sampler. Needing assistance, I picked up my phone and dialed Rachel.

Three rings later, she answered. "I just had an orgasm."

"Manual or with a certain tattooed hunk?"

"Tongue climax *without* the hunk. This Chardonnay is sinful."

Aazam's chocolate did the same for me. "I could use a drink about now. Probably a box of wine."

She coughed through the line. "Don't even joke about that. And why do you need this *box* of wine you will not be drinking?" I could practically see her give a heebie-jeebie shake. Total wine snob.

I traced distracted circles on my steering wheel. "Is your life perfect?"

She snorted. "No one's life is perfect."

I waved an impatient hand, as though she could see me. "I'm talking generalities. The big stuff."

"I don't know. I mean, I love living in Napa. Viticulture school is tough but rewarding. I'm an aunt to the cutest girl birthed this millennium, and, well...*Jimmy.*" She sighed on his name, no explanation needed.

Those two couldn't look at each other without every person in the room swooning or puking. What they had was intense. It was sweet and heart-melting and slightly sickening to witness. It also wasn't why I'd called her. "You fulfilled your birthday wish, didn't you?"

Silence answered me. Then, "I felt weird talking to you guys about it, not knowing if you'd worked on yours, but...I did. Why? What's up?"

"I just see everything in your life falling into place, and I wondered if that was part of the reason."

She didn't answer right away, and my mind tripped back to that night, as it often did. The night of our shared twenty-seventh birthday. Being born on April 12th had been as lucky as happening upon my first *Vogue* magazine. My two best friends had also come into the world on April 12th. Even luckier was finding the three of us coincidentally wasted and celebrating the start of our twenty-first year in the same bar.

We'd spent every birthday together since, but it was *last* April 12th that had plagued my mind the past six months: the wish each of us had made that night. No. Not a wish. *A life-changing resolution.* The type of change that would shake things up and trigger a domino effect of awesome. We'd linked our pinkies that night and had promised to fulfill our resolutions by our next birthday.

But I hadn't done a thing to realize mine.

Rachel broke her silence. "I believe fulfilling my wish played a part. Being a tad superstitious, I still don't want to hear yours before it's done, but mine was to find a rewarding career, which I'm working toward. So it's like carrying out that one big change affected everything else."

Exactly what I'd hoped for, yet I'd stalled. To fulfill my resolution, I had to become a better person, which meant making amends for my glorified-pimping job. "If you're right, I need to get my ass in gear. I only have six months left."

"Miracles happen all the time."

"True. There *was* that time my brother got laid."

She snickered. "No way. That chick took pity on him. It was for sure your housewarming gift."

"I'm an excellent sister." Who'd framed a condom with the tagline: In case of emergency break glass.

"You can do this, Ainsley." Rachel's soothing tone slid over my tense shoulders. "Regardless what you wished for, I know you've been down about work. A friend of Jimmy's volunteered at Habitat for Humanity. Not sure if he's still there, but he liked it. Doing something focused on helping others might make you feel better. Whatever you decide, I believe in you."

That made one of us. "I'll consider it."

"That's the spirit. Oh—and Jimmy went to the city last night to meet some restaurant people. I'm joining him tomorrow. I have to see my family and spoil my niece, but we'll squeeze in some girl time."

"Roger that."

I hit End and stared at my dashboard. The fact that Rachel sensed my wish without me breathing a word of it was a testament to our friendship. I was also a step ahead of her. I'd made a list of Ainsley-tailored volunteering:

Doing makeovers.

Helping fashion victims.

Saving discarded haute-couture items, one Dior at a time.

Soup kitchens involved touching meat. Animal shelters made me sneeze. Working with the elderly reminded me of my grandparents; I'd probably spend my time bawling on some granny's flower-print lap.

That left the Habitat build. Rachel had mentioned it once before. I'd been too anxious to sign up, but if Rachel—who'd held enough jobs to employ half the city—could fulfill her resolution and stick with a career, I could wear sneakers and dirty my hands. Plus, working on a Habitat project didn't require experience, and I'd be helping put a roof over a family's head.

Something I was already familiar with, but paying *my* parents' mortgage wasn't bettering society. It was taking care of my own. Like the framed condom.

Confidence growing, I turned my ignition and pointed my car away from Nob Hill's Victorian homes and headed for the address I'd driven past too often this month. Each drive-by had involved me slowing down, my heart revving up, then I'd peel past the construction site. It was ridiculous. I was an adult. Doing something new, by myself, shouldn't have reduced me to a stage five stalker. Still, each time I'd contemplate stopping, I'd be transported back to high school and the last time I'd stepped outside my element.

That shit show had involved a Chucky's Chicken paper hat, enough grease to drown a small country, and me praying to the porcelain gods before my shifts. Each yack fest was followed by a thousand screw-ups, then co-workers would lob insults my way, like they were spectators watching me die a glorious Roman Gladiator death, cheering for blood.

But I was done creeping the building site. I wouldn't drive by out of fear again, or put off volunteering by claiming I'd sign up online. No. This time I'd force myself out of the car. I would put the "con" in contractor and fake it until I made it. I would study my dictionary app and learn every construction term there was. I wouldn't make a fool of myself, circa 2006. (The Chucky's Chicken Maggot Incident was responsible for my vegan ways.)

By the time I parked at the curb, it was late afternoon and the Habitat build was winding down. When construction had begun a month or two ago, people were always scurrying about. Today there were only a few volunteers around, most looking ready to leave, but I wouldn't let that stop me.

According to their website, twelve two-bedroom townhomes and eighteen three-bedrooms were being built. Affordable houses for the less fortunate. A serious karmic opportunity. The orange hardhats were a concern—not my greatest color—but wearing one would be my first sacrifice.

I looked down at my cleavage and frowned. Walking up in my Michael Kors dress would have me labeled Pampered Princess next to the T-shirts and ripped jeans worn on site. The museum-worthy nails and Blahniks wouldn't help, either. They'd assume I dished out thousands on my wardrobe and appearance, when in reality I could sniff out sample sales better than a Chanel-trained bloodhound, a handy superpower when bartering for manicures and haircuts.

If I didn't look volunteer-ready, I would at least sound it. I scrolled through my dictionary app and studied up on construction terms.

Boom. Brace. Framing. Fuse. *Infiltration.*

The latter sounded more special ops than volunteer work.

Hammer. Circular Saw. Drill. Screw. *Nail.*

I laughed at the last one, horny-coverings quite the focus of my day today. English hadn't been my best class in high school, but the language had become a fascination since playing my crossword games. One word could have so many definitions. I even watched spelling bees and loved the part where they'd have to use the word in a sentence.

My manicured nails *deserved a two-page* Marie Claire *spread.*

I would hammer nails *like a regular* Bob the Builder.

As I gripped my door handle and prepared to earn my Girl Scouts' Good Samaritan badge, I noticed an unfamiliar man on the site, or, more accurately, an apparition in the form of a dirty, sweaty, panty-melting hunk.

If this were a music video, mist would be floating up from the ground, the sun setting, this man wiping his brow as Faith Hill sang about bare feet, country nights, and skinny-dipping in a rambling river. In worn jeans and work boots, he looked part-cowboy and all rugged. His ratty white T-shirt clung to his broad chest, biceps bunching as he lifted wood planks. Cheekbones I'd kill for upped his hot factor. He didn't talk to anyone, just went about his work. The pinched lines of his face hinted at a broody nature, and I liked me some tormented heroes.

My hormones sparked to life, Aazam's recent rejection and my dry-spell fanning the flames. A new definition popped into my mind, sending a smile skipping across my face.

I wanted to nail *that man.*

CHAPTER 2

OWEN

I should have joined the priesthood. Maybe I'd have been better off with my brother's genes, not that dating men came with any less drama. Still, my soon-to-be ex-wife could win a Tony for her theatrics. The melodrama made her a stellar attorney. It also made for a messy and long divorce.

With a grunt, I hefted a final wood plank to its new pile, readying the site for tomorrow's build. Studs to be put in place, framing to be done. I welcomed the tug on my muscles, the deep ache in my shoulders and forearms. It was honest work. A hell of a lot better than hunching over a desk for hours. Investment bankers didn't make things. They didn't even buy things. For eight years, I brokered sales and deals, not caring who got screwed along the way. Starbucks had been my life's blood, my chair an extension of my ass.

Now I could breathe.

Sawdust. Fresh-cut pine. Freedom drifting on the October breeze.

If my lawyer hadn't dealt me another blow this morning, I might have actually smiled as I inhaled a lungful of air. Instead I huffed out my breath, clamping my molars tight.

With the new delivery of lumber cleared to the side, I wiped my brow and stretched my neck. A cold beer would be heaven right now. A pizza even better. I took a mental inventory of my sparse fridge and added a trip to the store to my route home. Pick up a slice and a case of Pliny the Elder. Kick up my feet on my back patio. Just me, the squirrels, my neighbor's noisy Jack Russell, and a night with Victor Hugo. Forget about Tessa and her fucked-up accusations. The knots in my shoulders loosened a fraction.

"Do you handle the volunteers?"

I spun at the raspy voice, not expecting the blond bombshell in front of me. The *curvy* blond bombshell. Her massive purse and dangerous-looking heels weren't my style, but she oozed old-Hollywood elegance with her shapely hips and soft features.

I pulled off my work gloves and slapped them against my thigh, sending a cloud of dust between us. "No."

But the temptation of handling *her* teased my peripheral vision. That's what happened when you went without for over a year. Not that offering one syllable would get me far with a woman.

The blond twirled a lock of golden hair around her finger. Something about the action pushed up her breasts. I shifted, unsure where to look. I wasn't that guy. I tried to make sure women knew they were more than the sum of their parts. *This* woman's parts each deserved their own sonnet, curvy as she was, but I was out of practice—all awkward silence and no finesse—and she reminded me too much of the women in D.C. Superficial. Self-centered.

The life I'd kicked to the curb.

Rubbing the back of my neck, I forced my attention to her eyes, and my heart switched gears. *Blue.*

Blue was all I could see. Blue for a country mile.

Her eyes shone like the sun streaming through turquoise beach glass, pushing long-buried memories to the surface. Startled, I grunted at her, like a Neanderthal, and went to turn.

"So," she called, and I flipped back. "What's it like working here? I was thinking of signing up. Doing a couple of shifts each week."

I chuckled, picturing this pint-sized beauty dirtying her perfect nails. About as likely as my ex working less than an eighty-hour week.

Her luminous eyes narrowed. "For your information, I've done construction before. I'm not a total rookie."

She straightened her posture, daring me to challenge her. The only other person left on site was Nick, making sure all was locked up for the night. He needed to get done and get home, drive his son to karate. I stayed, grudgingly.

"Right." My tone came out nastier than intended. "You look ready to drywall the place." Nastier again.

She pursed her bee-stung lips, the plump beauties rich and lush. "Don't go getting all judgmental. I know the difference between fiberglass sheetrock and cement board." A smug grin settled on her face, like she was proud of herself. She eyed the backfilled construction site, studied the pipes poking their heads out of the earth. "Are you at the saddle and cripple stage?"

I nearly laughed again, but I reined myself in. I wasn't a contractor. I'd volunteered on Habitat builds since living in D.C. and paid my rent now with handyman jobs, but woodworking was my thing. I loved dragging my fingers against rough wood, knowing what was once a towering tree could be a rocking chair to calm a baby, a table for a family, a bed to help someone sleep.

What I *did* know about building a house, was people didn't toss around words like *saddle* and *cripple*.

"We're saddling," I said, playing with her. "I assume you have your own tools?"

"Yeah. Sure. Of course."

The pretty little liar was full of it. "Well, we have tools on site, but not always enough to go around. You'll need a tape measure and hammer and framing square, and don't forget the chalk-line clamp. You won't always have a partner to work with."

"Right. Chalk-line clamp. No problem." But the corners of her pink lips turned down.

"Safety glasses are a must."

The fear of God shone on her face. "I haven't seen anyone in safety glasses."

"We haven't started cutting wood yet. Face shield and respiratory mask, too." I had no idea why I was messing with her. Maybe because she was primped and polished and reminded me of my ex, a master manipulator who wove tall tales for a living. I doubted this woman deserved to be toyed with, but I'd been raked over the coals for months. My bullshit-meter had reached its limit.

"When you show up," I said, "no cuffs on pants or unbuttoned shirts. No jewelry at all. Safety comes first. We have hardhats and gloves, and you have to wear sturdy shoes." I shot a look at her mile-high heels.

Her reply: "You're kind of bossy."

Instead of the same evil stare I got when I'd laughed at her expense, her gaze dipped down my body, slow and languid, soaking me in. Something in me twitched to life, like a phantom limb reminding me hot blood once pumped through my veins. *All* my veins. My groin got heavy, heat flushing my thighs. Because she looked at me.

I let that notion marinate and did my best to keep my brain on target. "Just giving you the lay of the land. And if you plan on volunteering tomorrow, or any day, show up at 8:30 a.m. sharp. Nick will take you through the paces."

"Will you be here?"

"Possibly."

"Are you here every day?"

"Some."

"Do you often answer questions with one word?"

"Depends."

She tipped her head, those beach-glass eyes intent upon me. Suddenly, heading home for beers and pizza didn't sound as appealing. I dug my boots deeper into the earth.

She swiped her tongue across her full bottom lip. "All right, tough guy. I'll be here next week. Where you *may* or *may not* be, depending on if you *do* or *do not* decide to show up. I'll wear ugly clothes and get my gear, and maybe we'll see each other again."

Every word dripped with flirtatiousness, and I contemplated telling her I was messing around. That she only needed the face shield when working with flying debris. The way I'd all but grunted at her so far, probably better to keep my mouth shut.

So we stood there—her waiting on me to speak, a skateboarder barreling down the road at our left. *Me* unsure why she was affecting me.

I missed being with a woman. Missed the slide of soft skin and wet mouths, and locking my girl in my arms for the night. But I'd sworn I'd do it right this time. Not rush in. Make sure I dated someone with depth and interests outside of making bank. Everything about this spitfire girl read narcissistic.

When our silence slipped into awkward, she fluttered her fingers in my face. "It's been…interesting."

I offered her a curt nod.

Chuckling to herself, she spun around, but her right heel wedged into the loose dirt. Those damn shoes were lethal. She sank an inch and teetered, but seemed to catch herself. Then her massive purse fell. The thick strap landed on her forearm, tipping the balance. She shot out her hand, struggling to stay upright.

I lunged for her, clasping her trim waist to hold her steady. And close. Too close. Not near enough for her to feel how I was thickening behind my zipper, but the air swelled. It dilated with feminine scents. Something sweet. *Nice.*

She smelled like chocolate.

My hands spanned her waist from behind, her curves above and below all woman. Hour glass, like a modern-day Marilyn Monroe. Jean Harlow. Mae West. Over the years, I'd watched every classic movie there was, wishing I could slip to a time when men danced and women sang and loyalty and love were valued over getting ahead. An old soul, my nana always said. Or a romantic. Or just plain trouble.

Now I had my hands on a dangerous beauty. I shouldn't have been thinking about gripping her tighter or picturing my lips coasting over her jaw and down her neck. More began rising than my temperature. I noticed her foot then, the delicate sole having slipped out of her shoe, her toenails painted a soft pink.

Gripping my wrists for balance, she slid her shoe back on. "Thanks for the quick save." She turned to face me, but I didn't release her waist. "I'm Ainsley, by the way."

No woman should have a voice that sexy, as husky as a lounge singer in a smoky room.

"I'm Owen." *My* voice was nothing but rocks and gravel. Needing a breather, I stepped back. "Until next time."

"Next time," she replied.

She navigated the uneven ground cautiously, still managing to sway her full hips as she went. I turned and slapped my gloves against my thigh again, anything to busy my hands, distract my mind. Ease the blood flow to my groin. Going home solo was a bad idea. I'd either stew over Tessa's latest antics, or I'd stroke myself to the image of this pinup girl in all her natural glory.

I stopped at my truck and pulled out my phone. Half a ring later, my brother picked up. "Fine. I'll blow you. Get over here."

"Jesus, Emmett. Now I need to lobotomize myself."

His barking laugh bit through the line. "Fuck, man. Sorry. Thought you were Travis."

"Travis? What happened to Chris?"

"It ran its course."

Which meant he hit his one-month limit. Normally, I'd make a crack about him chasing a new guy for the shared-clothing benefits, or give him hell for sleeping around, but my patience wore past thin hours ago. I needed to drink beers or go for a run or take a cold shower. "I was thinking of kicking a ball around. You game?"

The sound of a can cracking open answered me. Then, "Sure. Travis plays, too. I can probably hustle up a couple more. Jimmy around?"

I ground my toe into the dirt. "Doubt it, but I'll check. Three on three would be good."

"You have no idea," he said.

Ladies and gentleman, my brother the manwhore.

"Meet you at the field in an hour," I said. Exactly what I needed. To run the soccer field. Chase out the messiness of the day. Shake the lingering heat left in Ainsley's wake.

We hung up, and I was greeted by a missed text from Jimmy.

In town for some meetings. Free for a beer?

Another lucky break. *How about kicking it at the park?*

Even better.

Reconnecting with Jimmy was one of the bonuses of moving back to San Francisco. As a teen, I'd been a recluse before him and our days playing soccer for the California Regional League. I still wasn't sure how Nana had paid for my spot on the team. Whenever I'd ask, she'd wave a dismissive hand, and say, "Not your concern."

Come middle school, mine and Emmett's clothes all came from Goodwill. Our lunches and dinners had been a study in stretching the dime—peanut butter measured, bread thinly sliced. Still, we'd crowd around the TV at night and watch Fred Astaire glide across the screen. Nana and Emmett would swoon, and I'd let my mind spin with the actor's effortless grace, imagining myself the fleet-footed Casanova, sweeping women off their feet. But I was a second-hand kid in second-hand clothes.

Instead of picking up girls, I'd read books and study and dance with Nana to Irving Berlin and Cole Porter. She schooled me in the ways of women.

You're always wrong.

You're always sorry.

You always *sleep in the wet spot.*

I split my gut laughing when she laid that last one on me. We did that a lot, at least—danced and laughed and forgot how far on the edge we lived. Made me feel fortunate, not shafted. Then came soccer and Jimmy and teammates slapping my back. I'd busted my ass for my scholarship, landed a beautiful wife, a great job, and thought I'd made it big.

Turns out big looks a lot like lonely nights lit by the pallid glow of a computer screen. Empty bottles of Scotch. Fights. Silent treatments.

Man, did I need that run.

Two hours later, my T-shirt was suctioned to my chest. Our group of six had morphed into ten. Some eager teens were working the field when we'd arrived and opted into our pick-up game, dribbling like pint-sized Pelés, fast as fuck. The action put a grin on my face. Especially when Travis executed a decoy run, and I sent a killer pass to Emmett, who smoked their goalkeeper.

The little shits still won, but Emmett gave Travis's ass a victory slap for the goal.

Followed by a cup and squeeze.

He'd often pull that move on me, grabbing my ass when we had an audience. With different fathers, we didn't look related, and Emmett loved exploiting the differences, hoping to embarrass me. Earned him a few blows to the ribs from me when we were younger. These days, I barely noticed it—an ass grab from my obnoxious brother was as normal as a hug.

"Hope you guys didn't get hernias!" one of the punks we'd played called. He nearly killed himself laughing as he kicked onto his bike.

"Ice those arthritic knees," razzed another.

Emmett saluted them. "Remember to change your diapers before bed."

We made our way to our pile of sweatshirts and bags, mopping our foreheads as we walked. Emmett stretched his torso, then cuffed the back of Jimmy's head. "Your feet were cement blocks out there."

Jimmy shoved him off. "I'd ask you to pass me a Gatorade, but you'd probably miss."

"Wouldn't want to watch you drink, anyway. Bet you dribble worse than on the field."

Jimmy snatched a Gatorade from the grass, wrenched off the top, and chucked the bit of plastic at Emmett's face. "Go suck a bag of dicks."

Travis shot his hand in the air. "Just one is fine."

We all tossed our heads back at that, except it sent my mind to the pretty little thing at the build earlier—her lips, my dick, and a whole lot of sucking. *Damn.* Not thoughts I should entertain while in workout shorts.

A sting of guilt followed the fantasy, cooling the heat stirring my blood. She may have been the opposite of what I was looking for in a woman, but she hadn't warranted my gruffness today. I shouldn't have coaxed her into showing up to volunteer wearing safety goggles and a face shield, either. She'd get laughed off the build, and I'd wind up feeling like an ass. Already did, as it stood.

We chugged our electrolytes, the evening air cooling the sweat on my skin. Emmett and Travis took off, leaving Jimmy and me, asses planted on a bench. We watched two kids playing Frisbee.

"How goes the wine world?" I asked.

His elbows fell to his knees, a content smile spreading. "Great. Really fucking great. Being back in Napa is better than I expected. Not sure who I was kidding, thinking I could live without the winery."

I knocked my knee against his. "And Rachel?"

"*Really* fucking great." His smile became something else entirely. "That woman is…everything."

Envy lassoed my heart, the squeeze uncomfortable. I believed in love at first sight. In happily ever after. I believed in touches that healed and kisses that could cut a man down. I also craved the steadiness I'd lacked as a kid. Unfortunately, it wasn't what I wound up with.

Jimmy picked a divot of grass off his sneaker. "Any headway on the divorce?"

Could I end world hunger? "One step forward, ten or twenty back."

He made a pained sound. "If I'd married my ex, I'd be where you are now. Drowning—trying to cut our ties and come up for air. Not sure how you do it."

"No choice, really. Tessa is smart and vindictive. She only knows how to win, and the word *divorce* isn't in her vocabulary. To her, it's a loss. A deficit."

"Sounds like a transaction, not a relationship."

"Pretty much sums up our last few years."

His penetrating stare had me counting blades of grass. "You sure you don't want to talk about it?" he pushed. "Things dragging like this can't make it easy to move on."

He didn't know the half of it. It wasn't just that Tessa didn't like to admit defeat. She never lost. Ever. Other lawyers called her the Sleeper, after those cichlid fish who played dead, then struck their unsuspecting victims. She was angry, hurt that I'd ended things. Now she was intent on ruining my name and sucking me dry in the process. Her accusations that I'd cheated on her were ludicrous, but you almost had to admire her tenacity.

Once her teeth were in you, shaking her was a bitch.

"I appreciate the offer. I *always* appreciate the offer. But we have an autocratic judge on the case. Insists we keep things quiet until the divorce is settled. Lawyer agrees. Anyway, as far as I'm concerned, we're done and over. The courtroom stuff is just semantics. I've moved on. I'm building a life. She'll clue in eventually."

Jimmy grunted, the two of us falling into the type of silence only old friends could abide. Hopefully I wouldn't be broke by the time my divorce was settled. Hopefully I'd meet a woman who wanted to *live* her life, not count her billable hours. A partner who preferred dancing on the beach to driving in rush hour, walking barefoot in the grass to winning the rat race.

A flash of Ainsley's polished toes and dainty feet filled that particular daydream until I schooled my thoughts, unsure why I'd crushed my Gatorade bottle. No point repeating the same mistakes.

CHAPTER 3

Eight letters for the discrepancy list made at the end of a
construction job.
Or what you'd like to do to the asshole who facilitates your
ridicule.
PUNCHOUT

AINSLEY

Sweat. Lots of sweat. Enough sweat to waterboard a platoon of soldiers. This was no delicate shine or attractive glow, either. I looked like I'd been sprinting in the Sahara, and it was all Rachel and Gwen's fault. I *may* have mentioned I should get in better shape. Keeping Rachel's superstitions in mind, I'd stayed mum about pursuing my birthday resolution and visiting the Habitat build, but my first volunteer session was tomorrow, ratcheting up my nerves.

Remembering how Owen had lifted and moved wood planks —forearms flexing, biceps bulging—had me flushing something fierce. It was also a reminder working on a Habitat site was no joke.

I needed to up my fit factor.

Now I was in Step Class Hell, a charley horse away from face-planting on the linoleum.

"Keep those knees up!" The perky fitness instructor with boobs up to her chin wasn't even glistening with a hint of perspiration. Not a measly drop. "Work that step, people. And don't forget to smile!"

Smile? As in slap a toothy grin on my face and pretend my heart wasn't a live grenade? If I was about to die, I'd do it snarling at Princess McGrin-a-Lot. I turn-stepped and muscled through my three-knee repeaters, glaring my fiercest glare.

An agonizing lifetime later, she flashed her pearly whites, and crowed, "Let's count it down now! Half-time. Nice and slow. Time to work those quads!"

Now it was time to work them? As if I'd been doing what? Sipping fruity drinks at the swim-up bar? If I could lift my quad, I'd shove my hot-pink Nike Free Run up this dictator's toned ass. Instead I did a zillion squats and over-the-tops.

"Okay. We're almost there! Keep it up while I help Cynthia for a minute."

Ex-squeeze me? Cynthia and her two left feet could die a painful, flesh-eating death for all I cared. Mussolini needed to finish this goddamn routine before I painted the floor green with the kale smoothie I'd sucked back earlier.

Gwen glanced at me and snorted. "You look like hell."

I directed my death-stare at her and tried to say, "Fitting, because I'm pretty sure that's where I am." Except it sounded like: "…be…cause…*am*."

The room was jam-packed with people panting and clomping, the wall of mirrors making me dizzy. My chest cavity was about to rupture.

Needing a diversion, I locked my eyes on Emmett, one step in front of me. We'd never traded two words, but I'd learned his name when Rachel used to work at this gym, because true friends helped friends creep potential crushes. I used to follow him around the like a lost puppy, until I learned he was gay.

The man owned his stepper, whipping around the thing like he was born to it. Not even the sight of his perfect body could ease my agony. Still, I looked. His rock hard calves balled and tightened. His thighs were strong enough to crush skulls.

And that ass. Glory, hallelujah…*that ass.*

I drooled. May as well add more liquid to the quarts of sweat pooling under my stair. With herculean effort, I lifted my leg, but I wobbled. My toe tripped on the lip of my instrument of torture, and I toppled forward. I landed knee first on the step as the class (thank God and every deity there ever was) ended.

The legs I'd been ogling appeared in front of my face. As did a well-endowed crotch that should have had a sign above it that read, *Sorry, ladies. I'm all about the cock.*

Him and me both.

He extended a strong hand toward me. I took it, grateful. Clumsy wasn't my usual MO, but that was twice this week a handsome man had helped me find my feet. Maybe I was on to something. Once I was upright, Emmett used his tank-top hem to mop the sweat on his forehead. All remaining oxygen vacated my lungs.

Holy abs of steel.

Slap a long wig over his dark curls, and he could be Tarzan's stunt double in a hot second. "Hard class," he said as he dropped his shirt.

Not as hard as his abs. I barely refrained from tipping sideways to watch each inch of delicious flesh disappear below his top. "That woman should be arrested for crimes against humanity."

He chuckled. "If you came more often, you'd get used to it."

God, how I'd like to come more often. Which sent my imagination to a certain construction worker, who no doubt had abs for days under his shirt. Owen also had strong hands. Big hands.

Hands that hammered things and *screwed* things, and had wrapped protectively around my waist the other day. I could have sworn he'd held on longer than necessary, was sure his broad chest had swelled faster as he'd gripped me.

Hopefully the sign above *his* crotch read *Ladies First*.

My savior smiled at me. "I'm Emmett, by the way."

"I know who you are," I said, practically admitting my unrequited crush. "I'm Ainsley."

Gwen slung a sweaty arm over my shoulder. "Hey, Emmett," she said sweetly.

Rachel appeared at my other side. "Emmett, hey. How's it going?"

He crossed his defined arms over his chest and tilted his head. "Do I know you ladies?"

That's when Gwen betrayed our sisterhood. "Nope. But Ainsley was sweet on you, so we've done some basic reconnaissance, which included discovering she's not your type."

A spark of mirth lit his dusky eyes. "I'm not sure if I should be flattered or call security."

"No need," I said. "I'll be revoking their memberships and putting hair-remover in their shampoo." If I weren't red-faced and drenched, he might have noticed my blush.

"Good luck with that," he said, laughing as he left.

I shrugged Gwen off and hefted my equipment into the corner, never to be used again. More often than not, my gym time was spent doing light weights and short stretches of cardio. I also loved leisurely hikes that allowed me to enjoy the scenery as opposed to intense climbs. Just enough exercise to allow me to eat Aazam's chocolate without worrying about my weight.

I wasn't toned like Gwen or tall and thin like Rachel. I was curvy and buxom—my mother's term of choice. I liked it, though. Enjoyed feeling womanly with curves to flaunt and hips to sway. I also loved spending this hour with my girlfriends, today notwithstanding.

Once my step and risers were away, I ended my silent

treatment. "I hereby remove you both from my will. Gwen, you will not receive my shoes if I die in step class. Rachel, you will no longer be the proud owner of my Coach purse collection."

Gwen mimed a knife wound to the heart. "How am I supposed to go on?"

I pushed past her and grabbed my towel from the floor. The crowd had mostly filed out, the three of us lingering in the humid room. Even the walls were dripping.

Rachel dabbed her freckled brow. "It was kind of funny."

"Because you weren't the butt of that particular joke." I stuck my towel down my cleavage, needing a squeegee not a swathe of cotton to deal with this deluge.

"I'm sorry," Gwen said, "but I couldn't resist. I mean, lusting after one gay man happens. But two? Next you'll be hitting gay bars, wondering why no one's buying you drinks."

Rachel's hilarious addition: "Maybe she'll join gaydar-dot-net to cruise for uninterested men."

"You should both write for Comedy Central." My tone was all aspartame as I pulled my towel from my boobs and tossed it at Rachel's face. "They were honest mistakes. Now, thanks to you two jokers, Emmett knows how pathetic I am. I really need new friends," I mumbled.

It was an empty threat. The three of us couldn't have been closer. We were there for Rachel when she'd lost her father, her struggles to keep her mother's spirits up, and through each of her ten thousand jobs. Gwen didn't bungee jump or skydive without messaging us first. When she had a tough day at the adoption agency, unable to place a child with a deserving family, we'd rally.

We lifted one another up, and made sure to keep one another grounded, but I'd wear a velour sweat suit before sharing my next crush with them. I'd keep a lid on things until I was sure of mutual attraction.

Rachel cringed, looking sheepish. Or maybe deerish. With

her big brown eyes, sun-kissed skin, and spray of freckles, she was more innocent doe than bleating sheep. "Now I feel bad."

"As you should, but you're forgiven. I expect a lifetime's supply of Chardonnay once you open your own winery."

She raised her right heel toward her bum and grabbed her ankle for a quad stretch. "Like that will ever happen. Maybe when I graduate, if I work up to head winemaker somewhere, I'll name a vintage after us."

Gwen ran a towel under her bobbed hair. "You'd have to call it The Ram."

Our shared zodiac sign.

We all grinned as we headed to the change room, but the horoscope comment was a reminder of our birthday resolutions. The resolution I'd start working on as of zero-eight-hundred hours tomorrow.

If this change could kick start other positives shifts in my life, like it had for Rachel, I needed to make it work. It might lead to an epiphany on ways to continue earning money while shedding my sleazy clients. Maybe I'd meet a contact, someone who could hire my father.

As long as I didn't encounter any supervillains along the way.

Nausea, familiar in its viscosity, coated my gut, thoughts of my teenage employment reducing me to a puddle of nerves. If I could have a magic do-over, I'd expunge those mortifying years. But there was no ctrl-alt-delete that could erase the ridicule I'd endured at the hands of Anton Bickley.

Light-headed from the workout and remembering my teen hell, I slogged into a bathroom stall but struggled with the lock. Gritting my teeth, I used my remaining energy to crank it in place. After barely holding my toilet-seat hover (yoga's chair pose should be dubbed the Public Bathroom Pose), my legs neared jelly status.

With my white camo Lululemon tights snapped in place, I

twisted the lock to leave, but it didn't budge. I tried again, and nothing.

My lungs constricted. Fresh sweat dotted my temples.

Nothing to worry about. This is just a glitch.

I used both hands and tugged until my thumbs were ready to snap.

No. No. *Nononono.*

My pulse thundered in my ears. The stall shrunk around me. In an instant, I was throttled back in time to the Chucky's Chicken walk-in fridge, locked inside. Stuck. Panicked. A budding fashionista working in a fast-food chicken joint had been a recipe for disaster. My coworkers had labeled me an airhead. An outsider. Someone to mess with, which included locking me inside the walk-in fridge while I slammed my fists on the door and screamed and cried for an endless hour.

Anton Bickley and his minions had been evil incarnate.

Now I was trapped again, my claustrophobia threatening to strangle me. I couldn't call for help or push enough air through my lungs to squeak. I fumbled harder, my saliva turning to glue. Then it unlatched.

I stumbled out of the stall and slammed my hands on the sink counter, head bent forward as I sucked back air. My eyes and throat burned. My legs trembled. Stupid step class and walk-in fridges and jammed locks. Stupid me for allowing Anton to best me all those years ago. Something that wouldn't happen at the Habitat build.

I was entering unknown territory again, the odd woman out. But I'd purchased my face shield, respiratory mask, and safety glasses. I'd even found a hot-pink tool belt and matching hammer.

I'd never apologize for reading *Vogue* instead of *Pride and Prejudice,* or wearing sunglasses and five-inch heels to turn an outfit into an attitude. I had a bracelet for every occasion, enough shades of lipstick to keep my lips guessing, and I could transform a Zara find into a runway show stopper with the perfect accessory.

Rachel's higher power was wine. Gwen was an adrenaline junky.

I knelt at Fashion Week's altar.

This fashionista wasn't about to go all granola in ratty jeans and a plaid shirt. Growing up was about owning who you were. But I *would* arrive at the Habitat site prepared, looking like I knew how to build a freaking house. Especially since Owen and his big hands might be there.

———

Monday had me hopping out of bed early. A shower, shave, and perfume later, I smoothed out my blond hair and tied it into a ponytail. I wriggled into my skinny jeans and fitted white tee, the Gucci logo hugging my breasts. No earrings were worn. No bracelets or rings. I tugged the laces of my pink Converse tight, hung my safety glasses and respiratory mask around my neck, then spent a few minutes browsing building terms in my dictionary app.

When I landed on crotch, I cackled to myself. *The "V" shaped assembly of skids that holds sections of pipe in place.* I could only hope and pray I eventually landed on Owen's "V" and "pipe."

Nerves buzzed through my belly as I drove to my first volunteering gig—partly frazzled, but mostly excited. This would be the start of a new me. A better me. Which meant my resolution would kick into action.

As I parked and reached for my face shield, my phone sang out "Daddy's Girl."

I hit Talk. "Hey, Dad."

"How's my princess?"

Most twenty-seven-year-old women would roll their eyes at the endearment. Instead, I chirped, "A client got me ballet tickets. How'd you and Mom like to see *Cinderella*?"

"With you?" His words always sounded more growled than spoken.

"No. I have *two* tickets, and Mom adores the ballet."

A love she'd passed on to me. She'd twirl me around the house in my tutu and tights while my brother, Jason, would groan and our father would lift me up for the big jumps. He was a bear of a man, my dad—tall and imposing, bushy blond beard, shaved head, tattooed neck. My dates would swallow hard when they'd shake his hand, but he was the man who'd play dress-up with his kids and sing me to sleep.

"Nonsense," he growled. "You should use them."

"They're already in the mail."

"*Ainsley…*"

"*Mason…*"

He chuckled. "Thanks, princess. Called to tell you I have an interview tomorrow."

I sat straighter. "Really? Where?"

"Tesla is hiring. Production line. Could be good."

It could be *amazing*. Auto manufacturing meant stability and good hours and solid wages. "What about your back?"

As he sighed, I pictured him kneading the strained muscles. "It's better. Definitely better. Doctor gave me the all clear."

"Then my fingers are crossed for you." And my toes. And arms. And legs.

Unless Owen got involved.

"I have to run," I said. "But tell Mom I'll drag Jason over for dinner soon, and I'm wiring money Wednesday."

A pause. Then, "Not sure what I did to deserve you kids."

We hung up, but his defeated tone lacerated my heart.

What he *hadn't* deserved was to lose two jobs to a crappy economy and injure himself twice. When Graham's Lumber had closed, and he lost his first forklifting gig, my ballet classes became too expensive. That day, I caught him crying in the kitchen. My father. *Crying*. Telling my mother he'd failed me. His massive shoulders shook. His gravelly voice cracked. My four-teen-year-old heart shattered.

I vowed then and there I'd move mountains to erase that tortured look from his face. Mountains I'd been lifting for the better part of my life.

I glanced at the clock. Owen had said to arrive at the morning meeting by 8:30 a.m. sharp. 8:29 glowed at me. My first impression might not go as smoothly as I'd hoped. Hurrying, I fitted my cell into my tool belt and straightened the safety glasses around my neck. I secured my respiratory mask over my mouth and put on the face shield, making sure its strap sat above my ponytail.

I was doing this. I was a strong, capable woman who would hold her own on this construction site.

Buoyed by my father's news and my fresh start, I crossed the street at a clipped pace. Trucks lined the road, the dirt-laden area covered in piles of wood and long pipes. Shovels leaned against a wooden workhorse. A couple of tent canopies offered cover, and wall-skeletons jutted from the ground. These would be the foundations of future homes, forever places for many families. If anything was done improperly, a wall could cave in. Mold could grow in a kid's room.

The damp air worked its clammy fingers over my skin. My mask scratched at my nose and cheeks. No matter how many words I'd studied, I didn't have the first clue about construction; my birdhouse in shop class had looked more like the Leaning Tower of Pisa.

Fuchsia hammer fisted in my hand, I forced my feet forward.

The morning sun blinded me a moment. Squinting, I made out a group of volunteers huddled together, orange hardhats on. Once I added one of those puppies to my face shield, mask, and glasses, I'd practically be bulletproof.

Still blinking away the glare, I didn't notice the stares at first, or realize these prepared volunteers weren't wearing the safety apparatus I'd been told was essential. It was the first laugh that clued me in. When the sun spots cleared from my eyes, I saw the whispering. The snickering. A few pointing fingers.

Just like that, I was back in high school, showing up at Chucky's Chicken, the words, "Stupid bitch," whispered so I could hear.

My mouth dried. No air passed through my mask.

Then I saw him. Owen. The traitor who'd put me in this position.

Last week he was all monosyllabic and moody, a little mysterious and a lot handsome as he'd listed the safety gear I "needed." If he'd hoped to embarrass me with his antics, he'd be gloating now. But he wasn't smirking, all pleased with himself. He cringed and hung his head, unable to meet my glare.

Whatever, asshole.

Instead of retreating, I rolled my shoulders back and sashayed toward the group, my adorable tool belt swaying with my hips. A few men went from amused to *interested*, their mouths dropping open.

I stood on the outskirts of the team. "Sorry I'm late. But you know, safety first." I knocked my pink hammer against my face shield. "Cap it before you tap it."

My audience laughed at my self-deprecating joke. All but one man. A man I had no intention of acknowledging.

CHAPTER 4

Eight-letter word for roofing material that protects a building
from water seepage.
Or when the woman you can't stop fantasizing about exposes
herself in public.
F L A S H I N G

OWEN

I'd seen Ainsley twice since the safety-mask debacle two weeks
ago. Both times, she showed up in her tight jeans and snug T-
shirt and her ridiculous tool belt. (Who knew those things came
in pink?) She'd studiously ignored me, and I'd hammered nails
within an inch of their lives. If I could retract our first meeting, I
would. Redo the whole encounter.

Most of it, at least. Kicking myself repeatedly for the fiasco
meant I'd also relived her near fall.

How her waist had felt in my grip.

That part left an imprint on me. Like muscle memory. The

way I could go years without kicking a soccer ball, then hit the field and weave between players and bend the ball into the net. My legs just *knew* how to react, and every time I neared Ainsley, my hands burned. They tingled with awareness of how her hips had flared below my touch. The soft give of her middle.

I'd remind myself she hated me, that I wasn't supposed to lust after a woman who wore name-brand clothing as a status symbol. But she was volunteering her time to help the community, and I kept thinking about her sharp tongue and what else it could do. Her quick wit.

Her smell—the one drifting toward me now.

Vanilla and chocolate and something flowery invaded my senses. Not sure how she smelled so sensual with all the dirt and sawdust kicking around the place. She always did, though. I sensed when she was near me. Behind me. Upwind from me. That's when my hands would twitch, wanting to latch around her again.

I swiveled as she and Sherise overlapped a section of synthetic housewrap. The older woman held it in place while Ainsley taped it down, securing the protective barriers that would shield the homes from mold and rot.

It made me think of my rainbow-walled home growing up, a ramshackle house in southern Texas, nothing protective guarding it. It didn't have visible mold, but there'd been no denying its shoddy workmanship. Or the fact that my mother had rarely been there.

The last time I saw her, she took Emmett and me to visit the beach. She had a faraway look about her that day. The one she'd get when high, before she'd disappear for a day or two or seven. She'd piled a collection of beach glass in her lap, while I sat across from her. "When glass is made," she'd said, "it's strong. If it breaks, the edges are sharp enough to cut, but they can be glued back together. Unless it's carried out to sea."

She'd held up a blue piece, and the sun had shot through it like a prism. "Those pieces get swept away. They turn soft from the push and pull of water. From drifting. Those pieces never fit together again."

She'd flitted down the coast then, her long dress and dreadlocks lifting in the wind. I could sense it—that something was different. I was twelve, Emmett ten. We didn't know our fathers, and we'd been cared for by her and the dozen or so hippies living in our commune, but there'd always been people to kick a ball with, fellow explorers to help search the woods for treasures.

Eternal children content to drift through life like shattered glass.

I'd scoured the beach after my mother had left. Gathered as many pieces of broken bottles as possible, determined to prove they could fit back together. They never did, and she never came back.

Now I was adrift, too, unmoored after a failed marriage, and I'd taken out my frustration on Ainsley, like some insecure jerk.

Sherise nodded to me, but Ainsley didn't glance my way. I busied myself, cleaning up a section of the site. I picked up discarded wood and stray nails, biding my time. Hoping for a minute alone with Ainsley, to finally apologize.

"A blue dress," Ainsley said to Sherise. "Like a deep sky, nothing too ultramarine."

Sherise swatted the air, dismissing her. "I usually wear neutral colors. Nothing too bold."

"Which is *safe*, but blue will highlight your skin. Your eyes will shine. And I know exactly where to go."

Sherise flattened her hands on the wall. "Don't go choosing something flashy. Jerome is my baby. My only child. Being part of the wedding means everything, and I want to look good, but we got to keep the price down."

They moved around a corner, and I inched closer, lurking like a creep. I wasn't willing to let another day go without making amends.

Instead of offering a pitying smile, Ainsley winked at Sherise. "Then it's a good thing you came to me. I'm a personal shopper, but I'm also the queen of sample sales. Looking this fly"—she gestured to her ample curves—"isn't easy."

Sherise coughed out a laugh. "If I had your figure, I'd wear a bikini to the wedding. As it stands, we'll look for a blue *dress.*"

Ainsley's grin widened. "You won't regret it, and I won't charge you my fee. It'll be my wedding gift."

I knelt to collect a pencil, watching Sherise gush over Ainsley from the corner of my eye. Not only did Ainsley volunteer at a Habitat build, she was offering her services for free to a woman she'd just recently met. The superficial girl I thought I should avoid was turning out to be anything but. And she wanted nothing to do with me.

Sherise smoothed down the last wrap. "Let's grab lunch."

"Lunch sounds amazing." Ainsley groaned—a sexy sound that lit a fire in my gut. She kept her focus on Sherise. "I'd say I'm so hungry I could eat a cow, but that would happen on a cold day in hell. I'll get my stuff and meet you by the bench."

Sherise left, and Ainsley raised her arms above her head, grabbing her wrist and stretching from side to side. She was likely sore, as I'd been my first month on the job. The good kind of ache. She arched her back, sending her hardhat tipping backward. It lifted and tumbled to the ground, and I didn't hesitate. Taking my opportunity to corner her, I dropped my wood scraps and snapped up her hat before she could bolt.

"I'm sorry." I rushed out the words.

She turned and crossed her arms. Her red T-shirt had a worn look about it—frayed at the bottom, a rip at her neck. The type of top designed to look old. Spending cash on that stuff confused the piss out of me. Like I could sell my jeans for a couple hundred bucks because the ass and knees were faded.

But it was the writing across her breasts that had my gaze locked on them longer than was decent:

A woman without curves is like jeans without pockets.
There's nowhere to put your hands.

Aw, hell. Now I was fantasizing again, picturing my hands sweeping over the rise of her hips, kneading her full ass as I sank in…

Nope. This was my time to apologize. Explain myself. Salvage some sort of friendship and end the awkwardness between us. She stood silent, not giving me an inch.

I shifted on my feet. "I'm sorry," I repeated. "That day, when you came by, was a rough one for me. It's no excuse. I shouldn't have told you to wear that stuff to the morning meeting. It wasn't cool, and I'm hoping we can put it behind us. We're a small group out here. Tension doesn't do anyone any good."

Stray blond hairs blew across her face. Her very stoic face. I hadn't been this close to her since that first day. I forgot how impossibly plump her lips were, how her eyes shone like blue beach glass. It made me wonder if her glass was the type to drift or stick or cut.

I inched forward, and her throat bobbed. Her shoelace was undone, her pink sneakers another cute thing about her.

"It sucked." Her husky voice took on a softer tone. "Made me feel pretty shitty. I'd wanted to volunteer for a while, and what happened is one of the reasons I'd waited so long. It's not nice being made the fool."

Talk about a left hook to the jaw. "The only fool here is me."

"You got that right." She studied my face, maybe searching for sincerity. Her shoulders lowered. "But thank you for apologizing."

Her phone buzzed from her tool belt, but she didn't grab it. She glanced toward the road, probably looking to escape. I wasn't ready to let her go. "It's dangerous to use cellphones on site. You could get distracted, and you should tie your shoelace."

"Is this you trying to give me handy-dandy tips again?" She backed up against the house, her chin tipped up in defiance. Her eyes still glinted, but not with annoyance. Her attention drifted down my sternum, and lower. It returned leisurely to my face. Warmth dusted my chest.

The construction area had cleared out, most people breaking for lunch. It was just her and me and this heaviness between us. And maybe something else...

I swallowed hard. "People get injured when they're not careful." I'd almost hammered my thumb earlier, watching her bend over.

"I'm not distracted. It's an alarm. I was playing my crossword app when Sherise went to get more tape. Sometimes I give myself a time limit. It's telling me I lost."

"Crossword app?"

"Yes, crosswords. Those games where there's a clue and you have to guess which word fills the space. Maybe you've heard of them?"

She was a snippy little thing. Feisty. I liked it. "I've heard of them. It's not what I expected, is all."

"Because?" Accusation lit beneath her raised brows.

Still holding her hardhat, I ran my tongue along the back of my teeth. I'd seen her on her phone at breaks, scrolling and tapping the screen. I'd assumed she was texting a boyfriend or checking fashion trends. Crossword puzzles were the last thing I'd have guessed.

"I'll let that question lie." I'd no doubt say the wrong thing. I didn't want to end this conversation, either.

It had been years since I'd flirted, and I'd never excelled at it back in the day. My mother had me at fifteen, something that scared the crap out of me. It had kept me away from girls awhile. Until I'd discovered sex. I may have been a late bloomer, but the studious kid I was, I'd made it my mission to uncover the glorious riches of a woman's body. Every canvas was different. Each woman had her own secrets, her body a treasure map.

Treasures I hadn't sought in ages.

Ainsley was the first in a long while to spark my interest, and I was about ready to forget my lawyer's no-dating advice. I'd also vowed to take it slow this time. Make sure I really knew someone before getting involved. If my flirting skills weren't on the corroded side of rusty, it would make getting to know her a hell of a lot easier.

"You're doing well," I said. "Making a difference on site."

Hope seemed to brighten her face, making her look younger, softer. "Really?"

"Pretty sure you've never used that hammer before, but you're catching on quick."

Her pointed look held more amusement than animosity. "Says you."

"You telling me I'm wrong?"

Instead of answering, she said, "Did you know hammer heads can come loose? That's where the term 'fly off the handle' came from."

I cradled her hardhat against my stomach. It had a worn bit of plastic on top, protruding. I ran my finger over the sharp edge. My hands had a sudden need to keep busy. "You don't say."

"I do. Know what else?" She arched her back, and that rip in her shirt shifted, revealing a tease of purple lace. Damn. *Purple.*

I shook my head in answer, didn't trust my voice to speak. But man, those eyes of hers were stunning, sucking me in again. I'd bet they burned into blue flame when she was coming. The possibility had me wanting to pin her against the wall, feel her surrounding me, grinding on me. Sweat gathered at the base of my spine.

"Well," she said, mischief lighting her face, "according to my online dictionary, there's also a peening hammer. It's used in metal work. There's a cross-peen hammer. A diagonal-peen. Point-peen. Chisel-peen. Like lots of peens that hammer things. Ever used one?" She batted her long lashes at me, dangling her teasing bait to see if I'd bite.

I sure as hell *wanted* to bite. To nibble and lick and kiss. Heat flooded my groin, my thighs flexing automatically. Time to dust off my flirting skills.

Unfortunately, as I opened my mouth, Sherise called, "You coming, Ainsley?"

The rest happened slowly, then all at once, like loose rocks setting off an avalanche. Maybe Ainsley was as flustered as me. Maybe her limbs felt as heavy as mine. Either way, she moved to face Sherise, but wound up tripping on her shoelace. I went to catch her—a habit with us—but somehow forgot I held her hardhat.

A hat with a sharp piece of protruding plastic.

The point connected with her "worn" T-shirt. She didn't make a sound as it snagged on the rip by her cleavage. She didn't wince as the fabric tore to her navel, exposing her lush breasts. A pained sound pushed from the back of my throat as I imagined how they'd feel in my rough hands, against my tongue. Her blue eyes popped wide, and her arms windmilled. A couple guys carrying brown bags glanced our way.

I dropped the hardhat and pressed her to my chest as quickly as possible, shielding her. "Sorry. I forgot I was holding that damn thing."

"It could be classified as a concealed weapon."

Her voice sounded strained, but she sank into me. The swells of her breasts against my chest made everything else rigid. My arms. My legs. My *cock*.

I kept my hips back and tried to swallow. Tried not to think about how sexy she looked in that purple bra. Not with the angry, red line blooming on her skin. I barely refrained from testing if she really tasted like chocolate.

Sherise arrived swiftly and pulled Ainsley aside. She threw a plaid shirt over her friend's shoulders, telling her she'd get something for the scrape. The women walked away, and I watched. Waited. Needed my galloping pulse to slow down. When Ainsley glanced over her shoulder with a seductive smile, it damn near killed me.

CHAPTER 5

Seven-letter word for warping that causes boards to curl up at
their edges.
Or when a man cops a feel of your construction hunk, proving
you've lusted up the wrong tree *again*.
C U P P I N G

AINSLEY

I breezed into the offices of Bega, Woodhouse, and Stein and placed a triple, venti, half-sweet, non-fat, caramel macchiato on their receptionist's desk. "Love the haircut."

"Love *you*." Hank blew me a kiss. "And that dress is fierce."

I blew his kiss back at him. My asymmetrical bandage dress *was* a great find. Conservative enough to fit into the law firm's dress code, it also hugged my curves in all the right places.

I sashayed down the long corridor and dropped a box of Aazam's peanut butter cups next to Cindy's phone. "You can thank me later."

My client's secretary snatched up the gift and hugged it to her chest. "You are a goddess."

No. What I was, was smart. Several of my clients worked here, including the philanderer, Thomas Arlington the *third*. Staying abreast of the comings and goings in these corridors was paramount to my business. If you wanted gossip siphoned your way, you didn't butter up the boss. You made nice with the veins of the business—the people who directed the flow of information. Luckily, I didn't have to deal with Thomas today. Today I got to see my favorite client.

"For you, anything," I told Cindy. "Can I head in?"

"You better. He's about to break into the Glenfiddich." But her attention dropped to my chest, and she cringed. "That looks painful."

I touched the scrape running down my breastbone. "It didn't tickle, but it was totally worth it." The Flashing Incident meant I could relive the feel of Owen's hard body against mine, how his intoxicating cologne of sweaty man and woodchips surrounded me, like pine and apples and masculinity rolled into a package as tantalizing as Aazam's chocolate.

Cindy raised a dark eyebrow. "Sounds intriguing."

"You have no idea. I'll fill you in another day." I pushed into Felipe Bega's office, three neckties in my hand.

He looked up from his stack of files. His dark hair was haphazard, like he'd been tugging at it. "You are a goddess."

I winked. "Seems to be the consensus today."

His coffee-stained tie had already been tossed on the couch by the windows. I took a moment to enjoy the floor-to-ceiling views, the nicest of any office I frequented. Something about the Golden Gate Bridge awed me: the marvel of modern engineering, how man could connect land and people with ingenuity. Kind of how I felt at the Habitat site. Like I was part of something bigger than myself. Bringing people together, instead of splitting them up.

I rounded Felipe's desk and held up the silk ties against his navy suit. The gray-and-burgundy stripes won, hands down. "Maybe try aiming for your mouth next time you're drinking."

He snatched the tie and had it fastened and tucked into his jacket in seconds. "I'll try to remember that." He tossed some folders into his briefcase, snapped it shut, then exhaled. "I hate being late."

"Better late and well dressed, than on time and sloppy."

"Which is why you're a life saver. Gabriella mentioned needing dresses for our Italy trip. Can you fit her in?"

Like he had to ask. Felipe was a gem of a client. He'd also been my first. He'd hooked me up with many of his colleagues (although slimeballs), and even better, Gabriella happened to be his *wife*. He didn't dally outside his marriage, as far as I knew. He worked long hours, invested time and money into outreach programs, and he made sure to treat Gabriella to a monthly romantic date.

"Consider it done," I said, placing the remaining ties on his desk. "These are for next time. You should have spares handy. And a shirt. I'll leave one with Cindy this week."

He ran a hand over his hair, smoothing down the wayward strands. "Like I said, you're a goddess."

"I prefer the Aphrodite of Fashion, but goddess will do." I glanced at his desk again, at the engraved glass pyramid commemorating his donation toward a rec center. He'd helped outfit the place with TVs and a sound system, all procured from his brother's electronics shop. Equipment the Habitat build would need, too.

That addictive pull to do more, give more, had me stopping Felipe before he left. "When you have time, can we talk about a community project I'm working on?"

"Sure." He grinned at me, dimples flashing on his clean-shaven cheeks. "Nice to see you getting involved."

He left, and warmth curled around my shoulders, better than if I'd pulled on a cashmere sweater. This do-gooder feeling should be bottled and sold.

Work was busier this week, which meant my two volunteer days had dwindled into one. Eight hours to make this world a better place, enjoy the swoopy feeling of philanthropy, and study Owen for signs of interest. I hadn't seen him since he'd apologized to me and glimpsed my purple bra. Pranking me wasn't cool, but he'd admitted the error in his ways, and the desolation in his furrowed brow spoke volumes. Plus, his hot factor put Emmett's and Aazam's to shame.

I'd also made a vow since then. I would not hit on him or ask him out or flirt shamelessly until I was sure he was straight. Two strikes were enough. This time I'd wait for him to make the first move.

Unfortunately, patience wasn't my strong suit. My strongest suit was a cream Chanel number with pencil skirt and blazer, accented by zebra-print Louboutins. So upon learning he usually volunteered on Tuesdays and Thursdays, I aligned my schedule with his. Today I joined the volunteers for our morning meeting, making sure to stand next to my construction hunk.

He smiled down at me. "Hey, Ainsley."

His grit-laced voice had warmth building under my vintage Levi's. I cleared my throat. "Hey."

I waited for his gaze to drop to my breasts, prominently displayed in a snug T-shirt. The inscrutable man never snuck a glance. I waited for his lips to curl suggestively while noticing my tight jeans. No cigar. Even when I'd flashed him my lace bra our last shift—the sheer material barely hiding my girls—he hadn't focused on my chest. Maybe for a second, but the La Perla cradling my 38 DDs had been more than glance-worthy.

Most men would gawk. Not mysterious Owen, who had covered me up instead.

With his rock hard body.

Sighing, I focused on our meeting. Aside from Owen and Sherise, I didn't recognize any other volunteers. Most shifts brought new workers, people helping out for one day only, or one or two a month. The site manager, Nick—whose thick mustache gave him a seventies porn star vibe—laid out the day's plan and began dividing tasks.

He pointed to Owen. "You'll be assisting me rough in a set of stairs." I immediately raised my hand. Nick smiled at me. "Yes?"

"If you need someone to lay out the line for the horse and carriage, I could help."

A muffled laugh came from Owen, and Nick snorted. "It's a stair horse *or* a carriage," our site manager said. "Not a horse and carriage."

Details, details. "I could still help."

Nick checked his clipboard. "Maybe next time. We need more people framing the roof."

That left Owen working far from my prying eyes.

The sun was intense today, a late October heatwave that had us all moving extra slowly. And perspiring. Not like Step Class Hell, but I was pushing past a delicate glow. The nutty thing was, I'd stopped caring about my sweat stains after day one. It was hard to focus on that while trying not to hammer my fingers. It was also tough to focus each time Owen (who I'd begun calling *unf*—the uncontrollable sound I'd make when spotting his fine self) emerged to cut lumber on the circular saw.

My current efforts involved holding a ladder so Sherise could take her turn helping frame the roof. The position allowed me to watch Owen, and the sight of him at the saw had fresh sweat trickling between my breasts.

When the veins on his forearms pulsed while pushing the planks through the blade?

Unf.

When his jeans stretched across his toned behind as he picked up a fallen piece?

Double *unf.*

He even rocked the face shield.

An hour later, the stifling temperature had intensified. Some of the newbies looked ready to call it quits. Hiking up and down ladders and sawing and hammering was exhausting when working on the surface of the sun. Their sluggish steps and yawns were bad signs, exactly how I'd dragged my butt around my first day. Levity was needed.

I climbed down my ladder and stowed my hammer. "My mascara has melted."

Sherise wiped her brow. "It's hotter than hell. I won't miss working in this heat."

But I'd miss her. This was Sherise's last volunteer shift, other things in her life taking priority. I hated to see her go, but at least we had our shopping expedition planned.

Nick was offering a pep talk to the other volunteers, so we joined the group. As he finished explaining how work got easier over time, I smiled sweetly, and said, "Will we be using caulking today? Because I love using caulking and hoped to get my hands on some *caulk* soon. It's been ages." I grinned.

Nick's rounded cheeks blushed crimson, and the other volunteers eyed one another, until Sherise cracked up. "Girl, you are too much."

That set them all off, the men and women wiping their eyes as they broke for lunch, hopefully ready to return with lighter spirits. Still snickering, Sherise left to meet her son for the break. That's when Owen's deep laugh rumbled from behind me, a bonus to my antics. That masculine sound echoed through the air and up my thighs.

It was clitoris catnip.

I didn't turn, not with my site manager giving me the side-eye. Nick removed his hardhat. "You've been a great addition to the team, Ainsley. Really glad you joined up. Even if you embarrass the heck outta me. Caulking…" he mumbled as he strutted off.

But I was a "great addition."

There was that cashmere again, working its way over my shoulders and wrapping my chest. Volunteering was nothing like I'd expected. Not only did I get all soppy when I'd remind myself these houses would turn into homes, but everyone accepted me for me.

We all had our reasons for being here: I wanted to atone for aspects of my job, Sherise was a cancer survivor looking to use her time for good. Some wanted it for their résumés, others hoped to learn construction. Whatever brought us out, no one teased me when I messed up. No one called me a stupid bitch for picking up the wrong tool or asking a question.

No one locked me in a confined space.

I hadn't made any connections that could offer my father a job, but the warm glow and comradery volunteering provided made my current job easier to bear.

As did Owen's deep laugh.

His long shadow fell over me. "You certainly know how to make Nick blush."

I turned, wondering if I'd made Owen blush, too. One glance and my breath stuttered. His high cheekbones were flushed, but it was hard to tell if it was me or the sun or the hard work setting his handsome face aglow. "Just lightening the mood."

"It was needed. They were looking rough." His steady gaze locked on mine. It was intense, the way he stared into my eyes at times. Unnerving. "You want to grab lunch?" he asked.

Curls of blond chest hair peeked out of his crewneck. I loved a man with a bit of fur. Something to nuzzle and kiss and rub against. I also wanted to grab the hefty bulge in his jeans and stroke him until he roared, but lunch could be a small step forward. "Since Sherise left, I *will* need a lunch buddy. So if you're offering…"

Again with that penetrating stare. "I'm offering."

"Then I'm in. I'll drop my hardhat and grab my salad." I crossed my toes, hoping more was on the table than food.

A few bungalows were across from the building site, old-growth trees towering on lawns, a canopy of leaves warbling in the wind. I'm pretty sure they were singing "Afternoon Delight" as we walked. A block down was a small park. Recently gentrified, they'd reused pipes and construction materials to make a playground. A couple kids crowed, all screeches and giggles as they wriggled through the shapes.

We sat at a picnic bench, both of us on the table top, our feet on the bench below. His hip was an inch from mine, his massive beige work boots dwarfing my pink Converse. Warmth radiated from his proximity.

Since I wasn't going to flirt first, I said, "Nice weather."

His reply to my riveting conversation starter: "Yep."

He unwrapped some godawful sandwich, the sliced bread barely containing piles of processed meats. I gaped as he opened his mouth impossibly wide and took a huge bite. His strong jaw worked. He settled his elbows on his knees.

I gagged silently. "You know bologna starts as liquid before it's solidified, right?"

Still chewing, he considered his revolting lunch, then swallowed. "Tastes good." He eyed my tofu salad. "Bet it tastes better than that."

My glass container sat on my lap, and I mixed the tofu with the cucumbers, chickpeas, olives, and Greek vinaigrette. Being vegan meant I had to work at my meals, find the right balance of protein, fats, and nutrition to keep my energy up, never skimping on flavor. Rachel would mock-choke when eating my desserts, but I knew she loved them. "Don't knock it until you've tried it."

"Okay." He laid his sandwich beside him and held out a hand. His strong fingers were thick and callused, his skin dry and peeling in spots. I'd bet my poppy-printed Coach purse they would feel sinful scraping up my inner thighs.

"*Unf.*" I startled at my needy sound, and he raised an eyebrow.

If this were six months ago (PBG—pre broken gaydar), I'd have scooted over until our hips touched. I'd have skewered my fork through a few vegetables and fed him my better-than-his lunch, watching as my fork slipped past his lips, my tongue (hopefully) following shortly. But this was *post* BG, and I still had no clue if Owen was just being nice, or if he found me attractive, or maybe he found *Nick* attractive. The seventies mustache was pretty cool.

Instead of acting on instinct, I placed my Tupperware in his large hand. He dragged my fork through the vegetables, wrinkling his nose when poking the tofu. He scooped a bite and looked at the blue sky as he chewed. "Flavor wise, really good, but I'll never get tofu. Tastes like bland mush."

A curious squirrel nattered from the ground, scurrying closer, then away. Probably scavenging for its next meal. "That's the cool thing about tofu. It's a blank canvas. With the right marinade, you can make it taste like anything. Even meat."

"Or you could just eat meat." He returned my lunch, ripped off a piece of salami from his sandwich, and tossed it to the squirrel. The rodent squeaked and squawked as it studied its find. Deciding it wasn't poison, he snatched it up and ran under the table.

"I'm vegan," I said.

Owen squinted at my fuchsia belt. "But you wear leather."

"It's not an animal-rights thing. It's more of a scarred-for-life thing."

That had him twisting toward me. "I'm afraid to ask."

I hadn't relived this particular story in years, never shared those humiliating days with friends, let alone a guy who had me all *unf.* Yet here I was, for some odd reason, going tell-all with Owen. "I worked this job in high school, at a fast-food chicken and burger joint. I didn't fit in with my co-workers, and my nemesis, Anton Bickley, liked to facilitate my embarrassment."

And call me Little Miss Priss when telling everyone I didn't know a chicken thigh from a leg. I ground my teeth. "So anyway, meat wasn't my favorite. I ate it, but working with it grossed me out. Anton knew it was an issue. He also knew when I formed our burgers that I'd turn my head when dipping my hand into the ground beef, unable to watch. Like when my blood is taken."

Owen stole an olive from my lunch and popped it into his mouth. "I do the same with blood," he said around his bites.

"Right? So I'd grab handfuls of seasoned beef and mush them together without looking. I didn't know there were maggots inside. When I finally looked, they were on my hands and wrists. I screamed and ran around like a chicken with my head cut off." I stabbed at a bruise on my wrist. "Anton must have set a batch aside, knowing my shift was coming up. Like room-temperature aside. I didn't have proof, but I caught him high-fiving people afterward."

"I think I hate this Anton kid."

Owen's voice roughening in my defense should have sent a dippy feeling through my belly, but a ball hardened in my gut. "It was traumatic, to say the least. I never ate meat again."

He didn't laugh, didn't crack a joke or brush it off. His cheekbones sharpened like they did when he seemed upset. "I'm sorry, Ainsley—for that first day you volunteered. I was as big of a jerk to you as that guy. Really feel like shit about it."

His knee swung wide, gently brushing mine. Like the leaves scraping against one another in the wind. He had no clue I was also upset over a revenge prank I should never have pulled on my nemesis, but something about his proximity, his deep voice, eased my guilt.

"Thank you. It was a crappy time in my life, for many reasons, but I know you didn't mean to be malicious. I also know it won't happen again."

He held up three fingers. "Scout's honor. But I still think tofu is nasty."

I picked up my salad. "Your loss."

Silence settled between us. He devoured his gross deli meat, while I munched on my veggies, sneaking the odd glance his way. The leaves above sent diamonds of shade cutting across our shoulders. Our squirrel poked its head out from below the bench and sniffed around for more food. My presumptuous hunk stuck his thick fingers into my lunch, stole a piece of tofu, and launched it for the little guy.

I elbowed his arm, barely making a dent. "Thief!"

He shook his head. "Scientist, not thief. Let's see what he does."

The squirrel squeaked and nudged the morsel. He paused. Then he repeated the inquisition. Next thing we knew, the cutie became irate, nattering at us in a high-pitched shrill that had us flinching. The rodent, who could double as a *Game of Thrones* villain, dashed for another picnic bench, ready to harass someone else.

Owen smiled at me, the first full grin I'd seen him unleash, and I nearly flew off the bench. That smile was a blast of sunshine. Joy in a rugged, dimpled package. It was riding in a convertible, the wind whipping at my face.

"Like I said, nasty." His grin turned smug.

I tried to contain my erratic heart. "Or your palate is as sophisticated as a squirrel's."

He chuckled, that delicious rumble amping up his hottness, and I clenched. *Clitoris catnip.* I also relaxed. Chatting with Owen was nice. I mean, his superhero smile and worn denim were as tempting as a Calvin Klein sample sale—I worked those sales hard and fast, and *always* came out satisfied—but this was different. A slow burn had warmth simmering low in my belly, promise in its lazy spin.

As we finished our food, both our cells rang.

"Jinx," I said as we fiddled to get our phones. His smile hit me full force again.

Thirty seconds later, we both said, "*Shit.*"

I repeated my "Jinx," but Owen's levity had vanished. He blinked his long lashes and tossed his cell onto the wood table harder than necessary.

I reread my father's text: **Good news and bad. Didn't get the**

Tesla gig, but I'm on their list now. If something comes up, they said they'll call.

"You okay?" Owen asked.

"Fine," I replied automatically. The way people said they were swell even if they'd just lost a limb. Social pleasantries. But this was the man who'd listened to my Maggot Incident. With him, the memory stung less.

"Actually, no. Not fine. My father has been out of work on and off forever. He had something lined up, but got passed over. Probably for someone younger, with a stronger body." I focused on my shoelaces, one bow tied larger than the other. "My mother works two waitressing jobs, and I've helped out since high school and pay their mortgage now. I think it makes him feel less of a man."

Owen's hand drifted to my back, his large fingers splaying from the band of my jeans up my spine. "Can't be easy for him, but sounds like he's lucky to have you."

I leaned into his touch, the action magnetic, so much heat focused in that one spot. "He says that all the time. Kind of breaks me."

"I never knew mine," he said quietly. His strong profile had become all sharp angles and serious lines. "My brother and I have different fathers that neither of us have met. We grew up on a commune in Texas with a hippie mother who couldn't handle being tied down by kids, so my grandmother stepped in. We moved to San Fran to live with her, spent our teen years here."

"Sounds like growing up was rough."

"At times. But my nana is great." His voice curled around the word *nana*, a lilting twang I'd yet to notice. It melted my remaining sanity. "I get it, though," he said, "supporting those you love and growing up faster than you should."

Owen's hand stayed on my back, his thumb drawing mindless circles. Circles I felt *everywhere*. He wasn't looking at me, but I could sense his attention, his understanding filling the cracks I rarely showed. Also, *unf*. Could he feel my breaths deepen? Did he sense how his touch sped my heart? If he didn't make a move soon, I'd have to risk rejection and ask him out.

When he glanced my way, our gazes snagged. Intensity shone again, like I was a riddle he'd been spinning, the answer out of his grasp.

"What about you?" I asked, trying not to sound as unsettled as I felt. "Your *shit* sounded as frustrating as my *shit*. And…wow. That came out way grosser than intended."

His answering grin didn't reach his eyes. "Also not fine, but something I'm dealing with."

He didn't elaborate, and I didn't ask more. This was casual, after all. Having had challenging childhoods gave us common ground, nothing more. And I wasn't looking for serious, not after the hell my ex had put me through. All I wanted was a fun night. Or two. Or three. Which meant it was time to forget my concerns and get this party started. Find out if Owen was picking up what I was putting down.

I struck a pose—chest out, lashes lowered. I unleashed my most seductive smirk. His attention focused on target.

Step one, a success.

Step two was the challenge. "So, I've been thinking—"

"Owen!"

We both rubbernecked in the direction of the voice…

And my ability to speak vanished.

What the frick is Emmett doing here?

"Give me a sec." Owen stood and jogged toward my gym Adonis, the two of them huddling on the curb.

Hot, meet hotter.

Emmett squinted my way, shading his eyes in the direct sunlight. He probably couldn't see me clearly, but I covered my face with my hair, just in case. Last thing I needed was him telling Owen I'd followed him around the gym. I watched them through my curtain of blond, stared as Emmett placed his hand on Owen's shoulder. It could have been nothing. Just two guys catching up. But they stood close. Too close? Like they were a couple? Boyfriends, maybe?

When Emmett dropped his hand to cup Owen's fine posterior and give him a squeeze, shock cramped my gut.

My construction hunk must be gay.

I was sure he'd been looking at me with interest before, a hint of lust or desire darkening his gaze. But my instincts in the sexuality department hadn't proven accurate thus far, and there was no denying the closeness between these two men.

How could this happen? A-freaking-gain?

My gaydar wasn't just broken. It was smashed, splintered, and had been set on fire. I could never trust my intuition again. At least I hadn't asked him out, and thank *God* I'd never mentioned my crush to Gwen or Rachel.

CHAPTER 6

Nine-letter word for an expert evaluation of property.
Or realizing the woman giving you mixed signals could be your
perfect fit.
A P P R A I S A L

OWEN

I thought Ainsley was into me. Attracted, at least. We shared a moment on that picnic bench, a connection beyond the build and me coming to her rescue. I could have sworn she was about to ask something personal before Emmett turned up. Then she bolted and barely spoke with me the rest of the day. Four weeks and seven lunches later, I still couldn't tell which end was up with her.

"I had no idea there was a vegan food truck in the area." She swayed side to side, a healthy distance from me, arms folded over her chest.

I smirked at her, ready for our usual banter. "There was an excess of grass from a nearby field. No point tossing it out."

"Or the mystery meat they used came to life and cannibalized the entire truck, leaving behind only things of nutritional value that don't birth maggots when left in the heat."

"Sounds plausible." I appraised the letters painted on the lime green truck: The Vegan Wagon. A brightly colored lettuce "man" was drawing a gun from his holster, ready to kill a rib-steak robber with a shot to the eye. It was a retelling of John Wayne's classic *The War Wagon*, complete with cowboy hats and metal spurs.

She glanced at me over her shoulder. "I could dig up some worms if the veggie fare isn't enough to fill you."

I rubbed my belly. "Had eggs and half a cow this morning. Should be good. I set aside some sawdust for you, though. In case you're hungry later."

"You're sweet."

"I know."

We grinned at each other.

I loved this, how easy joking was with Ainsley. How relaxed I now felt around her. Tessa's intellectual crowd hadn't always been my speed. I could put in the time, make conversation and have a decent evening, but I'd been a Clydesdale surrounded by Thoroughbreds, and Tessa would often shoot me scathing looks.

My fists clenched at the memory, a typical reaction when anything Tessa came to mind. But I was with Ainsley, and being with her was as easy as breathing. Except I wanted to do more than breathe. I wanted to explore and touch and hear how loud I could make her moan. If she felt the same crack and sizzle every time she looked at me, it would be a hell of a good time.

The line of five vegans inched forward while we studied the chalkboard menu. Her attention drifted to a woman in white nearing us. Tessa had a suit like that, but cut low in the front. She'd wear it when pitted against male attorneys. A master manipulator at every turn.

I flexed my hands again, tired of anger always following thoughts of my ex. Tired of her occupying my head space, period. My lawyer's e-mail this morning hadn't helped.

Tessa rejected last week's house offer, he'd written. *She believes it's below value, even though I sent comparative sales in the area. I'll dig up more data. Get prepared for next time.*

Sighing, I scuffed my boot over the asphalt.

Ainsley pulled a business card from her back pocket and held it toward the woman. "Jade pumps and a matching purse would be fierce with that outfit. Your eyes would look even more stunning."

The woman's face slammed into hard lines, probably unsure if Ainsley was insulting or complimenting her, but the comment had me relaxing. I knew Ainsley well enough to know it wasn't just a business tactic. Although she was trying to gain a client, it was nice being around someone who looked for the beauty in her surroundings.

I studied the woman's eyes. An intense green next to her red hair. "Have to agree. Your eyes are beautiful." And Ainsley was good at her job.

The redhead's hardness melted away. She plucked Ainsley's card from her hand. After scanning it, she then scanned *me*, a slow perusal from head to toe. "Thanks. Do you two work together?"

"She's my assistant." Couldn't help myself.

Ainsley shot me a scowl. "*He* struggles with basic math. We're working at a Habitat for Humanity build. I help him with his numbers." I bit back a laugh, but she didn't miss a beat. "My stunning ensemble"—she gestured to her clothing—"is purely functional, but personal shopping is my paying gig. If you're interested, call me. All I need is ten minutes in your closet."

My strangled laugh turned into a muffled groan. Ten minutes in a closet with Ainsley. *Damn.* Might have to hire her myself.

The redhead slipped Ainsley's card into her purse. "Maybe."

Her next glance at me held more heat, her attention lingering on my lips.

There was no spark. No moment where my mind went fuzzy and limbs turned heavy and chest grew tight like with Ainsley. What *did* have my temperature rising, were the daggers Ainsley was staring at her. Like she was jealous. Like she was ready to claim me as her own.

A notion I could get behind.

Except she crossed her arms and refused to look my way. Women were confusing as all hell, but I was partly to blame. Her hot-and-cold routine was tough to read. No denying that. If I got too close, she'd lean or step away. If I placed my hand on her back or arm or elbow, she'd shrug me off. But I hadn't asked her out to dinner, not even for drinks. After the Tessa fiasco, I wasn't sure I trusted my instincts when it came to women. Getting closer also meant explaining my divorce and the fact that my ex believed I'd cheated on her.

Would Ainsley trust that I'd never betrayed my wife? Or would she assume the worst like my D.C. friends and cut our ties?

Maintaining our status quo seemed less daunting.

Lunches in hand, we retreated to our picnic table and struck our usual pose—side by side, sitting on the table top, our feet on the bench below. Our white ash tree shaded us. Ainsley was eating a cactus and chili taco, while I crammed the first of two falafel pitas into my mouth.

Manual labor was hungry work, and truth be told, I missed my heartier lunch. Hopefully Nana was making her famous meatloaf tonight. Between Emmett and me, we could polish off two loaf pans.

A few quiet minutes in, our ornery squirrel made his appearance, nattering incessantly. Ainsley growled at the little guy. "I'm not tossing you a crumb so you can turn your nose up to it."

He screeched some more. The rodent really dug his meat, too. "We should call him Joe."

She scoffed at me. "More like Ivan the Terrible."

I tore off another bite and chewed. "Genghis Khan."

"Attila."

"Stalin."

"Definitely Lucifer," she said. "Or we could end the twerp. Put him and us out of our misery." She licked some sauce from her wrist. A slow slide of her tongue over her pulse point.

My heart rate kicked up. "Where I come from we don't shoot vermin when they get ornery. We tame 'em."

She cackled at my John Wayne impression. "Did the vegan food mess with your vocal chords?"

"John Wayne. It's a line from the movie the truck's named after, except horses not vermin. I took creative liberties."

"Still have zero idea what you're on about."

I shoved the last bit of falafel into my mouth, remembering nights growing up as I swallowed. "Instead of cartoons or sitcoms, my nana would put on black-and-white films —*Casablanca*, *It's a Wonderful Life*, *Singin' in the Rain*. Old Westerns, too. Loved those and the musicals best. We'd even dance sometimes."

"Is that so?" Her husky voice turned dreamy.

I bet spinning Ainsley around a dance floor would be heaven. "You dance?"

She crumpled her garbage and placed it next to mine. Avoiding my eyes, she plopped onto the far bench seat and lay down, blue eyes on the dancing leaves above. "I did ballet until high school. Loved it. I had to stop when it got too expensive, but it was everything to me."

Taking her cue, I lay down on the opposite bench, boots wide on the grass below. I laced my fingers over my stomach. "What were you like in high school?" I rolled my head to face her.

She frowned at the passing clouds. "It's the perfect temperature for hiking, don't you think? Not too warm."

She was evading my question, but her comment piqued my interest. "You hike?"

"Not as often as I'd like, but I try to get out once a month. I like the quiet, the fresh air."

"Really?" I winced at the surprise in my tone.

Ainsley shot me a look. "Yes, *really*. When money got tight at home, my family started going on weekly hikes. It was free and fun, and I still love it."

I wasn't about to admit I'd misjudged her again, that I wouldn't have guessed she'd choose trekking through mud over shopping the strip. I loved how she kept surprising me, each nugget I learned upping her appeal. "High school," I repeated, hungry for more.

"You're persistent."

"I'm interested."

Her brow pinched. "I was a loner."

Something I couldn't envision. She was snarky with a sarcastic wit all her own, always coaxing smiles from the volunteers. I couldn't picture her sullen or friendless.

I stared at her. She stared at the sky. Twisting her fingers, she seemed ready to ignore the subject. Then she stilled her hands. "My father had lost his job, and I worked as many hours as possible at Chucky's Chicken. That left me studying into the wee hours of the morning and spending my days trying not to fall asleep, only to deal with Anton's little shop of horrors in the evenings. All in all, high school sucked."

Hearing she'd been bullied at work still infuriated me. We all did senseless things as teens, but demoralizing others because they were different—no matter the reason—scratched at the memories of Emmett's struggles. *Fairy. Faggot. Queer.* My brother had made a pass at the wrong guy in high school. The fallout had ended with him enduring every slur invented, and one beatdown I wasn't around to stop. But I'd stopped a lot of them. Ainsley's melancholy made me want to hop back in time and pummel that Anton punk.

"What about after high school?" I asked, hoping to erase her frown lines.

They diminished slightly. "Post high school was an improvement. I landed a job at Barney's, which required no deep frying or paper hats. I also saved a man's life by finding his wife the perfect dress. His name is Felipe Bega, and he became my first personal shopping client."

Our conversation moved, expanding into the corners of our lives. I learned she never went to college and got a thrill out of jumping in waves. She yearned to visit Morocco and explore their leather tanneries. She had me talking, too. I found myself listing my teen jobs, how I'd searched out the only stables near San Francisco and had mucked stalls for cash.

"I loved the cowboy hats and boots," I said. "Was awed by the raw power the horses possessed."

"They are gorgeous creatures." Her blue eyes locked on me, warm and probing. "How'd you end up working a desk job?"

"I've always been good with numbers, analytics. It came easy to me, and I knew I could make money doing it."

"And now?"

I heaved a heavy sigh. "Now I'll be happy if I never see a computer again." Downright ecstatic. "When I moved here, I helped a neighbor redo his basement. That led to other odd fix-it jobs, enough to keep me afloat, but my plan is to build a carpentry business."

"While wearing a cowboy hat?"

I almost laughed, but she was cutting closer to a nerve than was comfortable. "I still love watching Westerns, but that was more of a teenage fascination. I was a bit lost back then."

She continued studying me intently. "How so?"

Someone had etched illegible initials on the underside of the picnic table. I picked at a splintered piece of wood cutting through what looked like an S. "Bill, who ran the ranch where I worked, was a real gentleman. He'd compliment the women and joke with the men. Always tip his cowboy hat. Guests would arrive early and leave late, because he treated them nice. I started emulating him. Made for some laughs at my expense, but I did that a lot. Watched men—in life and in movies—wondering how I was supposed to act."

"Did you ever ask your mother who your father was?" Her compassionate voice shrunk the distance between us.

"When I was old enough to realize the men who moved through my life weren't related, I'd ask. She'd answer something vague like, 'We're all children, together.' Probably hippie speak for *I don't know*." I stopped fussing with the splintered table and faced Ainsley, more truths tumbling out. "I actually thought my mother was a fairy for years, assumed she'd shrink and fly away when she'd disappear."

I'd never shared that silly childhood belief before. With anyone. Not sure why I was opening up to Ainsley. Not sure why my chest was warm and full and tight at once.

We stopped speaking, only watched each other, both of us breathing heavier. The table top between us made it feel like we were in an intimate fort. Our lunch hour finished five minutes ago. We both knew it. Neither of us moved. There was more awareness now. A better understanding of who we were.

Maybe this was what I'd been waiting for. To know this thing with Ainsley was deeper than an intense attraction. And it *was* intense. That spark and sizzle was back, crackling along my too-tight skin, snaking up my rigid thighs. Her tongue darted out to wet her lips, something like longing on her face. In that instant, I'd swear she felt it, too.

Then she shot to her feet. "I need to pee before our shift. I'll meet you there."

And she was gone.

———

"You keep sucking on that empty beer, you'll inhale the glass." Emmett tossed his napkin at my head. Nana flicked him behind his ear, and he rubbed his skin. "Jesus. That stings."

"It's supposed to sting." She collected his plate and came around to reach for mine.

I placed my hand on her thin wrist, nothing but bones beneath my touch. "Let me."

She flicked my neck too, and I winced. "If you treat me like I'm about to break, I *will* break. Let me do my thing."

I raised my hands in surrender. "Fine. But I plan on helping out."

Her eye roll was nothing but a ruse. This was our time, our thing. Emmett would stretch on the couch, lazy fucker that he was, and Nana and I would stand side by side at the counter.

Her house was narrow, an old Victorian home in the Dogpatch. This area may have been nothing but docks and industrial buildings when she'd first bought it, but it had transformed by the time she'd brought us here from Texas, breweries and restaurants popping up. Her house hadn't changed much, though. Lace curtains still hung on the windows, the yellow walls and green Formica table far from trendy.

Not much had changed, but it all felt smaller, the ceiling lower. Her tiny frame barely met my shoulders.

Etta James crooned from the CD player I'd bought her. She reached into the sink, suds swishing as she washed the dishes. "What's the latest from the hussy?"

Nana never minced words. She'd also never liked Tessa. "The usual."

Her rough scrubbing nearly sent the water sloshing on the floor. "Don't pull that tight-lipped nonsense with me, Owen Phillips. You may be all mum with your friends, but I've seen what happens when your frustration festers."

That she had. When she'd first taken us in, I didn't talk much. I thought I was fine. I said I was fine. But I'd felt numb. Nana had us doing chores, hours of homework, and she'd get to flicking our ears if we cussed. I'd tell myself I just missed the lax rules of our commune. It wasn't until she'd sat me down and stared at me in silence for hours that I opened my mouth.

What came out surprised the heck out of me: anger. *Outrage.* Frustration I'd never voiced about my mother's selfishness, all spewed in a choking rant...and Nana listened. She didn't defend her daughter. Didn't talk me down or wind me up.

She just listened.

When I'd had snot dripping down my face, my chest sore from heaving, she'd said, "It doesn't matter who your mother is. Your father could be James Dean for all I care. What matters is the boy you are. The man you become. Be good to your family, your brother. Treat women right. No one is responsible for your behavior and personality but you."

Simple words from a simple woman. I'd still spend time playing make-believe in my head, imagining myself a wrangler, Fred Astaire, a soccer star. Roles and stories that weren't mine. Trying to figure out how to be a good man, someone who wouldn't abandon his kids one day. I'd also worked hard to rid myself of my Southern twang and the memories that came with it. But Nana told me what I'd needed to hear at the time. A reminder now she'd always listened to me without judgment.

I still hadn't told her how off the rails Tessa had gone. The details would worry her and ratchet up her already-hateful feelings toward my ex. But I'd been slipping lately, getting down about the state of things. Maybe it was time to unload. "Things are rough with Tessa."

"Because of the assets? Selling the house?"

"Yes and no. Every time we have an offer, she refuses it. Claims it's too low, that she has no intention of giving it away. We have a few things that need appraising, too. She goes through the same routine each time. At this rate, we'll be divorced in three years."

"That woman doesn't need the money, so why drag things out?"

She passed me a wet plate to dry. More like rammed it into my hand. I eased it from her grip. "Because she's angry. Wants me to spend all my cash on lawyers."

"That little—"

"Yeah, I know." I cut her off, needing to say the rest. Get it out and off my chest. The way Tessa had dragged things out the past eight months, I'd heeded the judge's warning and hadn't discussed the proceedings. When my lawyer suggested I not date until it was all tied up, I'd listened, too. I hadn't been ready for a while, as it stood. Until Ainsley, even though her mixed signals were sending me for a loop.

It was time I regained some control.

Etta James's raspy voice vibrated through the room, the swish of the dishwater comforting. I flipped around and parked my ass against the counter. "Tessa's claiming I cheated on her. Telling everyone we know." Nana froze, and I hunched forward, the words tasting as bitter as they sounded. "She's a damn good actress, so most believe her, which hurts. But not as much as her vindictiveness. It's like she can't understand how I could have left her, was blind to the fact that we hardly talked anymore. Never spent time together. She believes, or claims at least, I was off having an affair. Blames me for us falling apart."

Lungs shrinking, I twisted my dishtowel until I'd tied it in a knot. Exactly how my insides felt. "I've been worried about telling you, didn't want you thinking less of me. And I just don't get how I could have loved her once. Or maybe I didn't. Maybe I got lost in feeling like I belonged to someone." I huffed out a defeated laugh. "When did I become so oversensitive?"

Nana paused at the sink. She waited. When she was sure I'd said my piece, she squeezed my bicep. "You've always been the sensitive one. And I would *never* think less of you. Would never believe filthy lies. You and your brother are stuck with me in your corner, like it or not. I just don't want this to taint your feelings toward relationships. You're a good man. A kind man. You deserve a sweet woman, and there is a lucky lady out there who will be deserving of you. Now let's wash these dishes."

She returned to the sink, dipping her wrinkled hands in the soapy water, swaying to the music. I dried the dishes and let her words wash over me. I hadn't realized how much I'd needed to tell her about Tessa's accusations, hear her indignation and know she'd never buy into that slander. Another reminder this divorce was barely progressing. Maybe I'd fly back to D.C. soon, see if face time could hurry things along.

"Is there mint chip in the freezer?" Emmett's booming voice blasted in from the living room.

"Get your lazy butt in here and check for yourself," Nana bellowed back.

A moment later, Emmett snuck up behind her and planted a kiss on her cheek. "You're scary when you're bossy."

She patted his ass. "Just keeping you in line. Speaking of which, have you found a nice man to settle down with longer than a week?"

"I'm having fun. Isn't variety the spice of life?"

"For now, maybe. Eventually it's the ingredient for a TV dinner cooked for one."

An hour later, she sent me home with leftover meatloaf and the soap she sold at a local market. Apple spice, she called it.

Before long I was hunched over the dinner table in my workshop. It had been my project the past month, a stunning slab of tiger maple. Perfect width, its live edges rustic yet clean. I'd kept the legs simple and elegant. They allowed the top to shine. I sanded every inch methodically, working from 120-grit paper to 220.

Tonight was when the magic happened. My first coat of Tung oil. The astringent, barnyard smells burned my nostrils, and I said a silent *thank you* for the wide garage doors.

One of the best things I'd done since moving back to the area had been renting this space. Oakland was close enough to San Fran that I could be in the city in half an hour, but far enough to find an affordable place with a workshop. The apartment above was small and clean. All I needed for now. Finding financial stability drove me for a lot of years. It was only in the past couple I realized I'd been happier with less.

Having made good money in D.C. meant I could take my time now. Pay my rent by installing countertops or fitting new doors or replacing rotting wood decks on the fly, all while building a small inventory of handmade furniture. When I had my finances sorted, I'd source out a shop or two to sell my pieces.

My business—by me, for me, from the ground up.

One stroke of my brush, and the table's colors flickered to life —sands and peaches and vanillas catching the light. I didn't use stains or dyes, preferring to retain the natural wood grain. I moved my body with each long stroke.

Not sure what time I finished the first coat. It was always like this when I worked with wood. I'd lose myself. Forget my worries. I chuckled, thinking of the dirty jokes Ainsley could spin about me working with my "wood," but man, did I *love* building things. The knowledge made me regret sticking with investment banking so long and giving my marriage more energy than it had deserved. I'd been nothing but restrained the past few years, and it was wearing on me.

Inside, I felt a little wild and desperate to break free. Itching to shed the past and seize my future. Which meant I should heed Nana's advice and not let my failed marriage stop me from trusting my heart. Not let this Ainsley opportunity slip away.

The more I got to know Ainsley, the more she seemed like exactly who I wanted to date. She was easy to talk to and generous with her time. She could make a trucker blush with her dirty humor and worked hard to support her parents. She was also sexy as sin, her smoky voice and swaying hips more sensual than listening to Etta James. There was a chance I'd read Ainsley's lack of interest wrong, my dating hiatus dulling my senses. Whatever the case, next time I saw her, likely two days from now, I'd toss my hat in the ring and ask her out.

CHAPTER 7

Six-letter word for specifications that limit property usage.
Or embracing your crush's (unfortunate) sexuality by redefining
your relationship from friends to sexual confidants.
Z O N I N G

AINSLEY

Today had been hairy. Not the kind where I got to run my
fingers through Owen's dusting of chest hair, as dreamy as that
sounded. This day involved me actually wearing my respiratory
mask while helping Nick cut insulation and push it into walls.

"How many of these caves do we have to fill?" I asked.

"Two more homes, and they're called cavities."

"That's what I said."

"Don't kid a kidder."

We went about our work.

I'd arrived late, stuffed a crap-ton of *cavities*, and was ready
to call it a day. Owen had spent most of his time helping the elec-

trician run wires, so lunch had been a solo endeavor. There was no one for me to nag about eating meat. No one to laugh with over Nick's newly gelled moustache. I even had to face Lucifer alone, the rodent nattering at me from his grass throne.

Spending time with Owen's *unf* self was challenging and mouth-watering and painful, but I missed him. I didn't normally do picnic-table lunches with men. Especially not ones where we lay on our backs, the wind kissing our faces, not an inch of our bodies touching as we shared personal stories. Owen Time was as thrilling as touring an uncharted clothing shop, new treasures at every turn.

I craved my Owen Time. I also had to get my cravings for *him* under control.

Glad to be done for the day, I whipped off my hardhat and mask. The fresh air was cool and damp, gray clouds frowning down. A few raindrops would be a welcome refresher. I spied Owen's fine behind poking out of the electrician's van, the two men rummaging through equipment. A familiar longing tugged at my belly, desire curling in a tight knot. I had a serious problem. Was becoming quite a creeper, stealing lusty glances at my new gay friend. He made me feel fourteen again, those yearning-filled days spent dropping red-lipped kisses on Justin Timberlake's *Tiger Beat* photos, no chance of ever dating my crush.

Assistance was required.

I fished my phone from my pink tool belt. Rachel's school hours made her less reachable these days. I dialed Gwen.

Two rings later, she said, "You have impeccable timing."

"Please don't tell me you're standing on a cliff edge." Last time she was about to bungee jump, she conference called Rachel and me, hollering, "I love you bitches," before she leapt off a mountain. The woman was certifiable.

"Nope. I was thinking the three of us should take a girls' trip. You know, for our twenty-eighth birthday next year. Roatán is on my radar. Killer snorkeling. I can scuba dive, and you two can sun on the beach. There's a cool town with bars and everything. What do you think?"

I either needed to earn more cash to make that happen, my father had to secure a steady job, *or* I could win the American Crossword Puzzle Tournament and make good use of that jackpot. "Love the idea, but not sure I can swing it. How about a solid maybe?"

Her answering sigh had me cocking my head. Gwen was generally upbeat. She loved her job at the adoption agency, was part of that weird CrossFit cult, and she could have her pick of men, if so inclined. She was also the one of us three girls who doled out the best advice. She called us on our bullshit, preferring to tell hard truths than sugar-coat them. That trait made her a savant when analyzing prospective parents for adoption. It also meant she was a doer, not a wallower.

"What's with the heavy sigh?" I asked.

Silence answered me. Then, "My mother is sick."

Sucking a sharp breath, I went to cover my heart with my hand, but I smacked my dangling face mask. "How sick?"

"The C word. So I went to see her, the first time in a couple years. We fought. Couldn't even have a normal conversation. Now I'm sitting here, trying to figure out if I'll be upset if she dies, and I'm planning a vacation because the idea of getting away from her and these uncomfortable feelings is the only thing making me feel better. I'm a horrible person."

"You're honest, love. That's more than most people can say. And I'm sorry. Do you plan to spend time with her? Patch things up?" As tough as things had been for me growing up, my family was close. Gwen and her mother had waged their own civil war. Partly because her mother was a crotchety bitch, but she'd also refused to tell Gwen who her father was. Just like Owen's mother.

They were both so well adjusted, considering.

"Unlikely. For now, I'll keep researching Roatán and

picturing beaches. Sorry to hijack the conversation. Why'd you call?"

My gaze drifted over the muddy ground, tool boxes, and piles of wood. It landed squarely on my construction hunk. *Creeper.* "I have found myself in a pickle, but if I tell you about it, you can't make fun of me."

"Hell to the no. I just told you my mother is sick. Making fun of you will distract me."

Not much I could say to that. "It happened again."

"You scored another Gucci purse?"

"Don't I wish. No. My recent pattern of male crushing has resurfaced."

She gasped. "Another gay man?"

"I have a problem."

Her cackle had me holding the phone away from my ear. "This is the best! I mean, maybe it's a fetish. Maybe, subconsciously, you want a threesome with a couple of beefy men. Or you're a voyeur and want to watch them. Which actually sounds pretty hot."

"Don't make me regret telling you."

She laughed harder, and I glared at a darkening cloud, wondering if I could telekinetically explode her head. I didn't mention I'd met Owen on a Habitat for Humanity build. My foray to realize my birthday wish was doing as well as the Titanic, and sharing it aloud could jeopardize it further. I was volunteering, finally contributing to the community, but I'd expected the rough edges of my world to align, too. Like they had for Rachel. But I still worked for cheating men, my father hadn't found a job, and my love life was beyond pathetic.

Apparently, I had to try harder.

"Okay, okay," she said, catching her breath. "So...he's gay. Move on. We'll go out to a club. I'll vet any potential cute men."

If only it were that easy. "I'm all for the clubbing, but my issue is bigger than that. I like this guy. Like, *like him,* like him. We're working together on a project, and I find myself telling him all sorts of things I never share. He's nice and fun, and he's crazy hot. Just…being around him is hard, so I keep him at a certain distance, but I hate the idea of losing him as a friend. I even show up when I know he'll be volunteering, like a glutton for punishment. It's a rock-and-a-hard-place scenario."

Meaning, I'd like to be pinned between a rock and his hard place.

"That's easy. Stop fighting it."

"Did you miss the part where I said he was gay?"

"Of course not. I get to make fun of you for at least a year with that tidbit. What I mean is, stop distancing yourself from him because you're a second from mauling the guy. Embrace the gay. You can shop together and dish about guys. It could be great."

Embrace the gay. *Huh.* I'd been avoiding physical contact with Owen, worried I'd accidentally/on-purpose cop a feel, but this could be liberating, allowing hugs and touches and cheek kisses, knowing it wouldn't go anywhere. Owen didn't seem like the shop-till-you-drop type, but I could get some guy intel. Real conversations about what sex is like for them. Learn some pointers.

He could be the Will to my Grace.

"You might be onto something. Sorry again about your mom."

She avoided the latter comment, and we hung up as Owen stood and stretched. Drool pooled in my mouth. His threadbare jeans emphasized his narrow hips and thick thighs. His ass was a gift from the gods. I continued my creeper staring as he scratched the back of his head, his T-shirt riding up just enough. Flat stomach. A trail of light brown hair. Hip bones. *Unf.*

Heat bloomed between my thighs, and I didn't fight it. If I was going to make this friendship work, I'd have to live with this constant ache or become accustomed to it. Sexy exposure therapy. Surely it would dissipate.

He spotted me and tipped up his chin. His long legs ate up

the distance between us, his movements purposeful, focused. Like he was about to lift me up, spin me around, and kiss me senseless. I bit down on my cheek, willing these fantasies to subside.

He stopped in front of me. "Sorry I missed lunch."

I wiped the corner of my mouth, worried the drool had escaped. "Lucifer was particularly ornery." Because I was embracing the gay, no longer avoiding sexual jokes or innuendo, I added, "I think he needs to get laid."

Owen tossed back his head with a hearty laugh. "You're probably right. Maybe we could hook him up on Match-dot-com."

I nodded thoughtfully. "His profile would read: 'I like hairy butts and I cannot lie.'"

"He also enjoys nuts by the mouthful," he added.

I guess Lucifer was gay, too.

We laughed. We grinned. We shared a moment of levity.

If I didn't know better, I'd say Owen had a sexy sparkle in his eyes. The kind that led a buckaroo such as himself to go all "giddy-up" and "ride 'em cowboy." But I was a cow*girl*. Still, this was nice. Easy banter. Jokes. I could even flirt with him, for shits and giggles, without consequences. I wouldn't have to worry about it leading somewhere. I opened my mouth to test this theory, when I spotted a man approaching Nick.

He was tall and thin, with short red hair. His thick-framed glasses looked familiar. I blinked once. Then again. I leaned forward and squinted until my eyes stung.

No way. No freaking way. It couldn't be.

The man twisted, taking in the building site, and I smacked my forehead with the heel of my palm. "Holy shit."

"What?" Owen spun to follow my incredulous stare.

He may not have been in a paper Chucky's Chicken hat, but fate had just dropped Anton Bickley at my feet. The boy who'd ridiculed me. The boy who'd caused my claustrophobia. Next, thunderstorms of fire would surely rain down. Or Hammer pants would come back in style. His attention shifted our way, and I gripped the back of Owen's shirt, ducking behind him.

His shoulders shook as he laughed. "Did I miss something?"

He tried to move, but I pressed closer against his back. "I'm hiding."

"I noticed."

"From that guy."

"Which guy?"

"The redhead. I know him."

Even with Anton across the site, being plastered to Owen was heavenly. The soft swells of my breasts met the hard planes of his "erector spinae" muscles. (Last week's crossword clue just got sexier.) He smelled like unadulterated masculinity. Like salt and apples and cedar. I leaned into his rigid spine and inhaled.

Did that moan come from me?

"Who is he?" Owen sounded like he'd swallowed gravel.

"Anton."

"No shit." His body stiffened.

"Yes, shit. And why are we always talking about shits? I need to get out of here."

And figure out what Anton's appearance meant. I still despised what he'd done to me as a teen, but I'd neglected to tell Owen how I'd sought revenge.

Anton had been a relentless bully. The villain had reduced me to cold sweats and nausea every work shift. Still, my innocent prank was anything but. Leaving him a cockroach-filled gift box on my last day should have been amusing. But I'd misjudged how apeshit Anton would go. His freakout ended with him burning his hand in the deep fryer and shattering his right leg.

I'd learned the hard way that getting revenge didn't feel good. My shame chased me to this day.

Seeing him now was worlds-colliding bad. I was doing better. Volunteering. I should be on my way to earning my wings and fulfilling my birthday resolution. Or was this karma sending me a swift kick in my DKNY-clad ass? Maybe I needed to do more to become a better person, including apologizing to Anton for my mean prank.

Either way, I was unprepared to face my nemesis.

"Come out with me," Owen said, his muscles still coiled tight. "That's why I came over. I thought we could grab an early dinner. Make up for our missed lunch. Have a drink."

I could seriously use that drink, except… "I'm not exactly dressed for it."

"You look great, Ainsley. You always look great," he said softly.

Belly, meet manicured feet.

Even in my construction outfit, I was powerless to his charms. "Okay. Let's take your truck."

Realizing my need to stay incognito, he spun and positioned me in front of him. Not nuts to butt, unfortunately, but his large hands curled around my hips, keeping me shadowed. And horny. But I could do this with him. Have dinner. Drinks. Become besties and figure out how to deal with the Anton Development.

Owen led me to the passenger side of his truck and held open the door. Ever the gentleman. It shouldn't surprise me, considering he grew up watching black-and-white films and dancing with his grandmother, just another dazzling thing about the man. Shaking off his awesomeness, I slid in and buckled up. I studied Anton from my perch. He was talking to Nick, likely asking about volunteering, which meant I could be working closely with him.

My stomach soured. Anton had never apologized to me, and I'd never apologized to him. Last I heard, the burns on his hand had left nasty scars, and he still limped.

Way to go, Ainsley.

Owen slid into his side and turned the ignition. Anton's attention flipped our way. *Crap.* I dove down, my face nearer to Owen's crotch than I'd ever have hoped. To avoid a broken nose,

I placed my cheek against his thigh and sighed. He cupped the back of my neck, those calluses as rough and sinful as expected.

His thumb sunk into my hair. "I got you, doll."

Slowly, he accelerated. At light speed, my heart revved.

Lord have mercy. *Doll.*

———

"It smells divine in here. How have I never been to this place?" Where most Indian restaurants had a cafeteria vibe with buffet offerings, this intimate room—full of soft lighting, gold-and-burgundy walls, and hanging swathes of sheer fabric—was sensual.

"I come here with my brother sometimes. Figured there'd be lots for you to order."

I scanned the vegan options. "Tons. This is amazing."

I sat across from him, eager to gossip and forge our new friendship. Redefine my Owen Time. The second our handsome waiter brought our drinks, I sipped my Riesling, enjoying the view as the man walked away. Our server was a looker. All chiseled and swarthy, his tidy beard and inky eyes reminded me of Aazam. Since Gwen wasn't here to help me deduce and assess a potential crush, I'd have to rely on Owen. Maybe he could assist in sussing out a good catch.

Even someone dateable.

Owen Time was pushing me to rethink my no-relationship motto. I liked getting to know him, sharing pieces of myself with someone again. Sure, most men were dicks like Thomas Arlington the *third*, who liked to park their cars in other women's garages. My last boyfriend, Brandon, had proven as much. But lately I'd sensed my faith creeping back. My father was devoted to my mom. My favorite client, Felipe, spent countless hours at his law firm, but he made his wife a priority. Jimmy was a winner too; Rachel was the happiest I'd ever seen her.

Putting my heart on the line again was terrifying, but I found myself craving that closeness. With someone like Owen—a man who put me at ease. I mean, I was in a public place, wearing dirty jeans, sneakers, and a T-shirt, and I didn't care. I kind of liked not sitting with perfect posture in a tight dress and heels. The ease of it reminded me of nights eating chips on the couch with my dad.

Before we could discuss my revelation, there was business to attend to. "Anton's for sure volunteering, right? I'm going to end up partnered with him, or something equally as horrifying."

Owen sipped his beer. "If I had to guess, yeah. He was talking to Nick, who organizes that stuff. But I could take care of him, if you want—shove him in a box and ship him to Antarctica. The prick deserves it."

"That's sweet, but I'd have to be deported, too." I went on to confessed my shameful stunt, describing how I'd forced my brother to collect cockroaches, not relenting until the "gift" box was full. I slumped as I admitted Anton's resulting injuries.

Owen scrubbed a hand over his mouth. "I get feeling guilty over that, but the guy had it coming. You also didn't mean to hurt him. And I know this isn't what you want to hear...but maybe Anton turning up is a good thing."

"Good because this is an alternate universe and everything is *opposite* to what I'm actually feeling?"

"No." He nudged my foot with his. "But that would be kind of cool. I was thinking more along the lines of a fateful push. If you're still upset over what you did, this could be life's way of offering you closure."

I stamped one Converse on the other, twisting uncomfortably. My birthday wish hadn't been made on the fly. I'd been down for a while, frustrated with aspects of my job, feeling badly about myself. But helping my parents took priority over ditching clients. As much pride as the Habitat project provided now, it didn't change my circumstances, and seeing Anton was a reminder that I had more to atone for than my work.

Apologizing to him could help with my resolution. I could

rise above the scars *his* bullying had left and be happier with myself, beyond my newest nail job—purple with white flowers, my pinkies dotted with rhinestones.

But the thought of confronting him had me tensing, a mental tally of every mean stunt he'd pulled locking my joints. I'd done one mean thing that had ended horrifically. He'd been the architect of *months* of my torment.

Overwhelmed, I turned my focus to Owen. Another drama I needed to sort. My first stride toward forging our touchy-feely friendship was admitting I knew his boyfriend. I'd avoided the topic, had sidestepped any subjects nearing our love lives. I hadn't wanted to confess I'd had a thing for Emmett, and I also liked pretending Owen was mine. A ridiculous notion.

Since I couldn't plow *him*, it was time to stop playing make believe and plow ahead. While admiring my horny coverings, I said, "I didn't mention it, but I know Emmett."

CHAPTER 8

Ten-letter word for a small elevator used to move objects
between floors.
Or the asshole who hits on your dinner date.
DUMBWAITER

OWEN

Visions of my brother sharing humiliating childhood stories with
Ainsley flooded my mind. I plunked my glass down harder than
intended. "What do you mean, you know Emmett?"

"I saw him a few weeks back, when he stopped by the build.
I kind of hid my face, so I don't think he recognized me. I was
embarrassed." Even now, she twirled a lock of blond hair around
her finger, avoiding eye contact.

"How exactly do you know him?"

She crossed her legs and bounced her foot. I could feel her
movements more than see much under the white tablecloth, but
our calves brushed. Even through our jeans, a spark of awareness snapped up my thighs. Like it had when she'd plastered
herself to my back earlier. I'd nearly growled when she'd

pressed her cheek to my thigh in my car. If I didn't get us naked soon, that spark would ignite and burn me whole. Tamping down the urge to drag her onto my lap, I waited her out.

She wasn't quick to answer. She flipped her fork in circles. She rolled her eyes as though annoyed with herself. "Thing is, I had a crush on him."

"On Emmett?" She nodded, a sweet blush dusting her cheeks. I'd have laughed, but she looked ready to crawl under the table. "How'd you even meet him?"

"At the gym. I work out with a couple friends there, and I'd seen him around. I mean, he's easy on the eyes, but he wasn't interested, obviously."

I didn't question that. Hearing she'd been into him irked me a bit, but it explained her mixed signals. Must be awkward to be interested in my brother, find out he's gay, then meet me. "You're not the first woman to fall for him, if it makes you feel better. I bet he got a kick out of it."

"Something like that. Anyway, I thought you should know. I enjoy spending time with you, and I didn't want it to make things weird with us."

Did that mean there was an us? I really hoped it meant there was an us. Either way, as new as I was to dating, talking about her feelings for my brother probably wasn't high on any win-the-girl checklist. "Thanks for telling me, but it's no big deal. And I like spending time with you, too."

"Yeah?" she asked, almost skeptical.

I stared into her blue eyes, losing a bit of myself each time they beamed me in. "Yeah," I said, my voice hoarse. The moment lingered. *Something* lingered. Until she looked down sharply, breaking the intensity.

I scanned the menu. "You want to share stuff or order on our own?"

"Share," she said, without looking up.

Sharing it was.

Two drinks and a stomach full of Indian food later, we both

leaned forward, elbows on the table. Nana would flick my ear if she saw my poor table manners, but the spices and conversation had me warm and hazy. Ainsley had me hazy.

"What would be your worst way to die?" she asked between sips of water. "Like, your most terrifying option."

"Zombie bite to the nuts."

She snorted out a stream of liquid, then slapped a hand over her face. It only made her cuter. "I can't believe I did that."

"Too bad I didn't have my phone out. I could have videoed it." Come to think of it, she hadn't touched her phone, either. Our conversation had been effortless, jokes and silly topics thrown between us. And there had been touching. Subtle brushes of her fingers on my wrist as she talked. My blood vessels swelled with each connection, her bright mood making my blood sing. Whatever barrier she'd thrust between us had toppled.

"Seriously though," she said. "Zombie bite to the nuts? Why?"

"If you'd ever been kicked in the nuts, you'd understand." I reached down and shifted my jeans at the agonizing thought. Ainsley's gaze followed my movements. The heat in her eyes had me adjusting for other reasons.

"Men have low pain thresholds. It can't hurt that badly."

"You have no idea."

She raised an eyebrow. "You'd probably skip a week of work for period cramps."

The one and only time I'd had a solid shot to the nuts had involved a soccer cleat, a missed kick, and me rolling on the ground. "If period cramps feel like being punched in the gut with Thor's hammer, followed by simultaneously wanting to puke and shit yourself, then yeah, you're probably right. I'd take a sick day."

"Baby," she mumbled.

"What about you? Worst way to die."

She tore off a piece of naan bread, scooped the last of our

chana masala, and hummed as she swallowed. "If we're talking fictional, then molten gold poured over my head."

I froze mid-sip of my beer. "As in *Game of Thrones*?"

"Obviously."

"I didn't peg you for a fantasy lover."

"I have eclectic taste in music and TV. My dad got me into fantasy stuff, and Khal Drogo boiling Viserys Targaryen's brain to give him his 'gold crown' was gruesomely awesome. Bad way to go."

She played word games, loved to hike, watched violent fantasy shows, her raspy voice exuded sex, and she looked like she walked off the set of *Some Like it Hot*. I couldn't have dreamed up this woman. "And if we're talking real life?"

She shuddered. "Death by submarine."

"Meaning a submarine falling on you, or dying in a submarine?"

She glowered at my teasing. "Dying *in* a submarine, smar- tass. Walking into one would give me an instant heart attack."

"You have issues with confined spaces?"

"I'm a tad claustrophobic. Tend to hyperventilate and thrash widely when boxed in. It isn't pretty."

Even now, her cheeks paled. The notion of her stressed and anxious did strange things to my chest. It had me wanting to run my thumb between her eyes, erase the crease settling there. "Do subways bother you?"

"I avoid them."

"Elevators?"

"I get sweaty."

Images of a flushed and dewy Ainsley flipped through my mind. Her curvy body under me. Over me. Locked in my arms. "Must make getting around tough."

"I deal with it. It just gets uncomfortable at times."

Like sitting across from her and not leaning over to taste her pulse point. A crumb from the naan clung to the edge of her mouth. Needing to touch her, I reached to brush it off. The tip of my finger dragged by her lips. Those plump, bee-stung lips. Her breasts rose on an inhalation, my nearness affecting her as much as it was me. My cock grew heavy, my body buzzing with desire. The urge to get our check and get gone was potent, but chatting with her was fun, too. Slowly, I sat back.

She seemed to bite the inside of her cheek, then she sent me a wicked grin. "Can I ask you a…" She chewed her cheek some more. "A personal question?"

I leaned into my chair, tipping onto its back legs. "Anything."

"What's sex really like for a guy?"

I dropped forward, and my chair *thunked* on the tile floor. That question was unexpected. Unexpected but intriguing. I liked it. Liked that Ainsley wanted to up the flirting a notch. "I need more specifics before I answer."

"Just…" Lilting Indian music drifted through the half-filled room. Ainsley swayed to the beat. "Is every orgasm the same? I mean, for girls it's different. Oral versus *sex* sex. Mood. Attraction. All those things affect how it feels. But guys, you know, just *come*. So, does it feel the same each time, or does it change?"

Jesus H. Christ. If I was hard before, I was iron now, thankfully covered by the tablecloth. She must have realized what she was doing to me. Must have been intent on killing me one sex-fuelled, husky word at a time. Delaying this gratification would make touching her that much sweeter. "It's always good." My voice was scratchy, and I cleared my throat. "Always blinds me. But some orgasms last longer, rock you harder, and with the right person, it's more intense." I held her gaze until she looked away. Her pale cheeks burned pink.

I had no doubt sex with Ainsley would blow my mind.

She dragged her teeth over her bottom lip and lowered her voice. "What about head? What's, like, really hot? What takes a blowjob from good to oh-my-fucking-God?"

My blood wasn't just singing now. It was roaring. It was demanding me to grab Ainsley, flip her over my shoulder, and carry her home to show her exactly what I liked, then spend the rest of the evening worshipping her curves. Every glorious dip and swell. I tugged at my shirt's neckline and sipped my water, never breaking eye contact.

"You want to know what I like?"

"I want to know what *men* like."

So this was a game. A hypothetical way to make me crazy. Getting her home tonight was going to be some kind of fun. "I can't speak for all men, but I love a nice, long lick. Teasing. Having my shaft and balls played with."

Her eyelids drooped and her lips parted. She made a breathy grunt, a sound she often released around me. Apparently Ainsley liked a dirty talker, and this extended foreplay was doing it for me. Getting me hotter than I ever remembered being. As soon as I told her all the ways I'd "theoretically" love her to suck me off, we'd be flipping this conversation onto her.

She nodded, expectant, waiting for me to go on. Practically panting for it.

Leaning closer, I obliged. "I like attention on the tip. A bit of teeth is nice, but not too much."

She whimpered.

"Also hands," I said, deepening my voice. "I like a firm grip. Lots of suction makes everything nice and tight. Wet and warm. Really love when I can watch, too."

Her reply: "I think I just came."

I barked out a laugh, unsure how I found this girl, but thanked my lucky stars her killer heels had sent her flying into my arms. I'd never had this much fun flirting and hanging out. Never experienced arousal so thick my skin itched. "You worried about your skills? Is that what this is about?"

She was glowing and nothing short of beautiful, her sultry smile sending an arrow through my heart. "I love sex." There was no hint of apology or embarrassment in her tone. "I love being with men and knowing what I like. I also love giving head. Some women find it degrading or, I don't know, *dirty*...but it makes me feel powerful. In control. I love watching a man's legs shake as he unravels, because of me. So, since we're friends, I figured this was a great opportunity. Like one of those 'The More You Know' public-service announcements. You're helping me do better." She shrugged a shoulder, like it was nothing.

Like she wasn't torturing me.

Forget getting her home. I was a second from fucking her perfect mouth right here and now. My dick pulsed, the room suddenly stifling. Soon I'd be jacking off under the table. "What do you say we get out of here?"

But she frowned. "You okay? You look flushed. Was it the food?"

Ainsley was playing with fire now. Toying with me. I'd bought condoms this morning, my first time in years. I'd felt like a teenager again, nervous and excited to ask her out, hoping I'd be making love to her soon. The nerves were gone. All that was left was raging desire. It was time to share how I planned to ravage *her* in the near future. Get her wet and ready for me. "Since you want to talk about oral sex—"

"Can I offer you any dessert?" our waiter asked.

Great fucking timing, dude. "Just the check."

Ainsley was all the dessert I needed, and she was eyeing me like she wanted a bite. Until her attention flicked to our audience.

She licked lips and flipped her hair over her shoulder. "I could be tempted."

Excuse me? Was that a seductive note purring in her voice? She was considering him now, her gaze taking in the man's physique. My confusion grew by the second. My fingers flexed, a second from locking around the asshole's neck.

Our waiter snuck a glance at me, then focused on Ainsley. "We pride ourselves on our variety here. Lots to offer." He winked.

Ainsley pushed out her breasts. "I like the sound of that."

What in the ever loving fuck? The asshole was flirting with

her, and she was playing along. No. Not playing along. She was instigating. Could be she was into kinky sex. Maybe she wanted a threesome with this joker. She knew Emmett was gay, probably figured I leaned that way, too. Maybe she'd hoped I was bi. As a teen, I'd debated the idea of being with men. Contemplated my brother's sexuality and wondered what it would be like. I even kissed a guy once. It never did anything for me, and threesomes weren't my bag. I liked being with a woman, and I didn't like to share.

Seeing this side of Ainsley was a bucket of ice water on my nuts.

Our server left to get dessert menus, and Ainsley bounced on her seat. "He's cute, don't you think?"

I guess things *could* get worse. "Not my type."

She swatted the air, unconcerned by my irate sarcasm. "Obviously. What about for me? I mean, his beard is hot and he has a bit of an accent. English, maybe? Should I ask him out?"

I crossed my arms, part fuming and *all* sexually frustrated. If she wasn't after a threesome, then what? More games? More hot and cold? Or maybe I'd been right from the start—she wasn't into me. She seriously just wanted to be friends. If that was the case, then fine. I liked her. She was fun to be with and easy to talk to, but right now I was riled up and needed space. If I confronted her and asked her outright, I'd wind up saying some- thing rude for leading me on. Better to end this night without putting my bruised ego on display.

"You were right before," I said, forcing my voice steady, my face placid. "I'm not feeling great. Best if we go."

She fussed over me for a beat, then proceeded to give our waiter her number as we paid. I sat there like a schmuck, swal- lowing my anger. Still burning with desire for a woman who wasn't interested in me. She was the first person I'd connected with since leaving Tessa, and my chest felt like it had been steamrolled. Disappointment sat heavy in my gut.

I drove her to her car, barely a word spoken between us; my

frustration didn't leave much room for conversation. She snuck furtive glances my way, but I couldn't speak. Wouldn't. I'd fallen for Ainsley. Beyond the attraction, I'd started imagining us eating breakfast in bed and swimming in the ocean. Doing dishes. Some people found day-to-day life mundane. I reveled in the idea of walking down a grocery aisle, teasing my girl, stealing kisses. I'd actually wondered if Ainsley was my missing piece of glass.

That dream would be a tough bubble to break.

Once I accepted she wasn't interested in me, I'd apologize. When I was sure I wouldn't say something hurtful, I'd explain. For now I needed to lick my wounds.

CHAPTER 9

Four-letter word for the part of a truck's crane used to hoist heavy materials.
Or the sound your heart makes when you realize your crush is straight.
B O O M

AINSLEY

Although I couldn't afford college and had missed the wild frat parties that accompanied higher learning, I'd come a long way since my teen years. I now ran my own business. I was still close with my parents. I'd since met Gwen and Rachel, two best friends who would take a bullet for me. I'd also found redemption with my pink tool belt.

Unfortunately, my life still felt like it was spiraling down a storm drain.

The waiter I'd met while hanging out with Owen hadn't wasted time asking me out. We'd met for drinks and talked about his burgeoning acting career and our shared love of *Game of Thrones* (aka: my love of Jon Snow), while a trio performed White Stripe covers, but it was work. *Effort.* Conversation would wane then disappear, awkward smiles traded, until we'd stumble back on track. He'd also use any excuse to brush his fingers against my arm. His flirting should have had my heart fluttering, but there wasn't so much as a limp flicker.

Nothing like my dinner with Owen.

I'd relived those details the past five days. The memory of him describing his ideal BJ still reduced me to hot flashes, and the way we'd laughed and joked had been as comfortable as chatting with Gwen or Rachel. Except it was *nothing* like chatting with Gwen or Rachel. With them, I didn't zone out, fantasizing about us kissing frantically. Or groping. Or groaning. Or fucking our brains out. I loved my friends, but I was all about the cock.

And so was Owen.

Which was fine. It really was. I was determined to ignore my raging attraction to the man and maintain our friendship, *if* he didn't currently hate me. I'd had a pit in my stomach since my dinner with him. Maybe I shouldn't have broached our sexual conversation. Maybe I'd crossed a line. All I knew was he'd shut down afterward, and his cold shoulder left me more confused than ever.

Then came my father's call this morning. Their house had mold. A dent in the bedroom wall revealed rotting wood and unhealthy spores. It had to be fixed. It would cost money. He'd refused my offer to cover it, so I suggested I find someone through the build to help out. Total lie. I would hire someone, pay them, and tell Dad it was pro bono. If it meant keeping his dignity intact, a little fib wouldn't hurt. It also meant putting any clothing purchases on hold for a while.

As pleased as I was to be volunteering in the community, my parents were sinking farther in debt, not digging themselves out. The Anton Bickley situation was a whole other ball of wax likely to plow over me. I hadn't seen him since that first sighting. I still wasn't sure what I'd do if he turned up. With my stress rising, I could have thrown in the towel and admitted bettering myself wouldn't alter my life in any grand way.

Instead I upped my game.

I found myself in my favorite client's office, asking Felipe to donate the stereos and TVs for the Habitat build. My motto: If at first you don't succeed, find a way to outdo all do-gooders. (Cue "Eye of the Tiger.") Following our twenty-minute meeting, I left Felipe's office in brighter spirits. The gold Jimmy Choos I'd scored at a recent sale certainly helped matters, but philanthropy was some high-level stimulant.

I strutted out the door like I was walking a Fashion Week runway, positive that things were looking up. Felipe's assistant, Cindy, was at her desk. Normally I'd gossip with her, bragging how Felipe had agreed to my request with gusto, but Cindy's dark eyes flitted about. She waved me over in a flurry of aggressive hand gestures.

Not her usual behavior.

If those who took stress in stride were considered "cool as a cucumber," Cindy was as chill as a margarita *on ice*. She was shorter than me, a petite Chinese woman with blunt bangs and bobbed hair. My first few months working for Felipe, she'd been all business with me, until we ran into each other at a club. Give Cindy a few shots of tequila, and the girl ruled a dance floor.

I hurried over and leaned close. "What's up?"

"You may have a problem." She lifted the small box I'd left on her desk while in Felipe's office. "Is this for Dean's wife or his mistress?"

By "this," she meant the gold Tiffany's bracelet with the hanging heart charm. The one I'd purchased on behalf of my client, Dean Linkletter, who worked down the hall. His office was beside Thomas Arlington the *third*'s. A despicable corridor of cheating men.

"Wife," I said.

"Shit."

"Crap."

"*Shhh.*"

I didn't know why we were cursing or Cindy was shushing me, but unease prickled my neck. "Spill the beans."

"Hank stepped away from reception, and the new girl, Letisha, let the mistress through, even though his wife is meeting him for lunch in twenty minutes." She snarled in disgust at this faux pas. "Dean's assistant messaged me that he's about to have an aneurism."

"Crap," I said again, *with feeling.*

If it weren't for Cindy, I'd have waltzed into the douchebag's office, brandishing the engraved gift for his wife in front of the mistress, who believed he was on the verge of a divorce. A misstep that would have damaged my business. I had five clients at this firm, each man sleazier than the next, Felipe aside. All were cutthroat attorneys who ate personal shoppers like me for breakfast and wielded their financial power like a khopesh. (Seven-letter word for an Egyptian sickle-sword.) If it got out that my lack of discretion—my fault or not—had brought ruin upon a man's personal life, I'd be toast.

I lowered my voice. "How long has she been in there?"

"Too long. He'll have her out before Mrs. Linkletter arrives. You can loiter here."

I forced a stiff smile and positioned myself near an abstract painting. My attempt to camouflage with the décor was unsuccessful. The gray-on-gray hallway and glassed-in offices exuded strength and dignity, two qualities seeping out of me by the nanosecond. Guilt weighed on my conscience. Culpability thickened my throat.

I was part of this deceit. Not the ringleader, but I eased the sting of Dean's betrayals with special gifts, false promises of devotion toward the mistress and his wife.

Belly roiling, I pulled out my phone and focused on my crossword app:

Seven-letter word for a disloyal person.

I'm pretty sure the answer was: A-I-N-S-L-E-Y, not *traitor*.

Another reminder of how far off I was from truly fulfilling my resolution. I may have been working at a Habitat build and had asked Felipe for donations, but there was no avoiding my continued contribution to the world's cesspool. Rachel's life hadn't turned around overnight. She quit her job right away, but things hadn't fallen into place until she'd made tough choices, enrolling in school months later. *That's* when her life had shot from "fine" to ticker-tape parade.

Which meant I needed to do more. Work harder. Find a way to shed my scaly clients in favor of the Felipes of the world. Not just for my resolution. Because this feeling, like raw sewage churned in my gut, didn't hold a candle to the swoopiness volunteering instilled. Leaving my folks to scrounge for mortgage payments on their own wasn't optional. My brother worked hard selling cars, but it didn't afford him enough to chip in.

I would make changes in my job. They just wouldn't happen quickly.

So lost in thought, I hadn't noticed the furious clickety-clack of stilettos or Cindy's mumbled, "Fucking Christ," until it was too late. I glanced up to find myself in the middle of a showdown. The mistress sauntered down the hall to my left…and Mrs. Linkletter strutted toward her on my right. Their collision was a matter of time, especially with the determination on the mistress's face.

Fucking Christ was right.

Sally Linkletter looked like a stereotypical Sally: curly blond hair, thin face, pointed features. Proper. Innocent. We'd met a handful of times, and she'd always been nice to me. The mistress was her polar opposite, all bright red lips and ombre-dyed hair, talons for nails. I plastered myself against the wall as Sally's attention flickered to me, her sweet smile the exact opposite of what her expression should be.

Oh God.

The mistress marched straight for her. "He's leaving you. He promised me he's ending it. So get ready for a divorce, because he loves *me*."

She shouldered past Sally, the angry *clack, clack, clack* of her heels as damaging as a spray of bullets. Mrs. Linkletter pressed her hand over her heart, caving forward. Dean peeled out of his office. He enveloped his wife, soothing her, going on about a crazy client who had it in for him. Somehow he guided her behind closed doors, not before her first tear slipped out.

My phone shook in my hands.

I'd been Sally once—duped, deceived, *humiliated*. Except my mortifying revelation had involved more show than tell.

Brandon and I had talked about moving in together, but I'd held out. The permanence of it was a big deal, and I wanted to be sure. Then he seemed to hesitate, too. In hindsight, I think I'd done it out of insecurity. I'd sensed him slipping away. Either way, I showed up at his place with my terminated lease. I'd stewed over it for weeks and decided Brandon was it for me. That moving in together would bring us closer. That we'd get married and have kids and ride off into the sunset.

On that particular rainy day, I'd also decided to use his spare key and surprise him wearing nothing but a white bustier, thong, and garters. I'd dropped my trench coat at the front door and walked toward his bedroom, where I'd planned to strike a sexy pose for when he came home.

My first clue my world was about to cave in was the grunting coming from behind his door. His "Yeah, baby, yeah" was horrifyingly familiar, but it was the feminine "God, yes, Brandon" that turned my knees to slush.

Shaking, I nudged his door open…and froze. I watched the two of them *fucking*, unable to look away. My terminated lease shook in my fisted hand, my lingerie pure humiliation. He was on top, each thrust a nail hammered in my heart. My throat constricted. My eyes burned. Then I screamed. Nothing specific, just an ear-splitting shriek.

Mortified, I'd grabbed my coat and tore out of the place. The second I hit the street, tears streaked my cheeks thicker than the rain plastering my hair. My stomach curled in on itself. I convulsed in shivery spasms, my skimpy attire barely covered by my trench coat. I wanted to disappear. Dissolve into the puddles collecting at my feet.

Now I ached for Sally, could feel the sting of disgrace that had seeped into my skin when in her position, and yet here I was, at the center of someone else's emotional hurricane.

If my parents weren't in the picture, I'd march into Dean's office and toss his wife's gift at his nuts. Cease being a pawn in this despicable game. He'd had me engrave Sally's bracelet with the word *Forever*. All to keep his public life intact. (Insert devil emoji here.) He placated the mistress with lies. She'd knowingly fallen for a married man. Now Sally knew the extent of his deception, unless she chose to accept his lies.

She might realize I'd helped him.

"Why don't I drop this off for you?" Cindy removed the gift from my clenched hand. The white box was now dented. "I'll give it to him when she leaves, tell him you couldn't wait."

I managed a few unsteady breaths. "I'd appreciate it."

Cindy really was a top-notch assistant.

———

Two hours into volunteering the next day, I was still off my game. The Mistress Encounter had undermined my concentration, and I kept expecting Anton to show up.

Then there was the Owen Issue. Upon seeing him this morning, he'd offered me nothing but a polite wave. He didn't make a move to stop and chat, when all I wanted was to confide in him. Talk through my financial options and ways I could build my client list, while shedding the diabolical assholes currently crowding my roster. I could have called Gwen or Ainsley, but Owen used to work in finance. He had experience.

It was also more than that.

He listened when I spoke, his replies always thoughtful and soothing. I could also use a hug from his gravity-defying arms. Friends could hug, after all. Friends could offer support. If I wanted to salvage things, I'd best start by apologizing for my forwardness at dinner.

Lunch was in an hour, but I couldn't wait. As soon as he came out of the house he'd been working in, I bee-lined for him. "How goes the dry walling?"

He wiped his hands on his jeans, leaving behind white finger streaks. "Good."

God, one word? He didn't ask me what I'd been slaving over or joke with me about the new volunteer with the misspelled tattoo. (Knawledge is Power.) I'd really messed things up. Not as badly as that tattoo, but Owen's distance worsened my already rising anxiety.

A muscle in his jaw ticked. He shifted his attention to the clouds blowing across the blue sky. Like he was frustrated. Like he couldn't look at me. He dragged his same hand through his thick hair, leaving a white smudge on his forehead. It was sweet, seeing a blemish on his handsome face. Being the Good Samaritan I was, I pressed to my tiptoes and swiped my thumb across the white streak, bringing us closer than intended. My breasts nearly grazed his wide chest, my senses filling with his intoxicating smell, an inhale I shouldn't have stolen.

Bad Ainsley.

Before I could snatch my arm away, Owen clasped my wrist. "What are you doing?"

He almost sounded angry, and I bit my lip, ashamed I'd made things weird again. There was no sweeping my behavior under the carpet. Brutal honesty was the only thing that would fix this mess. It would embarrass the crap out of me, but I'd made my bed.

Time to get cozy in it.

He still had my wrist in his hand. When I moved, he startled, releasing me.

I tucked my hands into my front pockets. "I'm sorry about the other night. It's just…" I looked down, unable to meet his eyes. Here comes the crazy. "I've never had a gay friend before, and I'm kind of attracted to you, like *way* more than I was with Emmett. I don't even know what that says about me. Anyway, it was tough for me, spending time together. But I like you, like really enjoy hanging out. So I thought, because I'm clearly an idiot, talking about sex and guys, and making those non-taboo subjects, was smart. That I'd get over my feelings for you. Turns out I made things worse."

My heart pounded an unsteady rhythm as I studied Owen's work boots, big and rugged like him. Unmoving, like him. Unable to handle his silence, I finally looked up. The fire in his eyes was unexpected. And odd. It was the kind of heat I'd expect from a lover, a person about to tear my clothes from my body. *God.* How did he expect me to stay friends with him when he looked at me like that?

"You think I'm gay?" was all he said.

I blinked a thousand and one times, and my heart raced faster. Was that disbelief in his tone? "Are you telling me you're *not*?"

And oh, that fire in his eyes sparked, his pupils blowing wide with intent. "I am not gay."

My life was not this lucky. Surely I had heard him wrong. I shook my head and dug a finger in my ear. "Sorry. I thought it sounded like you said you're *not* gay."

His right hand shot out, gripping my hip, spikes of fire zinging from each point of contact. "I am *not* gay."

I *was* having trouble breathing.

Maybe I'd harnessed some magical powers. Had somehow embodied Criss Angel or Hermione Granger, or that geeky kid from *Weird Science* (minus the tacky eighties outfits) and had conjured my ideal man with nothing but a pink hammer, orange hardhat, and good intentions.

Blinking was no longer an option. "But I saw you with Emmett. He grabbed your ass."

"You saw me with my *brother*. He thinks he's being funny with the ass grab, but that explains a lot. I also might have to kill him."

My pulse surged, my veins likely to burst from the rush of blood. "So, just to be clear, you're not gay."

Chuckling now, he flexed each finger on my hip, digging in deeper. "I'm not gay, Ainsley. I've been trying to figure out why the hell you'd go out with me and pick up another man on *our* date."

He wasn't gay. My gaydar wasn't broken, and by the sexy smolder aimed my way, I'd say my attraction wasn't one-sided. His thumb pressed under my hipbone, moving in a tortuous rhythm. Someone called his name, but neither of us flinched. We stared at each other, locked in some sort of carnal staring game. My eyeballs were getting a serious workout.

He stepped so close his belt buckle caught on my T-shirt. "I'm going to fucking ravage you."

A throb of want pulsed between my thighs. "I'm going to fuck you so hard the sheets will catch fire."

"I want to taste every inch of you."

"I want you to come all over me."

A pained sound tore from the back of his throat, and my body temperature shot to scorching. I was as wet as I've ever been, and I had no doubt if I gripped the thickening line in his jeans I'd find his cock was harder than the concrete footings.

"Owen! Need you inside." Nick's bellow was a harsh reminder we were at a busy worksite. Not alone. Nowhere we could unleash this woolly mammoth sexual tension.

Still, we didn't move. We breathed, I think. Once or twice.

Then Owen said, "Lunch." One gravelly syllable.

He didn't need to say more. Lunch was in one hour.

Although I had an avocado, white bean, and strawberry salad waiting in my car, I'd wager the only thing I'd be eating in fifty-eight minutes was Owen. I was ready to inhale this man.

"Lunch." My confirming syllable was pure whimper.

His hand dropped from my hip. We turned at the same time. Moved our feet in time, too. Suddenly, everything was in sync. The molecules between us vibrated—dusty particles floating on a cloud of lust.

We stopped at the entrance to the house, and he clutched the doorjamb. The marionette I'd become, I stopped, too. Waiting. Watching. Fascinated I'd soon be free to touch and taste my fill. His fingers turned white from gripping the wood. Or possibly from not gripping me. A dusting of hair spanned between his knuckles. I wanted to drag my nose over that blond fur, pinch the skin between each thick finger, nibble on his wrist bones.

Fifty-seven minutes and counting.

His brown eyes were usually rich with honeyed swirls lighting sections. Like Aazam's sixty-percent chocolate streaked with salted caramel. The dark brown stunners lasering into me now were nearing seventy-five percent, darker and more sinful.

What would it take to get them to a raw one-hundred percent?

I eyed the bulge striking a sharp angle behind his zipper. "Make sure not to hammer anything important."

He groaned, and the bulge twitched. We went about our work.

Seventeen minutes later, he eye-fucked me for thirty-eight seconds.

At the twenty-nine minute mark, I sucked a cut on my finger just for him.

Minute forty-one found us brushing horny elbows. I nearly came.

The last five minutes were the worst. My hardhat felt two sizes too small, my breasts two sizes too big. The earth's atmosphere had lost nine-tenths of its oxygen, and my tool belt weighed as much as the heavy ache between my thighs. Everything felt swollen. My T-shirt and skinny jeans would surely need to be cut off.

Then his large hand engulfed mine.

The volunteers had begun drifting off the site, heading for a quick burger or bagged lunch. Owen's fingers threading between mine promised more.

He tugged me forward, but I yanked him back. "Hardhat."

Sentences were no longer an option.

His eyes darkened to eight-five percent and a low growl rumbled from his chest, like he was pissed off. I felt the same. Angry to delay this for another millisecond.

We pried our hands apart for the time it took for us to leave our hardhats in the onsite tent and dump our tool belts in his truck. Then my small hand was enveloped by his again as we walked purposefully to our park. His strides were long. My short legs did small hop-steps to keep up. His grip tightened, nearly cutting off my circulation, and I unleashed a nervous-excited-when-did-this-become-my-life cackle.

Things were going to get fun fast.

Owen dragged me over the curb, the sprawling grass doing some sort of swaying tantric dance, the leaves above singing a chorus of "Let's Get it On." The pavement behind us swallowed the world. When we skirted our picnic table, he swung me around until my back hit our white ash tree.

He stared down at me, his eyes now at ninety-five percent. "You're so damn beautiful."

"Your hotness is at a nuclear level."

"Your eyes remind me of the beach."

"Yours are sinful chocolate."

"If you only knew how badly I want you."

Man, oh, man. "If you only knew how many times I came with your face burning the backs of my eyelids."

His hips jutted forward. Full lips parted, he cupped my cheeks and used his powerful quadriceps to press my thighs to the rough bark. Whatever sexy dance the grass was doing tickled along my fingers until I was running them up and down his sides. I was verging on delirious. "Do I get to kiss you now, sinful chocolate boy?"

He rolled his hips, and his erection ground against my belly. "Doll, you're about to get devoured."

CHAPTER 10

Eleven letters describing the amount of heat removed to keep a
space cool.
Or when your nuts ice over because you lie to the woman you're
falling for.
COOLINGLOAD

OWEN

My jeans pinched around my cock, not an inch of space between
Ainsley's sensual body and mine, but I needed more. Needed
her honeyed hair unfurled over my sheets, her clothes strewn
across my floor. Her skin shifting against mine. That perfection
would have to wait.

Heart hammering in my throat, I wrapped my hands around
the soft give of her waist and captured her lips in a crushing kiss.
When I'd imagined kissing Ainsley in the past, it was slow and
deep with little bites and licks snuck in. But her revelation of my
sexuality and my growing need the past hour had shaken me to

the point of explosion.

And I nearly did that. Almost came in my jeans. Tongues sliding hungrily, we kissed and moaned and groped while trying to shrink the nonexistent space between us. Her lips were full and soft, her body lush and yielding. I was all hard lines and painfully aroused. My balls had never been so tight, heat rushing my cock in fierce waves. My chest was the worst, a swirl of emotion cresting through me.

Ainsley wanted me. She'd been as frustrated as I had the past weeks, feeling our connection but not believing it was real. Dammit, it was real. It was wet mouths and breathy groans as our teeth bumped. Her fingers dug into my straining back muscles, her calf sliding around mine as if it could draw us closer. My knuckles chafed against the jagged bark.

A shriek from the playground had me jumping back, the outside world invading. Breathing hard, we watched a couple kids chase each other and giggle in an endless game of tag.

Ainsley unmolded herself from the tree and stood in front of me. She slipped her hands under the bottom of my T-shirt, letting her fingers trace my abs and the tops of my hipbones. "Where were we?"

I hissed out a strangled breath, each light brush of her fingers driving me insane. "You were throwing yourself at me."

She snickered, a sexy rasp sizzling with want. "Consider me your personal blanket."

Wrapping myself up in this woman sounded damn good. Her fingers continued stroking my stomach—up, down, side to side. My cock strained against my jeans, every muscle from my cheeks to my calves tensing. A blast of fire shot up my thighs. I clenched my jaw harder and flexed my quads, nearly spraining a muscle. It was time to slow things down. Savor the beauty before me. Not let things get out of hand.

Guiding her so the tree blocked us from the playground, I soaked her in. I touched her eyebrow, traced the smooth arch. She blinked, and her long lashes skimmed my palm. I felt that soft brush everywhere. I wanted to map every inch of her skin. I read her like braille instead, memorizing the curve of her cheek, the cupid's bow of her lips, the tiny divot under her chin.

She flattened her hands on my stomach and shuddered. "Are we dreaming?"

"If we are, I'd rather not wake up." Except the absurdity of our misunderstanding had me chuckling. "Can't believe you thought I was gay."

"Can't believe you're not kissing me right now."

"Demanding."

"More like undersexed."

Ainsley and her bluntness. But like her, I still couldn't fathom that we were standing here, her hands under my shirt, mine on her gorgeous face. The air snapping between us. We were like Ellie and Peter in *It Happened One Night*, but instead of a spoiled rich girl, I'd found myself a vegan fashionista with a love of crossword puzzles who'd upended my life. I looped my finger through the pink elastic holding up her hair, dragged it out, and tossed it on the ground.

A dangerous smirk lit her face. "I liked that accessory."

"You'll like my hands in your hair better." Not giving her time to reply, I threaded my fingers through the thick, golden layers, caressing her scalp and giving the strands a gentle tug.

She groaned. "I definitely like that better, but you're still not kissing me."

A travesty in need of reform. Noses brushing, I took my time. Barely grazed my lips over hers, mimicking the movement of her lazy fingers—up, down, side to side. I licked the seam of her lips, coaxing them open for me. Languidly, I twirled my tongue around hers, sucked on her bottom lip, teasing us both with light nips. Like I'd fantasized doing. We traded heady moans. Maybe traded promises, too.

We'd spent the past six weeks talking and laughing, both hoping for more. Could be this was the start of something amazing.

Her hands sketched a path over my ribs and up my back, her strokes quickening. Our kiss deepened—wetter, hotter, more tongue and teeth. But we weren't alone. I couldn't pop the top button of her jeans and work my fingers into her panties. I couldn't hoist her legs around my waist.

I kissed her softly on the corner of her mouth. "We should come up for air."

Cheeks flushed, she blinked before focusing on me. "Sorry, did you say something?"

Honest to God, this woman's unabashed humor. Every word out of her mouth had me falling harder. "You distracted?"

"I'm not sure I can feel my lips."

I ran my thumb over those bee-stung beauties. "They feel nice to me."

She tried to bite me. "What's this about air?"

Guess she was listening after all. "Unless you want to get arrested for indecent exposure, we need to take a break."

She removed her hands from under my shirt, then proceeded to smooth the cotton over my abdomen. "Can I touch you over your clothes? Because your body is ridiculous. I mean, I've pictured it a lot, like *a lot*, but you don't have an ounce of body fat anywhere."

Laughing again, I sat on the prickly grass and pulled her between my legs—my back against the rough tree trunk, her spine rounding into my chest. Our own slice of heaven. "When we're alone, you can touch me all you want, wherever you want. The ravaging I promised will happen. But tell me more about you picturing us naked."

"Aren't we supposed to be cooling things down?"

Her hair blew into my face, and I inhaled her scent. *Chocolate-dipped vanilla ice cream.* "Good point. How about telling me why you seemed so sad this morning." I'd watched her when she'd arrived, couldn't miss the frown lines sunk into her brow, her uncharacteristic bleakness. Still confused and irked with her behavior, all I'd mustered was a curt wave. Felt like an ass for it.

Turning sideways, she planted her feet on the outside of my thigh, wrapping her arms around her bent knees. "It's a few things."

I kissed her temple. Because I could. "I'm a good listener."

"You are." She pulled one of my hands into her grasp, traced the dips and curves of my knuckles. Ran her nails over the sparse hairs. I liked the simplicity of it. Ainsley plucking at my skin and calluses.

With my free hand around the back of her shoulders, I pulled her closer and nosed her ear. "Tell me."

Her shoulder pressed into my chest. "I want to fire ninety percent of my clients, but my folks have unexpected house expenses on top of their usual struggles, so I might be stuck working for assholes for the rest of my life."

I knew her clients were lawyers and had my own experience with that ego-driven crowd. "Let me guess, they toss their weight around and condescend to you."

Chewing her lip, she lined up our hands, bottoms of our palms even, like she was measuring me. "Attitude I can handle. These men are lying cheats. Most have mistresses."

My heart rate sped. Cheating meant they were looking for women to use and discard. Meant they might be hitting on Ainsley. "Are some of them inappropriate? Making advances you don't want?" The green grass clouded my vision, jealousy and protectiveness surging. If someone had made her uncomfortable or worse, they'd be having a conversation with my fist.

She shook her head firmly. "Nothing like that. I mean, it's happened. I've been propositioned. But it's never been uncomfortable, and I'd never get involved with a married man. Ever." Stiffness edged her joints. "I know how damaging that can be."

She didn't offer more, but her words were a reminder that, technically, I was still married, and Ainsley didn't have a clue. Tessa wasn't part of my life in any meaningful way, but the knowledge weighed on me. I also sensed something ugly in Ainsley's past. Without even knowing the details, it made me want to rewrite her story. Fill it with nothing but laughter and smiles and success. That wasn't real life, though. I knew what it was to be discarded, deemed not good enough. My mother leaving her kids wasn't the same as some prick sneaking around behind his spouse, but it all came down to loyalty.

Cheating was a hard limit of mine, too. Unacceptable. It's why Tessa's accusations were such a blow. She should have known me better. Believed I'd never treat my partner with that little respect.

Tired of poking those thoughts, I brushed Ainsley's hair behind her ear. "So these men you work for, you don't like being around them?"

Her jaded sigh was dredged from her bones. "It's more than that. I don't just buy clothes for them and their wives. They ask me to send gifts to their girlfriends, and I know it's wrong. Like so wrong. I'm facilitating their affairs, and I get sick every time I think about their wives finding out. I'm friendly with some of these women." She nuzzled her head under my chin. "I'm sorry. I'm ruining our we-just-found-out-you're-not-gay time."

Another laugh rumbled through my chest. "Baby doll, don't ever apologize. I don't like seeing you this stressed, but I'm glad you told me. I'll help you figure something out."

"Yeah?"

"We'll brainstorm. Try to find ways for you to expand your client base before making any rash moves. Get you away from those assholes without taking a pay cut."

"Can we do this brainstorming naked? Like tonight? I'm feeling a wave of insight coming on, but my clothes are distracting me." She placed two fingers on my chest and walked them toward my belt buckle. "Yours are distracting, too."

I exhaled a pained grunt. "As tempting as that sounds, I have bad news."

"You only have four hours left to live?"

"If you keep looking at me like that, I do."

She screwed half her face into a beastly grimace. "Like this?"

"Yeah, weirdo. Like that." I dropped a kiss to the end of her adorable nose. "A friend's in San Fran for a visit, and we have plans. Then I'm heading out of town for a few days." The way her face fell shouldn't have made me grin. The defeated slump in her posture shouldn't have had me wanting to run a victory lap. I was in trouble. "I need to head back to D.C., tie up some loose ends there."

Meaning I had to surgically remove Tessa's talons from my neck.

"Work stuff?"

My lungs stilled. Each nob of my spine scratched into the coarse tree bark.

Ainsley had never asked about my past. She'd obviously assumed I was seeing Emmett and left my romantic history at that. I should open my mouth and tell her about the clusterfuck of a divorce chasing me, but it had taken me months to tell Nana the lewd details, worried she'd believe the slander. Ainsley and I were just finding our feet. If I told her about my divorce, there would be questions, and I'd have to explain the extent of Tessa's accusations.

I offered her a partial truth. "I have a house that hasn't sold yet and some furniture pieces I have to ship."

"That sucks."

"It does."

Unaware of my unease, she pushed away from me and flopped on her back, pouting like a child. "I am not disappointed at all. I will not be using Blue Bunny while wishing you were between my thighs. Won't happen."

Leave it to this hellcat to ease my discomfort with her ridiculousness. I straddled her, pinning her wrists by her sides. "Who is this Blue Bunny? And do I need to be jealous?"

"You do. His stamina is remarkable."

"Explain yourself, doll."

"He's my fuck buddy, and he's rechargeable."

My blood burned hot again, and my grip on her wrists tightened. "Sounds like a busy bunny."

She tried to blow away the blond hairs streaking across her face. "You know what they say about rabbits. Plus I've had some issues to work through lately."

Her and me both. My recent evenings made my teen masturbation-athons seem amateurish. I could swing by her place later, after drinks with Jimmy, steal a few hours with her before sleep and waking for my flight. But that's not how I wanted things to begin with Ainsley. "If I can cut my trip short, I will." I pushed to my feet, then helped her up. "You need me to dust off your ass?"

She shoved at my chest, and her belly rumbled. "What I need is food."

What I needed was to get my life in order.

———

By the time I walked into The Blue Door, most of the unpretentious wine bar was full. Luckily, Jimmy and Emmett had already secured a table. The dim lights cast a glow on the wine collection filling the back wall as Eric Clapton drifted from the speakers. I found an empty place at the crowded bar and nodded to Cameron. "Hey."

He reached for a bottle of Pliny. "The usual?"

I'd been here enough that I could order with as little as a head nod, but my impending trip and my slight deception with Ainsley had me craving something harder. "Double Scotch on the rocks."

"Coming right up." Cameron was as tattooed as Jimmy, but instead of sporting a mess of wavy black hair, his blond pompadour was neatly styled. He poured my drink, then pushed my tumbler of amber liquid toward me. "Who's the new guy?"

I glanced at my friends. Jimmy had been a fixture here

awhile, introduced me to it when I'd moved back, but it was Emmett's first night here. "My brother."

"Seriously? You look nothing alike."

Emmett's wavy dark hair, olive skin, and darker eyes gave him a European look. As a kid, my sandy hair and square jaw often had people labeling me All-American Boy. "You mean I'm much better looking?"

His gray eyes cut to my brother, an appraising perusal that had my eyebrows inching up. Emmett attracted every available man in sniffing distance. I picked up my glass. "He's trouble. Don't say I didn't warn you." Cameron was a good guy, and I dug hanging out here. Last thing I needed was my brother the manwhore making the place uncomfortable.

Still, Cameron cast a searching glance at him. "Noted. You can settle up after."

I made my way to the boys and sunk into a seat opposite them. "Here's to a crazy day."

"Good to see you, too." Jimmy clinked his wineglass with my tumbler, Emmett following with his beer bottle. Jimmy swirled his glass. "To what do we owe the crazy?"

After the day I'd had, that was a loaded question. I hadn't mentioned Ainsley to Jimmy yet. Emmett didn't have much more dirt on the subject. Neither knew about Tessa's accusations and how painful seeing her would be on tomorrow's trip.

All this drama had my mind drifting to the one person who'd helped me when things had caved in with Tessa. *Summer Daniels.* Meeting her on my first Habitat build in D.C. had been a stroke of luck. We hadn't been in touch since before my divorce, and I hadn't thought about her in ages, but this trip to my past was dredging up all kinds of memories. The urge to contact her struck. Unfortunately, I wasn't sure she'd want to hear from me. Not with how our last talk had ended.

That left the boys.

My generous swallow of Scotch burned a warm path down my throat. "I've met a girl."

"Nice." Emmett grinned. "The one you were having lunch with at the Habitat build?"

"Yeah, but there's a funny story there." Guitar licks reverberated through the room, chatter rising and falling with it. The guys stared, waiting on me. This story wasn't just funny. It was downright ridiculous. "She was being all cagey with me, tossing out all kinds of mixed signals, because she thought…" I sighed, aware I was inviting ridicule. I looked at my egotistical brother. "She thought you and I were an item."

His grin spread until I could see his fucking molars. "She thought you were gay? That we were dating?"

All I could do was nod.

He released a roaring cackle. "Honestly, man, don't buy me anything for my birthday. We'll consider this my gift." He grabbed his ribs and tipped forward, laughing his ass off.

Jimmy joined in, nearly spitting out his wine. When the wheezing assholes finally calmed down, Jimmy dragged his wrist over his eyes. "Because I can't resist, what made her think that?"

Christ. I shouldn't have told them. Emmett would never let me live it down, and Jimmy would have enough material to make our soccer matches hell. I scrubbed my hand over my mouth as I mumbled, "She knew Emmett from the gym."

They both leaned closer, eyes squinting. Jimmy spoke first. "Didn't catch that."

Emmett's contribution: "Louder, fucknut."

I was so screwed. "She met *this* loser"—I jabbed a finger toward my giddy-ass brother—"at the gym and had a crush on him until she found out he was gay. So when he met me at the Habitat build and decided to grab my ass, she assumed we were a couple."

If they were wheezing before, the two of them were nothing but a pair of frenetic hyenas now, smacking the table and hooting. Every eye in the place was on us.

I sunk lower in my seat. "You two are such jackasses."

"Man—" Emmett spat out one word before dissolving again.

"Too damn good." Jimmy wasn't much better.

Emmett took a few deep breaths like a goddamn yoga instructor. "I remember her now. Didn't recognize her that day I visited you. But it's Ainsley, right? She's hot, man. Not great in a step class, but hot."

"Yes, it's Ainsley."

"Back up a second." All humor drained from Jimmy's face. "Her name is Ainsley and you met her through Habitat for Humanity?"

His intensity had me sitting straighter. "Yeah. She started volunteering there, like, six or seven weeks ago."

"Does she have long blond hair?"

"Yeah…"

"Curvy girl who looks like she should be toting a Chihuahua in her purse, sounds like a sexy chain smoker, and has a wicked sense of humor?"

I wasn't just ramrod straight now, the air was leaking from my lungs. "How do you know her?"

"You will not believe this."

"Try me." My curiosity was spinning into dread. Had they dated?

He waved his hand in the air. "It's nothing bad, just…wild. Sounds like she's one of Rachel's best friends."

"Like *Rachel* Rachel?"

"No, dipstick. My other girlfriend." He shook his head. "There are three of them, best friends who happen to have the same birthday. They met when they were out celebrating turning twenty-one. They've been close ever since. Ainsley had mentioned wanting to volunteer for something ages ago, and Rachel knew you were at the build and suggested it, but we didn't think she'd actually joined up."

What were the odds? Maybe there was destiny involved in our meeting. A reason we'd found each other. "Wild is an understatement. You know her well?"

"Just met a handful of times, but the girls are really close. I'm guessing Rachel doesn't know about you, or she would've brought it up."

I didn't imagine Ainsley would have gushed to her friends about the gay man she fancied. What about now? I hadn't told her about my divorce or why I was heading to D.C. If she confided in Rachel and they put two and two together, the things I'd avoided would sound way worse than they were. "Does Rachel know about my divorce?"

Jimmy's nose was in his glass, his eyes closed as he inhaled his wine's bouquet. He swished a sip around his mouth then swallowed. "No. She knows you were in a relationship and are single now, but nothing more. You've always been tight-lipped about it. Figured it wasn't up for public discussion."

I blew out a shaky breath. "Thanks. I haven't told Ainsley yet."

Emmett cleared his throat. Fixated on Jimmy's revelation, I'd happily ignored my obnoxious brother. Or maybe he was ignoring us—his attention was lasered in on Cameron. "I'm gonna get the next round." He scraped back his chair and strutted to the bar like he owned the place.

We watched him a minute. Emmett leaned his weight on the bar. Cameron looked shy as he smirked and rubbed the back of his neck.

Jimmy cocked his head. "Is Cameron gay?"

"Whatever he's into, he has his sights set on Emmett. I warned him about Casanova already."

"That'll be interesting." He turned his dark eyes on me. "Might not be my place to say anything, but if you're into Ainsley, don't you think you should tell her about your ex? Unless things are casual."

I had no idea what things were with Ainsley. When we'd left the park to get her lunch, we fell into step. Our arms had swung in time, the backs of our hands nearly touching. I wanted to interlace our fingers, fold her small hand over my forearm and hold her close. Except I had no clue if Ainsley wanted that kind of affection. We often laughed. We enjoyed our time together. There was no doubt our attraction was mutual. But she was a free spirit who spoke her mind, and the pain she'd hinted at in her past could have soured her toward relationships. A hookup might be all she was after.

"It's not casual for me. I'm really into her, but she works for a bunch of dicks who cheat on their wives, and I think she has personal experience with that hell. Not sure she'll take kindly to my divorce details. Haven't figured out how to tell her."

A few people stood from their table and squeezed by us to leave. Jimmy pulled his seat closer. "I can't help if I don't know specifics."

I'd already spilled all to Nana. I was ready to ignore my lawyer's advice and get involved with a woman before the divorce was finalized. There was no point continuing this charade. Head bent, I laid out the gist of it. How Tessa had freaked when I told her I wanted out. That she blamed me. Claimed I was having an affair. My anger and irritation rose with each word.

I'd picked apart our relationship countless times since it had unraveled. We'd met at college. She was beautiful—blond hair and red lips and full of confidence. I was away from home, missing Nana and Emmett, even my soccer team. Feeling at loose ends. Like I was a kid again, left to fend for myself. I got wrapped up in Tessa quickly. Her friends became mine. We spent our free time together. I proposed before we graduated, didn't hesitate moving my life to be with her. I craved building my own family.

That should have been my first clue things would fall apart. When I'd bring up kids, she'd sidestep the conversation. Her work hours extended. My job sucked. We'd fight. I wound up feeling more alone and discarded than I had since I'd stopped searching the beach for broken glass. Now here I was.

Jimmy finished the last of his wine. "Tessa sounds like a wack job."

"Vindictive, yeah. It's how she's been so successful at her firm. Thing is, Ainsley might not believe I'm innocent in all this. Since Tessa's spinning nothing but lies, and the divorce has to end sometime, I figured she didn't need to know yet."

He drummed his thumb to the music, nodding. "Just be careful. I won't say anything to Rachel, but you need to get this sorted before it bites you in the ass. And where the hell is your brother with our drinks?" He nudged his empty glass aside.

Another glance at the bar showed Emmett punching something into Cameron's phone, his number likely. Cameron was still smiling shyly, his hand lingering on my brother's as Emmett returned the cell. "Looks like drinks might be a while. But yeah, I'm trying to organize some face time with Tessa. That's why I'm heading to D.C. tomorrow. I'm hoping to talk some sense into the woman. Get our house sold and the papers signed."

"Sounds like an upward climb. I'd love to go out soon, though. With Ainsley and Rachel, when you're back."

Ainsley and Rachel. Still couldn't get my head around that. "We'll make it happen."

As long as Tessa didn't fuck everything up.

CHAPTER 11

Eleven letters to describe a knife or chisel's concave bevel.
Or seeking release when your hunky crush is MIA.
HOLLOWGRIND

AINSLEY

I didn't normally walk through life disoriented, barely able to coordinate my shoes with my belt, but yesterday's make-out session had rendered me intoxicated. Trapped in an endless state of horny inebriation. (Blue Bunny would need a heart transplant soon.) I couldn't stop imagining the situation going on below Owen's T-shirt. There was an undiscovered world under those wash-worn threads. He was a cityscape unto himself, all stacked bricks and polished marble. Miles of real estate to explore.

I was also dying for him to tug my hair harder and kiss me rougher, his thighs chafing mine as he thrust his length into me, but I found myself picturing other things, too. Us waking in bed together—those lazy mornings where you'd stretch and touch in the soft place between wakefulness and dreams. I'd always found that time intimate. Vulnerable. Sheets would rustle. Legs would tangle. Contented sighs would whisper along warm skin.

Missing that bond and imagining it with Owen had trepidation tapping restlessly in my chest. I wanted that connection with a man. Wanted it with Owen, specifically. But I was nervous. Scared to walk that open road again. Owen seemed perfect, but there was no such thing as perfect. Perfect usually came with secrets and skeletons in closets. Or I was just wary of repeating my mistakes. Which meant I needed a diversion.

Thankfully, Rachel was in town. I'd be able to seek oblivion tonight while drinking fruity cocktails with my friends. I'd made plans to take Sherise dress shopping tomorrow. Felipe's wife, Gabriella, was on the books for Sunday. She'd need easy dresses and comfortable yet stylish shoes for their Italy trip. I had several stores lined up.

That left today. I had no clients booked. No sample sales were in need of my perusal, and I couldn't afford my own shopping until things turned around for my folks. Normally, I'd head to the Habitat site. Volunteering had become my safe haven, a place to release my turmoil through manual labor. But it was Friday. Basic reconnaissance had informed me that Anton Bickley would be at the build on Fridays.

My arch nemesis was a school teacher now. He'd be at the site weekly, guiding his co-op students through the paces. I should have used the intel to head over and apologize to him for my awful stunt, but when I thought about how terrified I'd been in that walk-in fridge, how disgusting it had been to stick my hand in a maggot-filled bucket, my temper would flare. I was sick about the cockroach prank. I was angry about Anton's bullying.

I wasn't sure which emotion would rule me when I finally faced him.

I chose a hike instead. The fresh air cleared my mind, but not my Owen Restlessness. I checked my phone incessantly afterward, hoping Owen would send a flirty text, to no avail. I also creeped him on Facebook, but the mysterious man didn't have an account. My wariness increased. People with secrets avoided social media, like my ex had. But Owen wasn't Brandon, and I was letting my past affect my present.

Hanging out with Gwen and Rachel would be the distraction I needed.

Unfortunately, when I met them at the given address and realized where they were taking me, I nearly left. "Is this your idea of a joke? What kind of club needs an elevator?"

"A new swanky one," Gwen said. "Don't worry. I'll hold your hand."

"You'd be better off holding a barf bucket."

She tapped the toe of her turquoise stiletto, unimpressed, while we waited for Rachel to get off her cell. The girls knew I disliked confined spaces. They knew I'd be green by the time we reached the top floor. They also knew I'd recover. Checking out a new hot spot trumped my claustrophobia. "They better sell margaritas by the pitcher."

Gwen petted my hair. "I'll buy the first round. And we're doing you a favor. You can't spend your life avoiding your fears."

Except avoiding the Habitat build today proved I could.

Rachel hurried over, jamming her phone into her overflowing purse. "Sorry. Mother drama. She thinks my niece might have meningitis because the little peanut coughed." She planted her hands on her slim hips and exhaled.

I made the sign of the cross over my chest. "Let's get in that moving coffin and get my torture over with."

When the elevator doors opened on the thirty-eighth floor, sweat had gathered in my cleavage. My skin was likely more gray than blush. My lungs had shrunk to pea-sized and swallowing was an effort. Dizzy, I stepped into the bar. The massive windows overlooking San Francisco swayed, but the room was stunning. A spray of tiny lights exploded from the ceiling, mimicking the galaxy of city lights expanding across the night sky. The elevator sucked, but the view and ambiance were worth it.

Gwen slapped my back. "See? Piece of cake."

Said the girl who jumped off cliffs. "There should be a margarita in my hand."

Two and a half margaritas later, my Anton quandary and Owen Restlessness still lingered, but I maintained my game face. We chatted with Rachel about school and Jimmy and Napa Valley. Gwen regaled us with tales of rock climbing and bungee jumping that had me green again. We also tutted over her, making sure she was managing her mother's illness all right.

We laughed and commiserated at our high-top table. I managed to fly under the radar until Gwen said, "How did everything work out with your latest gay crush? You two besties yet?"

That had Rachel perking up. "Please don't tell me I missed another one."

I said, "Nope," and Gwen crowed, "Yep!"

Traitor.

Rachel sighed into her Chardonnay. "Honestly, the only crappy thing about living in Napa is missing all the little stuff. I need details."

They mirrored each other, chins in hands, waiting on me. They were about to get more than they bargained for. "That story is a doozy, but I need another drink before I open the vault." I drained margarita number three.

Rachel frowned at her almost-empty glass. "I'm not sure I should. Reckless Rachel hasn't been out for a while. I'm like the Hulk. Days Without Incident: Two Hundred and Twenty-five."

Except Reckless Rachel was a blast. Give my sweet friend four glasses of wine, and her inhibitions often vanished. Case in point: the Dildo Incident. If it weren't for Reckless Rachel dragging us into a sex shop, making a fool of herself, then running through the street with a dildo while screaming, "I have a penis!" I wouldn't have found Blue Bunny.

I fluttered my Lancôme lashes at her. "I rode the elevator. Drink up, girly."

Three men in slacks and button-downs, who had been circling us like sharks, finally moved in for the kill. The tallest led the way. "How about we treat you ladies to that round?"

I didn't blame them for hitting on us. I could strut through a *Sex and the City* rerun in my fluffy tulle skirt and pink strapless top as Carrie's stunt double. Rachel's red dress flaunted her tanned skin and freckles. Gwen was her usual rumpled-yet-styled self in a loose off-the-shoulder top and skin-tight black pants. Guys assumed we got dolled up to impress them. So adorably naïve. They'd never understand that women often dressed for women. I had to look my best for my girls.

Clueless, these men lingered. All three were fit and handsome. Business types with fancy watches, Crest Whitestrip teeth, and superhero jaws. Before Owen, I'd have flipped my hair and angled my cleavage their way. Before Owen, I'd have accepted their flirtatious offer. After Owen, I said, "Thanks but no thanks."

Rachel was taken, Gwen was on an asshole break, as she called it, and I was…

Big, fat question mark.

Defeated, the men went to search for other fish in this glittery sea, but Gwen leveled raised eyebrows at me. "Since when do you turn down drinks?"

"I don't know. Nothing. Whatever." God, I was pathetic.

Rachel nudged Gwen. "She's lying to us."

Gwen lifted her chin, studying me. "I know."

"Does it have to do with that gay guy?" Rachel asked her.

"Maybe. She was weird on the phone about it."

"You two suck," I said, reminding them I was at the table. But we often pulled this stunt, omitting one person from the conversation to make them squirm. It totally worked. "Yes, it's about that guy. There's a story. Get me my drink first."

Gwen saluted me and scurried over to the bar. Rachel grooved on her seat to the smooth R&B tunes. A Rachel groove looked like a giraffe on stilts trying to ice skate. It should have been enough to entertain me while I awaited my liquid courage, but thoughts of bars and flirting and buying drinks had me picking my newly polished nails.

Because *Owen, Owen, Owen*.

As maniacal as I'd been with him at our park yesterday, pawing at him like it was my job, insecurity had swept over me since. My history with Brandon kept rearing its ugly head, reminding me how painful relationships could be until my anxiety had stretched its wings, flapping fitfully through my belly.

Owen was in D.C., and his life there was a blank crossword with no clues. There could be an ex-girlfriend. He could be out with friends in his own ocean, circling schools of fish, buying drinks.

We hadn't discussed what we were, or if we were exclusive. We hadn't even been on a proper date. (Dinner with Gay-Not-Gay Owen didn't count.) Yet I felt like we were an item. Weeks of talking and laughing had set the stage for a romance that peaked yesterday. If he went out with another woman, it would hurt.

Gwen returned with our drinks. I downed half of mine, then blurted the whole story. Worried I'd impede my wish, I hadn't told them yet about my volunteering, but needing advice trumped that silly superstition. I finally admitted my Habitat for Humanity work. Meeting Owen. Then Gay Owen. Then Not-Gay Owen. I couldn't unpack the Anton Bickley situation yet and omitted that particular soap opera, but I bled out the rest.

Rachel spun her wineglass. "You met Owen at the Habitat build?"

"Yeah."

"Is he tall and fit, with a deep voice and sandy hair? Looks like he belongs at a rodeo?"

I narrowed my eyes at her. "Have you been creeping me?"

"Oh my God. Owen!" She smacked her hands together. "This is *insane*. He's friends with Jimmy. The one I mentioned volunteered at the build."

I blinked, dumbfounded. "*My* Owen is the Habitat guy, and he's friends with Jimmy?" I'd been reduced to repeating the obvious.

"From when they were teens. They played soccer together. They reconnected when Owen moved back to town. This means we get to double date!"

Gwen shook her head. "That's actually pretty nuts."

Absolutely crazy. It also meant Rachel might have intel. "So"—I sat on my hands before I picked my nails to death—"have you guys hung out?"

"A bit, but usually short chats after a soccer match. We did have lunch once."

"And?"

"And what?"

I rolled my eyes at the ceiling. After six years of gym workouts, drunken nights, and gossip sessions, I shouldn't have to spell this out. "I need to know *all the things*. Did he have a serious girlfriend in D.C.? An illegitimate child? Does he run a drug ring or work as a gigolo at night?"

Gwen snickered. "Shouldn't you know all this? You just said you guys have done nothing but talk for weeks. Why didn't you ask about his history?"

"Because he was *gay*." I needed to apply for new friends.

My soon to be ex-bestie tossed her head back with another wild laugh, pretty much all she'd done since I told them I'd flirted with another man after asking Owen to describe his ideal BJ. Once she'd gained control of her faculties, Gwen wrenched one of my hands from under my thigh and laced our fingers together. "I'm sorry, love. I will make fun of you forever for it, but I get that this is hard for you. I wasn't sure you'd let yourself fall for someone again after Brandon."

She kissed my knuckles, and we turned our attention to Rachel, who shrugged. "I wish I had more dirt. He did have a girlfriend or something in D.C. and is single now, but that's all I know. He seems like a good guy. Jimmy wouldn't be friends with an asshole."

There was truth in that, but it didn't lessen my turmoil. "I hate Brandon for ruining me like this. I shouldn't be this nervous to date again."

The girls traded sad, puppy-dog faces. To me, Rachel said, "Have you told Owen?"

I extricated my hand from Gwen's to sip my drink, curling in on myself the way I had with Owen yesterday when the words were at the tip of my tongue. "No. I almost did, but I chickened out."

There was nothing easy about admitting you were dumb enough to be duped.

"Well, I think you should," Gwen said. "Putting your trust in him is a big deal for you. If you're not honest, you guys don't stand a chance." Gwen never minced words.

Rachel's doe eyes softened. "From what I know of Owen, and what you've said, he seems like the type of guy who'll put your mind at ease. You deserve this, Ainsley. There are lots of jerks out there, but there are good guys, too."

They were right. I knew they were. I had to lay my dirty laundry out for Owen so I didn't wind up worse off than after Brandon's betrayal. Although watching my friends fill my ex's door lock with expanding foam while he was inside had made me giddy. Navy Seals had nothing on us.

As I'd done a hundred and seven times today, I slipped my phone from my purse to check my messages. My belly whirled at the sight of Owen's name. He'd texted me an hour ago.

My hotel room is lonely.

It was like he'd sensed what I needed to hear. With the time difference, he was probably asleep by now, but I couldn't resist replying. ***Don't they have gay porn?***

A second later: ***I've already watched it all.***

I could practically hear him chuckling from three thousand miles away, and I clenched.

Clitoris catnip.

You at home? he wrote.

At a club with the girls. The margaritas are flowing.

The girls in question made kissy faces at me and my phone. I could only imagine the goofy grin I was sporting. One word from Owen, and I was like a giant mop, swoopy and loose. Or maybe it was the margaritas. Rachel's fourth glass of wine was almost finished. She dragged Gwen to the dance floor, giving me some privacy. I snorted as Reckless Rachel made her appearance, busting an uncoordinated move. I should have been filming the moment for posterity, but my attention slipped back to my phone. To Owen on the other side of the country.

There was no reply. ***You still awake?***

We'll talk later.

My levity dropped, nothing but a chill in those words. A chill I understood. If he'd told me he was at a club with friends, I'd have shut down on him, too. God, I was insensitive.

Then I stooped to a new low. ***Guys came by our table. Asked to buy us drinks.***

His pause lasted an eternity. ***Don't know what you want me to say to that.***

Music thumping, heart racing, I wrote, ***I told them no.***

Another pause. ***Why?***

I didn't know where we stood, couldn't control what he was doing or thinking all that distance away. But I could be honest. ***Because the only guy I want to drink with is you.***

His next delay held more promise. Then, ***Ainsley.***

Yeah? My bated breath was practically fogging up my phone.

I miss you something fierce.

My heart pinballed. The stars and lights around me exploded

in my eyes. I needed more of him, something to get me through the next couple of days. He was three hours ahead of me, but he was awake. ***Don't move. Don't go to sleep. I'm heading home and want to hear your voice.***

I'm not going anywhere. I'd bet he was smiling.

I gave the girls sloppy hugs, braved the elevator down (only nearly passed out once), then took a cab to my place, slamming the door closed as I hit his number.

"Hey, baby doll."

I melted onto my white duvet at the sound of his voice. "If you answer every call like that, I'll be hitting redial all day."

A half sigh, half laugh tickled my eardrum. "Glad you called."

"Tell me again how you miss me?"

The rustling of sheets echoed. It was 3:48 a.m. his time. He was in bed. Did he slumber in the buff? In briefs? In pizza-slice printed pajamas bottoms? "I can't sleep. Keep thinking about kissing you."

"Just kissing?"

"No, doll. Not just kissing. The gay porn didn't help."

A yelp of a tipsy laugh burst from my lips. "Promise me we'll always joke about my idiocy."

"That's an easy promise to make. How was your night? Aside from assholes picking you up."

Jealousy edged his tone. I liked it. "Fun. Always nice to see the girls, and I found out a juicy tidbit about you."

Heavy breathing replied. Then quiet. He was probably exhausted. I grabbed my lattice Calvin Klein pillow and tucked it under my arms.

"What did you hear?" His eventual question sounded scratchy, his deep voice roughed up by the late hour. His twang made an appearance, too. That sexy lilt he often kept hidden.

"Looks like we have friends in common—Rachel and Jimmy."

A whoosh of an exhale slipstreamed from D.C. to my San

Francisco bedroom. "Yeah, I found that out before I left. That's who I had plans with." His tone lightened. Hopefully he was as excited about the notion as me.

But I was a teensy bit more than excited now. I had my construction hunk on the phone, his sensual voice purring through the line. Feeling wired and overheated and frisky, I kicked off my heels and attempted to get naked.

"What's that noise?"

I stopped thrashing around. "I launched my heels into the wall. Or do you mean the zipper sliding down the side of my dress as I dislocated my shoulder?" I'm sure I could have made that sound sexier.

He grunted—a low, masculine sound. "Ainsley…"

"Owen…"

My queen bed was a fluffy white cloud, my soft blue walls adorned with black-and-white fashion photos. It all looked hazy, probably hot-boxed by my heavy breathing. Zipper down, I shimmied out of my Carrie Bradshaw dress and dragged my pale pink panties and bra off. All that was left was a very horny woman. Blue Bunny was lounging on the duvet by my head, recuperating from today's workout. I snatched him up and let him buzz into my phone.

Owen answered with a "*Christ.*"

"You want to play with me, or should we hang up so I can play on my own?"

"Has your bunny been busy?"

"Is your wrist sore?"

His next guttural sound came out more like a pained sigh. "Turn it on and spread your legs for me. Nice and slow."

Holy Hannah. Dropping my head back, I let my knees fall wide and revved my little blue engine. "Are you touching yourself?" The need in my voice should have been embarrassing, but I was past the point of caring.

His baritone dropped an octave. "I'm gripping the base of my cock. I'm so turned on, baby. So damn hard. I'm stroking my whole length, slow but tight, picturing your luscious curves."

Odds are I wouldn't need battery assisted help to come. "Have you done this before? Because you could teach a class."

His muffled laugh was hot and hoarse. "You're my first. Now take that bunny of yours and press it to the top of your inner thigh. Beside your pussy. Don't get greedy on me. Tease yourself the way I'll be teasing you in a couple days."

Forget a class. He could earn a doctorate.

Following his rasped orders, I touched the edge of my vibrator to the juncture of my thigh. The buzz sent a spark to my center. "Oh. That's nice." So close yet so far from where I throbbed.

"I bet it is. Imagine how nice it'll feel when my face is buried in your pussy. I'm gonna plant wet kisses everywhere." His panting grew shallow. "Give you nice long licks and quick flicks and suck you until you scream. Now move your toy to the other side. Next to all that wet heat. Picture me between your thighs."

Molten lava dripped through me, his erotic words making me bubble and steam. I upped the speed but did as he asked— teased, tormented, and tortured myself. I pictured his dirty-blond hair tangled in my hands, could practically feel the scratch of his scruff on my sensitive skin. "More," I begged, the needy girl I was. "What are you doing?"

"I'm picturing your lips wrapped around my cock. Your tongue swirling and head bobbing. I'm stroking faster. Getting harder. So hard, baby. Because of you. Now"—a rough grunt sounded—"now press your blue bunny exactly where you need him. *Christ*, Ainsley, I'm close."

I was about to fly apart. The second I touched the buzzing tip to my nub of bundled nerves, I cried out. My hips shot up, my knees slamming together as I pressed down. "Owen." All breath trapped in my chest. "I wish you were here. I want you so badly." So much pleasure concentrated in one exhilarating spot.

"I'm going to spend hours exploring you. Fucking *hours*.

Now move your hips. Close your eyes and let go, because I'm… fuck…Ainsley, baby, I'm…" He roared from across freeways and cities and farmland. He called my name and growled, somehow closing the distance between us. His heavy breathing slipped through the phone, down my sizzling skin, urging my hips faster, and I burst open. Everything clenched as pleasure shot through me, currents of snapping heat. "Oh, Owen. God. *Yes.*"

My high crested, endless shockwaves knocking me senseless, until I was too sensitive for Blue Bunny. I was too sensitive for a light breeze.

Blissful, I turned off my bunny and pulled the lacy quilt from the end of my bed up to my chest. "I'm paralyzed."

Owen released a satisfied chuckle. "I'm sticky."

That was quite the visual, unbelievably hot. I was languid and loose, heading into a pleasure coma. "I wasn't kidding, you know, at the site yesterday. I want you to come on me. I've never wanted something like that before. Is it weird?" Although I often lacked a filter, my blunt honesty with him surprised even me.

"You trying to get me hard again?"

"Maybe?"

"Doing that to you, seeing it? It might ruin me."

Letting my heart go with him could obliterate me. My anxiety returned, a sudden rush of nerves churning the alcohol in my stomach. His breathing evened out, but mine sped up. I could hang up and never see him again. Quit volunteering— avoid him and Anton all the things that scared me. Return to a life that, although unfulfilling, didn't turn me into a panicked mess. That wasn't what I wanted, though. I wanted this. *Him.* Our lunchtime talks and easy ways. To learn everything I could about this man. Which meant I needed to be honest with him. I had to share my past so I didn't freak out and screw this up.

A familiar sting of humiliation closed my throat, an allergic reaction to memories of Brandon and heartache and my stupidity. Swallowing hard, I pulled my quilt higher. "My last boyfriend cheated on me."

"Oh, doll. No."

"Yeah. It was two years ago. I thought we were in love. Until I surprised him one evening. He was in bed with his coffee barista." I squeezed my eyes shut, a flash of his bare ass pumping between her legs almost making me heave. "We'd been talking about moving in together, and I wanted to surprise him and tell him yes. I'd already given up my apartment, and had to crash on Gwen's floor for a month. The man was a lying prick, but I've never felt so stupid in my life."

"I'd like to meet this prick in a dark alley."

His protectiveness curled around me, soothed me, as Owen's sweet understanding always did. "I'd like to watch that, but it's in the past." Still, I pictured Sally's shock when faced with her husband's betrayal the other day. Remembered my own tragic fall. Could I really risk experiencing that again?

My silence must have hinted at my worry, because he whispered, "I won't hurt you, Ainsley."

Again, exactly what I needed to hear. His promise had me happy and nervous and overwhelmed. Regardless, I wanted to try. Force myself to open up and let this sweet man more fully into my life. I twirled the corner of my quilt in anxious circles. "Are you my boyfriend?"

Not knowing if we were exclusive, or if he'd visit the D.C. habitat build and lay pipe with other hardhat-wearing do-gooders, was messing with me. My heart raced faster than Blue Bunny.

"Do you want me to be?" His Southern lilt pushed into his tired voice.

Sneaky bugger, answering a question with a question. "Yes." I relaxed deeper into my mattress. "I do." The simple truth of it.

"Good thing, because I got your name tattooed on my chest."

Contentment filled me. "You wouldn't be the first man." My father had my portrait inked on his forearm, mine and my brother's names branded over his heart.

"I don't like hearing about other men, Ainsley." His possessiveness was adorable.

A sleepy smile spilled across my face. "I'd like details about this ink, though. Do you have tattoos?"

"One."

"Oooh. Do tell."

A lion's yawn propelled through the line. "I need to sleep. Not sure if I'll make it back Monday. Things aren't going as smoothly as I'd hoped." He was silent awhile. Long enough that I worried he'd fallen asleep. Then, "I'll be back by Tuesday for sure. It sucks being away."

There was tension in his voice, and my untrusting radar pinged. *Owen was too good to be true*, my intuition taunted. I shook off my paranoia. He was just tired and missing me. "At least Blue Bunny is rechargeable," I whispered.

We breathed. We sighed.

"Goodnight, boyfriend."

"Sleep well, girlfriend."

CHAPTER 12

Seventeen letters for the part of a furnace where the burn occurs. *Or* getting locked in a room with the claustrophobic woman who drives you wild.
COMBUSTIONCHAMBER

OWEN

I spent the cab ride to Tessa's law firm coaching myself. *Don't lose my temper. Speak calmly. Slap on some Southern charm.* The fact that she'd cancelled yesterday's meeting and rescheduled for today was irritating at first, but I was over it. I replayed the good times we'd shared. I tried to picture us eating Chinese food on the floor of our house the night we'd moved in. I replayed snippets of Tessa's "soulmate speech" from our wedding, rehearsed though it had been. I remembered the early days when we'd go for evening walks, talking with ease.

We were together nine years, married for eight, but the last six had been a struggle. Like we'd agreed to refinish opposite ends of a wood table, only to realize we'd used different stains, separate visions guiding us.

It was time to strip our relationship down to its bones.

The elevator ride to her floor was more of me repeating my silent mantra. *Offer her a smile. Remind her of our history. Wish her the best for her future.* By the time my feet hit the firm's marble floor, positivity seeped from my pores. I would get this done. Convince her to tie up our loose ends. We'd loved each other once. We gave it a shot. All that was left was to torch our losses and move on. Especially when I had Ainsley waiting for me back home.

Ainsley and her toys.

I'd never had phone sex before. Never stroked myself so roughly or come so hard. It had taken all my willpower not to book a flight back to San Francisco the next day. But being with Ainsley meant dealing with Tessa, once and for all. Then I'd be free, and I could finally tell Ainsley about this mess.

It was a gift, her trusting me enough to open up about her ex, but I'd shut down afterward, couldn't confess that I was accused of the same sordid behavior. She worked for assholes who cheated on their wives. She'd been dealt the same harsh hand. If I didn't get Tessa to retract her claims, I'd likely lose Ainsley before we had a proper start.

I took a deep breath. Then two more. I straightened my tie and cracked my neck.

Treat her as good as Nana.

The office was a study in sleek, shiny surfaces, slicker lawyers to match. Everyone marched with purpose—briefcases swinging, arms pumping at their sides. I fell into step.

Tessa's office was at the far corner. Our meeting was scheduled for this afternoon at my lawyer's firm, but I wanted to have a private talk first. She didn't know I was here, and neither did my attorney. He'd have given me hell for facing her without him, but desperate times called for desperate measures. If Tessa and I could begin face-to-face, kind words offered, I was sure we could wipe our slate clean.

So focused on my end goal, I nearly smacked into my old friend. "Caroline, wow. It's been ages."

She stood, brown eyes wide, as though stunned to see me.

Of all Tessa's coworkers, Caroline was the one I'd adored. We'd often have dinner with her and her husband. Unable to convince Tessa to have kids, I'd doted on Caroline's two girls, even playing dress-up and letting them paint my nails. I'd coached the oldest in soccer, and had used Caroline as my wing-woman, bouncing plays off her on the sidelines.

Sad, the people I'd lost when Tessa and I fell apart.

"It's great to see you." I moved aside to let others pass. "How's Sam? She coaching her team yet?"

Instead of replying, Caroline's lips pinched tight. She was a head shorter than me, but her fierce glare had me stepping back. "Don't insult me by asking about my daughter." She inched closer and dropped her voice to a fiery hiss. "Do you know how hard it is for a woman to get ahead in this firm? How much we sacrifice? It only works if we have someone in our lives we can count on. It's not easy for Richard, being with me. But we made a promise to each other, and we fight to make it work. What you did to Tessa is an insult to all women. An insult to our friendship. I suggest not showing your face here again."

There was no waver in her accusation. No hint of disbelief that I'd cheated on my wife.

A slow boil started in my marrow, heat searing my neck and ears. I'd helped drive Caroline's girls around when her mother had passed away. She and Richard had invited us to their country home every fall. How could she swallow Tessa's lies? "I don't know what she told you, but none of it's true. Not a word of it."

Caroline's smooth ponytail and suit were as polished as every surface in the place. She sharpened her scowl. "Save the bullshit for someone who cares."

With that, she marched off, heels clicking, anger billowing. And my temper flared. No. Not flared. It erupted. All my serenity vanished, all positivity obliterated by white-hot fury. The emotion was potent. Raw. Tessa was the one who'd chosen work over me. She was the one who'd forgotten our anniversary and cancelled dates. Yet here I was, painted the villain.

I clawed at my tie, my breath coming hard and fast. Why would she ruin me like this? How could my close friends believe her? It all hurt so damn much.

Rage pumping through my veins, I plowed ahead and smacked shoulders with some asshole in a suit. I ignored Tessa's secretary as she called for me to stop. I barged into the office I'd visited hundreds of times prior, my vision darkening at the edges. Gone was my inner calm. Annihilated were all happy memories of our time before.

All that remained was *wrath*.

Tessa glanced up from her desk. Her blond hair was shorter, her blunt bangs framing a symphony of expressions flitting across her face—surprise, fortitude, and something that resembled...hope. Which was odd. Probably another tactic. *Manipulation Queen.* She went to open her red lips, but I was faster. Or my temper was.

I didn't speak nicely, couldn't find my voice of reason. I curled my hands into fists and shouted, "What the hell is wrong with you?"

"Me?" She reared back as though I'd slapped her. "You have some nerve, storming in here and hurling insults."

"Nerve. Honest to God, you could teach a course in nerve. And I don't get it. After years of neglecting our relationship, why the hell are you investing so much energy in it now?"

She leaned into her chair slowly and considered me. "I wasn't the only one in our house. It takes two to tango. Don't pretend like you hadn't checked out of our marriage years ago."

Always back to her same insanity. "I didn't cheat on you."

She steepled her fingers, exuding outward calm, but she

couldn't hide the telltale blotches at her neckline. "That's not what I said, but, as usual, you hear what you want to hear. It's amazing, though. After all this time, you're still clinging to your lies."

"Jesus, Tessa. We're *done*. Finished. And I never once betrayed you. The sooner you accept that, the sooner we can end this mess. I've met someone, am finally finding some happiness. It would do you some good to stop obsessing over me and do the same. Move on, for God's sake."

A calculated glimmer lit behind her darkening glare, the same sharkish feature she displayed when she had an ace up her sleeve in a big case. Before she'd execute the killer blow.

"I will be moving on. From my lawyer. She suggested I accept our recent house offer, a ludicrously low amount. I was debating it, but after this lovely conversation, I'm having second thoughts. I'm wondering if my counsel has my best interests at heart. I think I'll fire her." A grin slithered across her face.

I nearly punched a wall. Finding a new lawyer and getting him or her up to speed meant things would be delayed for another eternity. More games. More tactics. Just to infuriate me.

Mission accomplished.

———

My flight home was a blur. My gums and teeth ached from clenching my jaw. My shirt and jeans itched at my skin. A sharp headache pierced the base of my skull until my temples felt ready to rupture. Goddamn Tessa. And fuck me for letting her scheming screw with my head.

All I'd done the past hours was replay our argument, and my stupidity in giving her the upper hand. The urge to contact Summer Daniels had also resurfaced.

Since thinking about her at the bar with Jimmy, she'd been on my mind, but it would have been selfish. When we'd met on the D.C. Habitat build, we'd both hit low points in our marriages, confiding in each other as we'd weathered our respective storms. Talking with someone going through similar turmoil had given me clarity, but I'd overstepped my bounds and broke her trust back then. It was no surprise she'd shut me out, but it was because of her I'd found the courage to end my marriage. I needed to thank her for that one day.

By the time I landed and reached my truck, I could barely see straight. I moved by rote: Key. Ignition. Gas. Brake. It wasn't until I was nearing the Habitat build that I realized my headlights had been pointed there. I'd planned to go home, wash the fiasco and disappointment from my skin, but there was something I needed more.

I parked opposite the site and turned off my truck. I sat. The thrum of the engine subsided, leaving a heavy stillness in its wake. I dragged a hand down my face.

Then I saw her.

Workers had begun heading home. Ainsley stood with her pink tool belt on and pink Converse, grinning, ponytail hanging out the back of her hardhat as she chatted with a volunteer. She was a vision, all bright smile and cupid lips. She was a breath of fresh air.

She was also my girlfriend.

Such a juvenile word to define our relationship. It didn't come close to describing how one glimpse of her uncoiled the muscles in my neck and sent my heart beating back to life.

There was something else, too. It was unfamiliar, this intense ache migrating through me. A vise grip stopping my breath and clogging my throat. Not with anger. Not anymore. This was longing and rightness and fear that we were fleeting, too fragile to last.

I shoved open my door, needing to get her in my arms. Ainsley's attention shot to me. Without looking away, she said something to the volunteer, who then laughed—probably at some dirty joke—and left Ainsley waiting for me.

My girl's rounded cheeks shone, like she'd devoured a secret stash of Halloween candy. That vise grip on my lungs tightened. *Mine.* She was mine, and I wouldn't let Tessa or her lies ruin us the way they'd ruined the other relationships in my life. God, did I need Ainsley in my life.

Instead of giving Nick and the remaining workers a show, I grabbed her hand and hauled her after me toward the nearest townhome.

"You're back!" she squealed from behind me.

"You're too far away."

"You're holding my hand."

I walked faster. "I should be kneading your ass while I crush you against a wall and lick every inch of your body."

She whimpered.

This urge to devour Ainsley was a wild buzz, more intense than anything I'd ever experienced. It took root in my gut, splintered through my limbs. It made me feel untethered and famished. Crackling with desire. And *happy.* The simplest of emotions brimming until my disastrous trip was nothing but a distant memory.

I could hear her scurrying to keep pace. Our palms were dampening, my grip on her slender fingers unforgiving. She didn't seem to mind.

I led us into the half-finished building and tore into what would be a bathroom—a small space with a small window. The only room with a door. They must have installed the door since my last day, and the second I had Ainsley inside, I tried to shove it closed. It dug into the floor, jarring my arm. Guess I'd be leveling this out tomorrow. Today its only purpose was providing privacy for the sexual tension about to be obliterated.

Squaring my shoulder with the wood, I launched into its center, slamming it closed. Something rattled in the frame. My pulse rattled in my neck.

I spun around. "You're still too far."

Her blue eyes were heavy with lust. "Then get over here, cowboy."

I descended upon her, knocking her hardhat off and capturing her lips with mine, groaning at the contact. It was instant, how she made me soft and hard at once, melting my angst yet shooting me full of steel. I plunged my tongue between her plump lips, a little rough and a lot needy, each swipe searing my mind. I groped her ass and waist and breasts. So many curves. Too much clothing.

Her teeth sunk into my bottom lip as she tried to climb my body. "You're so tall."

"You're perfect." I hoisted her up, latching her legs around my waist, and swiveled, slamming her back against the door with a violent thud.

A strangled *oof* pushed from her pretty mouth. "That's sexier in the movies. I think I broke my spine."

Head thrown back, I chuckled. "Doll, I fucking—"

Whoa.

Love you. That's what I'd been about to say. In jest, maybe, an off-the-cuff fondness often offered to friends, but it was more. It was everything.

I'd only known Ainsley two months, not that long, but long enough to piece through my need to see her today and the whirl of emotions spinning through me and understand this was definitely *more* than infatuation. And she was in the dark about my past.

She had no clue I'd ever even been married.

Legs locked around me, she trailed wet kisses down my neck and along my collarbone, but I couldn't reciprocate. Her openness in the face of my duplicity was too much.

Her teeth bit, her tongue licked. I was riled up, dying to see her creamy skin, but it didn't feel right. She deserved to know. The basics, at least. She confessed a deep truth on the phone. I had to man up and offer the same. Find a way to explain Tessa's accusations without losing the first person in years to make me feel alive.

I returned her kisses, exploring the column of her neck, the delicate lines of her ear. Then I pulled back. "We need to talk."

"We need to kiss."

It was hard to argue with her breathy sounds and rotating hips, her body plastered against mine, but this was important. Honesty was important.

I inched away from the door, lowering her so she could find her feet. My shirt was twisted. Hers was halfway up her stomach. Her eyes darted to my hand as I adjusted myself in my jeans. "We do need to kiss," I said, "but I have some stuff I have to tell you."

She tapped an impatient sneaker. "I'm not sure what you're playing at, but I'm a tad horny, and unless you finish the job you started, and I get to strip you naked in the nearish-immediate future, I will die of blue bean."

"Blue bean?"

"Blue bean."

Even with my impending admission, this woman had me amused. "I don't follow."

"*You* get blue balls. *I* get blue bean. It's not fun, so wipe that ridiculous grin off your face."

I covered my mouth with my hand, unsure when my smile had gotten so wide. "Sounds painful."

"You have no idea. So get on with whatever conversation is more important than saving your girlfriend from an excruciating death."

I sobered quickly, shoving my hands in my pockets as I played the words in my mind. I had to say this right, not scare Ainsley off.

Before I could speak, she touched my cheek softly. "You're making me nervous. What's going on with you?"

Nothing. Everything. My life tumbling out of control. "I didn't tell you the real reason I went to D.C."

She snatched her hand back, like she'd been shocked. "You didn't have to sell your house?" Confusion sunk in a line between her eyebrows. There was uncertainty there, too. Wariness.

I forged ahead. "No. I *did* have to. I still do, but there's a reason it's lingering on the market." A stray nail was on the floor, and I rolled it under my boot. "I'm in the middle of an ugly divorce, and my ex is making things difficult. Including selling our house."

Recoiling farther, she blinked and shook her head. "You're married?"

God, the distress in her eyes. Her chest rose faster, while mine caved in. "No. I left her months ago. Nearly a year. It's just the law and paperwork getting in the way of ending things."

"Why didn't you tell me?"

"I should have, right away, but I was hoping to clear things up on this trip. Hoped I could tell you the divorce was final."

Her distrust was palpable, red blotches dotting her neck. Moisture glazed her beautiful eyes. It hurt worse than Caroline's disdain at Tessa's office and hearing Tessa's lies. I should be making Ainsley smile, not causing her pain, tossing roadblocks in our way. And there was still one left to wedge between us. A massive boulder. But the second I opened my mouth to explain how bad things were for me, a tear slipped down Ainsley's cheek.

Startled, she dashed it away. "God, I don't know why I'm crying. I'm really not that girl. It's just..." She fanned her face. "I think I need some air."

"Oh, doll. No." Unsure what to do, I pulled her into my chest. "It's over with her. I promise. On my life. Please, don't worry."

But she would. Worse than this if she got wind of the slander I'd been dodging. I couldn't risk it. Not this early. Not after Caroline's venomous insults and Tessa's newest antics. As long as Ainsley knew the facts, the *truths* of my divorce—that it existed, and that it was challenging—was all that mattered. The rest was fabrication, distortion. Lies that would be meaningless when our papers were finally signed.

Ainsley pressed her face into me, and wetness coated my T-shirt. She used it to wipe her nose. She could use me as her own personal Kleenex, for all I cared. Anything to make her feel better.

"Air," she said again. "I'm fine. I really am. I just need air."

I stroked her hair and kissed the top of her head. "Sure. We can talk about it after."

Releasing her, I took two steps and yanked on the knob. The door didn't budge. I gave it another hard pull. Nothing. Frowning, I gripped the damn thing with both hands and jerked with all my might. It moved a millimeter and jammed. "Fuck."

I examined the edge, bending down to feel the warp of the floor, the slight upward slope preventing the door from moving.

"Owen..." Ainsley croaked my name, her voice dripping with distress. I whipped around to find her breathing harder, pure fear on her face. "Why isn't the door open?"

That's when I remembered her claustrophobia.

CHAPTER 13

Eight letters for a device used to increase the static pressure of
fluid passing through a system.
Or a boyfriend who shares a humiliating story to distract you
from certain death.
DIFFUSER

AINSLEY

The walls inched closer, the temperature in the shrinking space skyrocketing. Moments ago I'd been fine. Better than fine, about to experience an *oh-my-God-yes-yes-yes* with Owen's hands on my body. Not through a battery-operated bunny or discovering a vintage Oscar de la Renta accidentally marked down. My construction hunk's sinful lips had been on my skin, my legs around his waist.

Now I was seconds from hyperventilating.

Owen held up his hands as though I were a rabid dog. "It's okay. We'll get out of here. It's just stuck. I'll get it open."

I pulled at my T-shirt's neckline and forced a swallow. "Okay."

But I wasn't. Not by a long shot.

His lie by omission still hung in the oppressive air, and there was nothing rational about claustrophobia. No concrete reason I could be in this room one minute, no thought to the size of the space, and a second from a panic attack now. It wasn't level-headed. Logic was no longer at play. It also didn't change the facts that forcing air into my lungs was becoming a challenge.

"Hurry," I managed.

His worried gaze darted over me like I was a stick of dyna-mite about to be lit, which sounded accurate. Swiveling, he began working furiously on the door. He kicked the bottom closed, yanked at it again. He studied its perimeter exhaustively. When that didn't work, he turned with another fierce, "I'll get you out of here," then proceeded to pound on the Evil Door and shout for help.

Not promising.

I walked backward, until my butt hit the far wall. I slid down its length. There were rough-ins for a shower, toilet, and sink around me, electrical wires protruding from the walls. The unfinished floor undulated as my focus swayed. My heart had never beat so loudly, a steel drum pounding in my ears.

If I weren't close to losing it, I'd probably come up with a fun crossword clue for the instrument, but losing it I was. My focus blurred as my mind tripped back to Chucky's Chicken and me slamming my body and fists into the unmoving exit of the walk-in fridge. Laughter had assaulted my ears that day—coworkers taunting me with promises of freedom, only to be denied.

Trapped. Imprisoned. Suffocated.

Today there were no derisive slurs, only Owen's increasingly frantic efforts and the dwindling oxygen powering my lungs. *I'm going to die wearing sneakers and a tool belt.*

I wasn't sure when Owen had crouched in front of me. I could barely register his gentle hands on my face. "I called

Emmett. He's on his way. We'll get it open together. He shouldn't be long."

My saliva had turned to sludge. "You called him?" It was then I noticed the phone on the floor by his boots.

He nodded. "I'm sorry, doll. This is my fault. I was so desperate to see you. I wasn't thinking straight."

"Maybe a striptease will help." My attempt at levity waned under my shaky voice.

He must have heard the panic coursing through my words, but that didn't stop Owen from standing and reaching for his belt. "Whatever you need."

"I need a football stadium's worth of air, and I was joking." I pulled my ponytail away from my neck, hoping to cool down. I closed my eyes and counted to ten, but everything seemed to shrink closer, spin faster. When I blinked, Owen was still hovering in front of me, a sly smirk on his full lips. He pushed the edge of his leather belt through the buckle and flicked the prong from its home. He released the ends slowly and popped the button of his jeans.

"Honestly," I said, "don't waste your *Magic Mike* moves on me today. The blue bean has turned gray. Fear doesn't increase my sex drive."

Ignoring me, he slid his zipper down and dropped his jeans to his knees, displaying black Hugo Boss briefs and the package they held in place. An impressive package. I should have been panting to crawl toward him and slip that thin cotton *down, down, down,* but I was sweaty and nauseous and hot and clammy at once. Still, his male review continued. He flipped around and dropped his underwear, flashing his toned ass.

And…what in the hell? "Is that a tattoo?"

"Yep."

Forcing my windpipe to function, I leaned forward and studied the spray of black ink on his left butt cheek. "Are they Japanese letters?"

"Apparently. You asked on the phone if I have any tattoos, and this is it. But I have no clue what it means."

I shocked myself by laughing. "I so need an explanation for this."

"Thought you would." He pulled up his briefs and jeans. Once facing me again, he jutted his chin in my direction. "Okay if I join you down there?"

His awareness of my discomfort, his concern, had me breathing slightly easier. "Sure."

Nudging me forward, he sunk behind my back, letting me lean on him without wrapping his arms around me and constricting my airflow further. He pushed my hair aside and kissed my neck. "It was, like, nine years ago. Maybe ten. Shortly before I met Tessa, my ex."

Hearing her name had the thickness in my throat expanding. It gave her life, made her real. It emphasized his exclusion of this important fact. I couldn't imagine Owen being like Dean or Thomas Arlington the *third*, spewing lies about divorces that would never happen. But Owen's blatant avoidance of the topic nudged at the damaged tissue guarding my heart, warning me not to trust men.

His chest expanded into my spine, his deep voice following. "I'd sometimes go out with Emmett, hit the clubs he liked. We always acknowledged the anniversary of the day our mother left us. Not sure why. A reminder of what we still had, maybe? Or a 'fuck you' to her. Either way, once we got fake IDs, we'd go out and get drunk. That night we went overboard. The club and the scene were nuts."

"A gay club?"

"Yeah. A wild one, with disco lights and men in crazy outfits. Pretty sure I danced a lot, and I made out with at least one guy."

"Seriously?" I didn't know why I found that so hot, but I did. Unbelievably sexy. "Did you like it?"

"It was nice, but it didn't turn me on. I never did it again."

I pictured my masculine man rubbing bristly cheeks and

hard bodies with Aazam (Because *Aazam*), and a glimmer of my desire sparked back to life. "Is there a video?"

His chest shook as he laughed. "No video, thank God. We kept drinking. Hard. It was the most wasted I've ever been. The last half of the night is a blur, but I remember waking up, my head as painful as it's ever been, then I spent the next six hours puking my guts out. I didn't notice the tattoo until I crawled into the shower the next evening. I also wasn't sure why my ass hurt so bad. At first, I freaked out. Thought maybe more happened with that man than a kiss."

Squealing, I covered my mouth and cackled into my hands. "Oh my God. If I didn't know the outcome of this story, I would not be laughing at you right now, but *oh my God*."

"Don't hold back. Emmett never does."

"I mean, they make movies about this stuff. Actually, it's something Rachel would totally do after four glasses of wine, but I digress. Continue your confessional."

I leaned my head back on his shoulder, giddy for the rest of his juicy story. I was still uncomfortable, but I could once again access the rational side of my brain. Thanks to Owen's distraction techniques.

Still giving me room to breathe, he traced shapes on the dusty floor. "All I know is what Emmett's told me. A friend of his back then was a tattoo artist. We ended up there, and I got inked. When I asked Emmett what the hell the Japanese letters meant, he busted his gut laughing. I endured that a few times, until I gave up. Whatever it means, it's enough to send my brother into hysterics. I decided I'd rather not know. If I had to guess, I'd bet Emmett had the guy tattoo something stupid like, *Ugly Bastard Eats Shit*."

He went on to talk about Emmett and him, two teen boys who'd wanted to ride horses and run soccer fields until the sun set. I listened. I breathed. More oxygen pumped through my lungs. The walls didn't press so closely.

I listened. I breathed. I fell harder for Owen Phillips.

I became aware of how much I'd missed him while he was gone. Still, he'd withheld vital information, reigniting my innate distrust. His admission had sent my mind careening to a disastrous time in my life, all of it jumbling together until a traitorous tear had pushed from my eye. I wasn't a crier. Yet there I'd been, rubbing my ruddy face against Owen's T-shirt.

Stupid Brandon and his stupid lies, messing me up like this.

Owen's stories ended, silence blanketing us. A soft place that cushioned my sudden vulnerability. I curled my toes in my sneakers. "Is there anything else, Owen? About this divorce I need to know? I want to believe you, that your ex isn't part of your future, but you should have told me when I asked about your trip. So is there anything else you've kept from me?"

His whole body froze. Not a smidgeon of air puffed against my hair. Then, "It's hard to talk about it, and my lawyer has been on me to keep quiet, so I'm not used to opening up. But that's the truth of it. My ex is bitter. She's giving me hell, getting in the way of selling our assets." Another pause stretched, this one speeding his heart rate. His pulse point raced against my cheek. "She's also been—"

Owen's cell phone leapt to life, and I shot forward. He reached for it, pushing to his feet as he spoke to Emmett. "First townhouse you see. Walk through the entrance, then down the hall to the right. You'll see the closed door. A safety floodlight is on inside."

I hadn't realized how dark it had gotten. Not with the muted glow seeping into the small room. It was bright enough to see relief etched on Owen's face, but I couldn't tell if it was because Emmett was rescuing us from this room or *him* from that conversation.

My panic resurfaced. Without Owen behind me, his rumbling baritone in my ear, the reality of our situation slammed home. We were still stuck. It was still too warm. The ceiling was still too low. It wasn't as intense as earlier, but I'd donate half my wardrobe if it meant escaping this coffin.

"You guys okay?" Emmett pounded on our door.

"Just glad you're here. On the count of three, you push and I'll pull."

The boys attempted to use their body mass to force the stubborn piece of wood into submission. My wilting temperature had reached a full-on sweat. Effort five was the clincher. Owen practically flew on top of me as the door busted open and fresh air wafted in. *Salvation!*

Crawling out on all fours, I rolled onto my back in the hallway and inhaled the entire atmosphere. "I almost died."

"You look okay to me, Stepper." Emmett towered over me, grinning.

"Is that a step class insult?"

"It is."

"I rocked that class."

"Your face nearly hit the riser."

"Details, details. And speaking of details, I need to know what Owen's tattoo means. I promise not to tell him."

He winked at me. "I'll take it under advisement." He smacked his brother's ass. "You guys need an escort home? Any kittens rescued from high places?"

"Fuck off." This from Owen hovering at my right.

"You're welcome. See you at soccer this week."

Owen crouched beside me and cupped my cheek, all his rugged handsomeness showering me with concern. "How you feeling?"

"Pathetically weak and embarrassed that something so lame reduced me to a panic attack."

"Nothing to be ashamed of, doll. Just wish it hadn't happened."

"You and me both. Actually...I'm still feeling drained. I might need a full fireman carry out to my car."

Dropping his head forward, he chuckled. "Think I can manage that. Up with you, then." True to my silly request, Owen slung me over his shoulder, turning sideways to avoid smacking my head into the wall.

I draped myself over him like a cheap dress and copped a feel of his jean-clad behind. "Next time we do this, you need to wear those fire pants and suspenders and no shirt, and oh…I'll smear charcoal all over you."

"Not on your life."

"What if role playing turns me on?"

I could sense him smiling. "I'll take it under advisement."

"You and your brother are no fun." I bumped against his back as he carried me to my car.

Gently, he lifted me up and over him, setting my feet on the pavement. "You want to come over tonight?"

Although we'd escaped certain death, tension still radiating from him, a point in his jaw ticking. Something felt off. Like it had while in the Evil Bathroom.

Owen had stiffened before Emmett cut our conversation short, poking my intuition that he had more to hide. Intuition I'd vowed wouldn't fail me again. But his tension was likely due to my claustrophobia display, and my distrust issues were surely messing with my mind. That must be it. Owen couldn't fake his sweet nature. He was a gentleman at his core. Kind. Courteous. Thoughtful. Sexy as a sweat-slicked cowboy drenched in sunset.

If I was going to move past Brandon's betrayal, I'd have to start with trust.

A rush of nerves fluttered through my belly. "I'll shower and meet you there."

CHAPTER 14

Seven letters for the surge of an electrical current in one direction.
Or giving into desire even though warning signs ring in your ears.
IMPULSE

AINSLEY

Apparently Owen lived in a garage. At least, that's where my GPS led me. A large steel door was open, light streaming out, along with old jazz tunes. Tools and a few pieces of furniture filled the stain-splattered space. The corrugated walls were rusted in spots, the concrete floors cracked. It had a vintage vibe to it. Classic, like something you'd see in a greaser movie.

It also housed a brawny man who was bending over a plank of wood, teasing me with his taut derrière.

"Did you pay extra for the view?"

He stood and twisted toward me, eyebrows pinched. "View?"

I gave him my best sleazy-stalker eyes as I focused on his lower half. "It's definitely nicer than at my place." This I could do. Flirt and joke as usual. Find our familiar rhythm and forget the conflict on his face at my car, the unease still gnawing at my gut.

Smirking, he dropped the sandpaper on his work-in-progress and smacked his dusty hands on his jeans, a stupid sexy move. He took long strides to reach me. "The view just got a hell of a lot better. Not sure they could put a price on it."

This man was some kind of dangerous. "Aren't you a charmer?"

"I'm honest." He proved his point with his lips on mine, his hot breath filling my chest. The kiss was slow and deep, more intimate than our desperate necking in the Evil Bathroom. Our tongues pirouetted in a perfect ballet duet.

Hopefully we weren't performing *Romeo and Juliet*.

His huge hands caressed my back as he rolled his hips into me, showing me how turned on he was. The Hugo Boss Package was indeed *large*. A solid line of granite jutting into my belly. "You make it hard to breathe," he murmured.

My purple satin panties were dampening by the second, my apprehension increasing, too. "Since I almost suffocated tonight, that would make us even."

He nosed my ear, the underside of my jaw. "Being even would mean forcing *you* to listen to all the ways I'm going to eat your pussy, then making you watch me flirt with another woman."

"Touché." His gentle explorations had me shivering, his dirty words firing the ache between my thighs. But it was all too much. A tug of war waged between my body and my mind, fear of getting hurt versus pent-up desire pulling at me.

I ducked around him and headed for the large table against

the wall. "Is that the piece you finished? The maple table?" I sucked in a lungful of air, urging my pulse to slow.

"Yeah." His voice grew quiet, and I glanced back. He dashed his hand through his sandy hair, a sweet blush dotting his cheeks. Was he nervous? Shy?

His humble uncertainty was endearing, and I gave myself a mental slap. I should be claiming him right now. Dragging him to a tattoo shop to have my name stamped on his other butt cheek. We could be making wild, passionate love.

Instead I walked the perimeter of his creation. I dragged my fingertips along the smooth wood, tracing the shimmering lines and colors tumbling through the grain, searching for my Zen.

During a few of our lunch confessionals, Owen had talked about this project. His eyes would go soft, his voice dreamy as he'd describe what working with wood meant to him. Working with *his* wood would likely plaster an equally blissful expression on my face, if I could get over myself. "It's spectacular," I said.

"Really?"

I wasn't expecting his voice to be so close, or to be so timid. Need for approval rang clear in his one hesitant word.

I spun around and had to look up to meet his bashful eyes. It hit home then, how much making furniture meant to him. How touching it was like touching his soul. "Better than stunning. It's real. It's what a table is supposed to be—strong, built with integrity and heart."

It was also the embodiment of this man.

"Thank you," he said softly. A beat later, a lecherous grin lit his face. "We should move this conversation and talk about my *wood* upstairs."

We should. We so should. So why was I still freaking out?

In seconds, he had the garage door closed and was pushing me up a narrow staircase. Each step toward our impending sexy time had my heart thrashing in my chest. I was horny as anything, wanting this sensitive yet powerful man moving inside me, but I still couldn't calm down. My adrenaline rush from the Evil Bathroom was surely messing with my mojo. It couldn't just be fear.

Before I could gather myself, we were in his apartment, his strong arms latched around me from behind. "You seem off. You still shaken from earlier?"

"Yeah, I think so." At least I hoped that was part of it. Stepping to the side, I twisted from his grasp. "I also didn't tell you, but I found out Anton will be at the build every Friday. I thought about confronting him, but I'm not sure if I'll yell at him or grovel for his forgiveness."

Owen scratched his jaw. "Considering what went down between you, I'd say that's a normal reaction, but this is eating you up. You'll regret letting it go."

He was right. I'd have to sort through my emotions and face my past. Just another dilemma to an increasingly melodramatic life. Theatrics that were wearing me down. But the larger concern, the more pressing issue, was the hunky man who wanted to discuss his *wood*.

"Also," I said, the stalling champion, "this is my first time in your place. I need to do a full recon mission. Make sure it's safe." Buy myself some time.

He cocked his head, amusement returning to his handsome face. "Did you bring a search warrant?"

"Matter of fact, I did." I lifted my top and flashed my double Ds.

Owen assaulted me with his sunburst smile. "I fucking love that purple lace. You have five minutes. Then we can talk about my wood, or, if you're not feeling up to it, we can watch a movie."

I wanted to be up to it. I wanted to be all over his Hugo Boss-clad *wood*. Our phone sex had heightened his hot factor, ratcheting up my fascination with his magnetising self. Maybe snooping in his place could help tame my crazy. I could confirm he wasn't hiding a second or third divorce, or a harem of exotic women.

I scanned the room, trying to decide where to begin. The space was small but neat. A leather couch and flat screen TV flanked a wood coffee table, a shelving unit made of something similar on the opposite wall. Likely built by his stalwart hands. The shelves were lined with books. Smarty-pants books. My English teacher, Mr. Lawrence, would have probably traded his first born for those well-worn volumes.

Shakespeare. Voltaire. Other long names I didn't recognize.

"Were you one of those kid geniuses? Like your grandmother skipped your grades and you wound up at university at fifteen and couldn't figure out why your facial hair was patchy?"

His rolling laugh filled the room. "Man, I don't know where you come up with this stuff. But yeah, I worked hard in school. I got a scholarship, but didn't fast track. I watch some TV—mainly HBO shows and movies. Otherwise, I built a deck off the back. I sit out there some nights to read." His attention flicked toward his stove. "Four minutes left."

Shoot. I hit his open kitchen next, studying the beer, deli meats, and condiments in his fridge. No girly vegetables or tofu or yogurt to be found. I kept up my peanut-gallery commentary, though, tallying up the items filling his apartment as if taking inventory. I then invaded his bathroom, scoping the space for fancy face creams and nail polish remover. His shower soap gave me pause. It smelled like him, like apple crumble steaming from the oven. I dragged my nail over the green bar, stealing a sniff.

Basically, I was acting like a lunatic.

"Ainsley."

Heart *pound, pound, pounding* in my ears, I plastered on my most innocent face and turned. "Yeah?"

"Is this because of what I told you earlier? My divorce?" Owen scrutinized my fidgetiness. He was on point. We both knew it. Once I slept with him, this connection we shared would go from intense to transcendental. There was something bigger here than I'd ever shared with Brandon, and my ex's betrayal had rocked me to my core.

If Owen hurt me—

I guillotined that thought. Owen was watching me, uncertain yet steadfast. A strapping man with a tender side who wanted me in all the ways a man could want a woman. It was time to start living and stop worrying. It was also time to get sexed up. "The fact that you never mentioned your divorce has thrown me for a loop, but I get that it might be hard to talk about. I'll get past it. It's just my issues rising to the surface."

He crooked a finger, beckoning me closer. "Come here."

He wasn't giving me bedroom eyes. He was laying down serious eyes.

Warily, I approached. When I was within reach, he ran both his hands through my hair, skimming my scalp until his palms rested on my cheeks. "I care about you a lot, and I'm sorry I didn't mention my divorce. If you just want to hang out tonight, count me in. I'm dying to be with you, but there's no rush. I also love the idea of squishing with you on my couch. We don't do anything more until you're sure."

His understanding loosened the knots inside me, reminding me how different Owen was from men I'd known. No matter his needs, he was putting me first. Only a good man would do that, and I was tired of letting Brandon infect my life. "My nerves are because of my past. Not my present. I trust you."

He kissed my forehead, my nose, my lips. "That means more than you know, but it doesn't have to happen tonight. When you're ready, just say the word."

My remaining reservation vanished. Everything disappeared but this beautiful man. "Word."

He pulled back, appraising me intently. "You're sure?"

"Positively." To prove my point, I took control of my life and chasséd my way into his bedroom. Owen followed closely behind. I pirouetted in the simple space, taking it in.

A photograph of a beach hung on one wall, a large window occupying the other. There was a simple closet and nightstands. Dark gray walls, lighter gray bedding. Large, cushy king bed. A cowboy hat on his dresser. Aside from a lamp and smarty-pants book on his bedside table, the only other item of note was a mason jar filled with what looked like shards of glass.

I picked it up and shook it. "Do you collect bottle caps, too?"

My immature humor usually tickled Owen's funny bone, but something in my comment hit a nerve. Darkness stirred under his sharp cheekbones. Closing the gap between us, he pulled the jar from my hands and set it back carefully. "We've done enough talking."

And he didn't want to discuss the glass. Not that I could blame him. His girlfriend of five days just tore through his apartment, cataloguing every inch of it. "I like your place."

"I like you." His chocolate eyes had reached ninety-five percent. Perfectly sinful.

I was horny and ready to indulge. "Then kiss me already."

I didn't have to ask twice.

He gripped my hips in a punishing hold, his fingers branding me with points of fire, and our lips fused. Our kiss rocketed to frenzied, both of us pushing against each other, deeper, harder, until my lips felt bruised. I was wet already, my panties likely soaked. I wanted his fingers there, his mouth, his *cock*. I needed him to alleviate this desperate tingling that threatened to burn my skin.

Pulling at his shirt, I shoved it up and almost wriggled my head into his black crew neck with him, stretching the cotton to get my greedy tongue closer to his abtastic body.

"You're ridiculous." He pulled me away and ravaged my mouth with his. The backs of my knees hit his bed, and I landed on my butt. I wore a cute pair of Juicy jeans and an animal print flutter top. The way Owen looked at me, I'd have guessed I was naked.

Chocolate eyes at ninety-eight percent.

Gripping my waist, he shifted me into the middle of the bed.

He knelt over me.

He pushed up my shirt.

He drew torturous circles on my belly, then lifted my top farther, over my bra, but not off. The cold air and his rapt attention sent goose bumps trembling over my skin. He traced my breasts, dragged his thumbs over my lace-encased nipples. His erection stretched his jeans.

"You're beautiful, Ainsley. Steals my breath."

He was stealing my heart, and my words. All my jokes and banter vanished, a swirl of emotion blooming in their place. I was going to fall hard for this man. I could sense the emotion refracting through me, the fragile beauty of a rainbow following rain.

Part of me still worried he wasn't as good as he seemed, but I was passed the point of no return. "Owen..."

"Yeah?"

"Don't hurt me, okay?"

Protectiveness surged in his fierce gaze. "You're about to become mine, and I take care of what's mine."

God, this man. Coiled tight as a spring, I pushed up and undid his belt buckle, tugging at it and shoving his jeans down. He stood and toed off his boots. His Levi's hit the floor next. Racing him, I lost my sandals, tossed my jeans beside his. His shirt joined the pile, mine following. We were both in our underwear, him in socks too, the sight almost funny if his body wasn't sapping my IQ. Every chiseled inch of him fogged my brain with lust.

"You're even hot in your socks," I said. Okay, it *was* funny.

"I could leave them on."

I shook my head. "Off."

He removed them deftly.

He stood at the side of the bed, eyes hooded as he stared down at me. He gripped himself over his briefs and dragged his palm along his erection, legs wide, body strung taut. It was the hottest thing I'd ever seen.

Steamed up, I flicked my bra clasp and tossed the purple lace at his head. He batted it away with his large paw, his eyelids sinking heavier. I slipped off my panties, twirled them in the air, and launched them at his lampshade. His answering groan was beyond erotic, deep and rugged and all kinds of wicked.

I'd never felt so exposed, or desired.

He shucked his Hugo Boss briefs, joining my birthday-suit party, and his erection sprang free. *Whoa.* That was a lot of man.

His cock was thick and hard, the head engorged. All for me.

He skulked closer, hunger burning bright. But he didn't ravage me. As though I might break, he caged me, lowering himself down in a tortuous descent. The edges of our bodies brushed—knees, thighs, hips, the flats of our stomachs, our chests. Miles of bare skin connecting. We both exhaled for an eternity.

Nothing had ever felt this sensuous. This right.

We lay still for a beat, then our pace surged. We couldn't explore enough, fast enough, rough enough. He rocked his length against my thigh as he squeezed one breast, sucking my nipple into his hot mouth and palming my ass. I writhed. One second I was tugging his thick hair, then I was pulling at his neck, his shoulders, his tattooed behind. Greedily fusing us closer.

It wasn't close enough. "I might die. I need you inside me."

"God, Ainsley. I've never wanted a woman this much."

Pausing, he pushed onto his forearms. The distance allowed me to trail my fingers through his scratch-soft chest hairs. I loved the feel of it against my palm, the hard lines of his pecs and corrugated abs. His cock stirred and slipped off my thigh, lining up with my entrance.

Hypnotized, I swayed my hips, not allowing him access, just loving the tease of all that power and rigid heat, knowing what was to come. Mainly *us.* "You're so hot."

My vocabulary had lost its mental thesaurus.

His cock twitched, making contact. He released a pained growl. "Fuck. Babe, I can't take it. I wanted to lick and taste you, and I will. But I need to be inside you."

Breathing hard, he nearly fell over as he fumbled with his end-table drawer, returning with a condom. My body turned hot and swollen as he tore the wrapper and rolled the latex down his hard length. Gripping the base of his shaft and squeezing as if to curb his arousal, he pushed one then two fingers inside me. I gasped at the sensation, clamping down on him while canting my hips up, needing him, needing more.

"You're soaked." His low voice sounded like it came from the abyss, a bottomless sea of lust. His gaze flickered then, as though hesitant, hinting to the sensitive boy behind the man. As though he was vulnerable, too, risking a nasty fall.

Maybe I wasn't alone in this leap of faith.

His fingers kept exploring me, his other hand clenched around himself. I could barely handle the sting behind my eyes. I bit my lip and pulled him down, his weight on me, his thudding heart next to mine. Hands tangled in my hair, he eased his hips forward, an undulating roll as he slid inside me, slow and gentle. He stretched me wide, while our lips met and tongues danced, my world reducing to the points where our bodies met.

Hips. Fire exploded between my thighs.

Calves. Bristly hairs caressed my legs.

Foreheads. Silent promises offered.

"Ainsley." He murmured my name, reverent, as his strokes quickened. I molded the bottoms of my feet over his calves, squeezing my knees into his sides, meeting his steady thrusts. Shuddering, he shifted his angle and lavished my breasts with attention, flicked my nipples with his tongue. His slight scruff scratched at my skin, spurring my arousal.

"I don't want it to end," I murmured.

I don't want us to end. They were still there, my irrational fears. The belief that love and commitment were fleeting things destined to fall apart. That Owen was too good to be true.

"This is just the beginning." His eyes were at a full one-hundred percent now, molten and fierce. Begging me to trust him. He planted his palm on my cheek, holding me firm, not allowing me to look away. Our connection deepened, causing a tear to leak from my eye. We were joined, our bodies moving as one, our emotions bared in this unguarded place of openness. We didn't kiss. We rocked and moaned and whispered each other's names as we neared the peak.

"I'm close," I panted.

"Let go, baby. I'm gonna explode."

He lowered his full weight on me, cradling me close as we bucked together and tensed. My orgasm hit me in a towering wave, my insides clamping on him as I shook. I dug my nails into his strong back. His release followed mine, a surge of heat pulsing between my thighs. He rolled his hips harder into me, a string of expletives growled in my ear, his legs shaking until he collapsed forward.

"Will you still want me if I'm blind?" I rasped.

He laughed, his weight dropping heavier on my chest. "Definitely. Especially since I've lost my sight, too."

"Blind leading the blind."

"As long as I'm with you, don't really care."

"You're heavy, cowboy."

"Shit." He pushed up and pulled out. His hair was sex-strewn, mine likely as tousled. We grinned at each other. "That was insane, and I'll be right back."

He disappeared out his door, and I starfished on the bed, enjoying the afterglow. My body felt well-used and languid, a light tingly sensation still fluttering through my belly. My heart had also grown. It was engorged, inflated with *Owen, Owen, Owen*.

I imagined us cuddled on his couch while we fought over the remote, his sink crammed with my toiletries, our coats hanging side by side in his entryway.

I imagined a future with him.

I hadn't let myself think beyond sex with a man since Brandon. That kind of hurt hadn't been worth the risk.

Even now, the possibility of getting in deeper with Owen

only to lose him to some awful deceit lingered. Time would ease this nagging doubt, the fear that he would hurt me. It also wasn't the worst idea to lower the intensity a notch. Wait for my over-thinking brain to settle. I still planned to enjoy our budding relationship, but a bit of space would do me good, calm my mind. I began gathering my clothes.

I heard Owen before I saw him. "Not sure if you like classics, but we could watch a movie. Or I could watch you while you tear apart the rest of my apartment. We could find a breakfast place tomorrow." He walked in as I finished dressing. He frowned when I stepped into my sandals.

"Actually, I think I'll head home. That was amazing. You're amazing. But I need to take this slower than I realized, if that's cool with you."

His gaze darted to the jar of glass by his bed, tension tightening his features. "Yeah. Sure. I get it." But he rubbed the back of his neck in agitated strokes.

He pulled on his boxers, covering up all the perfection I could have spent the evening exploring, but this was better. This was what I needed. This would allow me to get used to the idea of Boyfriend Owen, so I wouldn't pull another stalker move and ransack his place like a complete kook. In time, I'd get over my past and trust him not to break my heart.

CHAPTER 15

Thirteen letters for the internal pressure that causes tubing to
fail.
Or how your chest feels when your girlfriend learns your lie
from someone else.
B U R S T P R E S S U R E

OWEN

Like a pirate nearing a treasure chest, I approached the
lumberyard I'd visited a handful of times, greedily eyeing the
stacks of reclaimed wood—mountains of maple and walnut and
black ash. Trees salvaged from people's yards to be repurposed
into functional furniture or decorative art.

My Mecca.

The owner, Ellen, waved to me, her Rottweiler trotting at her
side. "You're becoming a regular."

"It's the woodchip fumes. Gets me high."

"If that were the case, I'd be rich by now." She nodded

toward the large barn flanking the property. "Another piece of tiger maple came out of the kiln today. She's a beauty."

"Is that so?"

"Thought of you the second I saw her. Actually wanted to pick your brain about something." Ellen wore heavy work boots and a tattered plaid button-down over loose jeans, her dark hair shoved into a messy ponytail. Her dog, Birch, loped away and nosed at a stick on the ground. The incessant grind of a wood planer whirred, kicking dust into the chilly air.

I loved the lack of pretension here. "Shoot."

"The way people are salivating for all things recycled, reclaimed wood is hot. I figured it was a good time to add a retail component to my business."

"Sounds smart."

"Yeah, but I'm not what you'd call artistic. I've been chatting with some clients, sussing out who'd be interested in selling pieces here. I have ins with a few designers looking for one-off stuff. Nothing factory made. You have a good eye for the nice pieces that come through. I'd have to see your work, make sure it fits with my vision, but I thought I'd check if you're interested."

If I was interested? I was practically frothing to convince her I was the man for the job. It would mean doing what I loved for a living, using my hands and mind to fashion beauty from nature. "Very interested. What would you need from me, besides seeing samples?"

She whistled on her fingers as Birch wandered toward the wood planer. Her dog trotted to his master, tongue lolling. "I want to start with three craftspeople. Which means, if it takes off, you'll have to produce the volume needed. I'm clearing the equipment from the front barn. I'll want enough work from each person to fill it. Make it impressive. Everything will be done on commission, so no cash up front. And you'd be free to do other jobs. I'm not expecting exclusivity."

Mentally, I calculated how much time I'd need to make

another few dining tables, maybe coffee tables and funky barstools, too. I pictured the modern shapes I'd imagined over the past months—sleek lines left rough and natural in spots.

I'd kill to jump on this opportunity, begin my business in earnest, but her talk of cash and commission had me hesitating.

I had a decent nest egg squirreled away, and I was okay not making the money I had in D.C., but I had no idea how much more cash my lawyer would siphon from my account, or when Tessa and I would finally sell our house and divide our assets. Getting pieces done for Ellen meant giving up volunteer hours and likely some of my paid handyman work. If I said yes to this venture and my divorce dragged on, buying materials could dwindle my accounts past my comfort zone. If I promised Ellen I could fill orders and wasn't able to come through, it would tarnish my name.

But I couldn't turn down something this perfect. "Count me in."

We shook on it. "I'll swing by your space soon. Check out your work in the flesh. For now, come see that sexy piece of maple."

I left with three stunning wood planks in my truck bed, a future prospect that should have had me on cloud nine, but keeping my precarious finances from Ellen felt like a lie by omission.

A pattern of mine these days.

Ainsley had been at my place five times the past two weeks. Always my apartment, never hers. We'd eat dinner together, spend time on my back deck—her with a *Vogue* magazine, me with Shakespeare—not to mention the hours spent charting each other's bodies. We'd even gone hiking, my little fashionista smiling as we meandered along a leisurely trail. Each date I'd ask her to stay the night, and she'd make a joke or brush me off, leaving me in bed alone.

I'd fucked things up not telling her about Tessa from the start. Her guard was up now, waiting for the other shoe to drop.

A shoe I could see hovering in midair, no clue how to force it to the ground without stomping on us. I kept hoping Tessa's new lawyer would, by some miracle, force closure to our never-ending battle. A childish wish, really.

Like believing Santa would bring me my mother for Christmas.

I pulled into my driveway and unloaded my haul. I stood, arms crossed over my chest, staring at the rough wood planks. My gaze blurred and cleared, blurred and cleared. This was my ritual, communing with the pieces, waiting for inspiration to strike.

"If you're hypnotized, does that mean you won't notice if I yank down your pants?"

My butt cheeks clenched at the sound of Ainsley's raspy voice. The woman oozed sex. "Give it a shot. We'll see what happens."

Her heels clicked closer. She dropped a takeout bag at my feet and snaked her arms around my waist. "I like this better." She pressed her face into my back.

My heart pressed into my sternum. Gripping her left hand, I channeled my inner Fred Astaire and twirled her out from behind me, then spun her back in. Her ass landed flush with my groin. "I like *this* better."

She twisted her head so she could see me, awe in her wide blue eyes. "Owen Phillips, you really *can* dance."

Exotic scents of Indian food curled thickly from the bag at our feet, but it had nothing on her natural musk, always smelling sweet. Like chocolate. I shrugged a shoulder. "Nana was a great teacher. And..." I caught myself before spilling that nugget. I had a habit of divulging my most personal stories to Ainsley. One whiff of this tidbit, and she'd flay me with her quick-witted humor.

She swiveled around to face me, still in my arms. She palmed my cock over my jeans. "And what? I sense another Embarrassing Owen Story. Don't hold out on me, cowboy."

"Nothing to tell."

She gave me another rough stroke. Heat flooded my veins, everything taut and pulsing.

"Liar." Smirking, she released me and wriggled from my grasp.

The bombshell fought dirty. "Get back here."

"I need convincing."

Prowling closer, I grabbed her wrist and placed her hand back on my aching cock. We moved together, my hand over hers as we both jacked me off over my jeans. My vision clouded. She cupped me tighter. Then she paused. "Let's hear it."

What I needed was to hear her moan and call my name in ecstasy, but she wouldn't give up easily. Ainsley was stubborn like that. "I took a year of ballroom dancing. Free classes at a community center."

Let the jokes fly.

She didn't laugh, though. Breathing harder she started fumbling with my belt buckle. "Just when I didn't think you could get any hotter, you go and tell me you took dance classes."

"If I knew it would turn you on, I'd have told you the first day we met."

"Then I'd have pictured you dancing with Emmett."

"Better that than picturing him and me in bed." An image I needed to bleach from my brain. Lust throbbing in my bones, I gripped her shoulders and forced her to a healthy distance. "What about our dinner?"

She eyed the bag, then my crotch. "I'm hungry, but not for food."

That's my girl. "Get upstairs and get naked. I'll close up here."

I slapped her ass to send her on her way. She squealed, tossing me a sexy smile as she took our dinner and her luscious curves upstairs.

She may not have been ready to open up fully, sleep over and risk getting hurt, but she was all in for the hours we spent together. Our dirty explorations between the sheets. Our lunches at the site. The endless texting in between. I was falling harder, deeper, but she seemed to be coasting, enjoying our moments, not asking for more. For now, I'd take what I could get.

I stalked through my shop, my loose belt buckles clanking with my hurried strides. My hands itched to get back on my girl, but as I reached up to drag the garage door down, I halted.

A black SUV was parked at the end of the street, one I'd seen a few times recently. Not the usual pickup or beat-up car cruising this area. This truck was too posh to blend in. As though aware of my stare, its headlights shot to life, engine turning over as it pulled out and disappeared around the corner.

Paranoia gripped me, like I was in some TV cop show, invisible bad guys staking out my home. I hadn't felt this unsettled since Tessa first accused me of the affair. It had taken a while to figure out I was being tailed back then, by a sleazy private eye hired to dig up non-existent dirt.

The same disquiet was back. It shot my mind to our last meeting—Tessa's comment about me only ever hearing what I wanted. Something about it didn't sit well. I'd also been stewing over the evil glimmer in her eye when she'd bragged about firing her lawyer. It left me worrying she had more planned. Or maybe this was her grand scheme: to play the part of emotional terrorist, leave me searching for strange cars, nervous to bring a new lover into my life.

Well, fuck that and fuck her. I had a woman upstairs who was hilarious and sweet, a pinup girl brought to life just for me. Ellen's offer today meant there was a chance I could turn my passion into a business. Good fortune was coming my way, long overdue, and I deserved the chance to enjoy it.

I yanked down the garage door, a loud *clang* ringing as the metal struck the concrete, then I hastened up to my apartment.

Ainsley was in my room, in nothing but a skimpy pink bra and thong, my cowboy hat on her head. A stunning vision. She was doing some sort of ballet move, heels together, knees bending wide. She kicked out a leg and pulled her pointed toe up her inner thigh, twirling in place. The ends of her blond hair flew in a circle. "Doll, you shouldn't do things like that. Makes me crazy."

She curtsied. The demure ballerina. "Crazy good?"

"Crazy amazing." I grabbed my T-shirt by the back of my neck and yanked it over my head. My jeans hit the floor, my socks next. My straining cock stretched my briefs at an awkward angle. "I have proof." I pointed at my dick.

She licked her perfect lips. "That you do." She removed the cowboy hat and placed it on my head. "How was the build today? I was bummed I couldn't make it."

Digging my fingers into her hips, I hauled her against me, stomachs flush, skin against skin. Heat licked my spine. "The first section of homes is looking great. More volunteers have been showing up. We'll be landscaping soon."

"I hate missing it."

I spanned my hands across her tailbone. "I hate missing you. You should come tomorrow, if you can."

But she frowned. Tomorrow was Friday. Anton would be there. I'd met the man who'd ridiculed Ainsley in high school, clocked some hours with him and his students. I hadn't been happy about it at first. Spent the first hour fisting my hands, but Anton was good with the kids, firm but well liked, it seemed. It bothered me, what he'd done to Ainsley, but people change. He also limped from his broken leg and had gnarly scars on his burned hand. He'd been through enough.

Ainsley kneaded my shoulders like they were stress balls. "I'm planning on ambushing him soon. The thought makes me feel like I'm stuck in the Evil Bathroom again, or the Chucky's Chicken walk-in fridge, but, like you said, I'll regret not doing it."

I rubbed her back, realizing just how hard this was for her. How much guilt she harbored from a prank gone awry. Under her dirty humor and perfect nails was a sensitive soul.

We were in our underwear, talking and touching, but neither

of us moved to take things further. She nuzzled her cheek against my thudding heart, and her gaze landed on my bedside table. On my jar of broken glass.

She hadn't asked about it since that first time, but whenever she came over, I'd find her staring at the shards, occasionally picking up a piece and studying it. I'd shared a lot with Ainsley, a woman who blew into my life with her painted nails and name-brand clothes—a stylish hurricane. Still, there was something about that glass. They were pieces of me. Fragments of my most intimate memories and misguided hopes for my future, another childish wish: to find the owner of my missing pieces. Someone who could make them whole.

Make *me* whole.

Possessiveness rushed through me, a hot blast of longing to brand Ainsley, mark her as mine. My hands moved as I walked us to the bed. I kissed her shoulder and neck, sucking and biting as I pressed my weight onto her in the middle of my sheets.

She purred. "Oh, I like that."

"You taste like chocolate." Decadent.

Her moan turned into a light laugh. "My favorite chocolatier sells a perfume. I dab it on my neck."

"That explains why I want to devour you." *But not why I'm halfway in love with you.* The unbidden thought had my next nip turning into a rough bite, and our hips lined up.

She took control then, flinging my cowboy hat to the floor and flipping us so she straddled me, a playful look of reproach spreading. "Is that the only reason?"

"Yeah."

She pinched the skin at my ribs. "Try again."

"Okay." I rocked my hips up, pressing against her from below, nothing but two bits of fabric between us. "The real reason I can't get enough of you is I worry about time." I wasn't expecting to reveal that much of my heart, risk her pulling away at my admission. I couldn't shove the words back in now.

She shifted her weight slightly, tiny ripples that teased us both. "Why time?" Hesitancy bit into her tone.

There was so much I wanted to say to Ainsley. Confess how often she occupied my mind, that our time apart was painful, and I wanted to watch every old movie with her nestled into my side, wash dishes with her *at my side,* cook with her, fight with her, make up with her, take her to Morocco like she'd dreamed, and find a thousand ways to tell her how her beauty hurt my heart.

I settled on a sliver of truth. "Because, after you leave, when I close my eyes I can almost feel you in bed, beside me. When I open them, and you're not here, disappointment sets in. The rough kind, like a hollow spreading in my gut."

She sucked in a breath, her chin trembling. She didn't speak, her unsaid words revealing as much as the moisture glazing her eyes. She felt it, too. I was sure of it—this unnameable connection. This sense of rightness. And she was scared. So Ainsley did what Ainsley did best: she changed the subject.

Blinking rapidly, she ghosted her nose along my chest, inhaling my scent. "You smell like apple pie."

"That would be my soap. Nana started making it a couple years back. She sells it at a few markets and sends me home with it every visit."

"I may need to buy a few bars."

Or you could stay over, I didn't say. *You could live here and shower here and use my soap and be mine.* But she wasn't, not with the one ugly truth I'd kept from her.

It was selfish of me, not telling her about Tessa's claims. The notion of speaking them aloud felt like breathing truth into the lies, giving them life. Still, it wasn't fair. If Ainsley found out some other way, it would undermine everything we'd built. Ruin it. Ruin us. Pretending the whole ordeal would blow over was a fool's errand.

She moved her hips faster, palms flat on my chest. I was

pumped with lust and an aching need to be inside my woman. To forget this one small, yet massive snag.

But this couldn't go on. "We need to talk."

"We need to fuck." With a sexy grunt, she slinked down my body, moving deliberately, teasing bites and licks tracing a tortuous path.

My thighs bunched, my abs contracting with each languid exploration. *Christ*, this woman. But I gripped her shoulders. "Seriously, there's something we need to discuss."

She nipped my hipbone. "I'm sure it can wait."

I should have tried harder to stop her, fought the pull to melt into this moment, but she felt too good, and we could be on a timeline. When I revealed I'd been accused of cheating on my ex, I could lose her. She was already halfway out the door as it was…

Her fingers lingered on my pecs as she descended, and I let her descend. I gave myself over to the perfection of her hot mouth on my skin. She toyed with my nipples, my chest hair, tracing a trail to my throbbing dick, pulling my briefs off on her way. She hummed against my shaft, ran her lips up and down the sides, fondling my balls with her skilled fingers in a blinding rhythm.

I didn't know if it was our blowjob conversation on that disastrous date, or her inherent expertise, but Ainsley Hall sucking me off was a one-way ticket to Nirvana.

Which was exactly where she took me.

Her full lips swallowed me, the head of my cock hitting the back of her throat. It was like she didn't have a gag reflex, taking me deeper, working me harder. Her small hands gripped and pumped while she sucked and used her tongue. I couldn't help but move my hips and fist her hair, knees wide as my balls pinched, so much heat flooding my groin. Too much heat. I needed to see her eyes when I came, feel her pulse around me.

Pulling my hips back, I eased her up. She looked wickedly pleased, her lips red and used, her cheeks flushed. I flicked her bra clasp and tossed the lace, taking her breasts in my hands, so big and lush. Absolute perfection. Touching wasn't enough.

Lifting up, I kissed and sucked her supple flesh, taking her nipple between my teeth as she tossed her head back, arching toward me. Her hips moved, searching for friction, but I wasn't done. I went to work on her other breast, feasting on her, like the desperate man I was, eventually rubbing my face between her tits, happy to drown in all things Ainsley.

Her husky laugh broke my spell. "So you're a breast man."

"I'm an Ainsley man. Want it all." I thrust upward, only her underwear between us.

She whimpered and rocked, her pussy so wet and hot, drenching the thin fabric. Flipping us so I straddled her, I continued worshipping her breasts, the soft skin over her ribs, the dip of her belly button, the swells of her hips, perfectly full and womanly. I couldn't touch her enough, open-mouthed kisses trailing her from end to end.

When I reached the valley between her thighs, she trembled. "*God*, yes."

"You a praying woman?"

"Only if it makes you work faster."

"Still so demanding."

"Stop talking and start licking."

I chuckled, then blew a stream of air over all that wet heat. Her hips kicked and knees trembled. I ground my own hips into the mattress, trying to tame my desire, but being with Ainsley, smelling her arousal, pungent and sweet, had my blood pounding.

I kissed her, exactly where she wanted me. I thrust my tongue into her, grinning as she pushed into my face. I wanted her to ride me, steal her pleasure. Submerge in my own. I held her open and flicked my tongue, working her in a steady rhythm, then pulled back, teasing her, taunting her. She nearly yanked out a fistful of my hair. When her frustrated groan dripped with hunger, I finally gave her what she demanded.

Taking my fill, I licked and sucked until she bucked, little shocks shaking her pelvis.

Eventually, she pushed me away. "If that's a form of religion, consider me a convert."

I lifted onto my knees. "I love tasting you. Could do it all night."

Her hooded gaze hovered over my dick, which jutted out toward her, hard and flush. "Sex now." She gripped my length, giving it a solid pump. *Fuck.*

I sheathed myself in record time, then pushed into her. I lost track of time, of space. There was no shattered glass by my bed, no divorce looming over me. No financial issues or impossible conversation on the horizon. There was just us, fitting together. Her hands were on me, messy kisses traded, my thighs slapping against hers as I lifted her up, pushing deeper.

Breasts bouncing, she clutched the sheets as I drove into her. I watched where we were joined—me sinking in and out, tight wet heat circling me. Desire blasted up my thighs, driving me from hard to titanium.

She bit her lip and pulled me closer, wrapping her legs around my waist. "You feel amazing."

"Heaven," I agreed.

Eyes locked, we rode the high until we crashed. She tipped over first, clenching so fucking tight around me I shot off like a firework, calling her name as the high pummeled through me. We were both shaking slightly, breathing hard. A thin sheen dotted her brow, and I could feel condensation on my lower back, where her fingers danced. My head was hazy.

"Owen?"

The quiver in her voice had my awareness creeping back. "Yeah?"

She pulled my hips farther into her, keeping us joined. "I never thought I'd meet someone like you."

Her face softened, trust and something more blooming...and my heart reared. I wasn't sure if it wanted to gallop closer to her or canter away, but this moment wasn't right. What I was keeping from her tainted it, corroded the beauty of her admission. My answering silence also had her frowning.

I kissed her lips, then pulled out and dealt with the condom. She was on the move, too, probably unsure why I was freezing her out. We got dressed in a distracted hurry. I mumbled something about our dinner. She didn't glance my way.

This was *her* pattern: have sex and close down. Get dressed and get gone.

I'd stopped asking her to stay over, the rejection stinging more with each rebuke. Except her confession just now could have been her reaching for a lifeline. If I'd asked her to sleep with me for the night, she might have said yes.

I paused in my doorway, one foot toward getting plates and the Indian food she'd brought and letting us go on like this. Staying in this space where we had unreal sex and laughs, not the intimacy I craved, but no risk, either. My other foot was stuck in my room. Stuck in my past.

Just plain stuck.

It was time to offer Ainsley the honesty she deserved.

As I opened my mouth to do just that, finally sit down and spill the truth, her phone buzzed. She grabbed it from my dresser and tapped the screen.

I'd seen a symphony of expressions cross Ainsley's face, from erotic rapture to stressed claustrophobia to simple joy. Her flaring nostrils and widening eyes were none of those things.

I stepped toward her. "Something wrong?"

The phone shook as she angled the screen my way. "Why don't you tell me?" Her usual raspy voice thinned and cracked.

Cupping her outstretched hand in mine, I read the text that had my girl upset.

From one woman to another, you should know that Owen cheated on his wife while they were married.

Fucking *hell.* Jaw clenched, I pulled the phone from her and checked the number. The D.C. area code had me nearly dialing

Tessa and yelling at my ex, but the familiar number wasn't hers. It took a second for it to click, to realize who'd decided to upend my life.

Goddamn Caroline. But why?

She'd been disgusted with me when I ran into her at the law firm, but ambushing my girlfriend was a whole other level of scorn. Unless she'd had some urging. I'd stupidly mentioned to Tessa that I'd met someone during our argument. Did she and Caroline have a girls' night out? Relive their rage over glasses of wine? Decide together to ruin my life?

"Owen?" Ainsley's voice was just a whisper, laced with pain. "Why do you look more mad than surprised?"

I tossed her phone on the bed. "It's not true. I swear to God, it's not true."

Her shoulders hunched forward, her breath coming faster. She was in slim black pants, a loose cream top hanging off one shoulder, always stylish and sexy. What wasn't sexy was how she was curling in on herself, looking at me like I was a stranger.

I gestured to my living area. "Can we sit and talk?"

She swallowed, but didn't answer.

"Ainsley, please. I know how this looks, but I can explain."

"God, Owen…did you read that text? I mean, I'm freaking out here. I don't even know what to think." She crossed her arms over her middle as though she might fall apart.

I was furious at Caroline for sending that text, but seeing Ainsley barely holding it together gutted me. My anger leached out. "Tessa thinks I cheated on her, like that text said, but I didn't. I've wanted to tell you, but with your past and every-thing I was scared to bring it up."

"So you kept it from me?"

"It was the wrong choice, but I'd decided to tell you tonight. That's why I asked if we could talk before we made love. Please, just hear me out."

I couldn't be sure if it was her remembering me asking her to talk or the reference to us making love, but she finally nodded. I all but collapsed. If I didn't fix this, I'd lose her. It would serve me right for keeping the details of my divorce secret, but the possibility was acid to my lungs.

Once her feet were tucked under her, both of us facing each other on my couch, I exhaled. "We'd been in a bad place awhile, Tessa and me. Years, really. She'd thrown herself into work, and I'd started volunteering at a Habitat build to escape my job. We rarely saw each other. Hadn't been intimate in ages."

I wanted to reach for Ainsley, hold her hand and feel our connection, but her unblinking gaze held me back. Throat thick, I forged on, "You're the first woman I've been with since her. She and I were basically strangers for our last year together, even before that hardly connecting. We fought regularly. It took an eye-opening conversation with a friend to make me realize I wouldn't be able to love Tessa again, no matter how long I held on, and when I ended things, she kind of…"

I gritted my teeth, remembering the animosity emanating from her that day. "She kind of snapped. She accused me of cheating on her. Refused to accept we were done, that I was leaving her to be on my own, not for someone else. To this day, I have no idea why she thinks I abused her trust. I'm not sure if it's because we weren't sleeping together. She's vague about it, but vehement. She's never even uttered a woman's name, whoever she suspects."

Except Tessa was cagey like that, treating us like we were in court, holding onto her best cards until they would do the most damage.

I couldn't imagine what fable she'd concocted, or what drove her sordid conclusion. In the end, I'd assumed it was her saving face with her friends and at her firm, shifting the blame to me. It still left me uneasy, had my mind back on that SUV outside and her battle-ready glint during our recent fight. Even this stunt reeked of Tessa—using an investigator to find out who I was dating would be child's play for her, securing Ainsley's number a cinch.

None of that mattered, though. And she had nothing left to hold over me. What mattered was Ainsley, the heartbreaking turmoil on her beautiful face.

"That's a lot to absorb," she said quietly.

At least she wasn't yelling or running away. I inched closer, dropped my voice lower. "I know. I should have told you, but I was worried. Your ex and the guys you work for—that stuff's a big deal. I figured you'd get one whiff of this and bolt. And my old friends all believe Tessa. They think I'm a lying sack of shit, which really hurts. That's who the text was from—I recognized her number. Caroline and I were close before, but I saw her on my trip to D.C., and she ripped into me. I don't know if she sent that text with Tessa or on her own. Either way, she probably thinks she's doing you a favor. So it's all just..." I focused on the stuccoed ceiling, wishing things weren't so damn complicated.

"Owen."

I couldn't face her yet. Not until I'd said it all. I kept my attention on the off-white divots and craters above our heads. "Thing is, Ainsley, you've kind of knocked me off my feet. I'm falling hard for you, but this is me—my shitty life right now. If you can't trust me after that text and what I've said, I under-stand. You've been through a lot. But the real truth, the harder truth, is losing you will hurt like hell."

I prepared for her to get up, grab her purse, and leave. Instead her fingers threaded through mine. "Look at me."

Steeling my nerves, I snuck a glance. Indecision flickered in her blue eyes. An unsettled sea. "Did you cheat on your wife?"

"No." One sure syllable. The only life preserver I had.

She stared at me, unwavering. I couldn't read a thing. But she held my hand and held my gaze and held my heart in her hands. Then she blinked. "Okay."

"Okay?"

"I don't like that you lied, and if you're lying now, I will cut off your nuts in your sleep, but I'm not ready for this to end."

I didn't dare ask if that meant she'd be sleeping over. "I'm not lying."

Her answering grin didn't reach her eyes. "Then we're good. Let's have dinner."

Her tone was abrupt, her movements purposeful, as though the momentum would keep her together. Her stiffness tore at me.

I needed to prove how much I cared for her. Show her I was a man of my word, faithful and true. I also needed to thaw this fresh ice between us. Her delight at my dancing admission earlier had been a thing of beauty, the way it had lit her up. A flame I could fan. Maybe it was time to pull out my rusty moves and make Ainsley Hall the star of her own Hollywood Musical.

CHAPTER 16

Three-letter word for the horizontal distance between the eaves
and roof ridge.
Or your natural instinct when facing the boy who bullied you.
R U N

AINSLEY

Half the fun of meeting the girls at the gym was wearing my favorite white camo Lululemon tights while watching them grunt and sweat from a safe distance.

Gwen dropped her ten-thousand-pound weights. "My shoulders are on fire."

Rachel finished her umpteenth squat. "My thighs might explode."

I fixed my ponytail. "I could totally go for a smoothie."

Gwen rolled her eyes and jumped up and down on a freaking *box*, as a few men snuck lusty glances her way. "Why do you even come here?" She shot the question at me, barely out of breath.

I pointed to my five-pound weights. "I'm practically Super Woman. You should feel my muscles." Posing like a body-builder, I flexed my biceps.

Rachel squeezed them indulgently. "Let's get that smoothie, Wonder Woman. Gwen can meet us when she's done showing off."

Gwen gestured rudely while still jumping on a box like a crazy person.

After a deep gulp of my coconut, pineapple, avocado smoothie, I slumped in my seat. The gym had a few tables nestled beside the juice bar. People hurried by with gym bags slung over their shoulders, occasionally blocking the view of the treadmills and the street beyond the windows. I watched the frenetic movement, slightly detached. Pretty much how I'd felt the past week. The seven days since Owen's big revelation.

"You seem quiet." Rachel knocked her smoothie against mine.

I shrugged and kept sipping.

She wrenched my cup from my hand, placed it out of reach, and faced me. "What's up?"

"Nothing."

"Seriously?"

"Seriously."

She made an annoyed sound at the back of her throat. "I rarely get to see you these days, which means time is valuable. If you don't start spilling all your secrets in the next five seconds, I'll tell Owen you also crushed on the hot chocolatier."

"You wouldn't."

"Try me."

I harrumphed. (Ten-letter word to express dissatisfaction.) But she was right. We didn't see each other nearly enough, and I'd done nothing but let my emotions fester the past week.

Although I'd visited Owen's apartment twice, our time together had been heavy. Thick with unspoken tension, weighing down our previously light banter.

We still couldn't keep our hands off each other, and I'd let myself enjoy flipping through a magazine while my construction hunk massaged my feet, lavishing me with attention. Like he couldn't do enough to prove his affection. Still, we'd avoid any and all topics involving his divorce and the details he'd withheld. There had also been a few nights where I'd texted him, but he hadn't replied until much later. Unusual behavior for him.

It was likely him feeding off my distance, but familiar anxiety knotted my belly. Maybe he was lying to me. Seeing someone else.

I needed to get my head together before I lost my mind.

My clutch purse was beside me. I fiddled with the zipper. "Do you know Owen's wife is accusing him of cheating?"

Rachel pressed her hand to her mouth. "*God*, no. I wonder if Jimmy knows."

I waved a dismissive hand. "I'm pretty sure it's all a fabrication. At least, that's what Owen says. That his ex is spreading lies. I mean, you should have seen him when he told me. He looked so defeated. I knew he was in the middle of a messy divorce, but she sounds like a nasty bitch."

Rachel leaned forward to get a clearer view of my face. "Do you believe him?"

Zip. Zip. Zip. I fiddled with my purse zipper as the background pop tunes chased my anxiety. There was no denying how he'd tried to tell me something important that night. I'd pushed him to relax instead, unwind. And his regret when confessing to me had been potent. But if he hadn't opened up about this, there could be more he was hiding.

"I think so," I said, clinging to Owen's best qualities, too many to name. He really had been distraught when talking that night.

"And how do you feel about him? Are things serious?"

The skittering of my heart said it all. "I love spending time with him, laughing and talking, and the sex is out of this world. Everything is just…easy." And there's that thing I couldn't describe—how one glance from him lit me up into a ball of energy.

She plunked my drink back in front of me like it was a double vodka on the rocks. "If he hurts you, I will drive over his nuts with my motorcycle."

"I already told him I'd cut them off. And when did you get a motorcycle?"

"Jimmy got it for me. It's way too much, and I tried to refuse it, but I couldn't rain on his parade. It even has sun rays painted on the tank."

Sun rays for his ray of sunshine. An adorable nickname for my adorable friend. "You picked a winner with that one."

"I sure did. But back to Owen. You say you believe him, but you seem wary."

"I *do* believe him, but my trust engine is running on empty. I keep replaying how clueless I was about Brandon, how foolish I felt afterward, then I hit meltdown mode." I was too drained to relive how horrifying it had been to get Caroline's text, how it still plagued me with doubts. But so much about Owen contradicted her claim, and I was too invested to walk away.

As Rachel made a clucking sound of compassion, my phone buzzed. I pulled it from my purse, my heart fluttering at the sight of Owen's name. No matter my turmoil, a simple text from him turned me back into a swoopy mop.

Jimmy and Rachel are in town. Let's all go out tomorrow.

I glanced at my friend to find her grinning at her phone, too. "You just get the same date request?"

"Is that cool? Or are things too weird right now?"

I stared at my phone. My gut told me it was what I needed: to go out with Owen and my friends and forget my nerves. I'd offered him my trust, accepting his version of the truth, so I either had to put the incident behind me...or I had to end things.

The latter riddled me with more anxiety, which meant it was time to forge ahead. Stop allowing my past to mess with my mind.

Come to think of it, there was another thing I could do to suss out Owen's intentions. My father had never liked Brandon. He'd been polite to him, but my dad was a cuddly teddy bear—a six-foot-five, tattooed teddy bear. For him, not liking someone meant no close hugs or bromance back slaps. Worried he'd upset me, he'd never mentioned his distrust of Brandon until we'd broken up. My sweet father felt partly responsible for the fallout.

Sounds great, I replied. *We'll bring Gwen if she's free. Maybe invite Emmett? And I have a request.*

Anything.

There was no hesitation in his reply. No concern over what I might ask. He really was the sweetest guy. A guy I could picture in my future, if I let my mind wander down that rose-colored road. Hopefully watching him with my father and my family would give me clarity. *Come to dinner with me before we go out, with my family.*

I tried to have a monthly Friday night dinner at home, but six weeks later, life had gotten in the way.

I like the sound of that. Mind doing me a favor too?

Cheeky bugger. But I warmed at his quick acceptance to meet my parents. *Depends.*

Come to the build tomorrow, he texted. *Talk to Anton. No matter how it goes, I'm here for you.*

My brief optimism disappeared faster than last season's horrific culottes trend. My neck prickled. A rock formed in my gut. There was no doubt the other thing fueling my recent dark mood had been my inability to muster an apology to Anton. I was afraid of facing the boy who'd ridiculed me. I was afraid of facing what *I'd* done to him in return.

I replied *Maybe* as Gwen joined us.

"That was an awesome workout."

I pulled out a chair for her. "You say that every time." Even after Step Class Hell. "How are things with your mom?"

She swiped a towel over her forehead, then hung it around her neck. "Not good. Chemo doesn't seem to be helping, and doctors wear that bad-news frown when they talk to her."

Rachel and I exchanged worried glances. She reached over the table to hold Gwen's hand. "How are *you*?"

"Also not good. I've tried to spend time with her, but we usually end up fighting. It's like me being there is making things worse. I'm going to take a break."

"You sure that's smart?" Rachel asked.

"I have zero clue what's smart right now. All I keep focusing on is the fact that she's going to die before she tells me who my father is. I brought it up last time, and our fight was pretty epic. We both need space, I think."

Whatever my relationship and life stress, it was peanuts compared to this. "We're going out tomorrow, with the guys and maybe Owen's brother. You should come. We can ply Rachel with wine until she gets on the dance floor and embarrasses herself."

Gwen snickered. "I wouldn't miss that for the world."

Somehow she perked up and chatted about her next death-defying stunt—rock climbing *sans* rope.

I once asked her why she tempted fate by jumping from planes and the like. Her reply: *Scaring myself makes me feel alive.* In the face of her mother's illness, she was still scaring herself. Still living, careening into the void. Dating Owen and ignoring that slanderous text certainly scared me, but confronting Anton also sent me into panic mode. I may never test my limits the way Gwen barreled through hers, but it was time to take control of my life. Facing my past seemed like a good place to start.

———

I'd skipped out on this week's volunteering sessions. Although I didn't have the willpower to turn down Owen's evening invitations, I'd studiously avoided him during the day, as though the sunlight would expose my nervous energy and he'd tire of my hot-and-cold routine. With tonight's ambush on the horizon, the notion was less unsettling, and it was nice to be back.

The familiar hustle and bustle of the Habitat build had me smiling: hammers pounded, saws whirred, voices shouted instructions and questions. I didn't spot Owen or Anton right away, but a handful of students were sitting on scaffolding, paintbrushes in hand, as they joked and painted window frames.

The first six townhomes were nearing completion, another six rising from the ground. Pride puffed up my chest at the sight.

Then a red-headed man slid into my peripheral vision, and my pride went *splat*.

Anton was talking with two girls, both teens grimacing. He was too far to see his scarred hand, but his arms cut stern lines as he spoke, maybe reprimanding them. The girls then faced each other, hips jutted out with attitude, as though they were forcing out insincere apologies.

If I could write thought bubbles above their heads, they would read:

"Sorry."

"Whatever."

"Fine."

"Fine."

The depths of teenage sincerity.

The two trudged off toward the build, and Anton rubbed his eyes, clearly exhausted. He didn't look like the guy who'd laughed as I'd stumbled, terrified, out of the walk-in fridge, or the villain who'd hissed *stupid bitch* when I'd forget to put a second tomato on a Chucky's Chicken Sandwich. But he did have a limp from the mean prank I'd pulled, a slight drag of his right leg.

I contemplated scuttling back to my apartment and hiding in

the dark for the rest of the day. Never showing my face onsite again. But I'd made a bold wish to better myself, which meant doing more than Habitat work.

Yes, Anton had been a dick. Yes, he had tormented me. But this was about acknowledging the cruel thing I'd done, provoked or not. Not hiding. Not pretending volunteering made it all better.

This was my trial, and I was as guilty as Anton.

He hadn't moved, likely enjoying a breather from his students. I chanted a series of yoga *oms*, searching for serenity. I'd been out scoping stores this morning and was still in my Donna Karan jersey dress and ankle boots. That left me dressier than I'd have liked for this encounter. The exact thing Anton had teased me about all those years ago.

At least my walk of shame would be fashionable.

I forced my spine straight, determined to face the music. (The soundtrack to *Jaws*, specifically.) I navigated the uneven ground until Anton was a foot away. Close enough that I could glimpse red, puckered skin on his right hand. His attention cut to me, maybe sensing my horrified stare. His eyes widened behind his glasses. Then they narrowed, slicing me down at my wobbly knees.

His stance slammed from relaxed to rigid. "Ainsley Hall."

I offered a timid wave. "That's me."

He stared. I cowered. Around us, the earth continued its slothful spin.

I was a breath from doing my fiercest runway walk away from there, but I'd come for a reason. There was no changing the prank I'd pulled. Nothing could undo the physical harm I'd caused. It was time to accept my punishment.

"I've been volunteering here and noticed you a while back, but was too cowardly to approach you." I cleared my throat twice. "Thing is, I was the one who left you the cockroach box. You weren't exactly nice to me, but there's no excusing what I did. And I don't expect you to accept my apology. I'm still sorry. You didn't deserve to get hurt."

His face glazed over like an unimpressed wax statue, but my heart was a battering ram. I couldn't tell if his blank expression was born of repressed anger or arrogance. He'd exhibited both as a teen.

He scratched his red hair, a move that put his burned hand in full view. "Are you done?"

If he'd let me apologize ten thousand times over, I would. "I guess. I've just always felt sick about it. Maybe knowing it's haunted me will make you feel marginally better." I didn't guilt *him* for what he'd done, or offer my sob story about working too many hours back then and struggling to keep my head above water while paying my family's bills. How it had all compounded with his cruelty, culminating in my cowardly act.

There was no justifying my actions.

"Good," he said, "because I'm the one who should be apologizing."

It was my turn to become a statue. As awful as he'd been, he'd never shown a lick of remorse. I hadn't hoped for it now. "You should?"

He watched his students a moment, then stared at his boots. "My father was a drunk—the nasty, abusive kind—and I took that out on you. You were an easy target, I guess. I'm ashamed about it, to this day. So, yeah…I should be the one apologizing. And thanking you. The cockroach stunt woke me up."

"But the scars…"

He held up his hand and smirked. "They're kind of badass, and they remind me what's important. I don't tolerate bullying in my classes. If I even get a whiff of it, I come down hard on the kids."

One of the moody teenage girls called, "Mr. Bickley!"

Anton raised a finger to tell her he'd be a minute. "Anyway, I'm sorry for everything I did. That fridge stunt especially. You tried your best at work, and I was a prick."

"You're forgiven," I said quickly, happy to say the words, thrilled to put this chapter of my life to bed. I wouldn't be sending him a friend request or swapping phone numbers, but grudges were poison. "Consider us non-enemies."

He smiled sadly. "Non-enemies sounds pretty great. See you around the build."

He joined his students, and I stood a moment, letting the reality of our conversation sink in. Shame still weighted me, but I felt light, too. Relieved the confrontation was over.

"How'd it go?"

I swiveled at Owen's sexy baritone, teetering like I had the first time we'd met. Muddy ground and high fashion were not a good combo. "When did you turn up?"

He slid his arm around my waist, anchoring me. "I saw you talking with Anton and waited until he left." His voice softened. "So?"

So, I faced my nemesis and apologized. *So*, I was still standing. "We both said what we needed to say, and he doesn't blame me for what I did. He actually thanked me, which is odd."

Pensive, Owen looked in Anton's direction. "How do you feel?"

Naming this riot of emotions was as easy as choosing one item at a Sephora sale. "Like I've been riding the Gravitron ride Gwen once forced Rachel and me on—exhilarated and nauseated. But I also feel badly."

Owen was in his usual work attire—worn jeans, gray T-shirt accentuating his broad chest, thick sandy hair askew from his hardhat. Untold tenderness warmed his eyes. "I don't follow."

"Apparently Anton was living with an abusive father back then. If I'd tried to understand him more, maybe I could have talked to him. Helped. But I was too wrapped up in my emotions to see beyond his pranks."

A sharp look crossed Owen's face, his features tightening.

My lungs constricted. "Do you think I messed up? That I should have done something?"

"Babe, no." He shook his head vehemently. "Nothing like that. Teenagers are ruled by their emotions, and he was awful to you. I'd have done worse than a box of roaches. It just made me think of something else. But I'm happy you've found closure."

I *had* found relief. As well as an idea.

Facing Anton had triggered a thought, a way to alter the focus of my current job situation. He'd found strength from my mean stunt, had used it to better himself. The way some women reinvented themselves after a nasty divorce. If I worked with women instead of men, people wanting to redefine their lives after a separation, I could make a difference. Help them find strength on their own.

Letting that notion marinate, I pressed to my tiptoes and pulled Owen down for a soft kiss. Someone wolf whistled, and I smiled against his lips. "We could give them a real show."

"Nick would have a heart attack." Another chaste kiss later, he said, "Looking forward to the club tonight. Emmett can't come, but I'm excited to meet your friends…and your folks."

Suddenly, so was I. Confronting my past-self had set my emotions awhirl. *All* my emotions.

I may have avoided sleeping at Owen's place, had kept him at a healthy distance this past week, but pretending my heart wasn't invested in him was foolishness. He'd pushed me to face my fear today, promising support no matter the outcome. He'd incorporated my vegan lifestyle into his, stocking his fridge with foods I liked. My man touched me whenever he was near, soft brushes that said: *you're mine, I'm yours, we're better together.*

He also fucked like a god.

The implications settled on me, just how hard I'd fallen for him. My father's opinion was still important, but I couldn't rely on him to confirm Owen's honesty. I had to take this plunge on my own and hope for the best.

A first step to stop dwelling on what-ifs could be having some enjoyment at Owen's expense. Watching him sweat while he feared for his life under my father's intimidating presence would be gold. He didn't know Mason Hall looked like a Hells Angels biker. He didn't have a clue Dad's tough exterior didn't match his gooey center.

My father and I had played this game before: the Make My Boyfriend Wet Himself game. I nearly released an evil *bwahahaha* laugh at the image. This was going to be some kind of fun.

CHAPTER 17

Four-letter word for the curved drain that prevents sewer gases
from escaping.
Or when your girlfriend sics her scary father on you for her own
amusement.
T R A P

OWEN

I stared at the e-mail I'd written to Summer, at the cursor blinking at the bottom of the page, wondering if it was smart to hit Send. I hadn't spoken with her since our days on the D.C. Habitat build. More specifically, since I'd punched her husband in the face.

I reread my message:

Not sure if you want to hear from me, but I'm struggling with some stuff, and you always helped me figure things out in the past. If you're around and can talk, let me know.

Ainsley's comment this afternoon, as innocent as it was, had knocked my scattered thoughts further askew. My last meeting (argument) with Tessa had been sitting with me, too. *You hear what you want to hear*, she'd said. Then Ainsley today, upset she'd been too wrapped up in her emotions to see what Anton had gone through as a teen.

I was beyond proud of her for finally facing her past, but her realization hit home. Maybe I wasn't seeing my past with Tessa clearly, either. I just didn't know how to sift through it all.

I flicked the mouse until it hovered over the Send button, paused, then clicked the damn thing, hoping I wasn't about to stir a hornet's nest. I didn't know if Summer had forgiven me for hitting her husband, but I didn't regret the impulse. I'd also never forget how that day had changed my life.

We'd both been struggling in our marriages and started sharing our woes at some point. At the time, she was the only one in my life who understood what I was going through. When our volunteer shifts overlapped, we'd commiserate. Then one day she got something in her eye.

Her chin had trembled as I leaned over her to carefully remove the wood particle. The second it was out, her tears spilled over and she collapsed into me. "He cheated," she'd said against my chest. "I saw a text and confronted him this morning, and… *God*, he cheated."

I held her and listened, all the while wanting to pummel the asshole. But it was her next comment that sucked the wind right out of me. "I still love him. I'm more afraid of losing him than forgiving him."

In that moment, I realized I had to let Tessa go. The love Summer still had for her husband had been palpable, even in the face of what he'd done, something I hadn't felt in years, if ever. Something I knew I'd never get back. Tessa and I both deserved better. So I'd wiped Summer's tears and kissed her cheek and told her to fight for her man, if that was what she wanted. What I shouldn't have done was punch him when he turned up that afternoon.

Now I was reaching out to her, seeking advice from the woman whose worst moment had given me clarity.

Her reply came swiftly: *I'm around now and would love to catch up. Send me your number.*

Relieved at her positive tone, I sent it off. My phone rang moments later.

"Summer Daniels."

"Owen Phillips. This is a pleasant surprise."

I bounced my heel. "Wasn't sure it would be after what I did."

Her laugh drifted through the line. "That day was nuts. But seeing you punch Mike in the face was a highlight back then."

I flexed my hand, as though it still throbbed. "Felt pretty good, considering. How are you?"

She paused, and I leaned back in my chair, spinning the pen on my desk. It was nice to hear her voice. The familiarity sucked time into a vacuum, like we'd never lost our friendship.

"I imagine you're asking if I'm still with Mike, and the answer is yes. We moved past what he did, with a crapload of therapy, but things are really good."

Not sure I had it in me to forgive a spouse that kind of betrayal, but if there was one thing my disastrous marriage had taught me, it was that there was no judging other relationships. We weren't privy to what happened behind closed doors. "Glad to hear it. I know you wanted to make it work."

"It's not all smooth sailing, and the distrust creeps up from time to time, but we both put in the effort we deserve now. What's going on with you? Why'd you reach out?"

Summer had always been a straight shooter. It was one of the reasons we got along so well. "I left Tessa shortly after the last day I saw you, and things have been…rough."

I launched into the whole mess: the cheating scandal that never happened, losing my friends, the divorce from hell, meeting Ainsley. The last bit came out soft and low, words I wanted to sink into.

"You sound smitten."

"Yeah." Even thinking about Ainsley had my stress ebbing. "But I need to end this standoff with Tessa if I want things to move forward with us. I didn't cheat on Tessa, but she thinks I did. Since you got past what happened with Mike, any chance you have advice on how to handle things?"

The sound of clanging bit out, then, "Sorry. Trying to cook a late dinner." More noises filled the pause. "Okay. The thing about Mike's affair was, it wasn't the cause of our problems; it was the effect. We'd drifted, as you know. We had money issues and his father had passed away, and a thousand other stupid things piled on until we didn't recognize each other. He knows if he ever cheats again, I'll be gone faster than he can blink, but I believed in us and wasn't ready to let go. Getting past what he did was about us *both* owning our part in the cause. So I guess the question is, have you done that? Have you apologized to Tessa? Have you taken ownership of your part in things?"

My heel was restless again, bouncing in time to my agitated thoughts. Tessa held a solid portion of the blame for our failed marriage. For years, I'd blamed her for it all:

Tessa didn't want kids.

Tessa chose work over me.

Tessa cared more about money than love.

Then came her accusations, and my anger had blocked out the rest, including my role in our collapse. I hadn't been able to focus on much besides my resentment and hurt. I would cast blame, and she'd bite back, an unending circle of animosity. Never once had I said I was sorry.

The more I spun the idea, the more it made sense. This was the wrench in our divorce.

I'd never accepted my blame.

"Summer, you're a genius."

"I try. Look, I've gotta go, but I'd also like to apologize."

"For what?"

"I meant to get in touch after the last day I saw you, but Mike assumed you and I were seeing each other. That's why he thought you hit him."

A wave of guilt rocked me. "I'm sorry if I made things worse."

"Don't be. Like I said, seeing that made me feel better, and he knows the truth now. But things were too fragile then to reach out to you, and time went on…"

"Don't think twice about it. I never messaged you, either. But it's nice to reconnect."

"It is. Don't be a stranger."

We hung up, and I stared at my phone. When Tessa had first accused me of stepping out on her, I'd racked my brain, trying to figure out why she'd thought I'd cheated and who she'd believed I'd been seeing. Summer had come to mind briefly, but we'd never gotten together outside the build, never talked on the phone. Tonight was the first time I'd even sent her an e-mail. It hadn't made sense, nor did any other acquaintance I'd had at the time.

Unless Summer's husband had said something to Tessa. Found out who I was married to and tried to start trouble.

If so, nothing to be done about it now. Now was the time to shoulder my side of the blame for my failed marriage. Sift through my actions and offer my own apology.

I kept my e-mail to Tessa short:

You were right that I only heard what I wanted when it came to us. There are things I've realized about our relationship, things you deserve to hear that I never said. It's time we talk instead of fight. I'd like to meet in person.

I steered clear of her crude accusations, Caroline's damaging text, and any divorce talk. I'd sent plenty of angry messages in the past. This was a new tactic. A last-ditch effort to find acceptance so we could both make peace.

I hit Send, then glanced at the clock. Ainsley would be here in half an hour. Her folks lived in a nearby suburb, so I offered to drive, suggesting she leave her car at my place. It would allow her to relax with her friends. Plus, if she drank too much, I wouldn't let her drive home. A prick move maybe, looking for any excuse to have her stay over, but I was greedy to sleep with her warm body tucked into mine. I wanted to wake her up with my mouth between her thighs, the best kind of breakfast in bed.

I got ready, nerves emerging as I dressed. She didn't know I'd taken private ballroom classes this week, preparing for tonight's clubbing afterward. I'd hated missing her texts, but dusting off my dancing skills so I could woo my girl had been more important. *Showing* her how much she meant to me was more important.

As long as I didn't trip over myself and blank on the steps.

By the time she arrived, I was fumbling while trying to tie my goddamn shoes, but one glimpse of my blond bombshell dispelled my nerves. Her golden hair fell around her shoulders, mile-high heels adding a sway to her step. Her purple dress was something from *The Great Gatsby*—shiny on the top half, fringed on the bottom. Sexy as sin. The sight made me happy I wore a vest with my slacks and dress shirt. I couldn't wait to spin her around a dance floor.

I clasped her fingers and kissed the back of her hand. "You're beautiful."

Her gaze slid down my body. "You're not so bad yourself. Love your shoes."

The black-and-white wingtips would hopefully serve me well when waltzing.

We didn't talk much on the drive, but the tension between us had thinned. Odd how silence had so many decibels, this one ringing with comfort.

Ainsley touched my thigh, and I covered her hand with mine, gathering her fingers in my grasp. I wanted to pull to the side of the road and kiss her senseless. I kept my foot on the gas. She gave me directions, seeming a bit fidgety on her seat, but not with unease. I sensed some kind of excitement, hopefully the idea of me meeting her family. If so, it meant she was finding it in her heart to trust me wholly. The notion made me pleased as hell.

Until I parked on her street.

Her white house was small and nondescript, the neighborhood a bit worse for wear. Some lawns were overgrown, others tended. Nothing was odd or out of place, except for the massive tattooed man leaning on her door frame. His thick arms were crossed over a Lynyrd Skynyrd T-shirt, bold ink splashed up his exposed skin, even his neck. His shaved head gave him a sinister look, and his thick blond beard accentuated the death glare launched our way.

I kept my hands on the steering wheel, ready to peel away if necessary. "Are you expecting someone else for dinner?"

Ainsley was all smiles. "Nope. That's my dad. My brother, Jason, should be here soonish."

"Your *dad*?"

"Don't worry. I had him lock up his guns. He's a pussycat, as long as he likes you."

My balls ran for cover while she hopped out of my truck and practically leapt at the intimidating giant. He lifted her up and flung her through the air.

I struggled to swallow.

Once inside the house, Mason Hall was even more intimidating. He nearly crushed my hand when he shook it, his steely appraisal unrelenting. Ainsley's mother was a different story. Colleen was as petite as her daughter, rounder curves, her blue eyes tired but warm. She fussed over Ainsley. "Your dress is lovely. Something new?"

Ainsley twirled and the bottom fringe fanned in a circle. "Found it at a vintage shop. Owen likes old movies, so I thought it would be fun."

The admission hit me square in my chest. I reached for her waist, to pull her closer, but Mason's scowl deepened. I froze and dropped my arm.

"I understand you just moved back to town, Owen." Mason growled more than spoke, his voice its own force of nature.

The women drifted into the kitchen, leaving me in the living room to fend for myself. The walls were a light yellow, a few family photos and dried flowers on a mantel above a brick fireplace. There was even a framed ballet poster over their brown couch. Mason Hall looked more of a brute in the slightly feminine space.

I cleared my throat. "I did, sir. I was living in D.C., but spent my teen years in San Francisco. I wanted to come back, be closer to my brother and grandmother." Unsure whether to cross my arms or let them hang, I shoved my hands into my front pockets.

"And you were married there?"

I bristled at the question, hadn't expected Ainsley to discuss my history with her father. Not that I had anything to be ashamed of, but his glower darkened with each passing second. "I was married for eight years. We got together young, and it didn't work out."

"So now you're dating around, making up for lost time."

Jesus fucking left field. "*No*. Now I'm volunteering at a Habitat for Humanity build, which is where I happened to meet your daughter. I wanted to contribute to the community while I figured things out." It was bad enough Mason thought I was a player. I didn't need him assuming I was a deadbeat, too.

He didn't invite me to sit, didn't make a move to be polite. "Sounds pretty convenient to me."

I widened my stance and scanned the room for those guns Ainsley had mentioned. "I don't have an agenda, sir. Coming home was a way for me to start fresh."

"Not with my daughter, I hope."

"Excuse me?"

"I know how beautiful my girl is. Know men see her as a prize. You won't be the first I run off, and you won't be the last. Ainsley deserves the world."

We were in agreement there, and I had every intention of

giving her just that. But he was about to get an earful. "All due respect, sir, I care for Ainsley a great deal. She *is* beautiful, but she's also smart and funny as hell, and I don't plan on letting her go, unless she doesn't want to be with me. But that's her decision to make, not yours."

A glimmer lit his gray eyes, a hint of…amusement? Then he cracked his knuckles. The ink on his forearms came into view: Ainsley's portrait beamed at me. This man was definitely devoted to his daughter.

The front door pushed open before he could pound me to a pulp, probably the other sibling joining us for this Cleaver Family Meal. Jason stopped at the threshold to the living room, assessing us with curiosity. "You must be Owen. I'm Jason, the better-looking sibling."

"Nice to meet you." His full cheeks reminded me of our chipmunk, Lucifer, but Jason was far from ornery. He had a bit of hipster to him with his plaid shirt and skinny jeans, grinning wide as his attention flitted between Mason and me.

Mason didn't move to greet his son. Not so much as a pleasantry offered. My girlfriend's father pulled up to his full height and stepped toward me. Christ, the man was scary. Jason's grin faded as he surveyed our mounting intensity.

Then he laughed.

Howling, he tossed his head back and smacked his thigh. Mason's lips twitched, a muffled snort escaping. I stood, baffled.

When Jason recovered, he slapped my back. "She's screwing with you, man. Dad's a total wimp."

What in the ever loving…?

Mason laughed outright, a guttural chuckle that bowled through the tension-filled room. "Sorry, but I can't say no to my girl. Even when she asks me to scare her boyfriends."

Ainsley stomped into the room and glared at her brother. "You ruined it. Dad hadn't even told him about the shallow graves yet."

Still on edge, I scrubbed a hand over my locked jaw. "Shallow graves?"

Mason planted his large mitt on my shoulder, leaning down close. "The ones out back, when the boyfriends get outta line." He blew out another snort, his shoulders shaking with humor. He tipped his head to me. "You did better than most. Nice to meet a man who'll stand up for himself." He regarded his daughter, a lifetime of fondness in his eyes. "Love you, princess."

Reeling from Mason's inquisition and chiding afterward, I hadn't quite found my feet, but the affection in the house began to set me right. They traded hugs and good-natured jokes. I didn't sense the irritation that lingered at some family gatherings. As hard as Ainsley's childhood had been, as much responsibility as she shouldered now, caring for her folks, there was no doubt she'd always been loved.

I stalked toward her, giving her my best playful glare. "You're in trouble."

Her eyes sparked with delight. "Punish me later," she whispered.

I'd be doing that and so much more.

Dinner really was a Cleaver Family Affair. Mason and Colleen teased Ainsley about her childhood Barbie fashion shows. They razzed Jason for having glued a piece of his model airplane to his chin. Vegan lasagna was devoured as Mason asked earnestly about my woodworking. Pride swamped me when Ainsley jumped in to praise my work.

I found myself staring at her across the table, losing trail of the banter, getting lost in her bright cheeks and easy manner. I even caught Mason watching me thoughtfully a couple times. Although no longer worried I'd be having a conversation with his fist, his attention was probing. Based on the closeness between him and his daughter, I'd guess he knew about Ainsley's ex. The cheating. How it had crushed her. I'd bet he was wondering if I'd hurt his daughter, too.

"I have an announcement." Mason tossed his napkin on his empty plate. He shared a tender glance with his wife, both clearly pleased about something.

Ainsley perked up, clueing into whatever I was missing. "Oh my God. Did something come through?"

Jason smacked the table in approval. "It was only a matter of time."

"I got hired at the Tesla plant. Another job opened up. Starts next week."

Ainsley squealed and hurried around the table, the four of them celebrating with laughs and more hugs. I sat back and soaked in their joy.

This was what I wanted one day, a family of my own. Accomplishments reveled, jokes shared, stories about Barbies and Super Glue remembered. I wanted stability and love, and I wanted it with Ainsley. I knew it in the deep ache anchoring my chest, the way my eyes followed her like a magnet. She was all I could see.

Shortly, she announced we had to meet our friends, not before we checked on the newly drywalled master bedroom—the work Ainsley had paid for but had lied about. I fell harder for her, watching her fuss over her tattooed father, who was wrapped around her finger. I couldn't count how many times he'd called her princess and had planted a kiss on the top of her head.

When her parents walked us to the door, Mason surprised me by pulling me into a hug. "Treat her nice," he said so only I could hear.

My throat tightened. I'd never had a father, let alone one whose world revolved around my happiness. I pounded his back. "Like a princess."

He released me, and Ainsley stood there, blinking rapidly—as though she might cry.

Once I had her buckled into her side of the truck, I trailed a finger along her jaw. "You okay?"

Still glassy eyed, she nodded. "Perfect."

I leaned down, stole a slow kiss, then gave her a wink. "Not perfect yet, doll. The night's just begun."

I'd visited The Scarlet Lounge yesterday and had cringed at the sight of the stark club in daylight. The cavernous space, worn couches, and nicked bar top weren't the backdrops I'd imagined for my romantic gesture, but it was where the girls wanted to go, so I'd powered on and had asked the owner for a favor.

Tonight the venue was ablaze with warm spotlights. A disco ball spun over couples and groups dancing. Others talked and flirted in clusters.

I placed my hand on Ainsley's lower back as we met the girls and Jimmy at the raised bar. Introductions were passed around, drinks ordered. Conversation flowed easily as our worlds merged. Hanging out as a group was fun…even when she gave them the play-by-play of her prank, at my expense. She could tease me endlessly for all I cared. I couldn't keep my attention from flitting to her beaming smile, her bright eyes.

Her quiet affection toward me.

Rachel placed her hand over her heart and said something I couldn't hear. "Sorry, what?"

She leaned closer and yelled, "You guys are so cute. I can't believe you're together."

In agreement, I squeezed Ainsley's hip. She pressed into me.

Gwen plucked the olive from her martini skewer and tossed it into her mouth. "The loud music and yelling reminds me of the night we first met Jimmy."

Rachel froze mid-sip of her wine. "Don't you dare repeat that story."

Jimmy was leaning on the bar, his shaggy hair and inked arms probably intimidating to strangers, like Mason's rough exterior had been. But my old friend was as solid as they came.

He wrapped his free arm around his girl. "Don't be embarrassed, Sunshine. I love that story." He nosed her ear and kissed her softly. "It was the best night of my life."

Rachel shrugged, feigning boredom. "If only I could remember it."

That sent them on a stroll down memory lane, the couple touching and joking about an alcohol-fueled one-night stand that turned into anything but. They were ridiculously in love. It made me want to hold Ainsley closer, have her pressed against me, under me, surrounding me.

"Speaking of wild nights one can't remember," she said, mischief in her voice, "Owen got his ass tattooed and has no idea what the Japanese words mean."

Gwen nearly coughing up her drink. "Can I see it?"

Ainsley went to answer, but I covered her face with my hand. "Not a chance. In fact, Ainsley made it up. She was hallucinating when we were stuck in a room."

"Whatever." Gwen eyed my belt buckle. "One night I'll get you drunk and pull down your pants."

Ainsley licked my hand, and I yanked it away, grinning.

"We'll tag team him," my traitorous girlfriend said. "It's hilarious."

Rachel raised her hand. "I'll help."

Jimmy crossed his arms, chuckling. "Can't wait to tell the guys at soccer."

These comedians. "You're all dead to me. And you…" I pulled Ainsley in front of me, her back to my chest, my arms secure around her. "That's twice tonight you've embarrassed me. I might need to spend more time with your folks, find out some dirt on you."

"You don't scare me, cowboy. Or should I call you Sinatra? Your outfit is a perfect throwback."

There was a time joking about my tendency to embody different personalities would have chafed. A reminder I used to search for stories that weren't mine. Any tale but that of being the second-hand kid abandoned by his mother, the teenager who'd been unsure what kind of man he should be.

I still valued the manners cowboys like my old boss, Bill, had inspired. I'd never tire of losing myself in a classic musical, watching love conquer all. But I liked who I'd become, an amalgamation of these experiences. Especially with Ainsley as my leading lady.

The music shifted, some remixed pop song that had the girls squealing. Gwen and Rachel snatched Ainsley from my grasp and disappeared into the crush of bodies on the dance floor. I settled against the bar, next to Jimmy. A glance at my watch told me my song would be on in fifteen minutes or so, and my stomach bottomed out. This was probably a stupid idea. There were a couple hundred people here, easy.

My lessons this week had been good. Irina was a great teacher, keeping things light and fun as she reinforced the basics I'd learned as a kid. But there'd been no audience those nights, no friends to laugh at us, no woman I'd been hoping to impress.

I took a lengthy pull on my beer.

"Looking kind of green," Jimmy said.

"Might have done something dumb."

"Care to share?"

"You'll know soon enough."

He didn't push, and I searched for the girls but couldn't find them in the growing crowd.

"Where's Emmett?" Jimmy asked.

I finished my beer and plunked it down. "No idea. I asked him to come tonight, but he was moody. Could barely get a word out of him."

"Did he end up dating Cameron?"

"Not sure. Why?"

He sipped his wine. "I was at The Blue Door last night, and Cameron seemed…subdued. I asked what was up. He said something about falling for the wrong guy, but I didn't know if that was your brother."

The intel gave me pause. Emmett was generally upbeat. Having him blow me off earlier hinted at something being wrong, but I'd had a dance to focus on and a dinner date with Ainsley's family looming. No time to force him to talk. I added that to my to-do list, along with convincing Tessa to wrap up our divorce, telling Ainsley I was madly in love with her without scaring her off, and getting my woodworking business off the ground. Piece of cake.

I searched for the girls again, still no luck, but my phone buzzed. An email from Tessa greeted me: *Talking sounds good. Why don't I come to you this time? I'm free in a couple weeks.*

I'd consider that a win. I replied for her to pick the time and day, then I caught sight of the girls. A couple douchebags were dancing too close, moving closer. Jimmy kicked off the bar, face darkening as he zeroed in on the same scene. Before we could make a move, Ainsley flipped around and said something to the tallest man. I was no lip reader, but there was no mistaking her sass and bite as the men raised their hands and slinked off.

Hot *and* badass—that was my girl.

"She's awesome," Jimmy said.

"I know, man. I know."

The music shifted then, the song I'd asked the owner to play strumming through the sound system. The dancing ceased, people unsure what to make of the mellow tune. Heart in my throat, I strutted toward Ainsley as the opening notes to Lighthouse's "You and Me" blanketed the room.

CHAPTER 18

Fifteen letters for the interlocking ridges and grooves that join
adjacent wood boards.
Or when your boyfriend busts out his inner Fred Astaire and
sweeps you off your feet.
TONGUEANDGROOVE

AINSLEY

My face felt flush, my armpits a tad dewier than ideal in my
vintage dress, but totally worth it after dancing with the girls. I
also wasn't ready to call it quits. But the funky pop mix blended
into a romantic song. The kind of music that had me wanting to
close my eyes and sink into my lover's arms. Not Rachel's or
Gwen's arms.

A tap on my back had my shoulders bunching toward my
ears. Some players didn't know how to take no for an answer.
They also didn't know who they were dealing with. Evil glare in
place, I swiveled. "You must not value your nuts, assho—"

Except he wasn't an asshole. He was Owen.

Bent forward at the waist, my charmer extended a hand in invitation. "May I have this dance?"

A small circle had formed around us, my friends looking like walking emojis with their heart eyes popping out. All I could do was stare. At Owen. I still couldn't get over how handsome he was in his white dress shirt, black vest and slacks tailored to his fine physique, those wing-tipped shoes pushing him from hot to hotter.

The Rat Pack had a new member.

I should have crowed *yes* on the spot, fallen into his inviting embrace. Instead I said, "If I have to lift my arms while dancing, I might clear half the room."

Not giving me a choice, he invaded my space. He placed one of my hands on his solid shoulder, the other in his outstretched hand. "You smell beautiful. You look beautiful. And you're going to dance with me, doll."

My breathy "Okay" was barely out when we began to move. Our first few steps were awkward. His body was stiff. My limbs were as graceful as a hippo's. All my ballet training disappeared in a whoosh. He tried to guide us to the left, but my instincts led me toward the right.

I cringed. "Shoot."

"Sorry."

"Sorry."

"Oof." He winced as I stepped on his toe. He tightened his hold on me, and whispered, "Let me lead, Ainsley. I got you."

Fred and Ginger we were not, but my lack of coordination wasn't because we were dancing our first dance in front of strangers. I just had to relax. Quit trying to halt the natural flow of our rhythm, exactly how'd I'd behaved in our relationship, stressing about Caroline's text and all the ways Owen could hurt me.

Inhaling his cologne of baked apple, musk, and man, I pictured my father giving him a bear hug. I remembered every time Owen had opened a door for me or asked me if something was wrong, sensing my sour mood. I stopped fighting his movements. Stopped trying to slow our momentum. I held my man, followed his lead, and gave myself over to the notion of us.

The disco ball above receded, the people and chatter fell away.

We didn't dance to the music. We *became* the music.

The romantic notes wove through my toes and twisted with my hair. The music strummed under my skin, binding me to him. Owen held me closer than a traditional waltz called for, but I loved how his heart whispered truths against my cheek, the heat of his hand on my back. We spun in circles as the sensual lyrics spoke of falling in love and tripping on your words and being overwhelmed by the woman in your life.

Did that mean Owen was overwhelmed by me? In love with me?

He slowed us down and changed direction, dipping me slightly, just enough for me to glimpse the affection in his warm eyes, then we were gliding again. Rising. Falling. Lights spinning. He turned me into the ballerina of my dreams.

As our confidence grew, he clasped my hand and twirled me in a circle under his arm, once. Twice. My fringe skirt whirled, my belly dipped. My hair was a riot until he caught me against his chest, not skipping a beat as our steps swept us in larger circles.

We were dancing on a cloud.

The song softened, the last chorus drawing us closer. A final dip sent me arching over his arm. A hush fell. My heart soared. He pulled me up slowly, meeting me partway. His lips closed over mine in a sensual rhythm, as spellbinding as our dance. His tongue stroked and swirled, mine following his lead. I never wanted to come up for air.

Someone hollered, "Get a room!"

Applause exploded, the room erupting into cheers as pop tunes returned. The dance floor filled up again, bodies crowding us. I tugged him closer, couldn't let an inch of space between us. "Get me to *your* room."

———

Our clothes disappeared in a hurry. We didn't make it to his bedroom, barely managed to get up the stairs. He lay sprawled on his hardwood floor, me on top of him. I was dazed, wild with lust, practically clawing at him. I wanted my mouth everywhere at once, a tigress come to claim what was mine.

He pushed up to suck a path down my neck and breast, working my nipple until I panted his name. All that remained was our underwear, the thick line of him rutting against me in the most delicious way.

I needed him inside me. Just plain needed *him*.

Rocking harder, I dug my fingers into his neck. His arms locked around my back as our next kiss turned dirty. Depraved. His teeth nicked my bottom lip in a sharp tug, a sting that had me pulling at his hair while trying to figure out how to get my panties off without letting go.

On a harsh inhale, I pulled back. Our chests heaved, his hungry gaze as savage as mine. There was warmth under the passion, too. A connection I never imagined finding with a man. We stared at each other, breathing hard, letting our eyes say everything we weren't.

You're mine.

I'm yours.

Don't you dare hurt me.

That last sentiment wasn't mine alone. A hint of censure darkened his gaze, a reflection of my own hesitation. It made me fall that much harder. I ran my hand over his brow, down his strong nose, ending on his flush lips. "I'm on the pill."

He stilled. "Are you asking me not to wear a condom?"

Swallowing, I nodded. "Ever since the stuff with my ex, I get tested regularly."

Because I didn't trust men, but I trusted Owen, with my body and my heart, and I wanted him to know it. I'd relived our magical dance the whole ride here, unsure how I'd found myself in a fairy-tale, starring my very own Prince Charming.

He flattened his palm on my chest, over my waltzing heart. "I'm clean, doll. There's no one else. So tell me you want this. That you want me to thrust my bare cock inside you."

"God, yes." A fresh wave of heat seared my thighs.

Grunting, he clutched me to his chest, stood, and walked us to his bedroom, my legs around his waist. I bit his shoulder and nosed his collarbone, even sucked on his chin. He tossed me on the bed, dragged my panties off and shucked his briefs, then he was on his knees, his intense gaze unrelenting as he admired my body while stroking himself.

Using his cock, he pushed my wetness around, teasing me, but he paused. "It's just us now, Ainsley. You and me."

My breath caught as I stared at his chiseled jaw and striking cheekbones, infinite passion in his heated gaze. If he were a lying savant who'd cheated on his ex, covering it with the acumen of a thespian, it would devastate me. It wouldn't leave me with the embittered distrust that still lingered after Brandon's deception. Owen's betrayal would breed the kind of hurt that would leave me broken.

But I was whole. And I was his, about to let him sink into me bare.

He pressed his tip into my opening, only an inch. "Okay?"

This. *Yes.* I wanted this. I wanted him and us. "Okay."

He swiped his thumb over my bottom lip. "Okay." Then he pushed in. The fullness was instant, all that warm pressure filling my body.

He moaned. "God, you feel good."

"More."

"More," he agreed.

We moved like we'd danced—me following his thrusts, meeting him in time. Rising. Falling. My heart spinning. It wasn't enough. He was so hard, each deep plunge stoking my desire. *More. More. More.* His skin was on fire, the solid expanse burning up. The weight of him was enough to make me lose my mind, and the edges of my pleasure took shape. My life took shape, around this man.

I grabbed his ass, arching as my vision went fuzzy, all my limbs hot and tingly. Tingles that sparked. "I'm there."

His mouth fell on mine. He kissed me harder, fucked me wilder, lifting my knee to force himself deeper. "I want to hear you come. Over and over. All night."

"If that's a dare"—I cried out as he tilted his hips, *wow*—"I'll take it."

His next move hit me just right, a spot of pleasure that nearly split me apart. "God, *yes*. Right there." My orgasm splintered through me, a burst of brightness behind my eyes, staggering fullness in my heart.

His release wasn't far behind, his last thrusts rough and sharp. His body shuddered as his heat rushed into me, and I held him closer, tighter. His voice was haggard as he whispered, "Never letting you go."

Sounded like a plan to me.

Eventually, he lifted onto his knees and pulled out of me. We both watched the slow drag of his exit. Still turned on, I grabbed his length, so flush and slick. "I want you to come on me."

His eyes hit their full one-hundred-percent rawness. "You're going to kill me."

"It would be a glorious death."

"That it would." His words were pure lust as I stroked him. I reveled in how he softened slightly then began moving with my hand, thickening, hardening.

A marathon ensued. He stayed on top, using short strokes to drive me wild, slamming flush when my nails bit into his neck. Over and over. The same rhythm. We didn't talk. We watched where we were joined until our eyes locked on a gasp, his pupils blowing wide. Then I fell. Ecstasy gripped me, each contraction clamping on his length, but he didn't come. He slipped out, and I released a cry.

More. More. More.

The need to stay connected shook me, and he was rock hard, nowhere near satiated.

I took charge, riding him—breasts bouncing, back arching—until I fractured again. His shoulder was pink from where I'd bitten him. My peaked nipples shone from his greedy mouth.

More. More. More.

He still hadn't come again. Grunting, he flipped us so my ass was in the air, and he plunged back inside me in one punishing stroke.

The force knocked me forward. "Are you going for a world record?"

"Can't get enough." More thrusts. Deeper.

A moan tore from my chest. "God, you're thick."

"You're so damn tight. Perfect."

He used his fingers, sliding them under me, rubbing maddening circles as our skin slapped. It took no time, my other orgasms feeding into this one. My arms quivered, my strangled cries an erotic symphony. He pulsed against my inner walls, a second from playing his own crescendo. Except he didn't.

Grunting, he flipped us again—me on my back, him over me —seating himself to the hilt. I should have been boneless, nothing left after the pleasure he'd wrenched from me, but a feral hunger flashed in his eyes. He was pumping fast, using my body to seek his pleasure. I *wanted* him to use me, to wring his own release from my body, because I was his to use, as he was mine.

I felt him swell, the hot length of him thickening into a steel rod. His strokes grew more frenzied. Sweat glinted on his brow. Then he pulled out. One hand branding my hip, he stroked himself with the other, coming on my belly and breasts and chest, long spurts that had him shaking.

His features sharpened, a primal growl rumbling from his

throat as he touched my stomach, dragged his fingers through his release. "So hot."

More like scorching.

Enraptured, I joined him, reveling in the odd sensation of his warm seed drying on my skin. I couldn't look away from his markings on me. "Watching you like that was unreal." His cock still jutted proudly, a job well done. "You better put that thing away. I'm tapped out. There's nothing left."

He grabbed his boxers and cleaned me up best he could. "Let's shower."

After a much needed soak, we flopped back onto his bed. The sheets were a mess, both of us naked and spread-eagled on our backs. Owen's solid muscle was spent and sprawled beside me. My body felt heavy, all the best places tender. "If we keep this up, I'll never have to visit the gym again."

"Challenge accepted." He lifted my hand to his lips and dropped a sweet kiss on my knuckles. "Best sex of my life."

My ego took a bow. "I mean, the sex was okay and everything, not my *worst*, but that dance was amazing."

He read my sarcasm plain as day, exhaustion coloring his laugh. "I know learning my divorce details was hard. I wanted to do something special for you—hoped to show you what you mean to me."

I loved how his lazy voice lilted into his often-hidden twang. "It was perfect."

Releasing a contented sigh, I lolled my head from side to side. My sights landed on the jar of glass on his night table. I hadn't outright asked about it since that first time. It seemed personal to him, something he didn't often discuss, but I wanted to know Owen. "Are the glass shards from where you grew up?"

The room was dark save for a glow from a corner lamp. A light *scritch* of leaves tapped against his bedroom window. He followed my gaze and reached for the container, bringing it to rest on his chest while tucking me into his side. "Yeah. The hippie commune. I collected them from a beach we visited, and then from others later."

He picked up a blue piece and turned it in his hand, then dropped it with a *plunk* back inside. More words followed, his quiet memories filling the room. He told me about the last day he'd seen his mother, and the riddle she'd spoken. Musings about feeling untethered in her world. How he'd scoured the beach for glass afterward, had collected it for the next few years, spending hours on sandy stretches, picking through twigs and rocks and garbage. He even shared how he'd bawled his eyes out to his grandmother, mountains of hate and hurt left in his mother's wake.

Gone was the intense desire from our evening, the air swelling with the wayward world of a lost twelve-year-old boy.

But he was older now, a strong man who'd been abandoned by the one person who should have loved him unconditionally. Somehow, he turned that tragedy around and became sweet and loyal and loving, but my heart squeezed for what he'd endured.

I took a piece of glass, letting the smooth edges bite into my thumb. "Why'd you keep it?"

Easing the glass from my hand, he moved the jar and shifted me on my back. He leaned on his forearm over me. Using the shard, he traced a line from my belly to my breastbone, painted invisible strokes along my lips and nose and brow.

He finished by placing it over my thrumming heart. "I kept them because I believed I'd find someone who had a piece of glass that would fit with mine. That I'd meet a woman who made me feel whole and loved and wanted. Probably some weird Oedipus complex I'd rather not interpret, but that's why I never tossed it." His voice roughened, scratched up with his history and the baring of his soul. "The second I saw your eyes, Ainsley, they reminded me of the glass. I get lost looking at you sometimes."

My throat burned, and I bit my lip. "What I feel for you scares me to death."

"Baby, I know. I'm nervous, too. But this is right. We're right."

Instead of agreeing or confessing the extent of my emotion, I said the next best thing. "Is it okay if I sleep over?"

Closing his eyes, he exhaled a long breath. "It would save me from cutting your spark plugs and tying you to the bed." His tone was light, but he swallowed hard, his Adam's apple traveling the length of his strong neck.

Since we'd started dating, every time I'd leave his place—never sleeping over, never offering him more—his thinly veiled hurt had cut me to my core. But staying meant trusting, as did sleeping with him without a condom. I was in this relationship mind, body, and soul, whether I was ready or not. "If you *do* mess with my car, I might have to miss work tomorrow. Spend all day in bed. And this piece"—I lifted the glass from my chest and set in on the bedside table—"is mine."

He placed the full jar next to my blue shard. "You can have it all. And this was my plan, you know. To woo you with the dance so you'd stay over."

Time for an admission of my own. "I packed a bag earlier. Before dinner at my folks. Before the dance."

"Yeah?"

"Mmmhmm."

His gentle smile said he approved. "I still plan to punish you for ambushing me with your father *and* your friends."

"Do your worst."

His worst turned out to be kissing me slow and deep until I nudged him off. "I need to grab said bag and brush my teeth. I don't want to have bad morning breath. I might not get invited back."

I went to move, but he placed a hand on my arm. The humor drained from his eyes, and the lull that followed sent my pulse racing. "I e-mailed Tessa today."

There goes my afterglow. God, I hated her name. Hated her vile accusations and the hold she still had on Owen. "About the divorce?"

He nodded. "I spoke with a friend from D.C. and sorted through some stuff. I think if I own part of what went down between us I can get the papers signed. She's coming here next week. No lawyers. Just us, to talk. I wanted you to know."

Acid burned through my gut. His honesty this time meant the world, but I didn't trust a woman hell bent on destroying a man, no matter their history. Even if the text I'd gotten had come from Caroline, Tessa's vindictiveness had been behind it. I also couldn't imagine why she thought Owen had cheated on her, had no idea what level of crazy she subscribed to.

Unless she wasn't crazy. Unless my instincts with Owen were as faulty as they'd been with Brandon.

Head spinning, I said, "Thank you," putting as much sincerity into the sentiment as possible.

Frazzled, I borrowed a T-shirt, grabbed my bag from my car, and escaped to the bathroom. *Not* cool. So not cool to be having a meltdown after the night we'd shared, but meltdowning I was. All the baggage I thought I'd released roared back, and I gripped the sink. Facing the reality of Tessa and her slander fed my insecurity, rational or not, but I wouldn't fuel it further. Not this time. I wouldn't let it ruin this beautiful thing Owen and I had. He also knew his ex. He had a plan.

As did I. I was one step away from becoming my best self and firing my sleazy clients. Facilitating their affairs had to stop, and losing my focus to insecurity could derail my efforts.

Soon I'd be starting a personal shopping business by women, about women, for women, turning the table on my unpleasant job. I'd target those recently divorced, wanting to reinvent themselves in the face of their losses.

What better way to do that than with my pals Dolce and Gabbana?

With Dad landing his job, I had a window of opportunity. He

could still get injured, or the factory could fold or cut jobs, so I couldn't sap my savings completely. But I had a shot.

Owen had even donned the hat of my financial (and sex) advisor recently. We'd sat down for a professional meeting, outlining how much money I'd need for a start-up business and ways to access my target market. I would decrease my volunteer shifts to one or two a month, use all spare minutes to build a website. It was the perfect distraction for my persisting paranoia.

CHAPTER 19

Nine-letter word for the deterioration of metal through
oxidization.
Or when your ex-wife's drama further infects your life.
C O R R O S I O N

OWEN

I hated being late. I found it rude and wasteful and generally made a point of watching the clock. But mornings the past couple weeks had been too sweet.

I'd slept at Ainsley's a bunch of nights, and she'd crashed at mine the rest. Each morning I'd tell myself to get up and get dressed, but she'd move in her sleep, snuggling up closer, and I couldn't let her go. I'd stroke her hair instead, tracing the smooth slope of her shoulder, mapping the three freckles set in a line. She'd shift and stretch. My touches would get more demanding until we were rocking together in an endless erotic dance.

Me and my girl.

My remaining time had been spent in my garage, building my inventory for Ellen's new shop. Volunteering had been put on hold, all my energy focused on producing the best work I could. Now I was late.

Not that it mattered when meeting Tessa. Her form of punctual was to arrive at meetings fifteen minutes past schedule. She claimed it set people off kilter, gave her an advantage.

Always a strategy with her.

This afternoon she was sitting in the coffee shop window, waiting on me. She'd traded her usual gray shark-suit for a red sweater and pearls. Her blunt blond hair and bangs framed her contemplative face as she sipped her coffee—likely the strongest they had, no cream or sugar.

It was odd, catching her in a candid moment. I could almost picture us eight years ago, a couple of kids who thought we knew what it would take to build a marriage. So naïve. So much lost time. I assessed how I felt, watching her. My anger bubbled below the surface, always there. Disappointment rang true, too, as did sadness. A heavy weariness that we'd wound up here.

Dragging a hand through my hair, I pushed through the doors and approached her table. "Tessa."

She pressed her hand to her throat. "Owen, you surprised me."

I shrugged off my jacket, rolled up my long sleeves, and settled onto the wooden chair opposite her. An espresso machine *shushed* and *whirred* as the line shuffled forward—business types on their handhelds, oblivious to the world. Tessa nudged a cup toward me. "Still take yours with milk and one sugar?"

I nodded. "Thanks."

Her tight smile showed signs of discomfort. I couldn't remember the last time we'd sat like this, no raised voices. No lawyers trying to keep the peace. Her attention drifted to my forearm. "Did you get in a fight with a grizzly?"

I glanced at the scratches and huffed out a laugh. "More like a fight with a rough wood plank."

"Does that mean you're pursuing your woodworking?"

"Trying to." Except I had no idea how much more money I'd spend on our divorce.

Gritting my teeth, I bit the words off before they could escape. I focused on my coffee, the warmth of it in my hand. I remembered the warmth of Ainsley in my arms this morning. I couldn't lose my cool today. There was too much at stake. I also couldn't do this small talk as though the woman before me wasn't trying to ruin my life.

I rested my weight on the small round table. "The reason I wanted to talk was I never said I was sorry."

Hope, similar to her expression the last day I'd barged into her office, colored her cheeks. "I'm listening."

It should be easy, to lay it out there, explain my struggles all those years ago, but I was suddenly burning up, the low hanging ceiling lamps casting too much heat. I tugged at my crewneck. "I wasn't happy in D.C. Never liked it. I moved there for you and thought I could make it work, but I felt like a fish out of water." The memories spilled over, all the frustrations from back then welling up. "My job wore on me. I missed Nana and Emmett. Most of my friends were friends of convenience—or they were yours. I think I shut down on you, and that's maybe why you started working so much. I'm sure there's more I did to piss you off, reasons for our slow decline, but I'm realizing now I hold some of the blame. So…"

I buried the fact that she'd turned Caroline against me. I put her recent game—firing her lawyer to toy with me—out of my head. I focused on what we once had, on the hurt I might have caused, and I said a genuine, "I'm sorry."

She shook her head, a small sad movement. "I knew you weren't happy. Not like we were in college. I got caught up in the politics at work, and you'd pulled away. I didn't know how to talk to you. Then you spent all your time on that Habitat project. And I…" Her lips flattened as she trailed off. Hurt sunk into her glossed eyes. "I didn't know what to do."

"We got married young, Tess. We were kids."

"But I was too driven. I worked hard because coming home to you was depressing at times, but it was also an excuse. I've been so determined to make partner. I couldn't see much past that goal."

"You're also good at what you do." Ruthless. The best of the best.

She studied her red nails. "I am."

Acoustic tunes floated on the coffee-scented air. We sipped our drinks, the tension between us less acute. "It's been a rough year."

Her voice grew quiet. "I don't think you know how hard."

I couldn't tell if that was a dig at my supposed cheating or our never-ending divorce. Either way, I didn't like being partly responsible for a woman's sadness. I never wanted us to end up like this. "I'm sorry, Tess. Sorry I couldn't make it work. Sorry I hurt you. Sorry for all the things that brought us here."

"I'm sorry, too. I've made it all harder. It's the fighter in me."

I wouldn't bet against her in a ring. "They don't call you the Sleeper for nothing."

She grinned at that. "I do kind of love that nickname." She lay her hand on the table, palm up. If I wasn't mistaken, her fingers trembled slightly. "What do you say we start over? Find our feet and try to move forward."

God, I liked the sound of that. Waving our white flags and surrendering our animosity.

I accepted her offering, placing my hand on hers and giving it a squeeze. What I didn't expect was for her to place her other hand on top of mine, too. For her to slide her fingers over my knuckles and trace the scratches on my forearm. "I've missed you so much." Her whispered confession held such longing. The type of angst spoken by a lover. "So much."

I froze. The hairs on the back of my neck stirred. I stared at her roving hand unsure where our wires had gotten crossed. Wires that needed untangling. I gave her another friendly squeeze, then twisted my arm and pulled my hand away. "We're talking about the divorce, right? Signing the papers and moving forward with our lives."

She winced as if I'd slapped her. "What did you say?"

"The divorce, Tessa. Selling our house and ending this standoff."

Her neck went blotchy as she scanned the mahogany walls as though she'd forgotten where she was. "Is that what this was all about? You offering fake apologies to end us?"

Just when I thought we were getting somewhere. "What else could this be?"

"I swear to God, I've never been this oblivious in a courtroom. But you"—her jaw flexed—"you affect me, Owen. Always have. You lured me here with false promises, all for what? To get hitched to your latest whore?"

Anger blasted through me, and I nearly tossed our flimsy table across the room. "Don't you *dare* talk about my girlfriend like you know her. And this wasn't a ruse. I *am* sorry. I fucked up. We both fucked up. This was me trying to admit my failure."

"To finalize our divorce."

"*Jesus.* Yes. To finalize our divorce." Patrons glanced our way, and I lowered my voice to an angry hiss. "Did you really think we could fall back in love after everything that's happened? The lies you've spread?"

Her brown eyes narrowed. "I was ready to forgive you *your* indiscretion, but I see clearly now. I won't make that mistake again, and you're right. It's time we both move on with our lives. We'll sell the house. I'll sign the papers. You'll never have to see me again."

Relief should have bowled me over, but venom bled through her tone. Vindictiveness. I offered a curt nod. "It's the best for both of us."

She scraped her chair back, plucked her purse from the window ledge, and smoothed her hands down her jeans. "It's the best for *you*, Owen. Everything is always about what's best for you. I wonder if your girlfriend knows what she's in for, how selfish you are."

Steel glinted in her pointed stare, then she strutted out the door, taking the oxygen in the room with her. I sat, cemented in place.

She'd agreed to the divorce, said she'd sign the papers. She could go back on her word, but that wasn't Tessa's style, and she'd never, not once, promised to come to an agreement. Still, worry pooled in my gut. Turning her down just now had hurt her. Her embarrassment had been palpable, and when Tessa felt wronged, Tessa lashed out. But she'd already done her worst. Caroline's text couldn't even ruin what Ainsley and I had.

Riled up and agitated, I headed home and sanded the coffee table I'd been working on within an inch of its life. I measured pieces for the black walnut stools I'd be building. Normally the steady labor cleared my mind. Today was a lost cause.

Ainsley's cute texting didn't even help. When I messaged her that Tessa had agreed to the divorce, she filled my phone with an alphabet of emojis, each more ridiculous than the last. Her silly humor didn't make a dent in my dark mood. I begged out of our usual evening plans, explaining the whole thing had left me drained.

I drove to Emmett's instead, soccer bag in my truck, hoping a hard run on the field would do me good. I'd ignored my brother the past couple weeks, or maybe he'd been ignoring me, but there was no answer.

I stood at his door, mulling over my options. I could go for a run on my own, but I'd end up chasing the uncomfortable dread I couldn't shake. Calling Ainsley and seeking her company would be the best kind of distraction, but she'd want to talk about my meeting. I needed to settle my mind before filling her in. My worry would only stress her out, when I was likely brooding for nothing. Instead I dragged my sorry ass to The Blue Door, hoping Cameron was tending bar.

My favorite thing about the dimly lit wine bar was its come-as-you-are vibe. I'd been here in dress clothes and in my shabby jeans from the Habitat build. Tonight I wore running sweats and a thermal long-sleeve, and I didn't give a damn.

I exhaled at the sight of Cameron's inked arms and slick pompadour. "Double Scotch on the rocks."

"This becoming your new drink?"

"It's been a wild couple months." I slid onto a barstool. The place was quiet, a handful of tables full, typical for a Thursday. A cool blast of air shot through the entrance as a few men hurried in. Cameron dropped my drink in front of me, and I knocked back a healthy swallow.

"That rough?" he asked.

"Not sure if today was good or bad, just glad it's over."

"Sounds intriguing."

I shrugged, effectively ending the conversation. There wasn't much for me to process besides needing to unwind. I was getting my divorce. Tessa misguidedly hoped there was a chance we could mend our fences and try again. It would never happen. Even if I weren't in love with Ainsley, there was no spark of affection I could fan for my ex.

Cameron filled a few orders while I nursed my drink. The heat of it burned my throat and chest, incinerating thoughts of Tessa and her diabolical games as it slid down. My muscles loosened. My mind uncoiled. It really had been a rough year. Or the best if I counted the Habitat build and meeting Ainsley, the girl with the beach-glass eyes and wicked sense of humor who turned my world right-side up.

I couldn't count how many times I'd wanted to pull her close and whisper *I love you*. I'd watched her face for signs she felt the same, but Ainsley was still coming around to the notion of us spending all our nights and mornings together, to her vegan food next to my "gross" deli meat in my fridge. At times she'd worry her lip when lost in thought, a sign I'd taken to mean:

What if this backfires in my face?

Cameron wiped a spot on the bar, then replenished a bowl of

pretzels, sneaking glances my way. I readied myself for prying questions, but he said, "You heard from Emmett recently?"

Maybe I wasn't the one who needed to talk. "Barely. When I text him, I get a curt reply. Went by tonight but no one answered."

"So it's not just me…" He spoke softly, as though to himself.

It activated my Brother the Manwhore Radar. "You ignored my advice, didn't you?"

He kept rubbing the same spot. "It had been a while since I'd dated. I thought having some fun would do me good."

"But you got in too deep?"

He scoped the bar, letting his gaze drag over the half-full tables. "Guilty."

One word filled with regret.

I hated my brother sometimes. "Don't take it personally. Emmett's only interested in casual."

Cameron gripped his cloth, his confusion and hurt plain as day. "That's just it—it wasn't casual. It was only, like, six weeks, and yeah, it was fun at first, but things got intense fast. The way I felt about…*feel* about him—I've never had that before. And he was right there with me. I'm sure of it. Then he disappeared. Slipped out of bed one night while I was sleeping. No goodbye. No note. He won't return any texts or calls." He rolled out his shoulders. "Is that normal for him? When you warned me not to date him, is that what you meant?"

Definitely *not* normal. "Emmett's flings usually last a month or so, but he's always made sure his partners are on the same page, and he's clear about where they stand when things end." Slipping out in the middle of the night was definitely not his MO. It meant something was up, and my frustration with him morphed into worry.

"That's what I thought." Cameron's forehead compressed, deep furrows framing his pained eyes. "I think he's freaking out. Just not sure how to help him."

If the tortured look on Cameron's face was any indication,

my brother may be falling in love. It also meant Emmett was probably spiraling, unsure how to deal with that kind of emotion. "I'll talk with him. See what I can find out."

"Thanks, man." He nodded a bunch. "Thanks a lot."

He retreated to work the bar, and I focused on my drink, on Emmett and me and all we'd endured. Our mother's abandonment had left its mark on us, all right. He was terrified of gaining affection, only to risk losing it. My damaged pendulum swung the other way. I craved permanence. I let my marriage linger years too long, afraid to be afloat. Now I had Ainsley. I was sure she was different. *We* were different. But if things changed, if she didn't want kids or we fell apart the way couples sometimes did, unable to find their way back, I wouldn't let it fester this time. I'd honor myself, not settle.

Emmett needed to learn how to hold onto the special people in his life, a lesson I'd have to drill into him, and I needed to remember how to let go.

If my instincts were right, though, I wouldn't be letting Ainsley loose anytime soon. Already, I regretted putting her off tonight. I could pull up her name on my phone, type *I love you,* and hit Send. Finally release the words I'd been holding hostage. Drive to her house and growl them as I came all over her creamy skin.

I'd loved marking her with my come. The act had felt intimate, in an odd way. Dirty yet binding. But there was no point texting or showing up at her place tonight. I'd let my day settle. See her tomorrow. And the next day. And the next. Finalize my divorce. Maybe get married again...one day. Relaxing for the first time in hours, I finished my Scotch.

CHAPTER 20

Thirteen letters for the machine that pumps wastewater from beneath the main drain.
Or when you're forced to evict your piece-of-shit boyfriend from your life.
SEWAGEEJECTOR

AINSLEY

Yawning, I rolled over in bed, blindly reaching beside me, a sleepy smile on my face. My happy haze vanished when I came into contact with empty sheets, not a construction hunk stealing my covers. Pouting, I pulled my pillow over my face.

It was wild how quickly I'd gotten used to our sleepovers and the weight of him against me—an arm tossed over my middle, his calf pinning mine. I'd also missed him terribly last night, drowning my sorrows in Aazam's decadent chocolate bark.

Until I'd gotten Owen's good news: the divorce. *Over.* The

papers soon to be signed. It meant he could pursue his wood-working in earnest and eject that bitch from his life, and I could stop worrying about the cheating scandal that never happened.

Pumped to start my day and celebrate with him, I tossed my pillow onto the floor and pushed my tangle of hair from my face. My sights landed on my piece of blue glass. I'd left it beside my alarm clock so I could see it every day. Sun beamed through my window, a ray hitting the glass just so, turning it from powder blue to turquoise. Like my eyes, Owen had said.

A glow burned inside me as I stared at it, all our lunch dates and kissing and sharing and dancing collecting into a bright spot under my breastbone until the truth of my feelings burned clear. I loved Owen Phillips. I loved him so much it threatened to crack me open from the pure joy of it.

I squealed like I was sixteen and flopped on the bed, grabbing the blue glass and spinning it through my fingers. I should make a necklace out of it, have a jeweler fasten something special. Owen would love it, and I could always have it close, just like him. Maybe take a few more shards, add some detail.

Practically floating, I rolled over and grabbed my phone to text him. *I forgot my favorite mascara at your place. Can I come by to steal it?*

His answer came shortly. *Only if I get to see you tonight.*

You drive a hard bargain. I'll pencil you in.

I'm around until noon but need to hit the hardware store, then I have a meeting at Ellen's barn.

I'll try to swing by before you leave. My fingers hovered over my screen, itching to hit the I and L and O and V and E. My belly felt bubbly, effervescence rising until I giggled. God, I was pathetically in love, but I wouldn't waste the opportunity for us to have ridiculous I-said-my-first-I-love-you sex by typing it on a phone.

I also had no intention of showing up while he was home. This was a stealth operation: Mission Mad Love. Show him what he meant to me by turning his most prized possession into a pendant I'd wear over my heart.

I texted Rachel instead, who texted Jimmy, who gave me Emmett's number, who then agreed to lend me his key. Next I called Volikov's and made an afternoon appointment. The jeweler was a gem virtuoso. He also owed me a favour. (Acquiring him Versace Medusa-strap sneakers at half price had been a miracle.) I could wait to steal some of Owen's glass tonight, but I was too pumped to get rolling. Plus, working on it might help balance the horrible-awful confrontation I'd planned for the morning.

My mood dipped. But if I truly wanted to fulfill my resolution and be a better person, there was no avoiding my fate.

A fate which began by writing e-mails to each douchebag client and firing their cheating asses. My website was almost finished, my calendar clearer to focus more attention on this new venture. I still had Felipe and a few upstanding clients. The rest could kiss my Miu Miu-clad behind. I sent the electronic pink slips, elation tickling my fingers. Next came the hard part.

———

I parked in front of Sloane's home, my hands gripping my steering wheel like it was the last Prada purse on a sale shelf. Thomas Arlington the *third*'s car wasn't there, but I'd pathetically hoped to find it. If he were home, I wouldn't be able to knock on the front door and tell a lovely woman, who had bought me ballet tickets, that her husband was scum.

I'd rather be locked in an elevator than face Sloane, or stuck on one of those reality shows where I'd have to eat bugs or bats or sheep intestines.

I hadn't developed as close relationships with the other duped wives, wasn't comfortable e-mailing them about their husbands' indiscretions. But Sloane was a friend. Breaking

Thomas's confidentiality could damage my reputation, but she deserved to hear the truth from me, in person.

I wiped my damp palms down the front of my gingham wrap dress, the same one I'd worn the first day I'd met Owen in all his manly glory. I considered it my lucky dress. I hoped it would give me strength to face my fears. *Here goes nothing.*

Attempting not to hyperventilate, I rang Sloane's doorbell. The kind woman answered and smiled, clueless that I was about to dismantle her life. I may have been in my lucky dress, stilettos, makeup and hair primped, but I was pretty sure I looked like a hideous troll.

"Ainsley, what a nice surprise."

She opened the door wider, but I couldn't step inside. The news I brought didn't deserve a warm invitation. "I need to tell you something. I should have told you ages ago, but...well, I won't make excuses, because there aren't any, and you deserve to know. It's just tough to say, and I've been a coward."

Already tall, her posture straightened farther, one hand on the door. "You're not making sense."

Because I was a babbling idiot, and there was no sugar-coating this atomic bomb. "Thomas is cheating on you."

Sloane's chin didn't tremble. She didn't choke on a sob. Her eyes darkened. "What are you talking about?"

Bile burning my throat, I confessed it all. How I'd met three women during my time with Thomas. That I was often asked to buy them gifts and clothes. That he was currently involved with someone and had spun a web of lies. "It's not your fault—I want you to know that. I worked for a number of men like him, and they thought they were beyond reproach or something, that their actions didn't—"

"Go." She spat the word, her stare hardening. "I don't know what your angle is, but I won't stand here and listen to such filth."

She moved to close the door, but I put my trembling palm on the wood. "I know it's hard to hear. I was in your position once, duped by a man. But I'm not lying. I have *met* these women. I have been in their homes. I have listened to your husband tell them he's getting a divorce. This isn't second-hand information."

She cocked her head, her disgusted gaze raking me from my honey highlights to my stilettos. "You've fallen in love with him, haven't you? Is this your way of getting me out of the picture? Forcing us apart? Well, it won't work. I love Thomas and he loves me, and you and your lies can go to hell."

She slammed the door in my face, the force of it blowing back my hair.

I winced. My knees weakened as I hurried to my car. I'd expected to face devastation—tears and anguish as the news I'd brought sunk in. Never had I considered she wouldn't believe me. The blind devotion was even worse. She either wasn't willing to risk a lifestyle change, or she loved him so much she couldn't face the truth. Such misguided loyalty, but it was her choice to make. Her life. I'd done what I could.

Frazzled, I picked up Owen's key from Emmett's mailbox. I drove home to spend a couple hours on my website, distracted the whole while. Making this gift for Owen was a smart move. I could focus on real love. Remind myself some men were devoted and true. When the clock read 1:00 p.m., I got ready.

He would be gone by now, and I could sneak in. Surprise him with the necklace in a month or so. Maybe I'd have them make him cufflinks, too. Something he could wear to think of me.

Buoyed at the prospect, I opened my door, but frowned. A manila envelope sat on the floor. Peeking my head into the hallway, I scanned left and right, but couldn't see a soul. Curious, I dropped my purse, scooped up the package, and turned it over. No address. Nothing written. I wasn't a prime target for terrorists, but I sniffed the edges. Did anthrax have an aroma?

Or Sloane could have sent a bomb to my home, but nothing protruded at sharp angles. I flipped open the flap to find photographs. Maybe Owen had thought of his own gift, dirty photos sent as a tease for tonight. I bit my lip as I pulled them out...

And nearly fainted.

My hands shook. My breath clawed at my chest. Lowering to my knees, I dropped the photos and pushed them around, sure my mind was playing tricks on me.

But no. No, no, no. The images were crystal clear:

Owen with his hands on a woman's face.

Owen leaning down, his back to the camera, but unquestionably *kissing* the woman.

The couple hugging.

The couple holding hands.

My head spun, pressure building at the base of my skull. A drop fell on the top image, my tear hitting the man I love on his chest. What were these? How? When?

A time stamp on the bottom sent relief crashing through me. These weren't recent. These were old, but Owen had left Tessa in March of last year, almost a year ago. These photos were dated February, while he was still married and living with his wife. Like Caroline's text had claimed.

My attention shot to my still-open door. Was *she* here? Caroline? Or Tessa? Had one of them followed me home and left these?

The violation of it slicked my palms, as did the reality of this evidence. Owen had promised he'd never cheated. I'd asked him point-blank, and he'd sworn the accusations were lies.

There had to be some mistake. A man who looked like Owen maybe. The images doctored so his ex could destroy him and what we had. Or maybe he'd played loose with the definition of cheating when we'd talked about his marriage. Cheating means different things to people, and he'd lied by omission before, hiding behind words.

Were these more secrets? His deceits come to life?

I wanted to dump the photos in the sink with a vat of acid

and pretend this nightmare wasn't happening, like Sloane had closed her ears to the truth. Choosing ignorance over fact.

More tears pooled, but I blinked them away before they spilled over this damning evidence. I would not full-on ugly cry. Not over a man. Not again. Full of trepidation, I picked up the envelope. Two photos were still tucked inside. I didn't want to look. I wanted to close my eyes and rewind time, but I was drawn to this car wreck, lured by the gory details.

Gut twisting, I pulled the last images out. Owen again, but with another woman, and they were dancing. He was holding her close, his face dreamy, like he was exactly where he wanted to be. In the next, he was dipping her like he'd dipped me in the club, bathing her in one of his glorious smiles. Those were my smiles. They were meant for me, and that was my dance. The time stamp on the bottom was the final blow. It wrenched a sob from deep in my bones.

Three weeks ago. While he'd told me secrets and promised me love and affection, while we'd had sex *without a condom*, he'd been with another woman.

My anguish hardened into a ball of fury.

He'd lied to me. Had used me. For what? It didn't make sense, but I'd seen men do this and much worse, always thinking with their dicks. I loved Owen, deeply, *painfully*. I couldn't hide from that sad truth. But I wouldn't be like Sloane, blind to reality. Believing my man's lies. I would surgically remove Owen from my life and never again trust a man.

The drive to his house was a blur of vengeance. I was Poison Ivy. I was Cersei Lannister. I was Maleficent and every raging villainess ready to set fire to the world. I would be nobody's fool. Except Owen's truck was in his driveway.

I slammed my foot on the brake, almost giving myself whiplash. *Oh God*. He'd said he'd be out. He'd asked me not to come by in the afternoon.

More lies. More deception.

This was Brandon all over again, forcing me to see my lover

in the throes of his affair. I should leave. I should hit the gas and drive, drive, drive. But I was stuck.

It was perverse, this need of mine to pull my car up next to his. To grab the envelope of treachery, put one foot in front of the other and walk through his door and up his stairs. But I couldn't stop my legs from moving or my heart from screaming or my throat from constricting.

It wasn't my intention to confront him. So raw and wounded, I'd never have dared face him yet. The plan was to leave the evidence on his counter, then drive to Napa Valley. Get away from this town and these lies. This devastating agony. Cry to Rachel until I was dehydrated, then find a way to reclaim my armor and resume my life.

Now that I was here, I couldn't turn away.

Nausea churned my stomach. I had to pause, hand on the stairwell wall until it passed. It took several deep breaths to find my resolve. Footsteps thudded above me, moving in one direction, then another, a low baritone following, as though Owen were talking to someone, but I couldn't make out the words. When I entered his place, he was leaving his room, head down, fully dressed. A small mercy. At least I wouldn't have to see his naked body loving on someone else.

I tried to look past him, into his room, but the door was nearly shut. He glanced up and jumped at the sight of me. *Surprise, asshole.*

He grinned, the brightness of his smile shattering what was left of my heart. His full wattage was aimed at me like we were the last beings on this planet, no mistress in his life. No betrayal about to rip us to shreds. It was also the same smile he'd lavished on the *other* woman he'd been dancing with.

His eyes roved over my face, his grin slipping into a frown.

I couldn't imagine how I looked. Rabid? Furious? Destroyed? He tried to close the gap between us with long strides, but the second he was close enough, I shoved him back. "Don't."

He flinched. "Ainsley, baby, what's wrong?"

He reached for me, but I batted away his arms. "I thought you were supposed to be out."

"I was…but I got caught up on staining a table and figured I'd hit the hardware store after meeting Ellen."

Lies. Nothing but lies. "Is she in here? In your room?"

Furrow sinking deeper in his brow, he glanced at his bedroom door, then back at me. "Who? What's going on?"

"Your girlfriend, that's who. Is she in there? Hiding in your goddamn sheets?" I shoved past him and smacked the door so hard it cracked against the wall. Empty.

Owen pleaded with me to talk, explain. I ignored the traitor. I tore through his closet, even though it was clear no one was inside. I made for the bathroom next. I checked behind his kitchen counter. The tears I'd struggled to keep at bay came hard and fast. The Ugly Cry in all its horrible glory. But there was no one here. No one but us and the envelope clutched in my hand.

With my back against his living room wall, I slid down. My butt hit the hard floor. I sobbed. I tugged at my dress, fighting to cover my knees. I felt so *naked*.

He crouched in front of me, his face twisted in distress. Like he cared. Like *my* tears were gutting *him*. "Ainsley, I need you to tell me what's happened." He reached for me, but drew his arm back when I glared. "Talk to me. I can't help unless I know what's wrong."

Unable to form the vial words on my tongue, I tossed the envelope at him.

He seized it, fumbling to get the photographs out. His eyes widened instantly, his broad chest rising and falling as fast as mine. He mouthed *what the fuck* as he dropped them on the floor and shifted them around, as though sorting through puzzle pieces. They were, in a sense. Each represented a jagged piece of my soul.

"Where did you get these?"

The bite in his tone had me shrinking. What right did he have to be mad? "They were left at my front door. Do you know these women?"

"*Fucking Tessa.*" Ignoring my question, he smacked the hardwood with the heel of his palm. "*Fuck!*" I jolted, horrified as he jammed his hand into the wood repeatedly. He crushed a couple photos in his fist, nostrils flaring as his tantrum ebbed.

"Do you know these women?" An odd calm claimed me as I repeated my question. My voice was even. The tears had ceased.

Sinking to his knees, he sighed. "Yes, I know them, but I can explain."

Like he'd *explained* about Caroline's text. "I have photographic evidence."

The anguish in his pleading eyes was almost believable. "This"—he picked up the one from last year with his hands on the brunette's face—"is Summer. We met on the D.C. Habitat build. This was the day she found out her husband was cheating on her. We were friends. Nothing more. Tessa had a private eye trailing me at one point, but I thought it was later."

He touched the image of his back facing the camera. The one with his large body leaning over Summer as if in a kiss. "I guess this is why she thinks I cheated," he murmured, slumping lower. Then his vehemence returned. "I kissed Summer's cheek, I think, trying to comfort her. But it was never more. Never. You can call her, ask her. I swear to God, Ainsley—I *never* lied to you."

I sat, numb, unable to reply or cry or yell.

Frantic now, he pointed at the shot of him dancing with the thin blond. A beauty with large eyes. "I took dance lessons. To prepare for the waltz. This is Irina. She turned her den into a small studio and does private lessons. I'll give you her number, too. Call *them*. Ask *them*."

His dark eyes were feral, desperate, and I nearly said, *okay, yes, I believe you.* I wanted to trust him so badly. The same way Sloane wanted to assume Thomas was true. Like I'd believed every work meeting Brandon had ever invented. These women could easily corroborate a lie. Talking to them would mean nothing.

I couldn't see past the pain. Or answer him.

"*Christ.*" He shot to his feet, pacing like a caged beast. "This is just Tessa playing her evil games. Don't let her ruin us. Don't let her destroy what we have."

"It's too much. The text. This…" I pressed my hand to my chest, willing the sharp pain to subside.

Owen speared his fingers through his hair, the tendons in his neck taut. "I didn't cheat on Tessa. I didn't cheat on you. I've never betrayed a woman in my life. It must have been horrible seeing those photos. I get it. But after all we've shared, what I thought we had"—he faced me and deflated—"how could you doubt me?"

I wrapped my arms around my middle, drowning in despair. His anguish felt thick enough to taste, so unbelievably real, and my anger morphed into confusion. If he was telling the truth, and I'd assumed the worst in him—my baggage messing with my head—then maybe I wasn't ready for a relationship. Maybe I never would be.

But the photos were damning, too, neither prospect painting a pretty picture.

Swiping at my tears, I pushed to stand, stumbling as I sought balance. "I don't know what to believe."

"Believe *me*. Believe in us."

"It's so hard."

"Baby, I know it's hard. But this is Tessa trying to split us up same as she turned my friends against me."

I hugged my waist tighter, sure I would crumble. I couldn't answer him or process a word he was saying. The longer I stayed silent, the more shadows drifted across his face. His cheekbones sharpened. His lips flattened into a grim line. "So this is how it is. My word, my assurance, means nothing."

"I don't know," I mumbled, faint and feeble. I couldn't form a coherent thought.

He scrubbed a hand down his face, looking as exhausted as I felt. "Thing is, Ainsley, I *do* know. I know exactly how I feel about you. And if you can't look at me and see past these lies, then maybe..." He trailed off, resignation thinning his voice. "Maybe we aren't worth fighting for."

His admission was a fresh blow, lancing the wind from my chest. One second I wanted nothing more than to neuter him like the dog I thought he'd proven himself to be, next the air rushed from my lungs. He was giving up. *He* was leaving *me.*

Is that what I'd wanted? For him to beg my forgiveness? Pledge his first born? Sacrifice himself at my altar? None of which I deserved if he was telling the truth. It was all such a mess. I needed to leave. Get in my car and drive. Stop my head from spinning.

"I have to go," I mumbled. Once. Twice. The same sentence over and over as I nearly tripped over my feet to reach the stairs. He didn't stop me or chase me out the door. He barely moved. I fled, and he did nothing.

CHAPTER 21

Five-letter word for the wetness of concrete.
Or your sad existence when you lose the love of your life.
S L U M P

OWEN

I'd been bucked badly from a horse once, slammed onto the ground so hard every bone in my body had vibrated. I was sore for months afterward, each inhale reminding me my ribs had cracked. Now each inhale reminded me my heart had fractured.

It had been five days since Ainsley walked out my door. One hundred and twenty hours of lying awake and cursing Tessa and working endless hours in my shop. Sawing and sanding and staining were supposed to give me peace, calm my frazzled nerves. Nothing worked. Then I'd happened upon Ainsley's tofu lodged behind my orange juice this morning and lost my shit. Doors were slammed. Curses yelled. My bookshelves hit the floor. My exhaustive run that followed subdued my misery, but not the constant ache in my chest.

Each day I tried convincing myself I'd made the right call, that not fighting for Ainsley was the smart move. I couldn't have a repeat of Tessa, I'd remind myself. Wouldn't get stuck in a relationship where I was more invested, more in love, more present than my partner. If Ainsley had loved me, she wouldn't have walked out the door.

The mental marathons were a losing battle.

Sweat coated my back from my exhaustive run. I stood, hand braced on my fridge as I chugged a Gatorade so fast it dripped down my chin. My phone buzzed from my counter. Wiping my forearm across my mouth, I glanced at the screen. *Jimmy.*

He'd been texting since Friday. First to tell me Ainsley was at his place in Napa, safe and sound, then to keep me updated on how she was doing. I never replied. Not to ask questions or to vent. Not to tell him to quit meddling. I was desperate for news of her, had to make sure she was okay. I almost hopped in my truck a thousand times to drive there and grovel at her feet, but I didn't trust my heart. I didn't trust hers.

That left me in this endless eddy, drowning.

I tapped on Jimmy's message as I always did, pulse spurring for news of my girl—an endearment I couldn't shake. He didn't mention Ainsley, though.

Gwen will be driving down to spend the weekend in Napa with the girls. I've been kicked out. Heading to The Blue Door on Friday. You should come.

No hint as to how Ainsley was doing. Did she wish she'd never met me? Was she cursing my name or hardly giving me a thought?

Earlier this week, Jimmy had said she was upset, struggling. An image that had gutted me. I'd barely slept that night and worked on a new maple table until the sun rose. Not mentioning Ainsley now might mean she was moving on, which was what

I'd said we should do. So why did the prospect make me want to punch the fucking wall?

Maybe, I replied, unsure I'd be better off in two days. Right now being in public and socializing was up there with watching reality TV. What did give me pause was his mention of The Blue Door. I'd forgotten about my chat with Cameron, hadn't spared my brother a thought during my seclusion. A fact in need of remedy.

A quick shower later, I tossed on jeans and a sweater and drove to Emmett's earlier than he'd prefer. Of the two of us, I was the morning person growing up, kicking a soccer ball for hours before he'd lumber from his room. Today's seven a.m. intrusion would annoy him, but being stuck in my place alone was unappealing. With my distracted state, I'd wind up cutting off my hand with my jigsaw, or I'd stare at my jar of beach glass again.

Another bleak ritual this week.

It took three pounding sessions on Emmett's door before he yanked it open. Flannel pants hung low on his hips, his tight wife-beater askew. His dark curls were plastered to one side of his face, and his exaggerated yawn forced him to squint. "What the hell, man?"

Without waiting for an answer, he scratched his chest and shuffled into the kitchen. I followed. His office door was open, giving me a glimpse of the posters on his wall—his most successful graphic design campaigns. My lazy brother was talented enough to work freelance, choose his hours, and never have to advertise. His place was nicer than mine, the open kitchen neater than was usual for him. His minimal furniture and coffee table were tidy, too. The way he'd been MIA, I'd expected the place to look like a crash site.

He hunched over his coffee machine while I leaned against his center island. I rubbed the exhaustion from my stinging eyes. "We need to talk."

"Apparently. You look like ass."

I felt like it, too. Assumed I'd look better than my brother, though. My brother, who was whistling as he poured us both steaming cups of coffee. A dash of sugar and milk later, we sat on the stools at his counter, side by side, eyes forward. "You've been hiding out," I said.

We sipped our coffee. The icebox in the freezer churned. "A bit. Had to figure some stuff out."

"And have you?"

A sly grin curved his lips. He didn't reply, but the sound of a flushing toilet came from behind us, and my anger surged. I couldn't keep it contained these days, but he was doing it again —using flings to avoid the one thing that truly mattered: love. It was bullshit, would only hurt him in the long run, when he had a shot at something real.

Lowering my voice, I hissed, "Fucking around isn't the answer. I spoke with Cameron. He's into you, and by the sounds of things, you feel the same. If you do this, start sleeping around again, he won't be there at the end."

"And what do you know about seeing things through?" he bit back. We faced each other, forearms on the counter, angry glares locked. "Jimmy called me this week, told me about Tessa's stunt and said you've dropped down a wormhole over Ainsley. I thought I'd give you time to wallow, but you look like utter shit."

"Fuck you."

"I had plenty last night, thanks." He winked, and I had half a mind to smack the smirk from his face. He barely paused. "You're as screwed up as me, by the way. Terrified to let people go, then scared to hold onto something real. Tessa is certifiable. I'm pleased as shit she's out of your life, but don't let what happened with her ruin your chance with Ainsley."

Except it wasn't Tessa who'd ruined us. Not really. Ainsley had let her past influence her present and couldn't trust me. She'd turned on me like Caroline and my other friends. Or did she need me to push harder, convince her I wasn't like her ex?

Drill it in that having faith in me wasn't repeating her mistakes. If I'd done that, maybe I'd have found a way to do the same—realize loving her wasn't repeating mine.

I wasn't sure when this intervention had become about me, but I found myself weakening, my hurt and confusion spilling out. "I love her. I've never felt anything this intense before." The truth had me sinking heavier on my stool. "But how do I know she feels the same? Tessa didn't. I've owned stuff that went down between us, but she didn't want me in the end, not until she couldn't have me. So how do I know I won't wind up here again, another breakup, more heartache? And Ainsley didn't believe me. I told her the truth, laid it all out for her, and she still couldn't trust me. If we don't have trust, what the hell do we have?"

Before he could answer, footsteps padded toward us. I gritted my teeth, reminding myself to be nice. Telling Emmett's latest fling to take a hike wouldn't help matters.

"You guys look serious."

I startled at the familiar voice and turned to see Cameron in his boxers, inked chest on display. He walked over to my brother, looped his arm around his waist, and kissed the back of his neck. He moved into the kitchen and poured a cup of coffee, smiling as though it were any ordinary Wednesday. "I'll have this in the bedroom. Leave you two to it."

I chuckled to myself as he left, then knocked Emmett's shoulder. "You sly dog. You're actually giving him a chance."

He spun his mug, a blush cresting his cheeks. "Took a while to realize he was worth the risk. And in answer to your question: you and Ainsley have love…and *love*, I've come to realize, is fucking terrifying. It makes trusting harder, because it means the fall if you get hurt could be crushing. It's how I felt when Mom left, and I didn't want to chance experiencing that again. My guess is Ainsley is dealing with similar crap over her ex. So, no—you won't know for sure she feels the same or won't freak out again in the future, like I don't know for sure this thing with Cameron won't backfire. But the idea of losing him was worse."

Yawning, he rubbed his eye. "Look, no matter what else happens, we both have Nana. And"—he lifted the side of his tank top, displaying freshly inked ribs—"we'll always have each other."

"You got a tattoo?"

"It's been an odd month." He dropped the fabric before I could puzzle out the four cursive words. "You don't need to read it though."

"Why's that?"

"You have the same tattoo. Only mine's in English and not on my ass."

Motherfucker. "I either stick you in a headlock right now, or you show me your tattoo."

"But it's been so fun, you not knowing what it means."

"Emmett…" My warning tone held no humor.

"Calm your tits." Instead of grinning his cocky grin, he lowered his voice. "The anniversary of Mom's epic display of motherhood is coming up, which fed into me pushing Cameron away and getting the ink. But the night of your ass tattoo…what was it? The nine year anniversary of her leaving?"

I huffed out a sad laugh at the passage of time. Nine years back then meant this anniversary would be eighteen.

"We were both sloppy drunk," he pushed on, "but you were worse. Fucking annihilated. You kept going on about how you'd never leave me. How you'd take care of me and make sure I was happy, as though you could fix what she'd done. Always taking on the role of mother and father."

"It was my job," I murmured.

"Self-imposed, maybe. But you admitted something to me that night. You were tanked and talking gibberish, but your eyes cleared at one point. You said something like 'I'm not good enough. Not for her. Not for some father I never met. Probably not for you.' It was the first time I saw the weight of what she'd done hit you."

As kids, it had been on me to make sure Emmett brushed his teeth and went to sleep at a reasonable hour when left afloat in our hippie commune. I'd force him to clean up after dinner, taught him to kick a soccer ball and ride a bike. Always being the parent. I may have cried to Nana after she'd come to claim us, but never in front of Emmett.

I had to be the strong one.

"Back to the ink," I said, my voice gruff.

He ran his thumb around the rim of his mug. "I don't remember how we wound up in Frederic's shop. I think he questioned if you really wanted a tattoo, and you were all over the idea, but didn't know what to get. You said you wanted something meaningful. Permanent. Always searching for things that stuck. Then out of nowhere, you grabbed my shoulders and told me to choose. You wanted something that represented us." He shrugged. "So I chose."

I was black-out wasted that night, but putting blind trust in my idiot brother was pure insanity. "And you chose Japanese words I couldn't read?"

He snorted. "That part was to screw with you. Couldn't resist convincing you to get it on your ass, either."

"Lift your goddamn shirt, Emmett."

Amusement lit his dark eyes. He teased me by lifting and dropping his shirt's hem half a dozen times. *Fucker.* When I cuffed the back of his head, the bastard complied. I read the words once, then again, gripping his far shoulder as my throat burned. "This is what mine means? The same thing?"

"Yeah." His voice was as quiet as mine.

I read them a third time, staring at the bold, clean lines:

Courage
Strength
Brothers
Forever

"Why didn't you tell me?"

"Messing with you was too much fun."

I traced the ink, the four simple words that defined us. We were courageous. We were strong. We'd have each other's backs for the rest of our lives. I pulled him into a crushing hug.

Emmett was dealing with his issues, growing up and risking his heart for the first time. What about me? Was pushing Ainsley away smart or cowardly? Was assuming she was taking the easy way out—not fighting for me, believing in me, truly loving me—my way of letting my fears run my life? I was scared I'd hold onto something wrong again. Thought I was too messed up to understand the difference, and I'd let the best thing to ever happen to me slip away.

The truth of it was a punch to the gut.

Ainsley needed space to process the lies Tessa had dropped in her lap, like Emmett had needed to find his way in his own time. I should have allowed her that, not given her an ultimatum. I should have fought for the woman I love.

Emmett pounded my back and returned to his coffee. "You okay?"

I exhaled a shaky breath. "No."

"You miss her?"

"Man, it's *killing* me." I rubbed the tender spot on my chest.

"Then stop being an ass and get her back."

"When did you get so smart?"

He glanced down the hall, to where his boyfriend was holed up. "Met someone who knocked some sense into me."

"Best if I follow your lead. I'd also like to hang out soon, get to know Cameron better. Maybe at Nana's next week?"

He smiled into his coffee. "She's gonna embarrass the piss out of me."

"Well deserved."

We talked awhile longer, filling each other in on our lives the past weeks, made plans to play soccer soon. Once in my truck, I debated sending Ainsley a text. It could be too soon. Seeing those photos and reliving her ex's betrayal wasn't something that would disappear overnight. But I couldn't wait.

We need to talk.

I pressed Send and dragged my hand down my face. I'd give her a few days, the weekend with the girls to do their girl thing. Commiserate. Call me every name there was, if that's what it took. Then I'd do what I should have done five days ago: fight for the woman I love.

CHAPTER 22

Eight letters for the vertical frames alongside window openings.
Or the hunky guy you're madly in love with.
KINGSTUD

AINSLEY

Clothing purchases were much like dating. Some items, once washed and worn, never fit right again. Some acquisitions were trendy, cool finds that became closet favorites until blacklisted to the kill-me-before-I'm-seen-in-public-with-this-again pile. Other purchases would sit folded in a drawer, overlooked time and again, until you tried them on with new jeans or shoes and realized, *wow—I had this gem all along.*

Then there was Owen.

Owen was the staple piece. The timeless classic. He was a steady pair of black pumps, the blazer that never went out of style. The Coach purse every woman coveted.

And I ran away from him.

I hadn't heard from him for the five endless days since I'd left his apartment. I'd replayed our time together ad nauseam. Had reviewed the honest conversations I'd shared with Gay-Not-Gay Owen during our many lunches, along with how our friendship had bled into passion and companionship. Those moments hadn't been imagined. Neither had the way he'd fit in with my family, or how much we'd laughed, or how intense our time in bed had been. Our dance had been the most romantic gesture this side of *The Notebook*.

But I hadn't given him the one thing he'd needed: my trust.

My phone rang from somewhere near me. I'd avoided it recently and had hijacked Rachel's couch, turning the cushy red sofa into my personal pity-party zone. Kleenex littered the cushions, fashion magazines overtook the floor. I'm pretty sure there was popcorn stuck in my hair. I felt around for my cell, wiggling like a depressed worm, until I found it smooshed between the seat cushions. The name lighting up my screen nearly had me launching it across the room.

Sloane.

I could flush the phone down the toilet or change my number, maybe run over it with Rachel's motorcycle. *Or* I could be a grown-up and answer the darn thing. Voting on adult, I hit Talk. My body tensed as I waited for a shrill scream to deafen my eardrum.

"Ainsley?" Sloane's quiet voice was barely audible.

I pressed the receiver harder to my ear. "Is everything okay?"

Her bitter laugh was answer enough. "No. But I owe you an apology."

Rachel had morning classes today. Jimmy was working at his winery. That left me in the quiet bungalow, hating how defeated this strong, vibrant woman sounded.

I lay back and stared at the ecru ceiling. "You don't owe me anything, Sloane. I just wish I hadn't let it go so long. I should have told you sooner."

She sighed heavily. "I doubt it would have made a difference.

It's funny, living your life with blinders on. Part of me believed you, when you came to my door. I'd had an inkling for a while, but I wasn't ready to hear it. Couldn't fathom my life without Thomas."

"Don't blame yourself. I did for a while, when I went through it. It only makes things worse."

Silence crackled through the line, then, "Men are such assholes."

"Those who cheat should have to walk around with a shit emoji on their heads." But I couldn't picture Owen wearing the offensive accessory. Deep down, in my gut, I knew he hadn't cheated on me, or on Tessa. Owen's pain and desperation when explaining the situation hadn't been fake, and the man practically bled loyalty. Yet I'd still bailed.

Sloane's breathing grew labored. "I hate how stupid I feel. I thought maybe he'd fooled around a time or two, but the extent of it? How long it's been going on? His business trips extended each year, he changed his phone password, and he worked late too often to be normal. But he always had an explanation, and I always bought it." Her voice fell to whisper. "I'm not sure how I'll ever trust a man again."

"You deserve happiness, Sloane. When it's the right person, you will."

"I don't know."

Her despondent words echoed my morose thoughts. I *had* let my distrust in men taint what I'd had with Owen. Brandon had started working longer, too, near the end. He'd been more protective of his phone and privacy. The memory of my ignorance had nursed my insecurity.

Insecurities I'd projected onto Owen.

When I saw his truck at his apartment last Friday, after he said he'd be out, I assumed he'd lied to me, that he had a woman in his bed. When he explained the damning photographs, I wouldn't listen. Caroline's nasty text and Tessa's diabolical package were bad, but I would have had a meltdown eventually.

If he'd missed a date because he was working late, I'd have second-guessed him. If his battery had died on his phone, I'd have wondered why he wasn't picking up, mind wandering, insecurity growing, until I snapped, just as Sloane worried she would.

My anxiety was ruining my life.

Sloane and I talked a short while longer, but I could barely focus. Queasiness clenched my stomach. We made plans to grab a coffee next week, and as soon as we hung up, I shot to my bare feet and paced a frantic line. I took deep breaths and a longer, harder look at myself.

Owen had proven his devotion time and again, but I couldn't see those photos for what they'd been—proof his ex-wife was a nasty, vengeful woman—because I'd been waiting for him to mess up the whole time.

Owen wasn't too good to be true. He was truly *good*.

Now here I was, another woman hurting him.

Shaken, I studied Rachel and Jimmy's bungalow, my safe haven the past five days. The large windows bathed the plants and overstuffed red sectional (and Kleenex and magazines) in sunlight. Stacks of her viticulture textbooks filled a bookcase next to her desk. Jimmy's badass motorcycle boots were at the front door, next to her Mary Janes. The couple also had a killer wine cellar in the lower level that had come in handy.

But my favorite was the framed quote hung in the entryway:

"If you obey all the rules, you miss all the fun." ~ Katharine Hepburn.

The space was warm and inviting, and I was thrilled Rachel had found contentment in her life. I'd only find my happy if I released the hurt I'd nurtured, quit assuming I wasn't capable of sustaining a healthy relationship. Owen wasn't Brandon. Trusting him would be so very hard, but living without him would be harder.

It *was* harder.

My mind clearer than it had been in weeks, I rescued my

phone from the couch and went to pull up his name, only to find a text from him. The ceiling pressed closer. The walls inched toward me. It was like I was back in the Evil Bathroom, air trapped in my throat.

Swallowing hard, I read his message: **We need to talk.**

I relaxed slightly. That better be the *I forgive you for being a moron* we need to talk, and not the *I need closure* we need to talk…unless he truly was seeking finality, wanting to put an official end to our relationship. It couldn't happen. Not like this. Not when I'd finally woken up and understood the extent of my baggage. And not the Samsonite carry-on variety. My issues would barely fit into a Tumi Alpha luggage set.

Rachel walked in as I was about to detonate. Eyes wide, she dropped her keys on her table by the door. "Why do you look radioactive?"

"I screwed up." So, so badly.

"Were you infomercial surfing again? Do I need to confiscate your credit card?"

"The Clever Cutter was a great purchase." The sauna pants were maybe over the top. And ugly. I had a problem. "This is an Owen emergency. He messaged."

She sat on her barstool and patted the one beside her. "Tell Auntie Rachel everything."

I rolled my eyes, but obliged. "I'm self-sabotaging."

Kicking my dangling feet like a child, I spewed my sad realization, reliving how I'd derailed my relationship. Each admission made my mistakes more blatant. Rachel sat in her chinos and ironed buttoned-down, nodding and listening. My chin trembled.

When I finished, she tucked a strand of my hair behind my ear. "You owe him an apology."

If he took me back, I'd owe him a kidney. "He was right to push me away. I mean, his mother abandoned him, his ex-wife is making his life hell, and I didn't stand by him. Why would he forgive me?" I spun my phone on the counter, my head spinning with it.

"Before you reach nuclear freak out, you should sit with this for a bit. I know you love him, and I'm pretty sure he loves you. But if you guys get back together, you have to trust him. Like I trust Jimmy. Like your mother trusts your father. Without that, it won't work. You need to be sure you can give him all of you, for both your sakes." When I didn't reply, she added, "Gwen will be here Friday. We'll have the weekend together, then you'll be back in San Fran Monday. That's another five days to get your head straight. Tell him you'll talk then."

"What if he decides I'm not worth waiting for?" Five days could be the difference between keeping him and losing him.

"He loves you, Ainsley. Give yourselves the time you both need."

Unsure it was the right move, I flipped over my phone and typed. *I'd like to talk. Meet Monday at noon at our picnic table?* I hit Send before I overthought it to death. *Please be the right move.*

I'll be there. The speed of his response buoyed my mood, but the reply was short. There were no sweet endearments. No clues as to how he felt.

It was the wrong move. Definitely wrong. I should have written more, apologized, grovelled. "I don't need time. Time is silly. I'll just tell him I'm madly in love with him and will never hurt him again and want to have his babies."

Rachel swiped the phone from my hand. "Consider this confiscated." She strutted toward the front door and ransacked my purse next, stealing my credit card. "And this. You'll get them both back Monday. No rash decisions. Nothing will change in five days."

So why did it feel like my vital organs were migrating to my throat?

———

My five-day sentence was a challenge. Gwen turned up on day two, and I pleaded with her to get my phone from Rachel. She compromised by returning my credit card, but the traitor parroted Rachel, claiming if I couldn't return to Owen with clear eyes and a full heart (*Friday Night Lights* forever) we'd be doomed to fail.

I was ready to open up to him, excessive baggage be damned, but they were right. Ten days apart was nothing in the scheme of life, and I hadn't fully decompressed from the past week's shock. It also gave me time to finally make my special gift for him.

So instead of professing my love to Owen, I worked on my website and drank and hiked and talked and laughed with the girls, beyond thankful to have them in my life.

Until Monday arrived and my ever-vigilant, supposed best friends still wouldn't give me my phone. I glowered at them. "You said five days. It's been five days."

Taller than me, Gwen held my phone in the air. "Now it's just fun. We have bets on when you'll start pulling out your hair."

I was about to launch myself at her, when my cell buzzed. We all froze. Then I lunged, but she used her CrossFit muscles to hold me at arm's length. She and Rachel crowded over *my* phone, the one not in *my* hands. They sighed in unison.

"He's such a dreamboat," Rachel said.

"Is it Owen?"

She grinned. "Yeah."

I reached for the tiny cellphone that housed my heart. "Give it here."

"Back off, buttercup. You still have two hours." Gwen held it at distance, the screen facing me. "But you can read it."

"This must be how Cinderella felt about her awful stepsisters." My irritable tone slipped into a whisper as I read Owen's text:

I can't live without you.

My pulse pitter-pattered, tears gathering in my eyes as I clutched my throat. More bubbles appeared below, but Gwen pulled my lifeline away before I could glimpse his next message. "Are you trying to kill me?"

Instead of continuing to humor them, I attacked. I pounced on Gwen, tickling her armpits until my phone flew into the air. My dive to capture it ended with me face-first on the plush couch. "Victory!" I crowed. Then I ran.

I locked myself in the bathroom, cradling my one tether to the man I loved as though it were Waterford crystal. I devoured his words greedily.

I plan to melt my glass into one sheet and break it in two. Half for you. Half for me.

If there was any remaining doubt he was devoted to me, it vanished. I was his matching piece of glass, and he was mine.

I pulled the silver chain from around my neck, a delicate strand with his blue shard hanging from the end. The top of the glass was encased in wisps of wound silver wire. I'd found the glass in my pocket the day I'd driven here. Had kept it close, hoping it could help me see the light. The day he'd texted, I'd evaded Rachel and had descended on a jeweler in town, begging for a rush job.

Unable to contain the swelling of my emotions any longer, I wrote: *I'm so sorry.*

Me too.

I love you.

What the fuck?

I shouldn't have written it in a text. Those words were meant to inspire enraptured kissing and voracious sex. *Wild*, voracious make-up sex. And I sent them in a stupid text. There were no bouncing balls to hint at a reply. I couldn't see his face or read his body language. No wonder the girls had kept my phone from me. Total self-sabotage.

When the dots showed, I pressed my fist to my mouth.

I had to read that ten times. My heart's about to bust through my chest.

Mine was pumping as hard. *Have we made up then?*

Doesn't count until I've seen you naked.

Sign me up for that extracurricular activity. *See you at 12.*

Vibrating as fast as Blue Bunny, I unlocked the bathroom door to find my friends squished in the same chair. They were facing Rachel's computer and my yet-to-be-live website.

"Who gave you permission to creep my work?"

Rachel waved an impatient hand at me. "Shush. We're reading."

I was a minute from having a stroke. This was my grand finale. My swan song. My chance to leave a positive mark in women's lives. And my friends were analyzing it.

I could only hope my new business would bring me as much joy as learning about wine brought Rachel, as much fulfillment as working at the adoption agency afforded Gwen. I hoped when reality set in with Owen and me, we'd truly be able to move past this painful speedbump.

For now, I fidgeted as my friends studied my website. When their silence became oppressive, I said, "Tell me if it sucks, already."

Gwen stood, nearly sending Rachel tumbling to the floor when her side of the desk chair dipped. She motioned me over. My friends flanked me as we studied my fledgling start-up.

CHERISH

It was the seven-letter word for caring for something dear, namely ourselves. Pushing through the hard times—whether personal or health related—and finding beauty again. It also paid homage to the queen of reinvention herself, Madonna, whose music inspired many solo dance parties in front of my bedroom mirror, thanks to my mom's CDs.

The homepage had a collage of client images, including one of Sherise at her son's wedding, beaming in the blue halter dress that fit her curves like a glove. I had tiered packages from full closet overhauls, to accent bundles—affordable options where key purchases could elevate a wardrobe. I also offered style consultations, facilitating hair and makeup appointments.

My favorite was our Screw the Ex Special: *Let us melt down your wedding ring and turn it into the design of your choice!* I'd also planned to give each client a personal gift from Aazam's Sweet Treats.

All I had to do was hit Publish.

Rachel kissed my cheek. "It's wonderful."

"So proud of you," Gwen said.

I inhaled deeply, then sent my business into the world.

The marching band I'd expected didn't show. No fireworks exploded. We stared at the unmoving screen, tapping our toes.

I shrugged. "I guess that's that. Now you two mother hens need to clear the way so I can get to my man."

Gwen did that observant thing of hers where she basically looked into my soul. "Do you trust him?"

"Yes." Not a lick of hesitation.

Rachel did a little bounce. "Are you ready for love?"

I snickered. "That's an Elton John song."

"And your point is?"

"Yes, I'm ready—for him, for it all. I'm sure I'll have my freak-out moments. We'll just have to work through them. But if I don't get in my car soon and kiss his beautiful face and neck and his entire body, I will implode."

Gwen raised her hands in surrender. "I'd rather not witness that." She swatted my behind. "Be gone with you."

My drive to the Habitat build was a tad loopy. I belted out the words to every song I knew, not caring when another driver could see me. I danced in my seat. I was high. Crazed. Filled to the brim with my life changes and the knowledge that a super sexy man would soon get attacked by *moi*. The sight of his truck near the Habitat build had me humming the chorus to George Michael's "I Want Your Sex."

I nearly jammed my toe into the curb as I hurried out my door...but I paused.

I hadn't visited the Habitat site in a while. People were milling about, none I recognized, but the first grouping of six townhouses had been freshly stuccoed in a mix of pastels, small patches of grass and bright green bushes warming up the exterior. I'd been coordinating the audio systems with Nick and Felipe, installation organized for a few weeks from now. Families would move in this spring.

I couldn't believe my hands had helped build those walls, that I'd had a part in changing someone's life. It also meant more knowing Anton had put his mark on the project. We hadn't seen each other since becoming non-enemies, but we'd both contributed to the community, together.

Feeling swathed in warmth, I turned my attention to the playground at the end of the street. My wacky energy from the drive returned. Owen was over there. So close, yet so far.

I speed walked. I ran. I raced the blowing clouds up above. My first glimpse of him stole my breath. He was tall and broad and handsome, pacing restlessly in front of our picnic table. He must have sensed me. Or maybe he heard me call, "Get over here!"

His head whipped my way, then he was moving, too. His jog pushed into a run that had us crashing into each other as he crushed me to his chest and spun me around. "So fucking sorry." His fingers dug into my ribs, his other hand tangling in my hair as he hugged the stuffing out of me. "I'm sorry as hell I let you walk out that door. Sorry I brought Tessa into your life."

I pawed at his back and shoulders, wanting to touch all of him at once, but there was something I had to do first. Still clutching him tight, I said, "I'm the one who owes you an apology. I should have trusted you. I *do* trust you."

"But I should have given you time. Not shut down."

Our hearts were pressed close, pounding out our apologies. "Can we kiss now?"

His rumbling chuckle vibrated through me. Angling his head down, his hungry lips went to work, coaxing mine open. His breath was hot, our mouths and tongues moving in sync. Everything about him felt *right*, destined. He tasted like goodness and loyalty and the type of man you fought for. Our level of PDA shot from mild to arrest worthy.

Panting, my construction hunk pulled away. "Come sit for sec."

"But the kissing?"

He licked his lips. "Doll, we're not done with the kissing, but we need to talk."

Ignoring my grumbles, Owen led me to our picnic table. He straddled the bench and had me sit opposite him, our bent knees touching. "I really am sorry, Ainsley. As much as I'm dying to make-out and get you home, I need you to hear me, *believe me*. Giving up on us was the wrong choice."

Such simple words, the candor behind them a balm to my healing wounds. I pushed my fingers into the front of his thick hair, letting my hands drag over his scalp, down the back of his neck and shoulders, coming to rest on his firm chest. "I know you are, but this is on me. I assumed the worst. Even though I knew you'd never cheat on me, I couldn't stop my mind from going there. Never again, though. I trust you." I pulled my necklace from under my cashmere sweater and placed the weight of it against my thudding heart. "I love you."

His forehead crumpled, emotion gathering in his eyes. He touched the glass, a gentle slide of his fingers down the pendant, then he gripped my ass and hauled me onto his lap. I linked my legs around his back.

"I love you," he whispered. A bruising kiss followed, leaving me breathless. "So damn much."

I needed more, those three words over and over. "Say it again."

Tugging me closer, he nosed my cheek. "So damn much."

I swatted his thick bicep. "Not that part, smartass."

"Oh. Okay." He nodded, a playful grin spreading. "I think I know what you're after." Reverently, he cupped my cheeks. "I"—he nipped to my earlobe—"love"—he dragged his lips along my jaw—"you"—he covered my face with a thousand soft kisses.

I sighed. "That's better." The urge to shred his clothing lessened, those words and his strong arms my perfect salve. I snuggled in closer. "My website is live."

"I'm so proud of you," he said into my hair. "I have no doubt you'll succeed."

I sure hoped so. "I'll advertise at gyms and salons, places women go when stressed. Tap into my target market like we discussed. I still have a few key clients who'll keep me afloat, but I fired the rest. It's a risk, but I'm happier for it." Like I was happier for allowing myself to find love.

He drew lazy patterns on my back. "I nearly finished that second maple table this week. Barely slept."

Guilt bloomed. "I'm sick that I left you, especially after what *she* did." She Who Must Not Be Named. "Can we throw her in jail? Send her on the first trip to Mars?"

"Unlikely. And it doesn't matter. She doesn't matter. She's done her worst, and we survived. But..." His hands paused their intimate strokes. "I have something to ask you. It might freak you out, and I want you to understand it's not something I want now, but it was an issue for me in the past. So I think I need to be clear about it this time, with you."

That didn't sound good. His heavy exhale when I leaned back to gauge his weighted expression didn't inspire confidence, either. "Consider me freaking out."

His attention shifted past me, to the jungle gym. It wasn't busy—a couple of tykes mucked about on the slide. "I want kids, Ainsley. Not anytime soon, but what we have is far from casual, and I can't get serious with someone without making that clear."

He wants kids. Kids with me, one day. How could I have questioned his fidelity? Believed, even for a second, his love wasn't true?

Awash with relief, I laughed. Giddy delight rolled through my belly in an uncontrollable wave. Owen caught my crazy, both of us laughing at absolutely nothing. Finally, I wiped my eyes. "We'll have ten, if that's what you want. They'll be stylish and read smarty-pants books, and...*oh*, the dancing. Two will be ballet stars, one will do the Hip Hop video circuit, and the rest will take the Broadway and ballroom worlds by storm. They'll make a reality TV series about us."

He wasn't laughing any longer. He pressed his forehead to mine. "I love you, Ainsley."

I bit my lip. "I love you so much."

There was no describing this thick swelling in my heart. I wouldn't want to, anyway. It was private. A slice of paradise just for us.

I inched my hands down his pecs, over the wonderland of his abs, to his waistband. I traced the ridge of his belt toward his back and dipped my hands inside his briefs, grazing the top of his fine behind. "To prove my valor, I plan to torture Emmett until he tells me what your tattoo means, then I'll torture *you* with the knowledge. Use it to demand sexual favors."

"How does messing with my mind prove your valor?"

"Just go with it."

He unleashed an impish smirk. "He told me, this week."

Ex-squeeze me? "How did I miss that?"

"I think he felt bad for me."

I squeezed my legs tighter around his back. "And?" When his smirk widened, I fisted the front of his shirt and pulled him close. "Now's not the time to hold out on me, cowboy. My form of punishment involves lack of sex."

He slapped my ass. "I'll take it under advisement. How about we go to your place and get naked?"

The bugger ignored my ultimatum, but my willpower waned. I was weak, needy. "Will you tell me eventually?"

Keeping me clutched to his chest, he kicked his leg over the bench and stood. He walked us to our cars while I did my best koala impression, legs hooked around his middle. "If you stick around, maybe."

I pressed my face into his warm neck. "I'm not going anywhere."

EPILOGUE

TWO MONTHS LATER

AINSLEY

A six-letter word for a place of ideal perfection.

I grinned at my crossword clue, an easy one that wouldn't require any cheating. Before I could type my answer, Rachel elbowed me. "They're finally starting."

"About time." I pocketed my phone and watched the group of fit men slap one another's backs as they spilled onto the soccer field. "It's a hunk buffet."

Gwen snorted from my other side. "You two aren't allowed to indulge."

"But we can look," Rachel said.

And we did. Thick thighs abounded. Broad backs filled out the yellow or blue shirts on either team, long socks suctioned to defined calves. There was one particular set of calves I was searching for—the pair attached to my favorite hunk…whose ass was being squeezed by another man.

His perverted brother flashed me a wink.

I glared at the jerk. "Emmett needs to get over the ass grab."

Rachel scrunched her adorable nose. "Why does he even do it?"

"Because he knows it annoys me. It's always the left cheek, the one with the tattoo. Neither of them will tell me what it means."

"I still can't believe Owen hasn't let it slip."

"I can't believe we haven't pantsed him yet to see that sucker." Gwen shook her head in disgust.

My scowl deepened. "He's staying mum. I figured it's better to focus my efforts on Emmett. He's likely to crack sooner."

"Good luck with that one." Cameron climbed the small set of bleachers, joining us for the morning festivities. He scanned the field. "It's a hunk buffet."

My words exactly. "You and I share a brain."

Gwen sat straighter. "Good thing I'm the only one of us available. Considering how long it's been, I might need the all-you-can-eat variety."

Rachel and I traded hopeful glances. Gwen had been on a break from men for over a year, focusing instead on work and CrossFit and her other life-threatening hobbies. She also hadn't been out much since her mother had passed away last month. The end had come suddenly, so swiftly Gwen hadn't spoken with her since their last fight. Gwen claimed she'd come to terms with the loss, accepting that her "mother" had gained said title by blood alone, not through any sort of proper relationship. She'd said losing her had felt like reading about a celebrity death in a gossip rag—a moment of sadness, followed by life moving on.

I patted her thigh. "If you go the buffet route, make sure the men all wear their *bibs* before entering your *restaurant*."

Cameron cracked up. "I need a book of Ainsley-isms."

I could totally rock that book. "We'll call it *Musings on the Love Glove*." Not that I had time to write such brilliance. My next two months were fully booked.

Aside from my growing client list, my weekly Habitat shift took priority, and I needed to add a before-and-after page to my website, showing off recent makeovers. One in particular would be front and center: Sloane. She'd progressed from a size celery to a size Italian eggplant and looked stunning in her less-conservative wardrobe. She was my ideal client, ready to shed her past with a new look and a new lease on life. She'd also made sure Thomas hadn't slandered my reputation.

I hadn't let her pay for my services.

The referee blew his whistle, and we all enjoyed the view as the throng of male magnificence ran and grunted and dripped sweat. We cheered. We leered. We had a blast.

"Have you ladies made birthday plans?" Cameron bent forward, elbows planted on his knees. He was a handsome devil, his mix of ink and fifties flair deliciously sexy.

Rachel sat between us. She leaned back so we could all talk. "We're keeping it simple. Going to a bar. Just close friends."

Namely him and Emmett, Owen and Jimmy, Rachel, Gwen, and me. Our little gang. Rachel and Cameron chatted about grabbing dinner beforehand while I watched the tail end of the match, but my mind was stuck on our birthday and all it meant.

I couldn't believe it had been a year. *Almost* a year. We'd be turning twenty-eight tomorrow, April 12th. Two years from thirty.

I'd never been this excited for our yearly celebration. Ringing in the occasion with Owen made it special. I planned to kiss him silly when the clock chimed twelve. I would also thank my lucky stars I'd made last year's resolution to become a better person, and had worked off my derrière to realize it.

Like spring cleaning, uncluttering one area of my life only made me want to streamline the next section, and the next. My work no longer made me feel like a bottom-feeder. I'd released my guilt over Anton. Owen and I had returned to each other, better, stronger. Ridiculously in love. Even my parents were doing better. Granted, my father's job at the auto plant wasn't my doing, but it gave him purpose each day, put pride into his voice. He and Mom no longer needed my help covering their mortgage.

Rachel had found her happy, too. She'd fulfilled her resolution and now had Jimmy and viticulture school.

Our happiness had my focus drifting to my right, to Gwen who was barely watching the soccer match. Her gaze was glazed, like she wasn't actually seeing it. A cheer rose up around us, shouts and claps blowing into the warm spring air. Gwen didn't flinch.

She was the strongest of us, could run a marathon, probably karate chop a cement block. She had the brass balls to jump out of airplanes. But losing her mother had been tough, and she seemed lonely these days, still enjoying her job, but…pensive.

I squeezed her thigh. "What was your birthday wish?" She'd never once said.

She didn't face me, just stared at a faraway point in front of her. "To know who my father was."

I pressed my hand to my throat, understanding sinking in. She'd asked her mother while she'd been sick and had gotten stonewalled. With her gone, she'd never know. She wouldn't find the peace that came with the knowledge she'd sought her entire life.

I wrapped my arm around her shoulder and pulled her close. "I'm sorry."

"Thanks." Her attention settled on her lap. "I'm still going through her house, hoping to find a hidden shoebox or something with a clue, but…" She shrugged. Gwen wore a ribbed tank top that showed off her toned arms and kick-ass physique, but inside she was soft, likely sinking at the prospect of never learning this one truth.

"I can help. Come by this afternoon maybe."

She didn't acknowledge my offer. "I want you to know how happy I am for you and Rachel. I know you stuck with your resolutions. It's impacted your lives, and you both deserve the best."

My DKNY-loving heart cracked. Gwen was no less deserving. More so for the year she'd endured…and the year wasn't quite over. "We still have until tomorrow night to fulfill your wish, not that the timeline really matters. But we'll scour your mother's place anyway. Tear it apart, if need be."

She shrugged me off. "You're sweet, but I'll pass. It was a silly wish to begin with."

Her eyes narrowed, focusing on a group of players preparing to take the field. They all jogged out, except for one man stretching on the sidelines. Gwen's attention didn't move from him. Owen and Jimmy had finished shaking hands with their opposing team and joined the guy. I had zero clue who'd won—aside from us who got to watch all the hotness—but I was more curious about the man Gwen was eyeing, especially when Jimmy and Owen clapped him on the back.

Gwen's jaw nearly dislocated. "Holy shit."

I squinted, checking the guy for familiarity. He was a looker with tanned skin and disheveled dark hair, short on the sides and longer up top. His toned body gave Owen a run for his money, but nothing about him rang any bells. "Do you know him?"

All she said was "Holy shit" again.

Cameron walked down the bleachers to join Emmett. Rachel leaned toward us. "Do you guys know who won?"

"No clue," I said, my attention fixed on my incredulous friend. "But Gwen is having a meltdown."

Rachel assessed Gwen's open mouth and unblinking eyes. "Do we need to call a doctor?"

I snapped my fingers in front of her face. "What's with the catatonic state?"

"It's him," was all she managed.

Again, I stared at the boys, all of them grinning as if they were old buddies. "Him who?"

"August."

Rachel and I drew a collective breath. *The* August. The neighbor Gwen had spent the majority of her childhood with, chasing each other across their joined yards. The one who'd taught her how to play guitar and had dragged her to his boisterous family dinners so she could escape her depressing home. The guy she'd been in love with.

"Was he that hot when you knew him?" Hot with a capital H.

"He's filled out," she murmured.

His gaze shifted, dragging toward us as though sensing our attention. The instant he saw Gwen, he froze. She squeaked. He opened his mouth, then closed it. Something dark passed over his eyes, but Gwen was already on her feet. "I need to go."

My usually fearless friend bolted from her seat, disappearing around the bleachers.

Rachel scratched her knee. "That was odd."

"Understatement. She's hiding something." I'd always sensed there was more to the August story than Gwen had let on. She'd given us the basics of their childhood and teen years, but when she'd skim over their relationship afterward, she'd always clam up and her eyes would get glassy. "If she doesn't spill the details, we'll pry them out of her."

With alcohol.

We stood, dusted off our behinds, and headed toward our sweaty men. Jimmy and Owen were at their duffle bags, chugging Gatorade. When Owen saw me, he prowled my way.

I held up my hands. "No. You're gross."

Unconcerned I was wearing an adorable Miu Miu floral dress, he wrapped his big, glistening arms around me. "Deal with it."

Unable to resist, I sunk into his embrace. Some things were more important than fashion. "Great game."

"You even know who won?"

"*I* did. I got to watch your ass and thighs flex. It was quite a show." I pressed my nose into his drenched shirt. His pungent musk of salt and man mingled with his usual apple pie. "I'd like to bottle you."

He released me far enough to plant a soft kiss on my lips. "You'll have to settle on living with me."

Excited, I did a jig and twirled in his arms. When he asked last week, I almost rented a truck that night to move my stuff pronto. I couldn't wait to blend our lives more permanently. "You'll need to build an addition with a separate walk-in closet for me."

"Might be tough, timewise. Ellen messaged to say she sold two of my pieces. I need to get to work."

I smacked his rock-hard chest. "Seriously?"

"Seriously." He couldn't hide the pride in his bright eyes, and the timing was perfect. She Who Must Not Be Named had signed the final papers on their house sale and divorce recently. Owen could stop paying his lawyer and invest more fully in his growing business.

I beamed at him. "Your designs will take San Francisco by storm."

"Here's hoping. And if I find time, I was thinking of building us a dance room. Solid wood floors. Mirrors so I can watch you twirl."

Or so I could watch other things. "Only if we can dance naked."

His answering grunt had my body humming, as did the way he palmed my ass. He moved to gather his bag, and I searched the soccer field, scanning the new group of men sweating it out on the field. When I spotted Gwen's old crush, I tugged Owen's arm. "How do you know August?"

He followed my line of sight and smiled. "He played soccer with us when we were in high school. On the California Regional League. Great guy. Haven't seen him since. Why?"

I could share Gwen's state of shock and their mysterious

history, or I could use this tidbit in my favor. "I have gossip. Tell me what your tattoo means, and I'll spill the details."

"Nope."

Damn him. "You're no fun."

"So you've said." He linked our hands, and we walked to his truck, the sun high, my spirits higher. He opened my door for me and helped me into my side, the eternal gentleman. Once I'd clicked my seat belt in place, he brushed my hair from my face. "You get more beautiful every day."

Heart, meet the moon.

Any other man, and I'd laugh at the cheesy sentiment, but this was Owen. A romantic who believed in finding his other half, and reminded me of his love daily. He kissed me hard and true. I nipped his bottom lip. "Us," I said.

His brows pulled together. "What?"

"Nothing." I shoved him out the door and pulled my phone from my bag. The writers of this crossword clue may have had *Utopia* in mind for their answer, but I knew better. The true answer was two letters. One word. My place of ideal perfection was wherever Owen and I were, together. Utopia was Us.

Thank you for reading Ainsley and Owen's story!

To learn how Gwen broke August's heart as teens, one-click *36 HOUR DATE* now, and keep reading for an excerpt.

36 HOUR DATE EXCERPT

Nine Years Ago
Aka Ground Zero for Gwen's Worst Terrible Fuck-up

Gwen

Dictators and loan sharks needed to rethink their torture methods. Sure, waterboarding and sleep deprivation could break a man. Pulling out fingernails and smashing kneecaps were reliable interrogation techniques. But if you really wanted to make someone suffer, to reach into their chests and yank out their proverbial hearts, simply force them to scroll through Facebook.

All seemed innocent at first. I sat on my too-hard chair and stared at my laptop, ignoring the Hello Kitty stickers affixed by the previous owner. The usual images floated by:

Fake smile.

Fake smile.

Kissy face.

Cat playing piano.

Drunk shirtless dude.

My attention darted between my laptop's flipping snapshots and my silent Blackberry, a cup of Jägermeister poised at my lips. Jägermeister was the butthole of birthday drinks. It tasted like cough syrup and bad decisions. It was a reminder of the bile-marinated blackout that would forever remain unspoken. An event that would *not* be repeated tonight.

Yet here I was, drinking Jäger, because underage beggars couldn't be choosers, especially at 10 p.m. on my nineteenth birthday, while alone in my apartment, wondering why my best friend hadn't texted me. The fact that we hadn't spoken in over a year should have been a clue.

I sipped the Jäger and grimaced.

Fake smile.

Faker smile.

Pouty face.

Cutest baby koala on the planet.

Drunk frat boy…in a diaper.

And how did Facebook know which bra I was wearing? I peeked into the front of my gray V-neck and back at the sidebar advertisement. That was seriously creepy. And depressing. The black lace looked miles better on the model than on my less-endowed 34Bs, but the sight had me imagining my breasts and my former best friend's large hands, our naked bodies, and a whole lot of heat.

A needy moan slipped past my lips.

Since the man in question had forgotten my birthday and had probably blocked my number, that particular scenario was as likely as me wearing pink nail polish. Not that I deserved a guy like August Cruz.

I poured another shot into my Badass Bitch mug and did the thing I pretended I wasn't going to do: I clicked on August's timeline.

A new profile photo filled my computer screen, and I bit my lip. The most pathetic sigh deflated my posture. His wavy dark hair was shorter these days, clipped at the sides and messily styled. His glasses were different—thicker frames than he used to wear, obscuring the gold flecks in his hazel eyes. He seemed to have bulked up, too. Unless his Lawn Enforcement Officer T-shirt had shrunk.

His clothing choice exacerbated my tipsy melancholy.

Had he worn that shirt because I'd given it to him? Did it remind him of me nipping at his heels and tossing clippings at his face as he'd cut our neighborhood lawns? Odds are it was nothing more than a comfortable relic—a T-shirt that would wind up in the trash one day, forgotten and cast away. Like me. Unless he'd consciously chosen to post the image, hoping I'd see it.

My next sigh was more heartsick than wistful.

I'd been down this unrequited-love road before. I'd walked it so often a permanent path had been forged behind my stinging eyes. I missed how August's rumbling laugh would infect me with giggles. I missed the way he'd dribble a soccer ball around me in an athletic blur. How he'd sit behind me, arms and legs around my torso, teaching me to play guitar.

I missed the only person who could soothe me when my mother's anger had burned through my lonely house.

These thoughts weren't new, but his profile photo and that T-shirt jostled them, a violent shove that shook my foundation. A strange awareness overtook me. He *must* have chosen that image on purpose, knowing I'd see it and think of us. He *must* have launched that sign through cyberspace so I'd catch it. It seemed obvious now—*Jägermeister obvious*, but whatever: August must miss me as much as I missed him.

I had to reach out and tell him I understood him and his subliminal message, the way only I could. Considering his stupid girlfriend, Kayla Morgan, was evil incarnate and the reason everything with August had gone to shit, she probably treated him like crap. I should have singed her blond hair in chem lab when I'd had the chance. Instead I'd let her vicious words infect my mind, poisoning all thoughts of August.

We'd been friends back then, Kayla and me. At least I

thought we'd been. *You drag him down*, she'd told me. *You're too needy. He pities you.*

Her words had hit their mark, feeding my insecurity. Fear of being a charity case had caused me to curl in on myself. Since I didn't do things half-assed, I shoved August away with the quietest silent treatment known to man...and Kayla, my supposed friend, gave him all the noise I'd sucked from his world.

She was still on his profile page. Still his girlfriend. I snarled at her picture filling my computer screen and grabbed my phone before my Jäger courage wore off.

Heart pounding in my throat, I pulled up August's name and rushed off a text. My fingers trembled as I typed, *I'm sorry.*

Who is this?

His quick reply almost had me launching my cell. My pulse went haywire, my hands too shaky to reply. But this was good. This was *right*. Of course he replied promptly. He wore the T-shirt! Fate was finally on our side.

Although he'd only been ten minutes away the past year, studying at SFSU while I killed myself cracking the books at San Francisco's City College, he'd felt so far. Not tonight. Not now.

I took a breath, then two more. I blinked away my Jäger fog and steadied my hands. *Hardy har har*, I wrote.

No. Seriously, August replied just as quickly. *The only Gwen I know hasn't spoken to me in a year and a half.*

His words were a knife in my chest, and the same wave of remorse I'd battled since I'd cut August from my life crashed over me. This wasn't the time to cower, though, the way I had the past year. This was the time to take charge of my life, beginning with an apology.

My thumbs went to work. *I'm sorry I was a bitch our last year of high school.*

Which time?

That knife twisted deeper.

Every time. All the time.

God, I wished high school had been the raging party promised in classic eighties movies. Instead it had consisted of me sinking into a jealous despair as I'd battled my mother's dictatorship and had struggled to get into college. I'd worked two jobs. Student loan applications had dogged me. All the while, my neighbor and best friend had coasted through life, then and now.

August's mother loved him. He had a father he actually knew and siblings to bond with, including an identical twin who had his back. Grades came easy to him. His soccer scholarship meant paying for college wasn't a stress. He played a mean guitar and had a crowd of hangers-on—friends who fed on his cool factor like pilot fish catching scraps from a powerful shark.

August had always had everything. I'd had nothing in high school but him.

Now I didn't even have that.

You ignored me, he shot back. *Stopped returning my calls and texts.*

Infection set into my festering wound.

I know. I'm the worst person.

Not good enough. You don't get off with a weak apology. What you did fucking hurt.

A heart transplant would be needed now. Or a heart amputation. Was that even a thing? Could a person live without her heart? Remorse fisted my rotting organ.

I knew I'd hurt August—I'd destroyed myself in the process —but hearing it firsthand had the burn in my eyes turning liquid.

He deserved some answers. *I was jealous. Your life kept getting better, and mine got harder. I felt like I was slipping into your shadow. I was resentful.*

What kind of bullshit is that? I never treated you as less. You were the most important person in my life, and you walked away like I meant nothing.

A tear leaked out, but I dashed it away. I wasn't a crier. I never let my emotions overrun me. Unless August was involved. He was also right: my actions may have made sense back then, but they had been a load of bullshit. The notion of dragging him down with my depressing life and crappy situation had seemed worse than shutting him out. It had been the wrong choice.

But it wasn't why I'd kept those invisible bricks stacked between us.

My fingers moved before I could stop them, before I could take a breath and collect myself and decide on the smart thing to say.

It was also because you started dating Kayla.

I stared at my sent message and smacked my forehead with the heel of my hand. *What the hell is wrong with me?* There was no ctrl-alt-deleting that horrifying confession. My stomach twisted, courtesy of the Jäger and my stupid fingers.

Kayla Morgan was still his girlfriend. Facebook reminded me of that painful fact daily. And I just kind of admitted I'd had the hots for him.

August didn't post much, but Kayla loved tagging him at every opportunity: selfies with her arm around his waist, candids of him studying or sleeping, captioned with things like: *I tuckered him out.* I would then "caption" my rude gestures with colorful expletives, all shouted at the screen. (Proof of Facebook's torture potential.) My roommate, Clean Your Damn Area Claire, would make a throaty sound and roll her eyes, then tell me to *clean my damn area.*

I stared at my silent phone, bouncing my heel, chewing my lip, wishing I could reverse time and suck that message back into my traitorous fingers.

His eventual reply didn't help: **What does Kayla have to do with this?**

Now he wanted me to bleed for him, eviscerate the guts of my hidden affections. All I managed was a partial truth.

I was jealous of her too. Because of her, we spent less time together. It wasn't rational. I'm sorry and I miss you.

I should have been more honest, admitted the depths of my feelings for him back then. My feelings for him now. Regret knotted my noodley insides as I waited for his reply. I contemplated moving to Mars or the jungles of Africa, a place where Facebook and stupid crushes wouldn't derail my life. My phone vibrated with August's reply.

You should never have dated Jared. Things would be very different now.

Holy hell.

Did that mean he'd wanted me in high school, too? Had we both read each other wrong? Jared and his leather jacket had been a distraction and nothing else, even though he'd barely kept me from fantasizing about August. The effort had been so dismal I'd broken up with Jared during prom.

Could I have spent that time kissing August's perfect lips instead of inhaling Jared's Axe Body Spray?

I typed a frantic reply, then deleted each letter. This was big. Huge. Like "winning all the blue jelly beans in a blue jelly bean counting competition" huge.

I'd been in Intro to Psychology with August's twin brother, Finch, all semester, staring at him with unhealthy longing. Aside from sharing August's dark hair, ridiculous bone structure, and gold-flecked hazel eyes, my belly had never flipped around him. The hairs on my neck had never shivered. That hadn't stopped me from ogling Finch, pretending and wishing he were August —the only man I'd ever truly *wanted.*

Up until one minute ago, I was sure my August ship had sailed, any chance with him destroyed by my childish behavior, but he was staring at his phone now, somewhere in San Francisco, not far from me, waiting on my reply.

This was do or die. This was the shot I never took.

This was my perfect birthday wish come true.

Holding my breath, I wrote out a careful reply, ensuring no typos waylaid my intentions. Brutal honesty was what this called for. Jäger honesty.

I dated Jared because you hooked up with Kayla. I had feelings for you back then and couldn't be around you guys.

I reread my reply. It didn't say how I *still* had feelings for him. Massive, crushing feelings. But it was more than I'd ever admitted. I swallowed hard and sent my heart through cyberspace.

One second passed. Two lumbered by. Five, ten, *fifteen* seconds dragged.

Heart pummeling my chest, I shot to my feet and paced. My eyes darted wildly, unable to focus on the guitar neck protruding from under my bed or my overflowing laundry basket or my King Kong Green Day poster. I felt like a science experiment, all vibrating molecules and firing synapses, a cataclysmic event away from full meltdown.

No message answered me. Not a one. The air in my lungs turned to glue. If I had a paper bag, I'd breathe into it.

Unsure what to do, I plunked down on my chair and scrolled through Facebook, a futile attempt to distract myself. It was either that or fill my bathtub with Jäger and go for a swim. The flipping images blurred, one annoying smiling face after another, until one particular face had my mouse stilling and my eyes bugging.

Kayla. Kayla tagging August in one of her flirty posts.

I wanted to slap my laptop shut and forget I'd ever sent that text or opened this Pandora's Box of awful, but I couldn't stop from leaning closer and studying the image. The glue in my lungs hardened into cement. I blinked several times, but Kayla still filled the screen. Her hand faced me, a band on her wedding finger.

The comment above read: *Guess who got a promise ring?*

———

Dazed and confused (not in the good way), I pushed into The Barking Owl. The student bar was jam-packed, sweaty bodies abundant, heat and pop tunes stuffing the pulsating room. An elbow jabbed me. Someone used my shoulders to keep from falling. Even in the oppressive space, I was relieved to be away from my computer and treasonous phone.

The second Kayla's post had sunk in, I'd hidden my Blackberry. There'd been no need to read whatever reply August would send. The sweet guy he was, he'd for sure let me down gently, and I'd marinate in my embarrassment, followed by a therapy session with my pals Ben & Jerry.

Better to cry on Jack Daniels' shoulder than poor Ben's.

"Gwen!" A waving hand caught my eye. When I noticed the hand was attached to Finch, I cursed the birthday gods for making this the suckiest birthday in the history of sucky birthdays.

My mother's curt phone call this morning had been as warm as a polar bear's ass. I used to get a yearly birthday card from my aunt, but those had vanished when I'd turned twelve. My grandparents pretended I didn't exist, and I'd just confessed my love to a boy who'd already given his girlfriend *a promise ring*. A freaking promise ring. Like it was 1950.

Now I had to spend the night looking at his identical twin.

A Jäger-bath and Ben & Jerry's chaser sounded better and better, but that involved actual effort.

Grumbling, I maneuvered toward Finch. Not an easy feat. A foot from my goal, some oaf in a Warriors jersey stumbled and dumped half his beer over my boobs.

"What the hell?" I attempted to shove him off, but the giant barely budged.

"Sorry about your shirt." His sleazy smirk suggested he wasn't particularly sorry.

I pinched the front of my sodden V-neck, the thin fabric fighting me as I peeled it off my chest. I could now add wet T-shirt contestant to this year's birthday of awesome. "Next time you wanna waste your beer, pour it over your head."

His lewd smirk graduated to vulgar. "It's not a waste if I get to suck it off you."

College students sure were classy.

Rolling my eyes, I flipped him the bird and squeezed toward Finch's spot at the bar. Considering most students crammed into the overheated room were underage, the San Francisco fake ID racket must have been thriving. Tonight mine was a godsend.

Finch squeezed my hip and raised his voice over the music. "Glad you made it."

I peered at him, unsure why he seemed to be on his own. "Did we have plans?"

"You didn't get my text?"

If it had been sent after I'd humiliated myself with his brother, his message would be buried with that damning evidence. "I haven't checked my phone in a bit."

"Then I guess this is fate, and I get to buy you a birthday drink."

I tried to smile at his sweet effort. When we were kids, he'd raised hell with August and me, but as we'd gotten older, August would often tell him to get lost. Finch would sulk, but I'd been too focused on his brother to insist he tag along. Alone time with August had been a valuable commodity.

The past year and a half, though, after having cut August from my life, Finch had been more present. The two of us were at the same school now. He'd make an extra effort to check in on me, inviting me to lunch, the library. He and August seemed to have drifted since high school, but my childish silent treatment meant I couldn't ask August why, and there was an unspoken rule between Finch and me: August was a classified subject. Any mention of him or his name would disqualify our friendship.

A friendship I'd begun to count on. Finch even remembered my birthday.

"What can I get you?" he asked.

"Shot of Jäger."

He cringed. "Who the hell drinks Jäger?"

"I do, apparently." Because Jäger was the butthole of birthday drinks, and today was a butthole of a birthday. "I should order a double."

His gaze dropped briefly to my wet T-shirt, to the now-visible black bra that had looked miles better on the Facebook model. He leaned closer. "Are you drunk, Gwen Hamilton?"

I met him the rest of the way, our noses an inch apart. "Not wasted enough."

The people and music and laughter swirled around us, so loud and distracting that for a second I was sure it was August's Roman nose nearly touching mine, his lips within biting distance. His scruffy jaw. His firm chest. But there was no scar on Finch's chin. August's scar had been acquired the night we'd snuck into the abandoned Wheeler home. Finch didn't have an untamable lick of hair that always shot heavenward or callused fingers from endless guitar sessions. He hadn't written songs for me while lying in the grass and staring at the sky.

But Finch was good for a laugh.

"You're lucky you found me." He pretended to tighten an invisible necktie. "We may have grown up neighbors, but I don't think you know I have a PhD in intoxication."

I rubbed my palms together in eager anticipation. "Do tell, Dr. Cruz."

"Well, if you're aiming for *sad* wasted, I'd suggest we start you off with tequila shots, followed by a keg of beer. If it's giddy wasted you're after, Long Island Iced Tea should do the trick."

"I was thinking more pissed-off wasted." Insane wasted. *Furious* wasted.

If I hadn't been so pathetically insecure during high school, I could be getting giddy wasted with August, instead of shooting the shit with his brother. The horrible choice to cut August off was a wake-up call if I'd ever heard one. Never again would I let a missed opportunity slip by. I wouldn't coast through life, cowering at challenges, afraid to rock the boat. I would scare myself. I would push my boundaries. I would make life my bitch.

Finch nodded sagely. "If pissed-off wasted is your mission, then stick with the nasty Jäger."

I almost did just that, but drinking more would dull this painful ache. I deserved to suffer every jab and twinge, each unforgiving pang. This was my fault. I should have admitted my feelings to August years ago.

Instead of walking the easy road of inebriation and oblivion, I ordered a Red Bull.

An insane amount of sugar-laced caffeine later, I stood in the crowded bar feeling more alone than when I'd been at home. The string of Red Bulls had done their job. I was painfully sober, and my revved brain kept reliving every different decision that could have resulted in a different outcome. Not this crappy outcome.

I was angry at myself. I was angry at August. And Finch was here for the entire show, doing his Finch thing, teasing my surly scowl and telling god-awful knock-knock jokes until I cracked a smile. Some song about booties blared. Two chicks acted out the lyrics, putting on a show for the bar. August barely glanced at them.

Dammit. Finch. *Finch, Finch, Finch.*

I kept doing that—thinking, wishing he was his brother.

Finch and his easy grin were facing me, like they had been all night. His chest rubbed my arm as he yelled in my ear about his summer backpacking plans, his voice battling against the loud tunes. I nodded automatically, barely hearing him.

Warriors jersey dude, who hadn't passed out yet, danced suggestively while ogling the bootie girls. The giant waste of space tripped into me again, sending my clutched Red Bull to the ground. Finch glared at him. Frustrated, I bent down to retrieve the fallen can being kicked to-and-fro like a pinball. Finch had the same instinct. At the same time.

Our heads smacked together.

"Fuck." I pressed my palm to my forehead.

"I'm not sure it'll help with the headache, but we could try."

We could…*what-the-what*?

Finch and I were crouched inches from a sticky floor covered in spilled beer and pretzel bits, a forest of legs surrounding our shoulders, and he was eyeing me like he wanted a closer inspection of my black bra.

What the hell?

I was strung out on Red Bull, my heart pounding a mile a minute, and my vision turned hazy. Blurred with sadness. I found myself craving more contact. Touch. Comfort in someone's arms. No matter how hard I looked at Finch, he didn't become August—the only person I wanted to fill that role. Did it matter?

Finch was nice, fun. He was the only one with me on my birthday, and he wasn't hurting in the handsome department, clearly. If August didn't want me, why not have fun with his twin?

Because August might find out and be upset, my unhelpful conscience whispered.

If August had really pined for me in high school, the way he'd sort of admitted, he'd have confided in Finch back then, when they'd been close. He might be pissed if Finch and I hooked up. But August had a girlfriend *with a promise ring*. A life that didn't involve me.

My decisions weren't his concern.

Tired of my lame wallowing, I grinned at Finch, returning his flirtations. I turned my brain to silent as we walked to my apartment. I moved on autopilot as I fitted my key into the door and dragged Finch inside. I closed my eyes when our shirts hit the floor, his bare chest pressed to mine.

His lips searched for purchase. "So long," he murmured. "I've wanted you so long."

My belly cramped at those needy words. Passionate words. Words I longed to whisper to August. *I've wanted you so long.* He wasn't here, though, and I was lonely. So, so lonely. Finch was undressing me, showering me with kisses. I tried pretending it was another man's mouth on my skin. *August. My August.* If I couldn't have the man I wanted on my birthday, I would steal a moment of abandon from his twin. Pretend. Dream. Live the lie.

It was a wasted effort.

The sex was mechanical, motions gone through, our bodies fitting together, my mind somewhere else. My faked orgasm sped the whole affair along. Finch, however, whispered endearments, hips relentless in pursuit of his pleasure. I was glad when it was over. And sad. Guilt returned as Finch kissed me gently and went to deal with the condom.

Did he have a thing for me? Had he been crushing on me the whole time I'd been crushing on his brother? Did August know? It was likely why Finch had been so attentive this year, and here I was, only wanting a mindless night. God, what a mess.

Letting him down after this would be another painful blow.

A knock at the door cut through my worry, and I groaned. Last thing I wanted was a witness to this sham, but Clean Your Damn Area Claire must have forgotten her key again. That emo girl would lose her black fingernails if they weren't attached.

Tossing on an oversized tee, I stood and breathed through the fog of bad decisions this night had become. I couldn't even blame the Jäger.

Unable to swallow past the lump in my throat, I hurried to the door and yanked it open.

I nearly passed out.

August Cruz was in my doorway, at my apartment, a crazed look in his stunning hazel eyes. "Happy birthday," he said, a slight pant to his words, as though he'd run here.

Then he kissed me. Callused fingers gripping my jaw, he crushed his lips to mine, devouring me like I was air in an airless world. This wasn't mechanical. This wasn't pretend. This was the love of my life twirling his tongue around mine sensually, moving his lips and body the same way he played guitar: with animal abandon.

It was too good. He was too good. And I let it all go on too long. I somehow managed to push him away. "You gave her a promise ring," was the first thing I said.

Not, *I slept with your brother*. Not, *your brother is in the next room*.

My brain cells had vacated the building.

He winced. "You saw that post?" Before I could answer, he breathed harder, talking over himself. "I'd bought that ring for *your* birthday, and she assumed it was for her."

He tugged at the back of his dark hair. "It's just, I've been thinking about you nonstop lately. Not sure why now—maybe it was your birthday coming up or the school year ending—but I knew I needed to set things right with you. I'd decided to end things with Kayla tonight. I got your address from your mother and planned to face you, then you sent me that text. And it was like…the whole thing kind of floored me."

Creases sank into his furrowed brow. "I'm sorry I lashed out at first. I wasn't expecting for all that shit to resurface. But I think it's good, you know? That we cleared the air. Now we can finally do this, be together. Because this thing with us?" He prowled closer and lifted the ring in question. "It's always been you, Gwen. No one holds a candle to you."

That's when Finch walked into the living area, nothing on but his boxers.

That's when I realized the extent of my Worst Terrible Fuck-up.

Start reading *36 HOUR DATE* today!

ALSO BY KELLY SISKIND

One Wild Wish Series:

He's Going Down

Off-Limits Crush

36 Hour Date

Over the Top Series:

The Snowflake Effect

One Degree of Perfect

Slammed into Focus

Showmen Series:

New Orleans Rush

Don't Go Stealing My Heart

The Beat Match

The Knockout Rule

The Bower Boys series:

Fall in love with the Bower brothers! A decade after being forced into Witness Protection, they're finally allowed to return home and fight for the women they lost.

Visit Kelly's website and join her newsletter for great giveaways and never miss an update!

www.kellysiskind.com

ACKNOWLEDGMENTS

Some books come easy, some come hard (that's what she said), and some are just plain fun to write. This book falls into the fun category. I knew a grand total of nothing about construction when I chose a Habitat for Humanity setting. I now know more than nothing, but I wouldn't hire me to build your next house. I also *whispers* suck at crossword puzzles. The beauty of creating worlds is being everything you're not!

A huge thank you to you, the readers, for allowing me to have fun. For reading my words. For being all around awesome people. The fact that you continue to buy and enjoy my books means the world.

Sending love to J.R. Yates, Kristin B. Wright, Mary Ann Marlowe, and Heather Van Fleet for being amazing friends, Beta readers, and critique partners on this project. I couldn't do this without you. Tammy Cole and Shelly Hastings Suhr, your feedback is always invaluable, and your cheerleading is just as appreciated. I adore you ladies. Thank you to Tamara Mataya for your top-notch editing skills, and to Sarah Henning for your keen proofing eye.

There are too many bloggers to mention, but so many of you have been unbelievably supportive. Thank you times a million for all you do.

ABOUT THE AUTHOR

Kelly Siskind lives in the wilds of Western Canada. When she's not out hiking or skiing, you can find her, notepad in hand, scribbling down one of the many plot bunnies bouncing around in her head. She loves singing while driving, looks awful in yellow, and is known for spilling wine at parties.

Sign up for Kelly's newsletter and never miss a giveaway, a free bonus scene, or the latest news on her books.

If you like to laugh and chat about books, join Kelly in her Facebook group, KELLY'S GANG.

Connect with Kelly on social media:
facebook.com/authorKellySiskind/
instagram.com/kellysiskind/
https://www.tiktok.com/@authorkellysiskind